Library of
Davidson College
VOID

# Authenticity Problems in Joseph Haydn's Early Instrumental Works

# Authenticity Problems in Joseph Haydn's Early Instrumental Works

## A Stylistic Investigation

by Scott Fruehwald

MONOGRAPHS IN MUSICOLOGY No.8

PENDRAGON PRESS
NEW YORK

Other Titles in the Pendragon Press *MONOGRAPHS IN MUSICOLOGY SERIES*

No. 1  *Analysis and Value Judgment* by Carl Dahlhaus, translated by Siegmund Levarie (1983) ISBN 0-918728-20-7
No. 2  La Statira *by Pietro Ottoboni and Alessandro Scarlatti: The Textual Sources with a Documentary Postscript* by William C. Holmes (1983) ISBN 0-918728-18-5
No. 3  *Alessandro Scarlatti's* Gli equivoci nel sembiante: *The History of a Baroque Opera* by Frank D'Accone ISBN 0-918728-21-5
No. 4  *The Interpretation of 16th-and 17th-Century Iberian Keyboard Music* by Macario Santiago Kastner, translated by Bernard Brauchli (1986) ISBN 0-918728-53-3
No. 5  *Classical Music of South India*: Karnatic *Tradition in Western Notation* by Kanthimathi Kumar and Jean Stackhouse (1987) ISBN 0-918728-42-8
No. 6  *The Art of Noises* by Luigi Russolo, translated by Barclay Brown (1987) ISBN 0-918728-57-6

**Library of Congress Cataloging-in-Publication Data**

Fruehwald, Scott.
  Authenticity problems in Joseph Haydn's early instrumental works.

  (Monographs in musicology ; no. 8)
  Bibliography; p.
    1. Haydn, Joseph, 1732-1809. Instrumental music.
  2. Instrumental music—18th century—History and criticism. I. Title. II. Series.
  ML410.H4f74  1988      785'.092'4   87-14931
  ISBN 0-918728-67-3

Copyright 1988 Pendragon Press

# Contents

|  | Preface | vii |
|---|---|---|
|  | Introduction | 1 |
| Chapter One | Literature on Stylistic Methods of Determining Authenticity | 17 |
| Chapter Two | Methods of Determining Authenticity by Style | 39 |
| Chapter Three | Keyboard Sonatas | 67 |
| Chapter Four | Accompanied Keyboard Divertimentos | 101 |
| Chapter Five | Keyboard Trios | 117 |
| Chapter Six | String Trios | 131 |
| Chapter Seven | Opus 3 String Quartets | 151 |
| Chapter Eight | Divertimentos | 165 |
| Chapter Nine | Concertos | 191 |
| Chapter Ten | Conclusion | 207 |

Appendixes

| | | |
|---|---|---|
| A. | Lists of Haydn's Early Works in Selected Instrumental Genres | 213 |
| B. | Editions of Authentic and Doubtful Works Attributed to Haydn and Hoffstetter | 223 |
| C. | Comments on the Non-Haydn Works and a Sample of Non-Haydn Works Used | 227 |
| D. | A Method for Drawing Up the Checklists | 231 |
| E. | Two Examples of the Analysis of Quantitative Ranges | 235 |
| F. | Selected Checklist Terms | 249 |
| | Bibliography | 255 |
| | Index | 265 |

# Preface

In the following study, I examine the authenticity of pre-1770 compositions attributed to Joseph Haydn that have not been proven definitely authentic or definitely spurious on documentary grounds. My method of authenticity determination consists of drawing up a stylistic profile for each genre comprising two parts: quantitative ranges and checklists.[1]
Quantitative ranges that I use most often include the rate of harmonic change, the rate of textural change, and the number of impacts (rhythmic attacks) per beat. My checklist includes traits that always or usually appear in Haydn's compositions and traits that never or rarely occur. Checklist characteristics can be seemingly minor aspects of style, such as "the texture changes three times in the first eight measures." All quantitative ranges and checklist entries are tested against a group of representative non-Haydn works to eliminate items that are too much a part of the contemporary vernacular. The completed profile is checked further with additional non-Haydn compositions to insure that no non-Haydn work will pass or score borderline.

---

The completion of this study brings with it the pleasure of being able to acknowledge those who aided in its writing. I wish to thank those individuals and institutions who helped me obtain rare materials, including William Shank, music librarian at the City University of New York; James Webster of Cornell University; A. Peter Brown of Indiana University; Georg Feder of the Haydn Institute, Köln; Horst

---

[1] A full explanation of my methods of authenticity determination appears in Chapter Two.

Walter, also of the Haydn Institute; the Moravské Múzeum, Brno; the Muzeum Céské Hudby, Prague; Kungl. Musikaliska Akademiens Bibliotek, Stockholm; the Princeton University Library; and the Staatsbibliotek Preussicher Kulturbesitz, Berlin. I also wish to acknowledge the aid of the staffs of the music divisions of the New York Public Library and the Library of Congress, and thank John Spitzer of the University of Pittsburgh for sending me the relevant chapters of his dissertation.

This study is a revised version of my Ph.D. dissertation, which was written at the City University of New York. I owe a deep debt of gratitude to my dissertation advisor, Barry S. Brook, which I shall never be able to repay. Special thanks also to the two principal readers of my dissertation, Joel Lester and Sherman Van Solkema, as well as the additional members of my defense committee, Allan Atlas, Rufus Hallmark, and Raymond Erickson. I also wish to thank Professor Richard Sackstedder of the Mathematics Department at the City University of New York for reading an early version of chapter two from a statistician's viewpoint. Finally, I am grateful to Bruce MacIntyre and László Somfai, who read this study shortly before I sent the final version to the publisher.

New York<br>December 1, 1984

# Introduction

Authenticity has been a central issue in Haydn research for the last fifty years. In *Die Haydn-Überlieferung*, Jens Peter Larsen laid a firm foundation for the study of Haydn authenticity problems by documentary means, based on the three Haydn catalogues (the *Entwurf-Katalog* begun c. 1765, the *Katalog Kees* compiled c. 1790-92, and the *Haydn Verzeichnis* of 1805), autograph manuscripts, and a critical evaluation of nonautograph sources.[1] Since the publication of Larsen's seminal study, research on Haydn authenticity questions using a documentary approach has been massive. Nevertheless, a large number of doubtful compositions still remain, especially among the works composed before 1770.[2] For example, in his catalogue of Haydn's compositions in *Grove*, Georg Feder lists fifteen harpsichord sonatas, dating from the 1750s and 60s, that are conceivably by Haydn, but which are not in the Haydn catalogues and do not exist in autograph or other unimpeachable sources.[3]* Similarly, all but one of Haydn's early keyboard trios

---

[1] Jens Peter Larsen, *Die Haydn-Überlieferung* (Copenhagen: Einar Munksgaard, 1939) and *Three Haydn Catalogues* (New York: Pendragon Press, 1979). In addition to the latter, important discussions of Larsen's work in English include H. C. Robbins Landon, *The Symphonies of Joseph Haydn* (London: Universal Edition, 1955) and Larsen, "A Survey of the Development of Haydn Research: Solved and Unsolved Problems," *Haydn Studies: Proceedings of the International Haydn Conference, Washington, D. C., 1975*, ed. Jens Peter Larsen, Howard Serwer, and James Webster (New York: Norton, 1981) 21.

[2] In the Haydn literature, any work that has not been proven definitely authentic or spurious is labeled doubtful. See George Feder, "Introductory Statement," *Round Table: Source Problems, Authenticity and Chronology, List of Works* in *Haydn Studies*, 74. Exceptions to this use of the term will be noted.

[3] Jens Peter Larsen, *The New Grove Haydn*, with worklist by Georg Feder (New York: Norton, 1983) 183-85. This monograph is an updated version of the Haydn entry in

## INTRODUCTION

(twelve compositions including two lost ones) fall into the doubtful category.[4] Clearly, new methods must be developed to deal with those authenticity problems that cannot be solved by documentary evidence alone. In this study, I shall examine authenticity problems in Haydn's early instrumental works, using a stylistic approach I developed for an investigation of Haydn's string trios.[5]

## THE NEED FOR THIS STUDY

The importance of establishing the authenticity of Haydn's early works that are presently considered doubtful is unquestionable. James Webster has declared that

> If we accept authentic works only, we guarantee ourselves 'Haydn and nothing but Haydn,' but we will almost certainly fail to obtain 'the whole Haydn.' Each type of authentic source [a musical source or document which derives from Haydn himself] testifies only to a fraction of

---

*The New Grove Dictionary of Music and Musicians*, ed. Stanley Sadie (London: Macmillan, 1980). All references are to the revised version. Feder's worklist is the most up-to-date and accurate inventory of Haydn's music.

*Because *The New Grove Haydn* is more up-to-date than the Haydn entry in the *The New Grove Dictionary of Music and Musicians*, all references are to the former. Since some libraries may contain only *The New Grove Dictionary*, page equivalents are as follows:

|  | NGH | NGD, VIII |
|---|---|---|
| Instrumental Works | 146-91 | 371-93 |
| Wind and String Concertos | 156-58 | 376-77 |
| Divertimentos | 158-61 | 377-78 |
| String Quartets | 161-65 | 378-80 |
| String Trios | 165-67 | 380-81 |
| Misc. Chamber Music | 174-76 | 384-86 |
| Keyboard Concertos/Divertimentos | 178-80 | 386-88 |
| Keyboard Trios | 180-83 | 388-89 |
| Keyboard Sonatas | 183-86 | 389-91 |
| Misc. Keyboard Works | 187-90 | 391-92 |

NGH=*The New Grove Haydn*
NGD, VIII=*The New Grove Dictionary, Vol. VIII*

[4]*Ibid.*, 388-89.
[5]Scott Fruehwald, "Textural Analysis as a Means of Determining Authenticity in the String Trios Attributed to Haydn," to be published in conjunction with the string trio volume of the *Joseph Haydn: Werke* (Cologne: Haydn Institute).

## INTRODUCTION

the entire body of authenticated works. It is therefore almost certain that some genuine works, especially from the early years and in the 'occasional' genres, have not survived in any authentic sources. These works cannot be authenticated today. If, on the other hand, we accept any work attributed to Haydn, whenever it suits us, we may hope to acquire 'the whole Haydn' but at the certain cost of including a great deal that is not by Haydn at all.[6]

Many writers have commented on the paucity of good stylistic studies of Haydn's music, and this is especially true for the early works.[7] It is clear from the above, though, that before we can do thorough, accurate stylistic studies of Haydn's early compositions, the authenticity problems must be cleared up. The resolution of authenticity questions would also help prevent works that are not by Haydn from being played on the concert stage or recorded under his name and expand the number of pieces that could be played.[8] Many of the doubtful compositions are excellent pieces that deserve to be performed. Finally, an accurate listing of Haydn's early works would give us a clearer picture of Haydn's early life in general. Our understanding of Haydn's interests in his early years will differ, depending on whether he wrote twenty-one string trios or eight-four, whether he wrote thirteen keyboard trios or one.

## WHY AUTHENTICITY PROBLEMS OCCUR

Reasons for misattributions in music vary widely, depending on the composer and periods involved. Newell Jenkins and Bathia Churgin believe that most of the conflicting attributions in Sammartini's works are due to confusion with other Milanese composers who wrote in a similar style; and confusion between Sammartini and his brother

---

[6]James Webster, "External Criteria for Determining the Authenticity of Haydn's Music," *Haydn Studies*, 77.
[7]A. Peter Brown, "The Structure of the Exposition in Haydn's Keyboard Sonatas," *Music Review* XXXVI/2 (1975) 102; James Webster, "Prospects for Haydn Biography after Landon," *The Musical Quarterly* LXVIII/4 (1982) 494-95; and Larsen, "A Survey of Haydn Research," 23-24.
[8]Perhaps this is too optimistic. Record companies and concert promoters tend to retain the original attributions of discredited pieces to attract record buyers and audiences thinking (probably correctly!) that Haydn or Pergolesi will sell while Hoffstetter or Gallo won't.

## INTRODUCTION

Giuseppe, other musical Sammartinis and composers with similar names.[9] On the other hand, Pergolesi authenticity problems were caused mainly by his posthumous fame. Marvin Paymer writes that

> The enormous propaganda value of this publicity [from the 'Querelle des bouffons'], and the vogue for music by a composer loved and revered throughout Europe, compounded by the dishonesty of eighteenth and nineteenth century copyists and publishers, resulted in a flood of newly discovered manuscripts and publications bearing the name of Pergolesi.[10]

Concerning the Renaissance chanson, Allan Atlas has hypothesized that many of the conflicting attributions arose from composers revising the works of other composers and the attribution switching to the reviser.[11] Among the evidence he marshals in favor of his theory is 1) many of the composers for whom there are conflicting attributions worked at the same centers sometime in their careers and 2) many of the revisions are too difficult for a scribe and would require a skilled composer. On the other hand, John Spitzer, using stemmatics combined with statistical methods, concludes that Atlas's theory explains some of the conflicting attributions in the Renaissance chanson, but that it does not explain all or even most of them.[12] Other possible explanations for the conflicting attributions in this genre that he gives include 1) confusion between pieces with the same or similar titles (both Josquin and Colinet wrote chansons entitled "Cela sans plus"), 2) confusion between similar names (Pietrequin and Pierre de la Rue), and 3) a "regional grapevine" (a chanson may be attributed to one

---

[9]Newell Jenkins and Bathia Churgin, *Thematic Catalogue of the Works of Giovanni Battista Sammartini* (Cambridge: Harvard University Press, 1976) 27.
[10]Marvin Paymer, *The Instrumental Music Attributed to Giovanni Battista Pergolesi: A Study in Authenticity* (Ph.D. diss., City University of New York, 1977) 12.
[11]Allan Atlas, "Conflicting Attributions in Italian Sources of the Franco-Netherlandish Chanson, c.1465-c.1505: A Progress Report on a New Hypothesis," *Music in Medieval and Modern Europe: Patronage, Sources, and Texts*, ed. Iain Fenlon (Cambridge: Cambridge University Press, 1981) 249-93.
[12]John Spitzer, *Authorship and Attribution in Western Art Music*, Ph.D. diss, Cornell University, 1983, 113-151. Although he does mention the problem, Spitzer probably underestimates the possibility that contamination may account for the discrepancies between his stemmas and the requirements of Atlas's theory. Still, Atlas's theory does not explain all the conflicting attributions in the Renaissance chanson. (For example, Pietrequin vs. Pierre de la Rue).

## INTRODUCTION

composer in Italian sources and to another composer in Northern sources).[13]

Jan LaRue has summarized the main causes of misattributions in eighteenth-century music:

1) clerical errors,

2) lazy inconsistencies of spelling,

3) similarities between names,

4) misreading sloppy handwriting,

5) vague title pages,

6) including a nonauthentic work with authentic ones to produce a published set,

7) anthologies that lack proper attributions, and

8) substituting the name of a well-known composer for a minor one to increase sales.[14]

Authenticity problems in Haydn's works are caused by several factors. Foremost among these, perhaps, is fraud; Haydn's name sold better than Pleyel's or Vanhal's or Hoffstetter's. This was especially a problem in publishing centers distant from Eisenstadt and Esterháza, but fraud also occurred in manuscripts copied in Austria.[15,16] Moreover, this problem was not confined to late works, but happened in early ones as well. Haydn's fame in German-speaking countries began in the early 1760s with the dissemination of his first quartets and symphonies.[17]

Probably more important for the early works is the attribution of a manuscript to a well-known composer because it resembles his style.

---

[13]Spitzer, *op. cit.*, 142-151.
[14]Summarized from La Rue, "Major and Minor Mysteries of Identification in the 18th-Century Symphony," *Journal of the American Musicological Society* XIII (1960) 181-85.
[15]Before 1780, music in Austria was usually disseminated in manuscript copies made by professional copyists and sold by music dealers. See Barry S. Brook, "Piracy and Panacea: On the Dissemination of Music in the Eighteenth Century," *Proceedings of the Royal Musical Association* CII (1975-76) 13-36.
[16]In fact, John Spitzer believes that more misattributions occur in manuscript sources than in prints. Spitzer, *op. cit.*, 152-242.
[17]H. C. Robbins Landon, *Haydn: Chronicle and Works—Haydn: The Early Years, 1732-1765* (Bloomington: Indiana University Press, 1980) 296-97.

## INTRODUCTION

The String Quartet in D Major by Albrechtsberger, which is attributed to Haydn in the Göttweig Abbey catalogue, appears to be such a case. Landon believes that it "sounds amazingly like the Haydn of Op. I and II."[18] Such mistakes are also probably the source for many of the misattributions in Haydn's string trios.

Confusion between names is also a major cause of authenticity problems in Haydn's music. Above all, there is the confusion with his brother Michael. Many eighteenth-century copyists included only the last name of a composer, and those who worked from these copies often made their own guess as to which brother it was. Probably in this way, a group of six Michael Haydn string trios was falsely attributed to Joseph (V:D2, E-flat1, E1, G2, A1, B2). Most of the time, Michael's music was wrongly ascribed to his brother, but, occasionally, the misattribution happened in the opposite direction: six of Joseph Haydn's string trios (Hob. V:11, 16, 18, 19, G1, A2) are sometimes attributed to Michael, as is the *Te Deum* (Hob. XXIIIc:1). One composer had a name similar to Haydn's, a Joseph Hayda, who was a follower of both Joseph and Michael and whom Landon includes in the "Third Haydn School."[19] Hayda's *Litaniae de Beata Maria Virgine* has been erroneously ascribed to both Haydn brothers.

Finally, numerous cases exist where Haydn may have become the "composer" of a work owing to the misreading of sloppy handwriting. Feder views this as a possibility in the conflicting attribution of the *Raigern Sonatas* (Hob. XVI:E-flat2 and E-flat3) to both Haydn and the obscure Mariano Romano Kayser.[20]

While conflicting attributions in Haydn's music concern composers from all over Europe, the majority of composers for which there are such conflicting attributions worked mainly in Austria. An examination of conflicting attributions for Haydn's symphonies in *Hoboken* reveals that most of the composers cited more than once are Austrians (see chart I). Many of the others, while primarily associated with other centers, had contacts with Vienna or Austria: Pleyel was a student of Haydn, Holzbauer spent his early career in Vienna before going to Mannheim, and the Netherlandish composer Maldere was patronized by Prince Charles of Lorraine, brother-in-law of the Austrian empress,

---

[18]Landon, *Haydn: The Early Years*, 298.
[19]Landon, *Haydn: Chronicle and Works—Haydn at Esterháza, 1766-1790* (Bloomington: Indiana University Press, 1978), 661-667.
[20]Georg Feder, "The Sources of the Two Disputed Raigern Sonatas," *Haydn Studies*, 109.

*INTRODUCTION*

## Chart I. Composers with at Least Two Conflicting Attributions with Haydn's Spurious Symphonies

| | | |
|---|---|---|
| *M. Haydn-23 | J. C. Bach-4 | Filtz-2 |
| *Dittersdorf-11 | Maldere-4 | *Gyrowetz-2 |
| *Vanhal-11 | *Holzbauer-3 | *Hoffmeister-2 |
| *Hofmann-7 | *Kerzel-3 | *Ordoñez-2 |
| *Pichl-6 | *Van Swieten-3 | Schmitt-2 |
| *Pleyel-5 | | *Zimmermann-2 |

*= composers who worked in Austria sometime in their careers.

## Chart II. Composers of Conflicting Attributions for the Haydn Doubtful String Trios

| | | |
|---|---|---|
| *M. Haydn-8 | Chiesa-1 | *Ivaschiz-1 |
| *Hofmann-8 | Enderle-1 | *Ordoñez-1 |
| Kammel-3 | Filtz-1 | J. Stamitz-1 |
| *Aspelmayr-2 | Gasparini-1 | *Vanhal-1 |
| J. C. Bach-1 | | Zappa-1 |

* = composers who worked in Austria sometime in their careers.

Maria Theresa. A chart of conflicting attributions for the doubtful string trios yields similar results (chart II).

## DETERMINING AUTHENTICITY BY DOCUMENTARY MEANS

James Webster has succinctly summarized the principal documentary approaches to determining authenticity in Haydn's music.[21] He distinguishes between direct and indirect authentication. Direct authentication is furnished by Haydn's handwriting or solid documentary evidence, including 1) autograph manuscripts, 2) the three Haydn catalogues, 3) manuscripts or prints signed by Haydn, and 4) works authenticated by letters or other documents. Among indirect authentic sources are 1) authentic manuscripts written under Haydn's control or with his approval, 2) printed editions, which are authenticated by letter, contracts, and business records, and 3) so-called good sources that

---
[21]Webster, "External Criteria," 75-78.

## INTRODUCTION

are similar to the best indirect sources for authentic works. The last category comprises a) early Viennese and Austrian manuscripts, b) catalogue entries that resemble those of other early genuine works (such as monastery catalogues or the *Breitkopf Catalogue*), and c) printed editions from Vienna after 1780 and from London while Haydn was there in the 1790s. More remote sources, such as those copied much later or in distant centers, are generally useless for establishing authenticity; in certain genres, more nonauthentic compositions are attributed to Haydn than authentic ones.

When a conflicting attribution is found, that work is immediately considered suspect and is generally assumed to be by the other composer. However, this is not always the case. The authentic keyboard concerto Hob. XVIII:2 was wrongly ascribed to Galuppi, and the keyboard divertimento Hob. XIV:3 was wrongly attributed to Leopold Hofmann.[22]

Any work that cannot be solidly documented as either by Haydn or another composer is considered doubtful. Considerable debate has occurred over whether there are subcategories of doubtful.[23] As far as documentary evidence is concerned, I prefer LaRue's distinction: "plausible, uncertain, and unlikely."[24] A proper stylistic study reduces the necessary categories in most cases to authentic and spurious.

Despite the rigorous methods used by Haydn scholars in establishing authenticity by documentation, many problems remain. Both the *Entwurf-Katalog* and *Haydn Verzeichnis* are incomplete,[25] especially for the early works, and the latter contains a number of compositions that are not by Haydn.[26] Concerning the *Entwurf-Katalog*, Larsen writes,

> Still, it must be recognized that the catalogue is not comprehensive up to this date [1765]. It is primarily concerned with works composed in Eisenstadt and with earlier works performed in these years or in any event still in Haydn's possession. Pieces from the 1750s no longer

---

[22]Feder, *The New Grove Haydn*, 178.
[23]See the discussion following Webster's article in *Haydn Studies*, 78-81.
[24]*Ibid.*, 79.
[25]The *Katalog Kees* contains only symphonies.
[26]Scholars have questioned the reliability of the *Entwurf-Katalog* in only one instance, that of the *Missa Rorate coeli desuper* (Hob. XXII:3). This conflict may be due to a similarity of incipits between a lost work by Haydn and a mass attributed to both Reutter and Arbesser rather than a mistake in the *Entwurf-Katalog*. In addition, the extant mass could conceivably be by the young Haydn instead of Reutter or Arbesser.

## INTRODUCTION

owned by Haydn could easily have been forgotten or even deliberately omitted since they did not relate to his activities as princely Kapellmeister.[27]

While scholars have often employed other eighteenth-century catalogues as sources for indirect authentication, it must be pointed out that such catalogues frequently contain many misattributions. Breitkopf himself warned of the authorship problems in his catalogue, and conflicting attributions appear throughout, sometimes within a few pages of each other.[28] Monastery catalogues have similar problems. Therefore, eighteenth-century catalogues should be used only as supporting evidence for establishing authenticity.

Some documentary evidence is misleading and even fraudulent. For instance, Haydn signed the title pages of two keyboard trios (Hob. XV:3 and 4) that are clearly not by him.[29] The only convincing explanation of this is that Haydn was trying to cheat the publisher. Other times, mistakes are due to failing memory or lack of communication. An apparently convincing case was made for the authenticity of the Opus 3 string quartets on documentary grounds. They appear in the *Haydn Verzeichnis*, they were included in Pleyel's complete edition of the string quartets, and Haydn himself asserted the authenticity of this edition. However, other documentary and stylistic evidence casts extreme doubt on the authenticity of these works.[30] Two possible explanations exist for the erroneous positive evidence: 1) Haydn's failing memory or 2) Haydn did not closely examine either the Pleyel edition or the string quartet entry in the *Haydn Verzeichnis*. These examples prove that one must critically evaluate *even the strongest* positive documentary evidence concerning authenticity.

Finally, no matter how reliable the documentary evidence, interpretations of that evidence can differ. For example, the sole copy of the

---

[27]Larsen, *The New Grove Haydn*, 26.
[28]Barry S. Brook, ed., *The Breitkopf Thematic Catalogue: The Six Parts and Sixteen Supplements 1762-1787* (New York: Dover, 1966) xiv-xv.
[29]Alan Tyson, "Haydn and Two Stolen Trios," *Music Review* XXII (1961) 21-27; Rita Benton, "A Résumé of the Haydn-Pleyel Trio Controversy, with Some Added Contributions," *Haydn-Studien* IV (1978) 114-117; and the discussion of these trios in chapter two.
[30]László Somfai, "Zur Echtheitsfrage des Hadyn'schen 'Opus 3,' " *The Haydn Yearbook* III (1965) 153-65; Alan Tyson and H. C. Robbins Landon, "Who Composed Haydn's Opus 3?" *The Musical Times* CV (1964) 506-07; and the discussion in chapter seven of this study.

## INTRODUCTION

keyboard concerto XVIII:G1 contains the inscription "Specht ad me J. H." One might assume that this inscription meant that Haydn had approved the manuscript. However, A. Peter Brown has demonstrated that the initials stood not for Joseph Haydn but for Joseph George Harold (or Haroldt), who was an inspector of manuscripts for a Viennese copying firm.[31]

While some of the problems connected with using external evidence occur in only a few cases, the lack of autograph sources, catalogue entries, and other solid documentary evidence are major obstacles in establishing the authenticity of many of Haydn's early works. For example, the *Entwurf-Katalog* and *Haydn Verzeichnis* include twenty-one string trios (three of which are lost) that may be considered authentic.[32] Sixty-three other trios exist that are also attributed to Haydn in some source; twenty-six that are attributed to him alone, and thirty-seven others that have conflicting attributions or are lost.[33] The scholars who have worked with these trios agree that some of them are authentic, but they often disagree on the authenticity of particular trios. For instance, Landon considers C1 indubitably genuine; Larsen regards it as possibly authentic; and Feder lists it as doubtful (in this case, meaning probably not authentic).[34] Furthermore, documentary evidence is of little help in establishing the authenticity of these trios. While the more plausible works exist in multiple copies, one cannot completely eliminate those trios that are unica; three of the Haydn trios that are authenticated by the Haydn catalogues are not extant at all. Likewise, the presence of a conflicting attribution is not completely reliable. V:G4, which is attributed to both Ordoñez and Haydn, is probably by Haydn.[35] To determine the authenticity of the string trios, then, one must rely on stylistic evidence or be left with an important

---

[31] A. Peter Brown, "Notes on Some Eighteenth-Century Viennese Copyists," *Journal of the American Musicological Society* XXXIV (1981) 333.
[32] Larsen, *Three Haydn Catalogues*, xvi. This does not include arrangements from other genres.
[33] Based on a list provided by the Haydn Institute and updated by the present author. Most of the string trios are scored for two violins and cello (or bass), with a few examples of violin, viola, cello.
[34] Landon, *Haydn: The Early Years*, 220; Larsen, *Three Haydn Catalogues*, xvi; and Feder, *The New Grove Haydn*, 167.
[35] See my discussion of the string trios in chapter six. Landon and Feder agree with this opinion (in differing degrees), as does A. Peter Brown in his article on Ordoñez's chamber music. "The Chamber Music of Carlos d'Ordoñez: A Bibliographic and Stylistic Study," *Acta Musicologica* XLVI (1974) 225.

## INTRODUCTION

early genre of Haydn's music in which there are almost three times as many doubtful compositions as authentic ones.

## THE EFFICACY OF EMPLOYING STYLISTIC METHODS IN AN AUTHENTICITY STUDY

Musicologists have traditionally viewed attempts to determine authenticity by style with great suspicion. In 1957, H. C. Robbins Landon declared,

> We have discussed the problems of this A Major Symphony [attributed to Haydn but by Ordoñez] in some detail, not to prove the fallibility of musicologists, but to show that internal, i.e., stylistic, evidence is a very subjective and—for purposes of drawing any definite conclusions—a very limited criterion. It does not matter how brilliant the critic is: when dealing with works of doubtful authenticity the stylistic element almost invariably leads to the wrong conclusion.[36]

James Webster expressed a similar opinion at the Hadyn Conference in 1975:

> . . . stylistic evidence can often persuade us that Composer X may have written a given work. But it can never prove that he must have composed it. Such an assertion would claim that nobody else could possibly have been the composer—not Composer Y, not Z, and not even W. None of us is in the position to risk this assertion, which would imply that we have scrutinized the music of every relevant eighteenth-century composer in exhaustive detail, and that our stylistic judgement is unfailingly accurate.[37]

On the other hand, as has been demonstrated above, many authenticity problems cannot be solved by documentary evidence alone, and

---

[36]H. C. Robbins Landon, "Problems of Authenticity in Eighteenth-Century Music," *Instrumental Music: A Conference at the Isham Memorial Library, May 4, 1957*, ed. David G. Hughes (Cambridge: Harvard University Press, 1959) 36. See also comments by Karl Geiringer and Edward Downes following the article.
[37]James Webster, "Problems of Authenticity—Opus 3: Relations Between the Documentary and Stylistic Evidence," *Haydn Studies*, 100. (Webster was paraphrasing an article by Jens Peter Larsen.) Also see comments by Christa Landon, George Feder, James Webster, and William S. Newman in *Haydn Studies*, 74, 77-78, 80, 118-19 and Wolfgang Plath, "Vorwort," *Wolfgang Amadeus Mozart: Neue Ausgabe sämtlicher Werke. Serie X: Supplement* (Kassel: Bärenreiter, 1980) xviii.

# INTRODUCTION

some musicologists have resorted to style analysis in their authenticity studies. For example, in their catalogue of Sammartini's works, Newell Jenkins and Bathia Churgin employed style as the deciding factor when determining authenticity.[38] Similarly, Marvin Paymer turned to stylistic criteria in his dissertation on Pergolesi authenticity problems because of the lack of external evidence.[39] Other scholars who have shown interest in using stylistic methods in authenticity studies include Jan LaRue, Eugene Wolf, and Barry S. Brook.[40]

Establishing authenticity through a properly developed stylistic method offers a promising approach on musical grounds. When a musically educated listener hears a piece of music that he does not know, he will often try to guess who the author is. While this listener is not always correct, the rate of accuracy for educated listeners goes well beyond random guessing and clearly indicates that composers have distinctive styles that can be accurately perceived by ear. Of course, a number of substyles may be associated with a single composer: Haydn's sonata style or Haydn's symphony style or Haydn's quartet style. Nevertheless, these substyles are limited enough that they are readily identified with the composer.

If we are able to recognize a composer's style by its sound, we should be able to identify his style analytically. That such an undertaking is not easy is suggested by the reservations on using style analysis in authenticity studies cited earlier; further problems in some of the existing stylistic studies will be discussed in chapter one. Nevertheless, it seems reasonable that methods can be developed to determine authenticity by style that are as reliable as certain traditionally accepted documentary means, if the researcher can discover those elements that turn up consistently in a composer's work.

My research on authenticity in Haydn's string trios and Renaissance secular music has demonstrated that stylistic methods can be effective in establishing authenticity.[41] The keys to a successful authenticity study comprise

---

[38] Jenkins and Churgin, *op. cit.*, 27.
[39] Paymer, *op. cit.*
[40] These and other relevant works will be discussed in detail in chapter one, except for the CUNY Haydn String Trio Project, which will be included with the examination of the string trios in chapter six.
[41] "Textural Analysis as a Means of Determining Authenticity in the String Trios Attributed to Haydn;" "The Three M. Ič Pieces in *Perugia 431*," unpublished seminar paper, City University of New York, 1982; and "Authenticity Problems in the Chansons of Pietrequin and Fresneau: A Systematic Stylistic Investigation," unpublished paper, 1984.

## INTRODUCTION

1) a well-planned method applied consistently to all compositions in a particular investigation,

2) careful comparison between the doubtful works and a group of solidly authenticated pieces in the same genre by the composer in question,

3) comparing movements that are analogous, such as minuets with minuets, not minuets with rondo finales,

4) examination of a properly selected group of contemporaneous works of the same type as the authentic and doubtful ones to determine which traits are a part of the musical vernacular of the time, and

5) a thorough cross-checking of the results by all possible means—documentary evidence, other stylistic factors, expert opinion, intuition, and studying several movements in multimovement compositions.

Also vital in an authenticity study are

1) concentrating on details of style that might seem insignificant in an analysis made for understanding the music, but which might be the key to determining authenticity and
2) using quantitative methods, which uncover "hidden communicators."

Both these techniques help separate what is consistent in a large number of pieces from what is unique to a single composition. Scholars working in the fields of art history and literature have often employed insignificant details of style in establishing authenticity.[42] For example, the nineteenth-century art-historian Giovanni Morelli attributed a painting to Botticelli, which was wrongly ascribed to Fra Filippo Lippi, based on the treatment of the fingers, fingernails, and nose.[43]

---

[42]See Bernard Berenson, "Rudiments of Connoisseurship," in *The Study and Criticism of Italian Art, Second Series* (London: G. Bell & Sons, 1902) and William J. Paisley, "Identifying the Unknown Communicator in Painting, Literature, and Music: The Significance of Minor Encoding Habits," *Journal of Communication* XIV (1964) 219-37. The Paisley study contains an excellent summary of the development of stylistic methods for determining authenticity in both art and literature. Selected examples of such studies will be given in chapter one.

[43]John Pope-Hennessy, "Connoisseurship," *The Study and Criticism of Italian Sculpture* (New York: The Metropolitan Museum of Art, 1980), 15.

*INTRODUCTION*

The term hidden communicator is adapted from William Paisley's term "unknown communicator" and indicates those aspects of a composer's style that are unconscious and therefore less likely to change from piece to piece. One can discern such hidden communicators by quantitative methods, such as studying the ranges of harmonic change and textural change.[44]

If stylistic methods can be so effective, why, then, has the stylistic approach raised such controversy? The answer lies in the procedures used in previous studies. In trying to define the style of the aforementioned Ordoñez symphony, Landon employed the following characteristics:

> The work has that strong rhythmic drive, that forward push that is so characteristic of Haydn's symphonic music in the early 1760's. There are several other confirming details: for instance, the nervous bass line, with its repeated quarter notes; the lean orchestration, in which oboes and horns are sparingly but telling used; and so forth.[45]

All these characteristics, however, were a part of the contemporary musical vernacular. No wonder, then, that Landon was unable to produce convincing results.

Webster's objections are on much more solid ground than Landon's, but they can be countered by using technique 4 from the list on page 13. One does not need to examine every eighteenth-century piece; a representative group should show which specific traits are characteristic of a particular composer and which are found in a large number of composers. After examining an extensive number of traits, a distinctive profile will emerge for a particular composer that clearly distinguishes his style from that of any other composer.

While it is obvious that the objections to stylistic approaches are due to oversimplification and a lack of consistent method, another question has to be answered because of the problem treated in this dissertation. This question is whether a composer's early works show enough consistency for stylistic methods to be effective. For example, Karl Geiringer during the discussion of Landon's Isham conference paper declared,

---

[44]The techniques mentioned in this paragraph will be discussed in detail in chapter two.
[45]Landon, "Problems of Authenticity," 33.

## INTRODUCTION

You [Landon] have clearly pointed out, and Mr. Downes has agreed, that it is dangerous to follow stylistic evidence in ascertaining the authenticity of a composition. I think that we all agree that works of the young Haydn are very similar to those of other composers, and by no means superior in quality. In such cases stylistic evidence is, as you have observed, of no value.[46]

The first objection to this statement is that it assumes the traditional opinion that Haydn developed as a composer only very slowly. This could not be further from the truth, except, perhaps, when he is compared to a Mozart. The first three symphonies Haydn wrote for the Esterházys (Nos. 6-8; ?1761) are generally regarded as being among his finest compositions, and these were written when he was about twenty-nine; Beethoven began his Second Symphony at the age of thirty-one. Numerous compositions from the 1750s are also very excellent (such as the Cassation in G, II:2; the early string quartets, op. 1 and 2; and many of the string trios), and Haydn's skill as a composer was evident very early in his career. Perhaps, some scholars have too glibly confused Haydn's growth as a composer of quality with the changes of style of late eighteenth-century music in general. Just because the post-1780 works are more in what we regard as the "classical style" doesn't mean that Haydn was not a mature composer in the 1750s and 60s.

My study of Haydn's string trios, some of which may date from the early 1750s,[47] turned up a great deal of consistency within the group, with the same set of criteria being equally applicable to earlier and later trios. In addition, my evaluation of other contemporary string trios revealed considerable diversity within the genre. Only those trios closest to Haydn's in style, mainly by Austrians, could be confused with his works, and the differences between Haydn and other contemporary Austrians showed up vividly on the quantitative tests. There is no reason that such methods should not work equally as well with Haydn's other early compositions.[48]

---

[46]Discussion following Landon, "Problems of Authenticity," 50.
[47]Landon believes that some date from the early 1750s and that they run at the most to the 1760s. Landon, *Haydn: The Early Years*, 219. Larsen concurs with this opinion, and quotes Carpani's statement that "A year after *Der krumme Teufel* [?1751; first performance Vienna May 29, 1753] Haydn began his real career and started it with six trios." Larsen, *The New Grove Haydn*, 14.
[48]Stylistic methods also work well when applied to the music of minor composers. This
*continued*

INTRODUCTION

## THE SCOPE AND FORMAT OF THIS STUDY

This study examines the authenticity of all those instrumental, multimovement compositions attributed to Haydn whose authenticity is in doubt and which were probably written before 1770 (not including groups of marches, minuets, or other dances). Works with Haydn attributions that have been proven spurious on documentary grounds are not considered. However, those pieces that are generally regarded as highly suspicious but which have not been conclusively established as nonauthentic, such as the Opus 3 string quartets, are studied. Compositions that are examined include sixteen keyboard sonatas, six accompanied keyboard divertimentos, ten keyboard trios, thirty-one string trios, six string quartets, nineteen miscellaneous divertimentos, a horn concerto, a violin concerto, and eight keyboard concertos.

This study falls into three parts: Part I (Introduction and chapter one) is an introduction to authenticity studies and a survey of the literature on authenticity, both documentary and stylistic, including fields outside of music, such as art history and literature; Part II (chapter two) presents my method for evaluating the doubtful works; and Part III (chapters three to nine) applies the method to Haydn's compositions. In Part III, a separate chapter is devoted to each major genre.[49] In addition to the stylistic tests, each chapter includes pertinent documentary evidence and a survey of previous opinions on the authenticity of the works in question. The final chapter (chapter ten) draws together my conclusions on the authenticity of Haydn's early instrumental works and discusses further my method for establishing authenticity. A revised list of Haydn's early instrumental compositions predicated on the results of the tests is included in Appendix A.

---

was very clear in both my M. Ič study and Pietrequin-Fresneau paper. See also the study of op. 3 in chapter seven.

[49]Those readers who wish to examine only one genre (keyboard sonatas, concertos, etc.) need not read the entire study, but should read at least chapter two, which explains the method.

CHAPTER ONE

# Literature on Stylistic Methods of Determining Authenticity

Following World War I, as a part of the efflorescence of musicological activity, a number of scholars presented authenticity determinations, based wholly or in part on style-critical evaluation, which were often less than scientific.[1] Larsen's source-critical approach, however, pushed the development of stylistic methods out of the mainstream of musicological research. Not until the 1960s did scholars attempt to develop new stylistic methods for authenticity determination, and the few studies that were done in the 60s and 70s were not well accepted by the musicological community. These studies were highly experimental, and, with one exception (see Paymer below), they were not applied on a large enough scale to prove their effectiveness. Nevertheless, an examination of these studies is useful because they recount the development of style-analytical approaches and may suggest further avenues for authenticity research.

Following a brief discussion of the use of stylistic methods in art history and literature, I shall examine and evaluate each major stylistic authenticity study in music (with the exception of the CUNY Haydn String Trio Project, which will be considered in chapter six). I shall present the methods of each study, then discuss any problems with the study. Criteria for evaluating the methods will include 1) consistency

---

[1]Such as C. S. Smith, "Haydn's Chamber Music and the Flute," *The Musical Quarterly* XIX (1933) 435-40. See also Larsen, "A Survey of the Development of Haydn Research," 20-21.

and thoroughness, 2) logical flaws, 3) usefulness of the method, 4) amount of testing of the method, and 5) how differences of chronology, genre, meter, and instrumentation are treated.

## ART HISTORY AND LITERATURE

The use of stylistic criteria in deciding authenticity dates from the eighteenth century in art history and the nineteenth century in literature. Jonathan Richardson the Elder (1719) first suggested the adoption of stylistic methods in art historical studies, but connoisseurship (the name generally given to the determination of authenticity by style in art history) became a method with Giovanni Morelli. William Paisley, writes,

> Whereas his colleagues were content to accept the testimony of Vasari and other early historians of art, Morelli contended that paintings sufficiently identified themselves, each work signed by its creator in dozens of little details, which no two painters executed alike. Traditional criteria based on the overall study of a work were entirely misleading, he claimed, since the student of any Renaissance studio soon learned the superficial marks of his master's style.[2]

Likewise, Morelli's student, Bernard Berenson, declared that

> Obviously what distinguishes one artist from another are the characteristics he does not share with others. If, therefore, we isolate the precise characteristics distinguishing each artist, they must furnish a perfect test of the fitness or unfitness of the attribution of a given work to a given master.[3]

Morelli's methods remained as the basis of connoisseurship in art during the early twentieth-century and into our own day. Roberto Longhi (1930) advocated the use of intuition in the attribution process, but Richard Offner (1927) wanted more reliable methods, stressing the importance of specialization. Concerning the value of connoisseurship in modern art-historical studies, W. Eugene Kleinbauer writes,

> Even though connoisseurship in the Morellian tradition is far less common today than it was in the first decades of this century, it is neverthe-

---

[2]Paisley, "Identifying the Unknown Communicator," 220-21.
[3]Berenson, *The Study and Criticism of Italian Art*, 123-24.

less here to stay, in spite of the recent advances in scientific techniques to assist in determination of authenticity and attribution. Of course, its need is now less pressing. With problems of attribution to major masters and groups or schools of artists no longer critical, historians have shifted their attention to other aspects of the visual arts and have applied different techniques of analysis.[4]

Of modern art historians, John Pope-Hennessy seems to have adopted connoisseurship most often.[5] In one study, he attributed a lost bronze statue (bronze casts survive) that had formerly been ascribed to Donatello to Antonio del Pollaiuolo.[6] He mainly based his determination on the eccentric construction of the statue—its use of three supports, the two feet and a cloak resting on the ground behind, which was similar to that of small bronzes of Pollaiuolo. Supporting evidence included

1) "the modeling of the arms and the attenuated, rather mannered forefingers, which have parallels in the reliefs of *Theology and Dialetic* on the Sixtus IV tomb;"

2) "the treatment of the temples, which are shown as indented planes receding sharply from the forehead in a way that recalls the treatment of the shoulders and shoulder blades of the *Hercules* in the Bargello;" and

3) "the heavy drapery which falls free of the spare, ascetic limbs in a way that cannot but remind us of the cloak of Hercules in the *Hercules and Antaeus* bronze."

Word lengths were the first criterion used for authenticity determination in literary studies. In 1851, August de Moran wrote,

> I should expect to find that one man writing on two different subjects agrees more nearly with himself than two different men writing on the same subject. Some day spurious writings will be detected by this test [word-lengths]. Mind, I told you so.[7]

---

[4]W. Eugene Kleinbauer, *Modern Perspectives in Western Art History* (New York: Holt, Rinehart, and Winston, 1971) 48.
[5]John Pope-Hennessy, "Connoisseurship," 11-38.
[6]Pope-Hennessy, *op. cit.*, 29-31.
[7]Quoted in Daniel Lawrence Brantley, *Disputed Authorship of Musical Works: A Quantitative Approach to the Quartets Published as Haydn's Opus 3*, Ph.D. diss., University of Iowa, 1977, 21.

Word-length studies written in the nineteenth-century include those by T. C. Mendenhall and Lucius A. Sherman.[8]

Among techniques modern literary historians have employed in authenticity studies are word-length frequencies; frequency of "favorite" words; the frequency of minor words such as the; and the absence of certain words.[9] One of the most interesting studies in literature is that of Frederich Mosteller and David Wallace on the authorship of the *Federalist Papers*.[10] These papers had appeared in various New York newspapers in 1787 and 1788 and advocated the ratification of the U. S. constitution. Most of the seventy-seven papers have been ascribed to Alexander Hamilton, James Madison, or John Jay, but twelve of the papers lacked attributions. Believing that the anonymous papers were either by Hamilton or Madison, Mosteller and Wallace set up four separate studies, each based on word frequencies and employing statistical methods. In their study, these authors examined the frequency of function words (less important words including articles, prepositions, and adverbs) in the writings of Hamilton and Madison. They used function words instead of more important words because both Hamilton and Madison adopted the contemporary rhetoric, which created many standard practices, and because filler words are nearly invariant under a change of topic. The results of all four studies pointed to Madison as the author of the disputed papers.

## PAISLEY STUDY

The first attempt to develop new stylistic methods for testing authorship in music came from a scholar who was not in music. William

---

[8]T. C. Mendenhall, "The Characteristic Curve of Composition," *Science* IX (1887) 237-249 and Lucius A. Sherman, "Some Observations upon Sentence-Length in English Prose," *University of Nebraska Studies* I/2 (1888) 119-30.

[9]These studies include George Yule, *The Statistical Study of Literary Vocabulary* (Cambridge: Cambridge University Press, 1944); Alvan Ellegard, *A Statistical Method of Determining Authorship* (Gothenberg, Sweden: Elanders Boktryckeri Aktiebolag, 1962); Bernard O'Donnell, "Stephan Crane's The O'Ruddy: A Problem in Authorship Determination," *The Computer and Literary Style*, ed. Jacob Leed (Kent, Ohio: Kent State University Press, 1966) 107-115; and Claude Brinegan, "Mark Twain and the Quintus Snodgrass Letters: A Statistical Test of Authorship," *Journal of the American Statistical Association* LVIII (1963) 85-96.

[10]Frederich Mosteller and David L. Wallace, *Inference and Disputed Authorship: The Federalist* (Reading, Mass.: Addison-Wesley, 1964).

Paisley, a statistician, advocated a system of discerning authorship by examining "minor encoding habits," which produce "unknown communicators."[11] His criteria for minor encoding habits include

1) "The detail to be studied should not be prominent, else imitators will appropriate it,"

2) "It should be executed mechanically (i.e., with little feedback from self-criticism), else the communicator consciously vary it for effect,"

3) "Its use should not be dictated wholly by convention (e.g., the halo in Renaissance paintings),"

4) "It should not be so rare that examples cannot be found in each disputed work," and

5) "The detail should remain consistent in frequency whatever the topic of the work, else topic difference will confound authorship difference."[12]

For music, Paisley tried to identify the minor encoding habits of five composers (Bach, Haydn, Mozart, Beethoven, Brahms), by studying the first five intervals of their opening themes.[13] In his first test, he tabulated two independent sets (two sets of Bach's works, two sets of Mozart's, etc.) of eight hundred two-note transitions (differences between two adjacent notes) from 160 themes ($5 \times 160 = 800$) in semitones, using the numerals 0 to 6 with 0 representing a unison, 1 a semitone, 2 a wholetone, etc. Intervals larger than a tritone were reduced to their simple forms (a m6 becomes a M3 or 4). Paisley discovered that the five composers agreed roughly in the frequency that they employed each interval but that the two sets of each composer tended to vary less around their own mean than around the ten-sample (works of all the composers) mean. To bring out these differences, he set up a statistic called the "chi-square goodness of fit test," which "provides an estimate of the probability that a given set of departures from theoretical frequencies could have occurred by chance."[14] The main formula for this test is

$$x^2 = \sum_n \frac{[nf(n) - F(n)]^2}{nf(n)}$$

[11] Paisley, "Identifying the Unknown Communicator."
[12] Paisley, *op. cit.*, 227.
[13] Unfortunately, based on Barlow and Morgenstern, which contains many errors.
[14] Paisley, *op. cit.*, 231.

From these chi-squares, he concluded that the Bach and Brahms samples could only have been written by their real composers, but that significant differences among the Haydn, Mozart, and Beethoven samples could not be made by this approach.

Paisley then tried another approach by making the classifications of two-note transitions more complex: twenty-five joint classes using the tonic, the third, the fifth, all other diatonic tones, and all chromatic tones. (Classes include tonic to tonic, tonic to third, tonic to other diatonic, third to fifth, etc.) The inconclusive results of this test resembled those for the first one. Next, Paisley made chi-squares from the above statistics. The results show that each of the five composers had at least a 50-50 chance to have written his own works, but more than a 1000 to 1 chance that he could have written the works of the other four composers. Paisley also tried four other groups of compositions (by Handel, Mozart, Beethoven, and Mendelssohn; 160 works in each group) against the last set of statistics. The chi-squares clearly demonstrate that none of the five composers of the original samples (Bach, Haydn, Mozart, Beethoven, Brahms) could have written the Handel or Mendelssohn samples, that the Bach, Haydn, and Brahms samples could not have been written by any of the four other composers (Handel, Mozart, Beethoven, Mendelssohn); and that Beethoven could not have written the Mozart sample or Mozart the Beethoven sample. Concerning the other two possibilities he states,

> . . . sample 2 [Mozart] could easily represent a chance deviation from Mozart's mean frequencies, while sample 3 [Beethoven] suggests a more outlying but quite possible deviation from Beethoven's mean frequencies. Foreknowledge of the authorship of samples 2 and 3 may dispose the investigator to attribute them to Mozart and Beethoven, but it seems that the chi-squares speak for themselves.[15]

While suggesting that composers have consistent ways of structuring melodies, Paisley's method has little practical application for authenticity determination. His system involves large groups of works (160 incipits compared with 160 incipits) and cannot be used for establishing the authenticity of individual pieces. Perhaps, his system would have had greater applicability if he had studied all the intervals in a work in a small number of pieces. Had he discovered in a sample of

---

[15]Paisley, *op. cit.*, 234-45.

twenty pieces that 5-10% of the intervals in each piece were unisons, 15-25% minor seconds, etc., and, if these patterns differed from those of other composers, then such figures would be helpful in evaluating doubtful works.[16]

## COMPUTER STUDIES

Several scholars have experimented with the computer to see if it is useful in authenticity studies. Arthur Mendel and Lewis Lockwood had Josquin's masses and 60-odd motets encoded into the computer, to answer a number of important questions about his music, including problems of musica ficta, range, and authenticity.[17] They discovered a number of difficulties with such an approach, including

1) how to change musical notation into computer language,

2) the many errors that occurred during the encoding process,

3) the large mass of undifferentiated data produced,

4) the computer's lack of critical discrimination, and

5) that they had to begin by asking extremely simple questions that often seemed irrelevant or inane.[18]

On the other hand, the computer quickly performed tasks that would take mere humans months or years, and it was unfailingly accurate as long as the information fed to it was accurate. Mendel sums up his first article by saying, "The computer can be, I am convinced, an im-

---

[16]Both the Paisley study and literary studies of word frequencies suggest that an interval frequency profile might be effective in establishing authenticity in music. However, such a study of the top voice of the expositions from the first movements of Haydn's piano sonatas from the early 1770s demonstrated that Haydn's interval frequency profile in these works is not significantly different from that of other contemporaneous composers. It remains to be shown whether compositions from other periods and genres yield equally disappointing results.

[17]Arthur Mendel, "Toward Objective Criteria for Establishing Chronology and Authenticity: What Help Can the Computer Give?" *Josquin des Pres: Proceedings of the International Josquin Festival Conference*, ed. Edward E. Lowinsky with Bonnie J. Blackburn (London: Oxford University Press, 1976) 297-308 and "Some Preliminary Attempts at Computer-Assisted Style-Analysis in Music," *Computers and the Humanities* IV (1969) 41-52.

[18]Of course, the work of Mendel and Lockwood was an early attempt at using the computer in musicological research and the process of encoding music has been refined since their pioneering studies.

mensely useful tool to the musicologist. But there is no danger and no hope that it will relieve him of the responsibility of hearing, judging, and thinking."[19] Yet, he also believes that "It is conceivable that our techniques of question-asking may some day develop to the point where we can program the computer to tell with a high degree of probability Josquin from Pierre de la Rue."[20]

Frederick Crane and Judith Fiehler undertook a computer study of twenty fifteenth-century chansons to test the computer's accuracy in establishing authorship.[21] They believed that "it is natural that analysts should look to the computer for assistance, as music lends itself well to alphanumeric notation, and because so much of analysis (counting chords and the like) is mechanical and tedious."[22] In addition, computers had performed successfully in other fields, including biology, psychology, ecology, archaeology, linguistics, and literary history, and such techniques could be applied to music.

For their test, they selected seven chansons attributed to Pierre Fontaine, five to Nicolas Grenon, and eight to Jacques Vide. The Crane-Fiehler method appears to be rigorous, comprehensive, and highly consistent. Their results produced three distinct clusters of compositions that are similar and predominately contain the works of one composer. However, they were disappointed with the results because six of the twenty pieces fell into the wrong group, and because two of the compositions did not join any cluster.

Daniel Lawrence Brantley based his computer study of the "Haydn Opus 3" on the methods of Crane and Fiehler.[23] He compared thirteen characteristics in Haydn's op. 9 quartets and Hoffstetter's op. 2 quartets, to try to determine which composer wrote the disputed op. 3. In his study, he separated fast movements from slow movements (and did not consider minuets because the Hoffstetter op. 2 quartets had none), yielding twelve fast movements by Haydn, twelve by Hoffstetter, and eleven in op. 3 and six slow movements by Haydn, six by Hoffstetter, and five disputed. The study assigned eight of the eleven op. 3 fast movements to Hoffstetter and three to Haydn, with a 79% probability

---

[19]Mendel, "Toward Objective Criteria," 52.
[20]Mendel, "Some Preliminary Attempts," 308.
[21]Fredrick Crane and Judith Fiehler, "Numerical Methods of Comparing Musical Styles," *The Computer and Music* (Ithaca: Cornell University Press, 1970) 209-22.
[22]Crane and Fichler, *op. cit.*, 209.
[23]Brantley, *Disputed Authorship*.

of success. It gave four of the five op. 3 slow movements to Hoffstetter and one to Haydn, but with only a 50% probability of success. From the above, Brantley concluded that all six quartets were by Hoffstetter.

Unfortunately, Brantley's study does not settle the disputed authorship of op. 3. That four of the sixteen movements (25%) were assigned to Haydn while twelve of the sixteen were ascribed to Hoffstetter, by itself, raises serious questions about the study. (Four of the six quartets contained movements attributed to both composers.) In addition, in a reliability check by Brantley, the computer misassigned two of the twelve Hoffstetter op. 2 fast movements, two of the six slow Hoffstetter op. 2, three of the twelve fast Haydn op. 9, and two of the six slow Haydn op. 9.

The most important problem with the study, though, is two major misconceptions: 1) that the quartets must either be by Haydn or Hoffstetter and no other composer and 2) that they are comparable to either Haydn's op. 9 or Hoffstetter's op. 2. Concerning the first problem, only the first two quartets can be assigned to Hoffstetter on documentary grounds; the remainder may be by Hoffstetter, but they could just as conceivably be by another composer or composers, including Haydn.[24] Therefore, Brantley should have included works by other composers in his study to insure the reliability of the results and also left open the possibility that some of the quartets may have been written by Hoffstetter and others by Haydn.

Concerning the second problem, the dating of the op. 3 quartets is uncertain; the only thing scholars are sure about is that they must have been written before 1777, the date of first publication, but they were probably composed much earlier. Because of the uncertain chronology, it might have been better to compare op. 3 to Haydn's op. 1 or 2 or, better still, selections from op. 1, 2, and 9 to insure that the profile applies to all possible years that Haydn could have composed them. More importantly, the Hoffstetter quartets that Brantley used are probably his latest ones; they were published in Mannheim c. 1780.[25] It would have been far preferable to employ the two quartets written c. 1765 or the op. 1 quartets (London, 1774). As it is, Brantley is comparing Haydn quartets from around 1770 with Hoffstetter quartets from about ten years later. Differences in style uncovered in Brantley's

---

[24]See the discussion in the Introduction in chapter seven.
[25]Date from Hubert Unverricht, "Roman Hoffstetter," *The New Grove*, VII, 631.

study could just as easily be due to differences in chronology as differences between Haydn and Hoffstetter. Brantley has not eliminated Haydn as the author of op. 3 and, even more so, the possibility that another composer may have written nos. 3-6. (I shall investigate the authorship of these works in chapter seven.)

While none of the above studies have conclusively proven the effectiveness of computers in authenticity determination, it is probable that further research will. I am not using a computer in my investigations, because I believe that the work involved in turning musical notation into computer language and developing the computer program for determining authenticity is much greater than the work involved in applying my present methods.

## JAN LARUE'S ACTIVITY ANALYSIS

Jan LaRue has developed the first quantitative approach to authenticity in music, which he calls "functional correlation analysis" and, in two later articles, "activity analysis."[26] In the first article, he assigns numerical values to activity in pitch, harmony, and rhythm in each measure, then compares the rates of change in these values. For harmony, he gives root movement up or down a fifth or fourth a value of 3; root movement up a second or down a second or a third a value of 2; and root movement up a third, over an organ point, or changes of mode a value of 1. For example, a measure that contains the harmonies I-IV-V would receive five points; 3 for the root movement of a fourth, 2 for the root movement of a second. With melody, he usually assigns each interval its own value (2 points for a second, 5 for a fifth) but a neighbor motion, such as C-D-C, receives 3 points instead of 4. Thus, a measure containing the pitches $c^1$-$e^1$-$g^1$-$f^1$-$c^1$-$d^1$-$c^1$ would get 15 points ($3+3+2+4+3=15$). One determines rhythmic values by adding two figures: a) the number of notes in a measure and b) the number of changes in rhythmic value. Thus, ♩ ♫ ♩ ♩ receives 7 points (five notes plus two changes in rhythmic value), while ♩ ♬ scores 6 points (five notes plus one change in

---

[26]Jan LaRue, "Mozart or Dittersdorf," *Mozart-Jahrbuch* 1971/72, 40-49; "Remarks on Activity Analysis," *Haydn Studies*, 102-03; and "Mozart Authentication by Activity Analysis: A Progress Report," *Mozart-Jahrbuch* 1978/79, 209-214.

rhythmic value). According to his method, LaRue uses the entire texture for harmony, but only the main melodic line for pitch and rhythm. Applying this approach to every measure in a composition (or section of a composition) results in the "correlation among harmony, melody, and rhythm." LaRue assigns values for the relationship of change in activity between two measure: 5 points, all three elements similar in activity; 4 points, two elements similar, one inactive; 3 points, two elements similar, one opposed; 2 points, two or three elements inactive; and 1 point, two elements opposed, one inactive. For example, a change from harmony 2, pitch 6, rhythm 4 in one measure to harmony 4, pitch 7, and rhythm 8 in the next measure would receive 5 points because all three parameters increase in activity, while a change from 2, 6, 4 to 1, 8, 4 would get 1 point because two elements are opposed while one is inactive. One adds the scores for each measure and divides by the number of measures then multiplies the total by twenty to turn the figures into percentages.

Another quantitative figure that can be determined from the above is the "activity plateau," "the percentage of bars that continue without a change in the level of activity."[27] One calculates this figure for each parameter—harmony, pitch, and rhythm. For instance, if the pitch of a measure and the following measure both have a value of 7, then the second measure is on the same activity plateau as the first. To establish the percentage of activity plateau, one counts the number of measures (for each parameter) in which the activity is the same as in the preceding or following measure and divides by the total measures. I have applied LaRue's method in Example I below, and I shall employ the same excerpt (Haydn's XVI:2/II) to illustrate the other methods discussed.

In LaRue's second authenticity article in *Haydn Studies*, he makes some important modifications in his system. First, he lists the activity for each parameter (again, harmony, melody, and rhythm) and looks for patterns, finding, for example, surges of activity in odd numbered measures in a Haydn string quartet. Next, he combines the totals of the separate parameters and again checks for patterns. The only important change in his third article is that he calculates by beats rather than measures.

Despite the importance of LaRue's work in developing a method for

---

[27]LaRue, "Mozart or Dittersdorf," 48.

# LITERATURE ON STYLISTIC METHODS

## Example I. Application of LaRue Method

| | | | | | |
|---|---|---|---|---|---|
| Pitch | 10 | 21 | 24 | 4 | 23 |
| Rhythm | 7 | 7 | 12 | 4 | 10 |
| Harmony | 0 | 3 | 7 | 0 | |

Correlation Score      4      4      3      3

Correlation quotient: 56

$$\frac{(4 + 4 + 3 + 3 \times 20}{5} = 56\%)$$

Activity Plateaus,

Harmony: 40.0
Rhythm: 40.0
Pitch:   0.0
Total:  80.0
$(2 \div 5 = 40.0\%)$

establishing authenticity by style analysis, several major problems exist in his system or his application of that system. First, he makes no comment about the effect of chronology on his method and little about limitations of instrumentation or types of movements. Second, in his first two articles, his system contains no way to treat different meters, and, even in his third article where he figures by beats instead of measures, one cannot be certain that the results apply to all meters. Third, LaRue does not test enough previously-authenticated pieces. In his Mozart-Dittersdorf article, he employs three Mozart and four Dittersdorf works as a control. In some cases, this might be enough pieces to establish authenticity, but not with the results that he obtained. The correlation quotients for the three Mozart works were 61, 60, and 62; for the Dittersdorf 36, 47, 56, and 72; and for the questionable piece 62. While the score of the questionable work does align it closely with the Mozart, one cannot eliminate Dittersdorf as the possible author; 62 lies between 56 and 72. His activity plateau figures more strongly indicate Mozart, but unfortunately LaRue has not shown the scores for each composition; he has averaged the scores of the three Mozart and the four Dittersdorf. It is still possible that while the average activity plateaus for the Dittersdorf and the doubtful composition differ significantly, the score of one of the Dittersdorf works could be close to the score of the doubtful piece. In his article on Haydn's op. 3, LaRue uses only one work of each type, an op. 2, an op. 3, and an op. 9 example, and, in his third article, he employs just three compositions by Mozart to determine if a symphony attributed to Mozart is by him.

The most serious flaw in LaRue's authenticity studies, though, is that he has not applied his method on a large-enough scale to prove it works. While there is no reason to say that it will not work, there is equally no reason to assume that it will. Some factors within a composer's output remain consistent while others do not, and the only way to prove consistency is by experimentation on a large-scale. It must be pointed out, however, that LaRue declared that his system was in the experimental stage, and he may correct these problems in the future. Despite these flaws, LaRue's system is a very important advance in the study of authenticity by style analysis.

Two of LaRue's students have adopted their teacher's method. Lester S. Steinberg employed activity analysis to understand the musical flow in Haydn's keyboard trios.[28] He simplified LaRue's system because he wanted to concentrate on large- and middle-dimension areas rather than foreground detail. He establishes melodic activity by adding the intervals between each pair of pitches, harmonic activity by calculating the number of chord changes, and rhythmic activity by counting the number of impacts, then he divides these figures by the number of measures. For example, if an eight-measure excerpt has 8 chord changes, 24 interval value, and 28 impacts, the harmonic density would be 1.00 ($8 \div 8 = 1$), the melodic density 3.00 ($24 \div 8 = 3$), and the rhythmic density 3.50 ($28 \div 8 = 3.5$). The "activity factor" arises from adding the three density figures. (In the preceding example, the total is 7.50) Steinberg applies this method to several sections (first-theme group, transition, second-theme group, closing, etc.) of Haydn's keyboard trios. He discovered that Haydn's trios show certain tendencies but "do not conform to any single pattern."[29]

Although his main emphasis is on understanding patterns of activ-

---

[28]Lester A. Steinberg, "A Numerical Approach to Activity and Movement in the Sonata-Form Movements of Haydn's Piano Trios," *Haydn Studies*, 515-22.
[29]Steinberg, *op. cit.*, 519.

ity, Steinberg does briefly use the system for authenticity determination, examining two keyboard trios that are attributed to both Haydn and Pleyel.[30] He concluded that "had it not already been established that they are not authentic works, this method would certainly have aroused strong suspicions."[31] However, Steinberg's figures do not conclusively prove the authorship of these trios.

A critical examination of Steinberg's tables reveals four important things about LaRue's method and about establishing authenticity in general. First, the wide range between his figures for single characteristics indicates to me that this approach (which is a modification of LaRue's system for purposes other than authenticity) is useful for reinforcing other information on authenticity but that it might be difficult to employ as a central factor in solving authorship questions. For instance, according to Steinberg's tables, in Haydn's late period trios (1790-96), the activity factor in the exposition varies between the extremes 15.19 and 38.43, a difference of 23.24, which translates into a combination of rhythmic impacts, changes of harmony, and interval variations adding up to 23 per measure, a range that seems too wide to establish authenticity.[32] Second, Steinberg's article demonstrates the importance of examining small sections; his figures indicate that different sections may have radically different activity factors. The activity factors for XV:16/I in Steinberg's chart are first-theme group 20.58, transition 16.40, second-theme group 22.13, closing 16.40, exposition 18.69, and development 19.62, while those for the same sections in XV:26/I are 13.63, 26.23, 47.71, 30.55, 28.51, and 41.56.[33] The only problem with examining small sections is that subsections are often difficult to define; it is clear, though, that having separate figures for sections that are less ambiguous, such as exposition and development or minuet and trio, might be useful. Third, Steinberg's charts show the importance of examining patterns. While he did not find one pervading pattern within all of Haydn's trios (such as activity factor always decreases for the second theme and always increases for the closing), he did uncover a limited number of consistent patterns. That a trio does not conform to one of these patterns may cast doubt on its authenticity or serve as a supporting factor within a larger argument.

---

[30]The Haydn-Pleyel trio controversy will be examined in detail in chapter two.
[31]Steinberg, *op. cit.*, 522.
[32]Steinberg, *op. cit.*, Table 4, 521.
[33]*Ibid.*

## OF DETERMINING AUTHENTICITY

Finally, Steinberg's work shows that, for his figures at least, there are clear stylistic differences among early, middle, and late compositions. For example, the average activity factors in Haydn's middle period trios are approximately one third lower than those of the early period.[34] Clearly, any authenticity study must consider chronology.

Eugene Wolf's article on the authenticity of a symphony attributed to both Stamitz and Richter is, in many ways, a model of what an authenticity study should be, evincing an excellent understanding of the problems involved, both documentary and stylistic.[35] He believes that the key to determining authenticity when dealing with stylistic criteria is seemingly insignificant detail, and that one way to determine such detail is by an analytical approach similar to that of LaRue. He began his study by examining the documentary evidence, including the number of attributions for each composer, the relationship among various sources (whether one is derived from another), and the reliability of each attribution. Next, he turned to general stylistic features, such as formal plans, instrumentation, melodic inventiveness, and textural variety. Finally, he applied LaRue's approach with certain modifications, employing an authentic symphony by Richter and one by Stamitz as controls. He first determined the correlation index (LaRue's correlation quotient) for the three works (doubtful symphony, Richter symphony, Stamitz symphony). Next he developed a new figure he calls the "activity index," which is calculated by multiplying the separate parameters in each measure. If the values for a measure are harmony 3, pitch 3, rhythm 2, the activity index for that measure is 18 (3x3x2=18). He then adds the totals for each measure and divides by the number of measures to obtain an average for a particular section. Wolf believes that the activity index "takes into account the actual degree of activity in each parameter and can thus produce greater discrimination between works."[36] Wolf also invented another quantitative figure, the "fluctuation ratio." For this ratio, he calculated the relationship of activity between measures by dividing the smaller figure into the larger one. If two adjacent measures have activity indexes of 4 and 12, the fluctuation ratio would be 3 (12÷4=3). Again, he em-

---

[34]Steinberg, *op. cit.*, 520.
[35]Eugene Wolf, "Authenticity and Stylistic Evidence in the Early Symphony: A Conflicting Attribution between Richter and Stamitz," *A Musical Offering*, ed. Edward H. Clinkscale and Claire Brook (New York: Pendragon Press, 1977) 273-94.
[36]Wolf, *op. cit.*, 291.

ployed the average of the ratios for a section. One may also determine the width of the fluctuation ratios between measures. For instance, one can calculate the percentage of measures in a section that had a narrow fluctuation ratio from the preceding measure, say 1 to 1.5. An application of Wolf's various methods can be seen in Example II.

## Example II. Application of Wolf Method

| Pitch   | 10 | 21 | 24 | 4 | 23 |
| ------- | -- | -- | -- | - | -- |
| Rhythm  | 7  | 7  | 12 | 4 | 10 |
| Harmony | 0  | 3  | 3  | 7 | 0  |

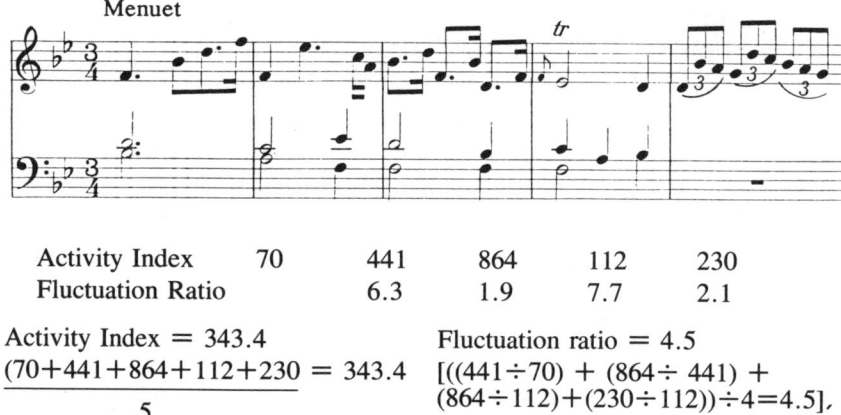

| Activity Index    | 70 | 441 | 864 | 112 | 230 |
| ----------------- | -- | --- | --- | --- | --- |
| Fluctuation Ratio |    | 6.3 | 1.9 | 7.7 | 2.1 |

Activity Index = 343.4
$$\frac{(70+441+864+112+230)}{5} = 343.4$$

Fluctuation ratio = 4.5
$[((441 \div 70) + (864 \div 441) + (864 \div 112) + (230 \div 112)) \div 4 = 4.5]$.

% of measures with a narrow fluctuation ratio (less than 2) = 20.0 $(1 \div 5 = 20.0\%)$

Note: Wolf determines the figures for pitch, rhythm, and harmony slightly differently than LaRue, but to avoid confusion I kept the LaRue type figures in the chart. In calculating the activity indexes, zeros were disregarded.

Wolf concluded his article by examining activity plateaus.
   One important flaw exists in Wolf's article; he employed only one Stamitz and one Richter symphony as controls in the quantitative sections. Still, the fact that all evidence—documentary, general stylistic features, and quantitative analysis—points to Richter creates a convincing case for Richter as the author of this symphony.

*OF DETERMINING AUTHENTICITY*

## PAYMER STUDY

In his dissertation on the authenticity of Pergolesi's instrumental works, Marvin Paymer refined LaRue's method and combined it with other tests, producing the first truly comprehensive stylistic approach to authenticity.[37] Paymer's system consists of six major criteria:

1) a checklist of positive characteristics,

2) a checklist of rare characteristics,

3) a checklist of characteristics that never appear in Pergolesi,

4) a study of the percentage of similar activity in a work (based on LaRue's method),

5) the concept of the "Pergolesi style" as a "synthesis of elements," and

6) external evidence.

From the above, he developed five categories of authenticity:

Category A: authentic, met all five stylistic criteria;

Category B: probably authentic, met three or four of the stylistic criteria;

Category C: doubtful, passed only one or two of the stylistic criteria;

Category D: probably spurious, failed all five stylistic criteria; and

Category E: spurious, failed at least three stylistic criteria and criterion 6.

Paymer modified LaRue's system, because, like Wolf, he believed that it does not adequately quantify the amount of change of activity.[38] He uses the same method for figuring activity in individual measures, but simplifies relationships between measures to only two categories: 1) similar activity and 2) opposing or nonactivity. When the three parameters (melody, harmony, rhythm) move in the same direction be-

---

[37]Paymer, *The Instrumental Music Attributed to Pergolesi.* Paymer developed his method in conjunction with his dissertation advisor Barry S. Brook. Brook's major contribution to the study of authenticity by style is his notion of using three groups of works: 1) the doubtful works, 2) authentic works by the possible composer, and 3) works not by the composer. For more on Brook's authenticity work, see chapter six.
[38]Paymer, *op. cit.*, 163-70.

tween two measures (all either increase in activity or decrease in activity) or when two parameters move in the same direction and the third is inactive, they fall into the former category (similar activity); and when two or more parameters are inactive or parameters move in opposite directions (one increases in activity, another decreases) they fall into the latter category (opposing or nonactivity). For example, if the figures for two contiguous measures are measure 1: harmony 6, pitch 8, rhythm 8 and measure 2: harmony 7, pitch 12, and rhythm 8 that is similar activity because two of the parameters move in the same direction while the third is inactive; while a change from 6, 8, 8 to 4, 12, 8 is not because two of the parameters move in opposite directions. To calculate the percentage of similar activity for a piece or a section of a piece, one adds the number of measures that show similar activity and divides by the total number of measures (minus the first measure), producing a percentage between 0 and 100. Paymer also determines whether the similar activity shows an increase (+) or a decrease (-), so the results of a sample using Paymer's system might be PSA: 50% (+30, -20). An example of Paymer's approach appears in Example III.

## Example III. Application of Paymer Method

| | | | | | |
|---|---|---|---|---|---|
| Pitch | 10 | 21 | 24 | 4 | 23 |
| Rhythm | 7 | 7 | 12 | 4 | 10 |
| Harmony | 0 | 3 | 3 | 7 | 0 |

PSA=50% (+50, -0) (2÷4=50%)

+=increase in activity, -=decrease in activity, x=opposing or nonactivity

For his checklists, Paymer examined the authentic Pergolesi sinfonias (the only instrumental works that are definitely authentic on documentary grounds) and determined which traits appeared frequently and which appeared rarely.[39] Checklist A contained positive characteristics that appeared in 50 to 100% of the works, Checklist B traits that appeared in 1 to 25% of the works, and Checklist C characteristics that were never present.

Paymer's "concept of the Pergolesi style as a synthesis of elements" was an attempt to compensate for the other tests, which treat Pergolesi's style as isolated traits.[40] Among the elements Paymer surveyed were phrase syntax, harmonic structure, the presence of the minor mode, baroque vs. classical texture, and the use of contrast. He summed up the Pergolesi style as ". . . an effort to reconcile high baroque elements with proto-classical tendencies."[41]

Paymer's study is admirable for the great advances it makes over previous attempts at establishing authenticity by style analysis, but it contains several, perhaps unavoidable, flaws. The first is that he determines Pergolesi's style based on six sinfonias, with limited reinforcement from authentic vocal works. While the situation is complicated owing to the limited number of previously-authenticated compositions, he was unable to take into account that different types of movements and instrumentations are normally treated differently by most composers; one cannot assume that Pergolesi's sinfonias and trio sonatas (if he had written any) will produce the same stylistic profiles. Second, Paymer's percentage of similar activity is of only limited use because it encompasses such a wide range (37-62%). This covers one quarter of the possible range, and one would expect most compositions to fall within the middle of the range (as Pergolesi's do) and avoid the extremes near 100% and 0%.

The third problem with Paymer's study is that his checklists need refinement. Many of his characteristics are too much a part of the contemporary vernacular for use in an authenticity study. In his positive list I would delete seven (out of thirty) characteristics and question seven more. Among those traits I would eliminate are "Range of keys from four flats to four sharps in major keys and four flats to three sharps in minor keys," "Proportion of second key area to length 10-45%," and "Relative key of slow movement in major works: ii, iv, IV, i, flat-vii, V, VI, flat-VI, flat-vii."[42] Moreover, some of Paymer's

---

[39]Paymer, *op. cit.*, 157-62.
[40]Paymer, *op. cit.*, 183-93.
[41]Paymer, *op. cit.*, 188.
[42]Paymer, *op. cit.*, 159.

cut-off points seem much too liberal. The positive checklist, for example, includes traits that appear in 50 to 100% of the Pergolesi works sampled. I believe that the cut-off point for positive traits should be, at most, 75%. Finally, Paymer's method would probably be more effective if he could tighten up his criteria so that he could limit himself to three (probably authentic on stylistic grounds, probably not authentic on stylistic grounds, stylistic evidence uncertain) rather than five categories of authenticity.

The true test of Paymer's approach lies in its effectiveness in establishing Pergolesi authenticity. Of course, because of the documentary problems with Pergolesi authenticity that led to Paymer's study in the first place, such an evaluation can only be tentative, but one can examine Paymer's system for its consistency and compare his results against the documentary evidence and other Pergolesi scholars' opinions. Paymer placed 15 works in Category A, 2 in Category B, 6 in Category C, 13 in Category D, and 43 in Category X.[43] Because Category X required the failure of only three criteria Paymer found it unnecessary to study all five stylistic criteria for these works. Of the remaining 36 compositions from all categories, 28 agree on all stylistic tests (Categories A and D, 77%), while 8 show conflicting results (Categories B and C; 23%). In a tighter study, one should not allow such a high percentage of compositions that show conflicting results.

On the other hand, Paymer's conclusions generally agree with the limited documentary evidence and previous scholar's opinions. Especially notable is that out of 56 compositions he labels spurious or probably spurious, 43 also fail Paymer's external evidence criterion. Concerning the 13 other pieces that Paymer considers probably spurious, most of the existing literature also doubts their authenticity. Only one work that he places in Category A (authentic) can be questioned—the Concerto for Two Harpsichords and Strings in C Major (P240-A). Charles Cudworth considers it "rather unlikely" and Helmut Hucke calls it very questionable in *MGG*.[44] Also questionable is the Concerto for Violin and Strings in B-flat Major (P36-B) in Category B (probably authentic), this time on stylistic grounds. While it does fit Paymer's requirements for Category B (it passed three criteria), it failed the neg-

---

[43]Paymer, *op. cit.*, 477.
[44]Charles L. Cudworth, "Notes on the Instrumental Works Attributed to Pergolesi," *Music and Letters* XXX/4 (1949) 323-24 and Helmut Hucke, "Pergolesi," *Die Music Geschichte und Gegenwart*, ed. Friedrich Blume (Kassel/Basel: Bärenreiter, 1962) X, 1058.

ative checklist and scored 50% (26% or more is considered failing) on the rare checklist, scores which cause one to question the work's authenticity. My conclusion regarding Paymer's approach is that, as applied in his dissertation on Pergolesi, it should be accurate between 80 and 90% of the time. Refinement could raise its accuracy considerably. Paymer's dissertation lays a good foundation for further authenticity research, and his approach must be considered by anyone studying authenticity.

## CONCLUSION

None of the previous studies on establishing authenticity by style are completely satisfying. Flaws found in the studies include

1) major logical flaws (Brantley),

2) characteristics used too general or a part of the contemporary vernacular (Paymer),

3) the effects of genre, instrumentation, meter, or chronology ignored (all the studies to a certain extent),

4) too few authentic works examined (Brantley, LaRue, Wolf, Paymer),

5) method not useful for application to most authenticity problems (Paisley),

6) inconsistency of the results (Paisley, Crane-Fiehler, Brantley, Paymer), and

7) the method was not tested on a large-enough scale (all except Paymer). Of the various studies, LaRue's is the most innovative, Wolf's the most convincing, and Paymer's the most comprehensive and promising methodologically.

CHAPTER TWO

# Methods of Determining Authenticity by Style

The approach employed in an authenticity study depends on the circumstances of the particular problem: the number of doubtful compositions, the number of previously-authenticated pieces, the genres and composers involved, and the presence or lack of conflicting attributions. The approach to be discussed first has the widest applicability for the problems covered in this study. It is limited to pieces from a single genre and works best when there is a large number of previously-authenticated compositions.

### MAIN APPROACH TO DETERMINING AUTHENTICITY

My main approach entails four groups of compositions:

*Control Group I*, which is a set of previously-authenticated works of the same genre as the doubtful ones by the composer in question;

*Control Group II*, which contains pieces of the same type as Control Group I by a wide variety of composers, but not including the composer of the works in Control Group I;

*Test Group I*, which also contains works by a wide variety of composers sometimes including the composer in question and which is used to check the validity of the tests, and

*Test Group II*, which comprises the compositions whose authenticity is in question.[1]

For example, in a study of Haydn's doubtful string trios, the four groups might be:

*Control Group I*—the eighteen previously-authenticated Haydn trios (those trios listed in the *Entwurf-Katalog*),

*Control Group II*—twenty non-Haydn trios by such composers as M. Haydn, Hofmann, Gassmann, Boccherini, Le Duc, Pugnani, etc.,

*Test Group I*—an additional group of twenty non-Haydn works, and

*Test Group II*—the thirty-one doubtful string trios (string trios that are ascribed to Haydn in some source, but that are not listed in the Haydn catalogues, autograph, or other unimpeachable sources and that are not convincingly attributed to other composers).

The first step in an authenticity study is to set up a profile for the previously-authenticated works in Control Group I. Because a composer treats various types of movements and genres differently, and because a composer's style may change with time, the profile should be formulated for a well-defined type of movement, such as fast sonata-form movements in string quartets. Unfortunately, even a well-defined group may occasionally produce two or more distinctive profiles. For example, Haydn treated texture in two different ways in the fast binary or rounded-binary movements of his string trios: one that involves a great deal of imitation and another that employs only short bits of imitation. A movement of one type would obviously fail the profile of the other type, so one must create two separate profiles or look for characteristics that are common to both types. Usually, though, a single profile for each type of movement that is limited by genre and period is sufficient.

My profile consists of two types of criteria (Tests I and II): quantitative ranges and checklists. Examples of quantitative ranges include the

---

[1]The works in Control Group II and Test Group I should contain as much variety as possible, but also should include several pieces that are similar in style to the works in Control Group I. Ten to twenty compositions are sufficient for Control Group II or Test Group I. In most cases, any more than twenty would increase the amount of work without significantly increasing the accuracy of the results. The profiles in this study will generally employ ten works in each group. More information on selecting the non-Haydn pieces is given in Appendix C, along with a sample of non-Haydn pieces used.

rate of textural change, harmonic rhythm, percentage of measures with more articulations than beats, percentage of measures with ties over the barline, etc. For instance, the scholar could study the harmonic rhythm in the expositions of a composer's sonata form first movements from string quartets. He would simply count the number of changes of harmony in this section for each piece in Control Group I (in this case, consisting of all the composer's previously-authenticated string quartet movements in sonata form) and divide by the number of beats.[2] Say in a particular composition in 4/4 with a thirty measure exposition, the harmony changes sixty times. One would divide 60 by 120 (4 beats per measure x 30 measures), yielding a rate of harmonic change per beat of .500 (=one change of harmony every two beats). By doing this for the exposition of every work in Control Group I, one would produce a range of what is normal for the composer in question, say .450- .550. (Scores of Control Group I pieces, for example, .450, .471, .489, .490, .491, .500, .515, .526, .537, .550). If the resulting range is narrow enough, and if by testing the works in Control Group II (in this example, the same sections of contemporaneous string quartets not by the composer of the Control Group I works), one discovers that most of these pieces do not fall within the range, then the range is very effective for determining authenticity; if not, the range should be rejected. A range of harmonic change per beat of .20 to 2.00 (one change of harmony every five beats to two changes of harmony per beat), for instance, is too wide for authenticity determination. Also, what is narrow in the music of one composer may be too wide in the works of another composer, so different ranges may have to be used with certain authenticity problems. Furthermore, one should try to find several ranges that are valid, since a single factor in itself is not enough to decide authenticity. The ranges can be for any sized section of a composition. It is often useful to check more than one section, such as calculating separate rates of harmonic change for the exposition and development of sonata-form movements. One could argue that scholars might analyze changes of harmony or other aspects of style in different ways. While this is true any reasonable approach that is consistent is sufficient. Of course, this requires that the entire study be done by one person to insure consistency, and that this person applies the same analytical criteria throughout his investigation.

[2] For works in $\frac{3}{8}$ or $\frac{6}{8}$ one multiplies the answer by two. $\frac{2}{2}$ is treated like $\frac{4}{4}$.

In the preceding example, I employed the number of beats, not the number of measures, to divide the number of harmonic changes, because measures are of different lengths in different meters. However, when it is not the length of the measure but the content that matters (such as with the range "percentage of measures containing eighth notes"), it is preferable to divide by the number of measures. One must test all ranges against Control Group I to insure that they are valid for all relevant meters (all meters found in the doubtful works).

The other half of my profile (Test II) consists of a checklist of "positive characteristics" that always or usually appear in the works in Control Group I and a checklist of "negative traits" that rarely or never appear. As was true of the quantitative ranges, one trait by itself cannot establish authenticity or nonauthenticity, only a combination of traits can. The characteristics should be expressed in the most precise language possible. As mentioned in the Introduction, the components of the checklist do not have to seem analytically significant. For example in my study of the M. Ic̄ pieces in Perugia 431 (see footnote 41, Introduction), I employed the following entries: 1) "the lower voices touch but don't cross," 2) "a rest of a semibreve in all voices at least once in a work," and 3) "more than two octaves between the highest and lowest notes on a single simultaneity at least once in a work." One finds the characteristics by going over the control group for stylistic features that seem to be consistent. However, one need not search for every consistent trait. Twelve to twenty significant items in the final checklist are sufficient to establish a distinctive profile. Also, redundant or partially redundant characteristics must be eliminated. A study of string trios should not include both "double-stops used in the first eight measures" and "at least one simultaneity of four or more notes present in the first eight measures." In some cases, quantitative figures may function better in a checklist than in a range. (In my M. Ic̄ study, I placed the entry "at least 15% of the measures contain sixteenth notes" in the checklist.) Finally, some of the the checklist entries may be a composite of several traits. For a particular entry to pass, a work must contain all parts of a positive composite trait and no part of a negative composite trait.

After creating a list of possible traits, one must test them against Control Groups I and II. When Control Group I is small, positive characteristics must appear in all works and negative characteristics in none, but, with larger groups this is not possible: experience has shown that positive traits should appear in 85% or more of the compositions in Control Group I and negative ones in 15% or less. One then checks the characteristics against Control Group II (works not by the composer of the Control Group I works) to determine if they are too much a part of the vernacular of the period. To say that Haydn's string trios always adopt keys between five sharps and three flats is useless for authenticity determination since this is true of most contemporaneous works. The scholar calculates the percentage of works in Control Group II that contains a particular trait and rejects those items that turn up in too many pieces. The exact cutoff point depends on the particular authenticity problem. (In my M. Ič study, I rejected all positive characteristics that appeared in 35% or more of the works in Control Group II and all negative ones that appeared in 65% or less.)

Because certain characteristics are more significant than others, weighting plays a vital role in drawing up the checklist. In the scoring process, each trait (generally twelve to twenty) is usually given one point. However, an item that seems more important can receive two points instead of one and less important traits can be given a half point. Criteria for weighting can include

1) a trait that is especially distinctive for a particular composer,

2) a characteristic that appears in a small percentage of the Control Group II works, and

3) a trait that helps differentiate the profile of a composer from those composers who have similar profiles.

(It is usually preferable to put the weighting on an objective basis, weighting, for example, those traits that appear in all Control Group I works and no Control Group II work.) In addition, certain items permit different degrees of failure. For example, one may have an entry that reads "no more than 15% of the measures contain rhythmic doubling between the two violins." Clearly, a score of 16% on this characteristic is much different from a score of 75%. In such a case, I would probably subtract a half point (instead of a whole point) for the 16% and subtract a whole point for the 75%. (Additional information on drawing up the checklists appears in Appendix D.)

After the components of the two tests (quantitative ranges and checklist) have been established, one must decide what passing and failing will be. With the quantitative ranges (Test I), I usually require that a composition fall within all ranges to pass. However, since a doubtful group may show slightly more variance than the control group, I also create a borderline category that changes with the type of range. A doubtful work that scores borderline on the quantitative ranges can then be passed or failed by the checklist.

For the checklist (Test II), I have developed two methods for determining passing, borderline, and failing.

*Method I.*

When there are additional previously-authenticated works available, I take the lowest score of the previously-authenticated works and consider that the lowest passing score. I then determine the midway point between the lowest passing score of the authentic works and the highest score of the pieces in Control Group II and regard everything below that as failing and everything between that and the lowest passing score as borderline. For example, if the lowest score of an authentic work is 23 and the highest score in Control Group II is 13, I would make 23 or greater passing, 18-22 borderline, and below 18 failing.

*Method II.*

If there are no additional authentic pieces available, I take the difference between the maximum score and the highest Control Group II score, and give each of the three categories one third of the total. When the maximum score is 20 and the highest Control Group II score is 8, 17-20 would be passing, 13-16 borderline, and 9-12 failing. (20-8=12; 12x1/3=4; each category receives four points; for failing add the four points to the highest Control Group II score.) If the difference cannot be divided evenly by a third, always give the passing category the largest number of points. In addition, the passing category must include a minimum of three points. If it doesn't, the difference must be made up from the other categories.[3] If the highest Control Group II score is higher than or equal to the lowest passing score (possible only with the first set of scoring criteria), the profile is not distinctive enough; more work needs to be done. Moreover, it is preferable to have several points separating passing and failing.

Based on the two tests (quantitative ranges and checklist), one can develop three categories in relation to the profile:

---

[3]In determining passing, borderline, and failing, a certain amount of arbitrariness is unavoidable. This arbitrariness will not affect the results if the profiles have a wide separation between authentic and not authentic. It matters very little if the passing category is a point or two too large, when the highest failing score is 7 and the lowest passing score is 13. In addition, the scoring criteria must be checked with additional non-Haydn works (Test Group I; see below).

*Category A*, passed both tests or borderline on one test and passed the other, fits the profile;

*Category B*, borderline on both tests, uncertain; and

*Category C*, failed at least one test, does not fit the profile.

In a well-constructed study, no work should fall into Category B.

One should test the completed profile to insure that it is distinctive for the composer in question but still contains enough flexibility to allow for variation in a composer's style. Test Group I may consist of two types of compositions: previously-authenticated works of the composer and works not by him. In some studies, one may not have any of the former, because they were needed to produce a large enough sample for Control Group I. In any case, it is vital to confirm that pieces not by the composer do not fit the profile or fall into Category B (results uncertain). If any do, one must try to discern the flaws in the profile, and, after the profile has been revised, test it again.

With the efficacy of the profile insured, one can evaluate the doubtful works. The tests determine only whether a composition fits the profile or not; it is the conclusions that one draws from this that decide authenticity. If the profile is truly distinctive for a particular composer (confirmed by the fact that none of the works not by the composer in Test Group I or Control Group II fit the profile or appeared in Category B), then one may consider any piece that fits the profile (Category A) to be authentic.[4] However, since any style-analytical study establishes the norms of a composer's style and may ignore that which is unique, the compositions that appeared in Category C must be carefully re-evaluated before they may be regarded as spurious. Reasons for re-examining the works include:

1) the work contains a single element that in itself might cause a movement to fail the tests,

2) the work could possibly be a member of a previously-unknown subtype,

3) the movement contains details that seem to be typical of that composer,

---

[4]The way the method is set up, if all the steps are followed, the chances are extremely slim that a work not by the composer of the profile would fit the profile. This has been confirmed by extensive experimentation.

4) the other movements of a multimovement work might be by the composer.

Using these criteria in my Haydn string trio study, I discovered a subtype of texture treatment in the fast binary or rounded-binary movements that did not occur in the previously-authenticated trios (see chapter six, chart VI). I authenticated these three doubtful trios by a detailed comparison with a group of Haydn baryton trios that treated texture in a very similar manner. I believe that instances where an entire subtype would not appear in a large sample group to be relatively rare. In addition, the vast majority of works that fail the tests do not fit the four requirements from the previous paragraph and may thus be regarded as spurious.

Based on the above, it is necessary to examine only one movement of a multimovement composition to establish authenticity but best to study at least two to determine non-authenticity. Works that contain a movement that passed the tests may be regarded as authenticated, while a composition that has movements that failed the tests and that has been carefully reevaluated using the above criteria may be considered spurious.[5] *This does not mean that the tests are 100% accurate.* While the method used in this investigation is highly effective, it is possible that the method might fail in a small number of cases. Still, I believe that the results from a study using a well-formulated stylistic method can be just as reliable as those of most documentary studies, especially when several movements of multimovement compositions are tested.

The parameter that seems thus far to be most effective for determining authenticity is texture, especially when setting up the quantitative ranges. I have based my method of analyzing texture on that of Wallace Berry, who has developed a system of notating texture by using numerical symbols that represent both the number of "sounding voices" and the number of "real voices."[6] *The number of sounding voices* are the total number of voices sounding at a particular time. When two flutes, an oboe, and a bassoon are playing, there are four sounding voices. *The number of real voices* are the total number of independent parts, regardless of the number of sounding voices. Independence is determined by intervallic, directional, and, especially,

---

[5]Of course, an authentic work may contain spurious movements that were added later.
[6]Wallace Berry, *Structural Functions in Music* (Englewood Cliffs, N. J.: Prentice Hall, 1976) 184-300.

rhythmic factors. Two lines that employ different rhythms and melodic contours are independent, while two lines that use parallel thirds or sixths are dependent.

In Berry's system, the symbol 3/1 (not to be confused with a fraction) indicates four sounding voices but only two real voices. The four sounding voices are arrived at by adding the 3 and 1; the two real voices are represented by the two numerals (3 and 1), with three sounding voices on one part and one sounding voice on the other. Similarly, 3/1/2/1 represents seven sounding voices with four real parts, 5/1/1/2 represents nine sounding voices with four real parts, and 3 represents three sounding voices with one real part.

One analyzes the texture of a work, producing a chart like the one below (see Chart I and Example I).

### Chart I. Texture in Haydn's Op. 54, No. 1, m. 1-12

| *1* | *2* | *3* | *4* | *5* | *6* | *7* | *8* | *9* | *10* | *11* | *12* |
|---|---|---|---|---|---|---|---|---|---|---|---|
| 1/4 | 5 | 1/3/1 | | 2 1/1 1/1 | | 1/1/1 | 1 | | 2/1/1 | | 4 1/3 |

Such a chart may also include other aspects of style, such as formal symbols, harmonic rhythm, etc. From the chart, one can discern quantitative ranges for a composition: the rate of textural change as well as the percentage of measures containing a particular type of texture. One determines the rate of textural change by counting the number of changes of texture in a section and dividing by the number of beats.[7] (In Chart I, the rate of textural change per beat is .166; 8 changes of texture divided by 48 beats.) Examples of a particular type of texture include 1) percentage of measures with less than full texture, 2) percentage of measures with $\frac{2}{2}$ texture, 3) percentage of measures with 3 or 4 texture, 4) percentage of measures with four real voices, etc. The charts may also be helpful in drawing up the checklists. For example, in my Haydn string trio study, it became apparent that all the previously-authenticated trios had at least three changes of texture in

---

[7]As was true for calculating the rate of harmonic change per beat, one must multiply the answer by two for works in $\frac{3}{8}$ and $\frac{6}{8}$.

### Example I. Haydn's Op. 54, No. 1, m. 1-12

1/4=5 sounding voices and 2 real voices (the first violin presents one real voice, while the three lower strings including double stops in the second violin present the other real voice); 5=5 sounding voices and one real voice); 1/3/1=5 sounding voices and 3 real voices, etc.

For further examples of the analysis of quantitative ranges, see Appendix E.

## DETERMINING AUTHENTICITY BY STYLE

the first eight measures, a trait that was important in establishing authenticity. (As was true for analyzing changes of harmony, different scholars will analyze changes of texture differently, but this is not important as long as the one doing the study employs the same analytical criteria throughout an investigation.)

While texture was the most effective parameter for the quantitative ranges in my previous studies, the textural ranges are not always consistent, so other parameters must be tested to determine their reliability for establishing authenticity. Extensive experimentation with Haydn's piano sonatas from the early 1770s revealed that, for Haydn at least, harmonic rhythm shows considerable consistency. An analysis of the expositions of the first movements of the six op. 13 piano sonatas (XVI:21-26) yielded a range of harmonic change per beat of .549-.804. Of nine piano sonatas and four string quartets by composers other than Haydn tested against the range, only one fell within it (Sonatas: J. C. Bach .274, Pleyel .396, Paradisi .446, Clementi .337, Mozart .622 [passed], Mozart .373, Mozart .545, Mozart .258, Mozart .357; Quartets: Dittersdorf .358, Mozart .443, Mozart .319, Mozart .317). On the other hand, all of Haydn's next set of sonatas (op. 14, XVI:27-32) fit the range (.579, .597, .658, .775, .739, .607). The above suggests that the range of harmonic change per beat is a significant factor in separating the style of Haydn's piano sonatas of the early 1770s from those of other composers. With those authenticity problems where the textural ranges are not sufficient, I shall also employ harmonic rhythm ranges.

## EXAMPLE OF MAIN METHOD

To illustrate my method more fully, I shall examine the authenticity of two keyboard trios attributed to both Joseph Haydn (XV:3 and 4) and Ignace Pleyel (Ben 428 and 429). This is an especially good test of the method because Pleyel was a student of Haydn, who often wrote in a style similar to that of his master, and because many conflicting attributions to both Pleyel and Haydn exist in other genres. In 1784, Haydn sent the two trios, along with a third definitely authentic trio, to the London publisher William Forster, who issued them as op. 40. In his dealings with this publisher, Haydn clearly indicated that the two trios were by him, and he wrote on the title pages of the fair copies of both trios "di me Giuseppe Haydn." Such an inscription is usually regarded as *indisputable documentary evidence* that Haydn was the composer. However, the trios later appeared under Pleyel's name as op. 24 (earliest extant edition Le Duc, c. 1800?, although there are indications that Longman and Broderip published them under Pleyel's name contemporaneously with the Forster edition), and other documentary evidence points strongly to Pleyel as their author. Moreover, neither trio appears in either the *Entwurf-Katalog* or the *Haydn Verzeichnis*. Both Alan Tyson and Rita Benton believe that the trios were written by Pleyel, and Georg Feder marks them as probably by Pleyel in his *Grove* worklist.[8] Because of the strong documentary evidence pointing to both Haydn and Pleyel, the only way to test the authorship of the two trios further is by stylistic means.

As my Control Group I, I have chosen fast first or second piano trios movements in some kind of sonata form, written by Haydn in the 1780s. Seven such movements exist, but I am only using five of them to set up the profile, so that two authentic works remain with which to test the profile.[9] I also decided to limit my study to the expositions of these movements, since this part of the movement shows the most consistency in the control group. In addition, I shall employ texture as the only criterion in the quantitative ranges, but shall use all parameters of style in the checklist.

The quantitative ranges that seemed most significant for authenticity determination are listed in Chart II. To fit the profile on the quantitative ranges (Test I), a trio must fall within all six ranges. To be borderline, a trio must not exceed the ranges at either end by more than .02 on the textural change range or 2.5 on the other ranges. Any other score is failing.

### Chart II. Ranges for the Control Group I Works

1. Textural change per beat: .154-.165

2. % of measures in which at least one voice rests for more than a beat: 32.0-54.2

---

[8]Alan Tyson, "Haydn and Two Stolen Trios," *Music Review* XXII (1961) 21-27; Rita Benton, "A Resumé of the Haydn-Pleyel Trio Controversy, with Some Added Contributions," *Haydn-Studien* IV (1978) 114-117; Feder, *The New Grove Haydn*, 182.
[9]It was possible to limit Control Group I to only five compositions, because all the previously-authenticated works and the two doubtful pieces were in duple meters. If there had been a greater variety of meters, Control Group I would have had to have been larger.

3. % of measures containing more than five notes in a single simultaneity: 21.4-33.9

4. % of measures with four real voices: 3.3-15.3

5. % of measures with only one real voice: 21.4-28.8

6. % of measures with two and only two real voices: 32.3-54.1

Next I drew up a checklist of positive and negative traits. Because there were only five trios in Control Group I, it was necessary that all items be valid for all five trios. I then tested the characteristics against ten Control Group II works (see Chart IV), which were drawn from a set of trios for keyboard, violin (or 'flute or violin'), and cello written in the second half of the eighteenth-century. I included three of Pleyel's earliest trios (Ben 431, 432, and 435; also dating from the mid-1780s) in Control Group II to produce a clear distinction between Haydn's and Pleyel's styles. I retained all positive traits that appeared in none of the Pleyel trios or 50% or less of the entire group and all negative ones that occurred in all Pleyel trios or 50% or more of the group. This process produced seventeen entries, which are listed in Chart III. (The first figure following each item indicates the percentage of Pleyel trios it appeared in; the second figure the percentage of the entire group.) On those characteristics that allowed different degrees of failure (Nos. 3, 10, 13, 16, 17; marked * on Chart III), I subtracted a half-point instead of a point when a trio barely failed. Also, I weighted those positive traits that occurred in 10% or less of Control Group II (Nos. 7 and 10; marked # on Chart III), giving them two points each. (Thus, No. 10 receives one or two points, depending on whether it passed or barely failed.)[10] I then tested the works in Control Group II against the profile, and all failed on the quantitative ranges and scored low on the checklist (see Chart IV; the cut-off point for the checklist will be determined below).

### Chart III. Checklist for the Expositions of the Opening Movements of Haydn's Keyboard Trios from the 1780s

#### Positive Traits Appearing in All the Haydn Works[+]

1. The melody in the first four measures presents the tonic triad horizontally, uses sixteenth notes by the second measure, contains the second

---

[10]There were no negative characteristics distinctive enough to warrant weighting.

## DETERMINING AUTHENTICITY BY STYLE

and fourth degrees of the scale, and has the first or fifth degree in different octaves. 33.3%/30% (Pleyel/entire group)

2. The same note value, either quarter or eighth, is repeated at least twenty-six times without a break in the cello. 33.3%/20%

*3. At least 59% of the measures contain a note value shorter than an eighth note. 0%/50%

4. The highest note in the cello does not exceed the highest note in the left-hand of the piano more than once in a work. 0%/40%

5. Violin tessitura of at least two octaves and a third. 0%/40%

6. Tessitura in the violin from a ninth to an octave and a sixth in the first eight measures. 0%/40%

#7. At least five changes of texture in the first eight measures. 0%/10%

8. All four parts (vn., vc., pn. rh. + lh.) sound on the downbeat of the first measure. 66.6%/40%

9. At least one seven-note simultaneity in the first seven measures. 33.3%/30%

*#10. 61% to 79% of the measures contain pitch and rhythmic doubling between the left-hand of the piano and the cello (octave placement not considered). 0%/10%

### Negative Traits Found in None of the Haydn Works[+]

11. Dominant seventh chord used in the first three measures. 100%/50%

12. Pedal points in the bass lasting more than seven measures. 100%/40%

*13. 15% or more of the measures contain a whole note in the violin or cello. 100%/70%

14. Thirty-second notes on the second half of a beat (not including ornaments or the resolution of ornaments). 100%/40%

15. Use of ♪ ♩♩♩ ♪ ♩♩♩ pattern in the piano (length of bass note may vary). 100%/50%

[+](In this case meaning the five authentic Haydn keyboard trios from the 1780s in Control Group I.)

*16. More than 45% of the measures contain patterned accompaniments in a least one voice. 100%/70%

*17. More than 12% of the measures contain octave doublings in the left-hand of the piano. 100%/50%

## Chart IV. Results for Control Group II

| Composer | Test I-Ranges | | | | | | Test II | Results | |
|---|---|---|---|---|---|---|---|---|---|
| | 1 | 2 | 3 | 4 | 5 | 6 | Ch | R-Ch | Conc. |
| J.C. Bach | .087 | 4.7 | 2.4 | 9.4 | 11.6 | 16.5 | 11 | f-f | C |
| Beethoveen | .258 | 20.3 | 10.9 | 10.9 | 14.1 | 25.0 | 7 | f-f | C |
| Filtz | .180 | 10.0 | 0.0 | 0.0 | 4.0 | 26.0 | 9.5 | f-f | C |
| Kozeluch | .081 | 47.3 | 29.7 | 0.0 | 14.9 | 28.6 | 9.5 | f-f | C |
| Mozart | .122 | 39.0 | 26.8 | 7.3 | 4.6 | 52.5 | 7.5 | f-f | C |
| Pleyel | .098 | 45.3 | 44.5 | 0.0 | 11.9 | 21.4 | 3 | f-f | C |
| Pleyel | .093 | 58.6 | 21.2 | 0.0 | 24.2 | 21.2 | 3 | f-f | C |
| Pleyel | .075 | 67.7 | 26.4 | 0.0 | 25.0 | 38.2 | 2.5 | f-f | C |
| Schobert | .240 | 11.5 | 9.6 | 0.0 | 11.5 | 48.1 | 11.5 | f-f | C |
| Toeschi | .312 | 25.0 | 0.0 | 15.6 | 12.4 | 31.1 | 12 | f-f | C |

Scoring. Ranges: see Chart II; Checklist: passing 17-19, borderline 14.5-16.5, failing below 14.5.
Ch=checklist, R=ranges, Conc.=conclusions, p=pass, b=borderline, f=fail, A=passed both tests or passed one and borderline on the other; fits the profile, B=borderline on both tests; results uncertain, C=failed either test; does not fit profile.

To test the profile more fully, I examined the two Haydn trios from the 1780s that I had withheld from Control Group I. Both trios passed Test I, quantitative ranges, and scored 17 or 18 (out of a possible 19) on the checklist, Test II, scores that indicate that the profile is effective (see Chart V). Based on these two Haydn trios, I decided that passing on the checklist would be 17 (the lowest a previously-authenticated Haydn trio had scored). Since the highest a work in Control Group II scored was 12, I made the midway point between 12 and 17 (14.5) the lower end of the borderline category. Thus 14.5 to 16.5 is borderline, 14 and below failing. All authentic Haydn trios passed both parts of the profile; all non-Haydn works failed both parts. I then checked the validity of the profile further with ten more non-Haydn works, all of which failed both tests (see Chart V).

# DETERMINING AUTHENTICITY BY STYLE

## Chart V. Results for Control Group I

| Composer | | | Test I-Ranges | | | | Test II | Results | |
|---|---|---|---|---|---|---|---|---|---|
| | 1 | 2 | 3 | 4 | 5 | 6 | Ch | R-Ch | Conc. |
| Haydn[1] | .162 | 52.3 | 23.3 | 3.9 | 22.1 | 51.9 | 17 | p-p | A |
| Haydn[2] | .157 | 41.2 | 23.1 | 11.7 | 23.3 | 37.3 | 18 | p-p | A |
| Abel | .130 | 8.0 | 24.0 | 28.0 | 0.0 | 16.0 | 10 | f-f | C |
| C.P.E. Bach | .107 | 54.3 | 14.3 | 0.0 | 28.6 | 57.1 | 11 | f-f | C |
| J.C. Bach | .113 | 39.1 | 1.1 | 8.7 | 3.3 | 26.1 | 9.5 | f-f | C |
| J.C.F. Bach | .125 | 20.0 | 4.0 | 4.0 | 22.0 | 10.0 | 10 | f-f | C |
| Eichner | .079 | 15.9 | 24.6 | 49.1 | 3.5 | 24.6 | 10.5 | f-f | C |
| Kozeluch | .077 | 19.7 | 32.1 | 0.0 | 22.2 | 22.2 | 10.5 | f-f | C |
| L. Mozart | .077 | 0.0 | 6.9 | 2.6 | 0.0 | 48.3 | 7 | f-f | C |
| Mozart | .144 | 53.3 | 4.4 | 13.8 | 10.9 | 25.5 | 7.5 | f-f | C |
| Richter | .504 | 9.6 | 0.0 | 0.0 | 0.0 | 21.3 | 12 | f-f | C |
| Rosetti | .132 | 39.3 | 16.4 | 8.2 | 9.9 | 18.0 | 12.5 | f-f | C |

Scoring. Ranges: see Chart II; Checklist: passing 17-19, borderline 14.5-16.5, failing below 14.5.
[1]XV:9/II, [2]XV:10/I

Finally, I tested the two doubtful works (XV:3 and 4) against the profile. Both trios failed both parts, supporting the general consensus that they are not by Haydn (see Chart VI).

## Chart VI. Results for the Doubtful Works

| Work | | | Test I-Ranges | | | | Test II | Results | |
|---|---|---|---|---|---|---|---|---|---|
| | 1 | 2 | 3 | 4 | 5 | 6 | Ch | R-Ch | Conc. |
| XV:3 | .077 | 71.5 | 12.0 | 0.0 | 24.6 | 23.1 | 4.5 | f-f | C |
| XV:4 | .100 | 62.2 | 21.1 | 0.0 | 14.4 | 35.5 | 6 | f-f | C |

Scoring. Ranges: see Chart II; Checklist: passing 17-19, borderline 14.5-16.5, failing below 14.5.

The ultimate test, though, is whether one can verify that they were written by Pleyel. I used the three Pleyel trios from Control Group II plus two other contemporaneous trios by Pleyel to set up quantitative ranges for early Pleyel trios, to compare his ranges to those of Haydn and the two doubtful trios. Chart VII provides very strong evidence that Pleyel is the author of the two trios.

## Chart VII. Hob. XV:3+4: Haydn or Pleyel

*Range 1.* Textural change per beat: Haydn .154-.165; Pleyel .075-.105; XV:3 .077, significantly exceeds Haydn range, falls within Pleyel range; XV:4 .100, exceeds Haydn range, falls within Pleyel range.

*Range 2.* % of measures in which at least one voice rests for more than a beat: Haydn 32.0-54.2; Pleyel 45.3-72.4; XV:3 71.5, significantly exceeds Haydn range, falls within Pleyel range; XV:4 62.2, exceeds Haydn range, falls within Pleyel range.

*Range 3.* % of measures containing more than five notes on a single simultaneity: Haydn 21.4-33.9; Pleyel 12.0-44.5; XV:3 12.0, falls within Pleyel range, exceeds Haydn range; XV:4 21.1, falls within Pleyel range, barely exceeds Haydn range.

*Range 4.* % of measures with four real voices: Haydn 3.3-15.3; Pleyel 0.0-3.6; XV:3 0.0, exceeds Haydn range, falls within Pleyel range. XV:4 0.0, exceeds Haydn range, falls within Pleyel range.

*Range 5.* % of measures with only one real voice: Haydn 21.4-28.8; Pleyel 11.9-30.0; XV:3 24.6, falls within both ranges; XV:4 14.4, exceeds Haydn range, falls within Pleyel range.

*Range 6.* % of measures with two and only two real voices: Haydn 32.3-54.1; Pleyel 21.2-38.2; XV:3 23.1, exceeds Haydn range falls within Pleyel range; XV:4 35.5, falls within both ranges.

*Conclusion:* XV:3 exceeds five of the six Haydn ranges and falls within all six Pleyel ranges. XV:4 exceeds five of six Haydn and falls within all six Pleyel ranges. XV:3 and 4 fit the Pleyel profile and fail the Haydn profile.

## MODIFICATIONS OF MAIN APPROACH FOR APPLICATIONS TO OTHER AUTHENTICITY PROBLEMS

One can modify the main method of determining authenticity to deal with other types of authenticity problems that involve a single genre. First, when there is a conflicting attribution (as in Chart VII), one can set up separate profiles for each of the composers in question and test the doubtful work or works against both profiles. Conflicting attributions are probably the easiest type of authenticity problem to treat because, if the study has been designed properly (and assuming that still another conflicting attribution has not been lost),[11] the questionable piece should clearly fall within the profile of the real composer and differ markedly from those of the other composers. In a study of conflicting attributions, one should exclude from the profile all traits that are shared by the possible composers. Also, one may eliminate one of the two tests (either quantitative ranges or checklist), because the built-in check of having separate profiles for each of the possible composers makes retaining both tests unnecessary. Second, in those instances where there is a small number of doubtful works that are obviously by the same composer and that are similar in style, one can design the profile for the doubtful works and test previously-authenticated pieces by the possible composers against it.[12] Owing to the nature of this approach (and assuming that the profile is distinctive), if one of the previously-authenticated pieces by a particular composer fits the profile, the author of that work is also the author of the doubtful ones. Finally, when there is only a small number of previously-authenticated compositions or even a single one, a stylistic comparison can still be made; but to draw definitive conclusions the comparison must be detailed enough and the similarities striking enough that there can be no doubt that the pieces were written by the same composer, which may not be possible in many instances.[13] When there is only a limited number of previously-authenticated pieces available, nonauthenticity is especially difficult to prove.

## CROSS-GENRE METHODS OF DETERMINING AUTHENTICITY

In the preceding studies, a group of previously-authenticated compositions in the same genre as the doubtful ones was required to draw up the profiles. There are many cases, however, where there are not

---

[11]If the correct attribution has been lost, the work should not fit the profiles of the other possible composers. To insure this, it is best to test a group of pieces by a wide variety of composers against the profiles.

[12]I employed this approach in my M. Ic̄ study. I set up a profile based on the three M. Ic̄ works (three pieces in *Perugia 431* that were identified by the initials M. Ic̄) and tested compositions by the two composers that Renaissance scholars thought might be M. Ic̄—Icart or Isaac—against the profile.

[13]For example, see my discussion of V:F1/I, G1/I, and G4/II in chapter six (Chart VI).

enough previously-authenticated works in a genre to produce a distinctive profile, and, in such cases, one must use compositions from other genres.

I experimented with Haydn's music from the early 1770s in an attempt to develop a cross-genre method. I discovered that quantitative ranges were not effective for establishing authenticity in a cross-genre study when the instrumentation is markedly different. For example, the range of harmonic change per beat in the expositions of fast first movements of the keyboard sonatas was .549-.804, in the string quartets .416-.620, and in the symphonies .303-.430. Clearly, each genre has its own range. A composite range of the three (.303-.804) is too wide for establishing authenticity; eleven of the thirteen non-Haydn works discussed on p. 50 fall within the range.

The failure of quantitative ranges in a cross-genre study can be demonstrated further by examining the number of impacts (rhythmic attacks) per beat in all voices (composite rhythm) in various genres. To determine the number of impacts per beat, one counts the number of impacts in a section (composite rhythm) and divides by the number of beats. For example, if in a measure from a string quartet the four voices have the rhythms ♩ ♫♩, ♫♩, ♫♩, and ♩., the total impacts for all voices in that measure would be five and the number of impacts per beat 1.67 (5 impacts ÷ 3 beats). The range of impacts per beat for the expositions of the fast first movements of Haydn's keyboard sonatas from the early 1770s is 3.02-5.71, for the string quartets 1.70-3.54, for the baryton trios 2.76-3.10, and for the symphonies 1.94-2.55. Clearly, the piano sonatas evince a greater amount of activity per beat than the other genres. Unless the instrumentation is similar (such as with works for keyboard accompanied by two strings and works for keyboard accompanied by three strings), quantitative ranges probably cannot be employed in a cross-genre study for Haydn.

Cross-Genre Study of Haydn's Instrumental Works, c. 1770-75

While quantitative ranges are not generally usable in a cross-genre study, checklists did prove effective for determining authenticity across genre boundaries. I set up a profile for the first movements of ten of Haydn's works from the early 1770s (3 string quartets, op. 20, nos. 1, 3, 4; 2 baryton trios nos. 100, 101; 3 piano sonatas, XVI:21-

23; and two symphonies 50, 54) that is applicable to other compositions from the period. I tested a large number of traits both against the Haydn group and against a group of ten non-Haydn works (Control Group II), with traits that were valid for less than 90% of the Haydn works or more than 60% of the non-Haydn group being rejected. Only nine traits remained (see Chart VIII), but the resulting profile was effective for authenticity determination.

### Chart VIII. Cross-Genre Profile for Haydn's Instrumental Works c. 1770-1775

### Positive Traits Appearing in at Least 90% of the Haydn Works

1. Same rhythmic value repeated at least thirty-two times in the bass without interruption.

2. At least three changes of texture in the first eight measures.

3. Texture space of movement's final sonority two or three octaves.

4. Use of phrase lengths other than two, four, or eight important in the exposition.

5. a) Range of the first two phrases in the top voice each an octave or more but less than two octaves, and b) ranges of first and second phrases differ by no more than a 2nd. (When the second phrase has an extension at the end, only that part corresponding to the first phrase considered.)

6. Use of melodic seventh in the bass.

### Negative Traits Appearing in 10% or Less of the Haydn Works[14]

7. In opening theme, a) use of | ♪♪ ♩. , Mannheim sigh, chromaticism, more than five repeated notes in a row or ties over the barline in the first eight measures; b) the same rhythm in consecutive measures except all eighths, all sixteenths, or a whole note; c) hammer-stroke opening or two eighth-note pickup at the beginning; or d) the third and fourth measures repeat the rhythm of the first two.

8. Patterned accompaniment at beginning or near beginning.

---

[14]As mentioned earlier, if a movement fails one part of a composite trait, it fails the entire trait.

9. a) In the exposition, patterned accompaniment lasting for more than twenty beats, accompaniment pattern like |♩♪ ♩ ♩ ♪| (except symphonies in minor), or use of Alberti bass for more than a measure, or b) lacks patterned accompaniments completely.

I added five more Haydn works to the original ten pieces to determine passing, borderline, and failing. Since no Haydn work (of the 15) scored less than seven points (out of a possible 9) and no non-Haydn work scored more than 5 points (see Chart IX), 7 or above was considered passing, 6 borderline, and 5 or below failing. To validate this approach further, I tested the profile against five more contemporaneous Haydn compositions and ten more non-Haydn works. All twenty Haydn works fit the profile, while all twenty non-Haydn failed (see Chart IX). It is especially significant that two baryton octets, a genre not employed in drawing up the profile, passed the profile.

### Chart IX. Results of First Cross-Genre Study
#### A. Non-Haydn Works

| | | |
|---|---|---|
| J.C. Bach PS-2 (f) | M. Haydn Q-5 (f) | Mozart Q-3 (f) |
| J.C. Bach S-3 (f) | M. Haydn S-3 (f) | Mozart S-4 (f) |
| Boccherini Q-4 (f) | M. Haydn ST-5 (f) | Ordoñez ST-5 (f) |
| Cannabich S-2 (f) | Kammel ST-5 (f) | Paradisi PS-3 (f) |
| Clementi PS-4 (f) | Le Duc ST-5 (f) | Pleyel PS-3 (f) |
| Dittersdorf Q-2 (f) | Mozart Qu-3 (f) | K. Stamitz WQ-3 (f) |
| Eichner KT-5 (f) | | Wagenseil ST-5 (f) |

#### B. Haydn Works

| | | |
|---|---|---|
| BO X:1-7 (p) | BT 108-7 (p) | Q 20/6-7 (p) |
| BO X:6-7 (p) | PS XVI:24-9 (p) | S 55-8 (p) |
| BT 103-7 (p) | PS XVI:25-7 (p) | S 56-7 (p) |
| | PS XVI:26-8 (p) | |

Scoring. Checklist: passing 7-9, borderline 6, failing below 6.
BO=baryton octet, BT=baryton trio, KT=keyboard trio, PS=piano sonata, Q=quartet, Qu=quintet, S=symphony, ST=string trio, WQ=wind quintet, p=pass, f=fail.

In the above experiment, I would have preferred to have come up with a larger number of characteristics and a wider borderline span; I do not feel completely certain that some non-Haydn work would not eventually pass. However, the results clearly suggest that a cross-genre method based on a checklist can be effective. Moreover, the effectiveness of such a study would be greatly enhanced if one limited the genres involved. In a study of doubtful string quartets, one may wish to include string trios, string quintets, piano trios, or even piano sonatas in drawing up the profile, but one need not include symphonies or concertos.

## Cross-Genre Study of Opening $\frac{3}{8}$ Movements

In a series of meetings of the CUNY Haydn String Trio Project, the participants generally agreed on the authenticity or non-authenticity of the trios discussed (see chapter six). A few compositions did, however, produce conflicting opinions, especially the string trio V:C3. C3 failed my authenticity tests of the first movement and the phrase tests of another student, but several members of the group argued convincingly for its authenticity, and H. C. Robbins Landon also considered it genuine.[15] It was suggested that the work had failed my tests because its first movement was in $\frac{3}{8}$ meter. I had employed several triple meter movements, including one in $\frac{3}{8}$, in creating the profile, but the presence of only one $\frac{3}{8}$ movement did leave some room for doubt. At the end of the meeting we decided to include the trio in the complete works stating that there was some question about its authenticity, unless we discovered new information before the volume went to press.

The authenticity of the trio can be tested further by doing a cross-genre study of the $\frac{3}{8}$ opening movement. Four $\frac{3}{8}$ opening movements by Haydn from the 1750s and 60s exist in genres similar to the string trios: two baryton trios (nos. 26 and 70) and two string quartets (op. 1, nos. 2 and 4). In addition, I added the last movement of a string trio (V:8) to the group of works used in creating the profile.[16] Twelve characteristics were valid for all the Haydn works but for 60% or less of ten non-Haydn works in Control Group II (see Chart X; figures following each trait are the number of non-Haydn works a trait appear in).[17] Be-

---

[15] Landon, *Haydn: The Early Years*, 220.
[16] The profile, however, is valid only for opening $\frac{3}{8}$ movements, because there are not enough sample $\frac{3}{8}$ finales in the profile.
[17] I used $\frac{3}{8}$ finales in Control Group II and Test Group I to provide a large enough group of works. This turned out to be an advantage rather than a flaw. While Haydn's $\frac{3}{8}$ finales could not be required to pass the profile, it is still possible that $\frac{3}{8}$ finales by other composers could pass if the profile is not distinctive enough.

cause certain traits appeared in a large percentage of the non-Haydn works while others turned up in none, each item was weighted: traits appearing in five or six non-Haydn pieces were given 1/2 point, one to three pieces a full point, and no works two points. Since 12 1/2 points was the maximum score and 4 points the highest Control Group II score, I made 9.5-12.5 passing, 7-9 borderline, and below 7 failing (giving each category one third of the difference between 4 and 12.5).

## Chart X. Profile for Opening $\frac{3}{8}$ Movements from Haydn's Instrumental Works from the 1750s and 60s

### Positive Traits Appearing in All the Haydn Works

1. Texture changes at least two times in the first nine measures. 50%:1/2 point (trait appears in 50% of the Control Group II works; weighted with a half point).

2. a) Texture space by second beat at least an octave and a fifth and b) texture space of final sonority two octaves and does not contain the fifth of the chord. 30%:1 point.

3. Eighth notes for a least seven measures without a break in the lowest voice. 60%:1/2 point.

4. In the bass, at least one instance of three eighth notes of the same pitch class with the first and second notes being in different octaves in a single measure. 60%:1/2 point.

5. In the opening measure, there are three impacts (composite rhythm), at least one part has only one note, the melody has three notes, and there is only one harmony (with or without nonharmonic tones). 20%:1 point.

6. In the first eight measures of the melody, the rhythmic pattern ♪♪♪ is present, a two-measure rhythmic pattern is repeated at least once, notes of the same pitch class are adjacent, and at least six notes of the diatonic scale are present, but with steps six and seven not appearing in the first measure. 30%:1 point.

7. 38% to 70% of the total measures contain note values shorter than an eighth note, between 6% and 14% of the measures contain less than three impacts (composite rhythm), and the first four measures contain no more than three impacts per measure. 10%:1 point.

# DETERMINING AUTHENTICITY BY STYLE

**Negative Traits Appearing in None of the Haydn Works**

8. a) Presence of ♪♩ , ♫𝄽𝄽 , or ♩. ♩. ♩. in upper voice, or ties over the barline in this voice (other than those beginning on the first beat of a measure); b) opens with a pickup; c) thirty-second notes on the first or third beats of a measure; d) ♫♪♪ more than twice in a movement (not counting ornaments); or e) lacks ♩♬ . 100%:2 points (trait appears in 100% of the non-Haydn works in Control Group II; weighted with two points).

9. Use of melodic chromaticism before measure twenty and use of non-diatonic note in upper voice before measure fourteen. 80%:1 point.

10. Dissonance on a downbeat in the melody in the first ten measures other than a dominant seventh chord or doesn't include a dominant seventh chord in the first ten measures. 80%:1 point.

11. In upper voice, an interval of a fifth, sixth, or seventh in the first four measures, an interval larger than an octave in the first ten measures, or does not contain at least one third and an interval larger than a perfect fifth in the first ten measures. 90%:1 point.

12. a) Opening or closing harmony lasts more than two measures, any harmony in first eight measures sustained longer than two measures, or more than two different harmonies in a measure in first eight measures or more than one harmony per measure in first five measures or b) more than two measures in a row with more than one harmony in first eight measures. 100%:2 points.

I then tested additional non-Haydn pieces with no movement scoring more than 4 1/2 points (see Chart XI). The only comparable $\frac{3}{8}$ movement by Haydn that had not been used in drawing up the profile, II:22 (best known in its string quartet arrangement as op. 2, no. 5), was also tested, and it scored 11 1/2 points. From the above, one can see that the profile is very effective in differentiating Haydn's authentic $\frac{3}{8}$ opening movements from the 1750s and 60s from those of other composers. Finally, I tested String Trio C3 against the profile. Its score of only 1 1/2 points provides strong evidence that Haydn is not C3's composer (see Chart XI).

## Chart XI. Results of Second Cross-Genre Test

| | | |
|---|---|---|
| Haydn II:22-11.5 (p) | M. Haydn ST-1.5 (p) | Mozart Q-3.5 (f) |
| Boccherini Qu-2 (f) | Hasse ST-4.5 (f) | Mozart PS-2.5 (f) |
| Clementi PS-2.5 (f) | Holzbauer ST-1.5 (f) | Richter S-2 (f) |
| Dittersdorf S-3 (f) | Mann ST-1.5 (f) | Stamitz S-2 (f) |
| Filtz S-1 (f) | Monn ST-2.5 (f) | Wagenseil S-1.5 (f) |
| Gassmann Q-3 (f) | L. Mozart ST-1.5 (f) | Zappa ST-4 (f) |
| Gluck ST-1.5 (f) | L. Mozart ST-4 (f) | ? V:C3-1.5 (f) |
| | Mozart Q-3 (f) | |

Scoring. Checklist: passing 10-12.5, borderline 7-9, failing below 7. Conclusion: V:C3 not by Haydn.

## THE EFFECT OF CHRONOLOGY ON THE PROFILE

A final factor to be considered in this chapter is the effect of chronology on the profile. Is it reasonable to assume that a profile for a group of works from the 1780s is just as applicable to compositions from the 1760s and 1790s? The answer to this question depends on how much the minor details of style and hidden communicators in a composer's music change with time.

As a first experiment, I tested a keyboard trio from the late 1760s (XV:2) and one from the mid 1790s (XV:27) against the profile for Haydn's keyboard trios from the 1780s used earlier. Both trios failed: XV:2 failed five of the six ranges by large margins and scored only 11 points on the checklist (passing 17), while XV:27 exceeded all six ranges and scored 13 points on the checklist. Clearly, this particular profile applies only to works from the 1780s. The application of the c. 1770-75 cross-genre profile to earlier and later works yielded similar results. Only one of the four works passed the profile (XVI:50-5 points, failed; op. 2, no. 2-6 points, borderline; op. 2, no. 4-7 points, passed; Symphony No. 1-5 points, failed).

If a factor was to remain consistent over a long period of time, it seems most likely that it would be one of the quantitative ranges, since quantitative ranges are the most effective tests of hidden communicators. However, no quantitative range was found that remained within a narrow enough limit throughout Haydn's career to be useful for establishing authenticity.

My experiments with chronology have indicated that a profile is valid only for the time period of the compositions used in drawing it

## DETERMINING AUTHENTICITY BY STYLE

up. A profile can encompass a large number of years, but only if it includes a representative number of works from each part of the period.

Note: Abbreviations are given on the first relevant chart in each chapter. Appendix F gives unusual or often ambiguously-defined terms that are used in the checklists in chapters two to nine.

CHAPTER THREE

# Keyboard Sonatas

INTRODUCTION

Haydn's keyboard sonatas have been among his most studied works.[1] Yet, unlike the other two instrumental genres that have received close attention—the symphonies and string quartets—a large number of authenticity problems still exist for the early sonatas. Only eight complete extant sonatas that were (probably) written before 1770 (XVI:3, 4, 6, 14, 19, 45, 46, and 47 bis) can be solidly authenticated by documentary means, either by entries in the Haydn catalogues or by the existence of an autograph. In addition, a fragmentary sonata (XVI:5a) survives in autograph, while seven lost sonatas (XVI:2a-e, g, h) are listed in the *Entwurf-Katalog*. Sixteen more sonatas (XVI:1, 2, 5, 7-13, 16, 17, G1, XVII:D1 and the Raigern sonatas XVI:E-flat2 add. and E-flat3 add.)[2] fall into the doubtful category because of the lack of documentary evidence.[3] In this chapter, I shall test the authenticity of these doubtful sonatas.

[1] In the index of the Brown-Berkenstock bibliography, the keyboard sonatas have the third largest number of entries under the instrumental works with seventy-three. This is in comparison to thirty for the wind and string concertos, twenty-six for the keyboard trios, eleven for the keyboard concertos, five for the accompanied keyboard divertimentos, and only two for the string trios. A. Peter Brown and James T. Berkenstock with Carol Vanderbilt Brown, "Joseph Haydn in Literature: A Bibliography," *Haydn-Studien* III/3-4 (1974) 35-51.
[2] Those works marked add. were not listed in the original Hoboken (Volume I) but were included among the addenda in Volume III.
[3] All other early sonatas that have been attributed to Haydn have been proven spurious or are arrangements. Among these, XVI:15 is an arrangement from the divertimento II:11.

The most important documentary evidence concerning the authenticity of the pre-1770 doubtful sonatas are statements made by Haydn in the years 1799-1803 for the preparation of the Haydn *Oeuvres Complettes* by Breitkopf & Härtel. These statements appear in the papers of C. F. Pohl in the Gesellschaft der Musikfreunde in Vienna, based on lost documents in the Breitkopf archives. According to Pohl, Haydn accepted 5, 7-12, and 17 as his compositions, while his opinions concerning 13 were contradictory.[4] However, Haydn's statements in this source have often been questioned; his judgments were based solely on thematic lists and were made in his later years. Moreover, as we shall see below, the scholars who have previously examined these works doubt the authenticity of three of the sonatas (XVI:5, 11, and 17), including one (17) that is very probably by Schwanenberg.

Concerning the source situation of the doubtful sonatas, 1 and 2 exist in good copies from the former Artaria collection (strong indicators of authenticity), while 5 and 7-13 are preserved in early copies in various libraries. In addition, the *Breitkopf Catalogue* lists the incipits of 5 and 7-13 under Haydn's name.[5] The six remaining sonatas (16, 17, D1, G1, E-flat2, and E-flat3) lack documentary evidence other than attributions supporting their authenticity.

Six modern scholars have made important statements about the authenticity of the early sonatas: Georg Feder, Jens Peter Larsen, Christa Landon, H. C. Robbins Landon, A. Peter Brown, and Anthony van Hoboken. Feder's opinions appear in several sources and show a certain amount of change owing to new discoveries.[6] In *Grove*, he lists fifteen works under the category "Early harpsichord sonatas attributed to Haydn," marking 5, 16, E-flat2, and E-flat3 as "doubtful," the first movement of 12 as "? doubtful," and 11 as "? a combination of G1/III and two other movements" and he also questions the authenticity of 11's third movement trio.[7] He makes no comments about the

---

[4]Feder, *The New Grove Haydn*, 185-86.
[5]Barry S. Brook, ed., *The Breitkopf Thematic Catalogues 1762-1787* (New York: Dover, 1966) 120, 251, 283. As stated in the Introduction, attributions in eighteenth-century catalogues are often unreliable.
[6]Georg Feder, "Probleme einer Neuordnung der Klaviersonaten Haydns," *Festschrift Friedrich Blume*, ed. Anna Abert and Wilhelm Pfannkuch (Kassel: Bärenreiter, 1963) 92-103; "Vorwort," *Klaviersonaten, 1. Folge-JHW* (Munich: Henle, 1970) i-xi; "Zwei Haydn zugeschriebene Klaviersonaten," *Bericht über den Internationaler musikwissenschaftlichen Kongress Kassel 1962*, ed. Georg Reichert and Martin Just (Kassel: Bärenreiter, 1963) 181-84; "The Sources of the Two Disputed Raigern Sonatas," *Haydn Studies*, 107-11; and *The New Grove Haydn*, 185-86.
[7]Feder, *The New Grove Haydn*, 185-86.

authenticity of the nine other sonatas and places 17 in the spurious category. In addition, in an article in *Haydn Studies*, he includes 1, 2, 16, G1, and D1 among "early keyboard compositions that require further proof of authenticity," and, in his critical edition of the sonatas (one of the two modern critical editions; see C. Landon below), he writes that the minuet of 5 may be authentic.[8]

Larsen believes that ten sonatas (1, 2, 5, and 7-13) are rather well-documented, although they cannot be regarded as definitely authenticated.[9] He also asserts that the Raigern sonatas (E-flat2 and E-flat3) are poorly documented and stylistically questionable, that 16 is dubious, and 17 spurious.

Christa Landon prepared the other modern scholarly edition of Haydn's sonatas. In the preface, she considers 1, 2, 5, 7-10, 12, and 13 to be genuine but adds that "although in the case of the early works, leaving aside the inferior sources for some sonatas, the determination of authenticity on the grounds of style is severely handicapped by our complete ignorance of the music of the period."[10] She doubts the authenticity of 16, and says that 17 is probably by Schwanenberg. She also includes E-flat2, E-flat3, G1, D1, and 11 in her edition, although she regards 11 as a combination of three unrelated movements.

H. C. Robbins Landon lists eleven of the sonatas as authentic (1, 2, 7, 8, 9, 10, 11, 12, 13, D1, G1).[11] He asserts that 5 is doubtful, although the minuet may be authentic, and that the Raigern sonatas are not by Haydn. One may assume that since he does not mention 16 and 17 he considers them spurious.

A. Peter Brown's study of Haydn's sonatas, including the keyboard trios and accompanied keyboard divertimentos, is the most thorough stylistic examination of this genre. In this study, he questions the authenticity of 5, 16, and E-flat3.[12] He adds that 5 and 16 could be manifestations of Haydn's very early style but that E-flat3 does not fit into any of Haydn's keyboard styles. Furthermore, he believes that 11 is an

---

[8]Feder, "The Sources of the Raigern Sonatas," 110-11 and "Vorwort."
[9]Larsen, *Three Haydn Catalogues*, xvii-xviii.
[10]Joseph Haydn, *Sämtliche Klaviersonaten*, ed. Christa Landon (Vienna: Universal Edition, 1963) Ia, xvi. In *Haydn Studies*, she declared that if she did another edition, she would have reservations about E-flat3 and omit E-flat2, the finale of E-flat3, 5, and 11. *Haydn Studies*, 119.
[11]H. C. Robbins Landon, *Haydn: The Early Years*, 224-25.
[12]A. Peter Brown, *The Solo and Ensemble Keyboard Sonatas of Joseph Haydn: A Study of Structure and Style* (Ph.D. diss., Northwestern University, 1970) 21-22.

arrangement because 1) the opening movement is clearly a finale type and 2) the second and third movements belong to a later style. Finally, Brown excludes 17 from his study completely.

Hoboken's determinations are usually obvious from his system of numbering. The works that he includes under key designations, in this case G1, D1, E-flat2 add., and E-flat3 add., he considers spurious.[13] He mentions statements by Larsen and Rudolf Steglich against 16 and presents the evidence for Schwanenberg as the composer of 17, although he enters both sonatas among the authentic works.

From the above, one can see that there is considerable difference of opinion concerning the authenticity of the sixteen doubtful early sonatas (these opinions are summarized in Table I). The scholars who have given opinions regarding their authenticity agree that while most of the sonatas are probably authentic, none of them can be regarded as definitely authenticated. All six scholars think that 7-10 and 12 (except for the first movement of 12) are probably genuine, and the documentary evidence supports this conclusion. Most of the scholars also believe that 1 and 2 are probably authentic, although Feder would like to see more evidence. For the remaining sonatas, there are opposing opinions or conflicting external evidence, especially concerning 5, 11, G1, D1, and the Raigern sonatas (other opinions on the Raigern sonatas will be presented below).

## THE TESTS

I employed four separate profiles to study the authenticity of the early keyboard sonatas: 1) fast first or second movements in binary or rounded-binary form, 2) minuets, 3) slow movements, and 4) $\frac{2}{4}$ and $\frac{3}{4}$ finales. The use of four different profiles insured that at least two movements of each sonata would be tested and that all individual movements that were questioned separately from the complete sonatas (5/II, 11/II, 11/III, 12/I) could be evaluated. So many tests were necessary because of the wide variety of approaches found in the early sonatas, especially in gross form. Despite this variety, it was possible to employ only one profile for each type of movement.

---

[13]Hoboken, *Haydn Catalogue*, I, 733-81 and III, 349-50.

## Table I. Previous Opinions on the Authenticity of the Sixteen Doubtful Sonatas

|    | Feder Grove | Feder other | Larsen | C.Landon | R.Landon | Brown | Hoboken | Con. |
|----|-------------|-------------|--------|----------|----------|-------|---------|------|
| 1  | -           | fpn         | wd     | pa       | pa       | -     | a       | pa   |
| 2  | -           | fpn         | wd     | pa       | pa       | -     | a       | pa   |
| 5  | d           | II:?a       | wd     | pa       | d,II:?a  | d     | a       | mixed |
| 7  | -           | -           | wd     | pa       | pa       | -     | a       | pa   |
| 8  | -           | -           | wd     | pa       | pa       | -     | a       | pa   |
| 9  | -           | -           | wd     | pa       | pa       | -     | a       | pa   |
| 10 | -           | -           | wd     | pa       | pa       | -     | a       | pa   |
| 11 | ?arr        | -           | wd     | arr      | pa       | arr   | a       | mixed |
| 12 | I:?d        | -           | wd     | pa       | pa       | -     | a       | pa   |
| 13 | -           | -           | wd     | pa       | pa       | -     | a       | pa   |
| 16 | d           | fpn         | ps     | ps       | -        | d     | a       | ps   |
| 17 | s           | -           | s      | ps       | -        | ps    | a       | ps   |
| 2  | d           | -           | ps     | ie       | ps       | -     | s       | ps   |
| 3  | d           | -           | ps     | ie       | ps       | d     | s       | ps   |
| G1 | -           | fpn         | -      | ie       | pa       | -     | s       | mixed |
| D1 | -           | fpn         | -      | ie       | pa       | -     | s       | mixed |

'-'=no clear opinion, arr=arrangement, d=doubtful (probably not authentic), a=authentic, s=spurious, fpn=further proof needed before being declared authentic, wd=well documented, pa=probably authentic, ps=probably spurious, ie=included in edition without comment, Con.=consensus.

---

Profile I: The Expositions of Fast First or Second Movements

I drew up the first profile for the first part (exposition) of fast first or second movements in binary or rounded-binary form. All eight previously-authenticated compositions (Control Group I; XVI:3, 4, 6, 14, 19, 45, 46, 47 bis) contain such a movement, as do twelve of the sixteen doubtful works.

For Test I: Ranges, I found three ranges that were effective for determining authenticity: 1) textural change per beat (TC/B) .119-.180, harmonic change per beat (HC/B) .420-.640, and impacts per beat (I/B) exceeds 2.75. The last range was especially significant for certain movements in the keyboard sonatas because they use a large number of sixteenths and thirty-seconds. To pass, a movement had to fall within all three ranges. A movement was borderline if it did not exceed the textural change range by more than .020 or the harmonic change range by more than .040; no borderline was allowed for the impacts per beat range owing to its special nature.[14]

I included twelve traits in the checklist, with all traits being valid for all eight previously-authenticated movements (see Chart I). Eleven of the characteristics were valid for 40% or less of the ten non-Haydn works in Control Group II; the other one (No. 7 a negative trait) was retained because it is very uncharacteristic of Haydn's movements of this type and because it helps distinguish his style from those composers who do use it. I gave Trait No. 3 two points because it appeared in none of the Control Group II pieces and the remaining traits one point, yielding a total of 13 points.[15] The maximum a piece in Control Group II scored was six points.

## Chart I. Profile I: Checklist for the Expositions of Fast First or Second Movements

### Positive Traits Appearing in All The Haydn Works

1. Uses triplets and thirty-seconds (not including grace notes). 20% (trait appears in 20% of the non-Haydn works)

2. a) Opening harmony lasts at least one half measure but less than four measures, b) closing harmony of exposition no more than three and a half beats, and c) V-I cadence ends the exposition with 2-1 or 7-1 in the top voice. 40%

*3. a) First four measures include a dominant seventh chord but lack a submediant harmony, b) fourth measure includes a tonic chord at the beginning or end, and c) diatonic notes only in the melody in the first four measures. 0%:2 points

4. Treble clef used at some point in the left-hand and either the left-hand goes above middle c or the right-hand below middle c by measure four. 20%

5. a) First four measures in the melody have the tonic or dominant pitch

---

[14]Borderline on the other two ranges was determined by extensive experimentation, both within this study and from previous investigations. Borderline for a specific range may vary from study to study, depending on the particular profile and the width of the range.

[15]As mentioned in Chapter Two, a work must contain all parts of a positive composite trait and no part of a negative composite trait to receive credit for a particular composite trait.

in different octaves; b) first and third measures, second and fourth measures, and third and fifth measures have different rhythms; c) triplets, eighths, or sixteenths repeated no more than one and a half measures without break during the first four measures; and d) the first measure contains a value of a sixteenth or shorter by the first beat of the second half of the measure, including ornaments. 20%

6. At least two consecutive measures of 1/2 texture and lacks three real voices for more than a measure. 30%

### Negative Traits Appearing in None of the Haydn Works

7. a) Presence of murky bass, repeated accompaniment pattern 1-3-5-3, or repeated chords (at least three notes) as an accompaniment pattern anywhere in the exposition, or b) Alberti bass used during the first theme. 70% (trait appears in 70% of the Control Group II works)

8. Chords to mark opening, more than one texture in the first measure, less than two impacts per beat in the first full measure (composite rhythm), both hands begin simultaneously, or only one sounding voice in the first measure. 70%

9. In melody, a), presence of [♩. ♫ ♩. ♫], [|♫ ♩.], [♩], [♩], [♩.. ♫. ♩], or [|♪ ♩ ♪] in all meters or b) more than two quarter notes in a row that are not ornamented in duple meters. 40%

10. Eighth or sixteenth note runs or arpeggios (Most of Haydn's filler material in these movements involves triplets). 70%

11. In bass, [♩.] or [𝅗𝅥.] or more than twenty-two eighth notes, three quarter notes, or two half notes in a row during the first theme. 90%

12. a) Mannheim sigh during opening theme, b) the first two measures of the second phrase identical to the corresponding measures of the first phrase, or c) all seven notes of the scale present in the first measure and a half or the third of the scale is not present in the melody by the first half of the second measure. 70%

(Figures following each item in this chart and the other charts in this chapter indicate the percentage of Control Group II works containing the trait.)

*(In this case, the eight authentic movements in Control Group I.)

I employed those doubtful works for which there was complete agreement regarding their authenticity (7, 8, 9, and 10; henceforth called "consensus sonatas") to establish the lowest passing score. The use of a strongly-supported doubtful composition to determine passing is valid as long as the lowest passing score is significantly higher than the highest score from Control Group II and as long as the scoring criteria are tested further with additional non-Haydn works (Test Group I). Sonatas 7, 8, and 9 all scored 9 points on the checklist, and I used 9 as the lowest passing score. Since 7.5 is the midpoint between 9 (the lowest passing score) and 6 (the highest score of a work in Control Group II), I regarded 8 as borderline and 7 and below as failing (see first set of scoring criteria in Chapter III). I then tested the validity of the profile with ten more non-Haydn works (Test Group I). All twenty non-Haydn pieces in Control Group II and Test Group I failed the checklist and scored borderline or failed the ranges (see Chart II).

### Chart II. Profile I: Results for the Non-Haydn Works

| Composer | Test I-Ranges | | | Test II | Results | |
|---|---|---|---|---|---|---|
| | TC/B | HC/B | I/B | Ch | R-Ch- | Conc. |
| *Control Group II:* | | | | | | |
| C.P.E. Bach | .063 | .103 | e | 5 | f-f | C |
| C.P.E. Bach | .125 | .327 | de | 4 | f-f | C |
| J.C. Bach | .132 | .274 | e | 3 | f-f | C |
| J. Benda | .063 | .875 | e | 3 | f-f | C |
| F.X. Dussek | .162 | .600 | de | 3 | f-f | C |
| Galuppi | .083 | .425 | e | 2 | f-f | C |
| Mozart | .184 | .525 | e | 2 | b-f | C |
| Mozart | .166 | .403 | e | 4 | b-f | C |
| Platti | .126 | .516 | de | 6 | f-f | C |
| Scarlatti | .060 | .390 | e | 3 | f-f | C |
| *Test Group I:* | | | | | | |
| C.P.E. Bach | .204 | .545 | e | 7 | f-f | C |
| J.C. Bach | .112 | .435 | de | 6 | f-f | C |
| W.F. Bach | .031 | .825 | e | 7 | f-f | C |
| G. Benda | .222 | .820 | e | 7 | f-f | C |
| Cimarosa | .021 | .615 | e | 4 | f-f | C |
| Hasse | .200 | .076 | e | 7 | f-f | C |
| Paradisi | .148 | .334 | e | 7 | f-f | C |
| Platti | .094 | .710 | de | 4 | f-f | C |
| Rutini | .195 | .484 | e | 7 | b-f | C |
| Wagenseil | .145 | .705 | e | 6 | f-f | C |

Test I: TC/B .119-.180 (borderline .020), HC/B .420-.640 (borderline .040), I/B exceeds 2.75; Test II: passing 9-13, borderline 8, failing below 8.

TC/B=textural change per beat, HC/B=harmonic change per beat, I/B=impacts per beat (composite rhythm), Ch=Checklist, R=ranges, Conc.=conclusions, e=exceeds, de=does not exceed, A=fits profile, B=results inconclusive, C=does not fit profile.

A test of twelve doubtful movements showed that nine movements (2, 7, 8, 9, 10, 13, E-flat2, E-flat3, and G1) fit the profile, while three (1, 5, and 17) did not (see Chart III). Those movements that failed the profile failed both parts. As mentioned earlier, the movements that passed the profile may be regarded as authentic, while those that failed must be re-evaluated before being designated as spurious. (This will be done for each separate composition in the last part of this chapter.)

### Chart III. Profile I: Results for the Doubtful Sonatas

| Sonata | Test I-Ranges | | | Test II | Results | |
|---|---|---|---|---|---|---|
| | TC/B | HC/B | I/B | Ch | R-Ch-Conc. | |
| 1 | .118 | .389 | e | 5 | b-f | C |
| 2 | .139 | .615 | e | 9 | p-p | A |
| 5 | .104 | .655 | de | 5 | f-f | C |
| 7 | .166 | .500 | e | 9 | p-p | A |
| 8 | .155 | .590 | e | 9 | p-p | A |
| 9 | .166 | .670 | e | 9 | b-p | A |
| 10 | .190 | .545 | e | 12 | b-p | A |
| 13 | .150 | .630 | e | 9 | p-p | A |
| 17 | .046 | .460 | de | 6 | f-f | C |
| E-flat2 | .150 | .607 | e | 10 | p-p | A |
| E-flat3 | .164 | .625 | e | 9 | p-p | A |
| G1 | .160 | .565 | e | 9 | p-p | A |

Scoring. Test I: TC/B .119-.180 (borderline .020), HC/B .420-.640 (borderline .040), I/B exceeds 2.75; Test II; passing 9-13, borderline 8, failing below 8.

Profile II: Minuets

The second profile applied to minuets, not including trios. Four of the previously-authenticated works (Control Group I; XVI:3, 4, 6, 14) and fifteen doubtful ones included minuets. The only quantitative range (Test I) that was narrow enough for authenticity determination was the range of harmonic change per beat (.470-.606; to be borderline a minuet must not exceed the range at either end by more than .020). Because only one range was employed, it is possible that a non-Haydn movement might pass Test I. Nevertheless, Test I is still valuable because it is an excellent indicator of nonauthenticity.

The checklist of positive and negative traits in Haydn's authentic keyboard minuets (Test II) comprised eleven items (see Chart IV). All traits were valid for the four authentic sonatas and 60% or less of the ten non-Haydn compositions in Control Group II. The maximum score was 12.5; Nos. 7 and 9 were given two points, because they turned up in one or none of the Control Group II works, while No. 5 was awarded only a half point because it appeared in six of the ten pieces. The highest a Control Group II work scored was six, while the lowest one of the consensus sonatas (see above) scored was 8.5. Therefore, I made 8.5-12.5 passing, 7.5-8 borderline, and 7 or below failing. That twenty non-Haydn works in Control Group II and Test Group I failed the profile supports its effectiveness (see Chart V). In addition, I tested a Haydn movement (XVI:5a) that I had not included in Control Group II, and it passed.

## Chart IV. Profile II: Checklist for Minuets

### Positive Traits Appearing in All the Haydn Works

1. a) Opening harmony no more than a measure and closing harmony two or three beats, b) dominant seventh present in first four measures, and c) a dissonance on the first beat of a measure in the first four measures. 20% (trait appears in 20% of the non-Haydn works)

2. At least one measure in the melody repeats the rhythm of the preceding measure (not including straight quarters, eighths, or sixteenths). 40%

3. Rhythmic patterns | ♫♪ ♪ | or | ♬♪ ♪ | present. 30%

4. In the melody, first and second measures, third and fourth measures, and second and fourth measures have different rhythms. 30%

#5. Texture of 2 (two sounding voices, one real part) on beats 2 + 3 at least once and texture changes at least twice in the first part. 60%:1/2 point

6. Trills used at least twice in the first part. 40%

*7. a) In top voice, range of first part between an octave and two octaves; b) maximum texture space between two octaves and a third and three octaves and a fourth on a single simultaneity, and c) left-hand range of at least g to g$^1$. 0%:2 points

**Negative Traits Appearing in None of the Haydn Works**

8. In the left-hand, a) presence of two or more eighth notes in a row, b) ties over the barline (except those beginning on the downbeat of a measure), or c) more than eight sixteenth notes in a row. 70% (trait appears in 70% of the Control Group II works)

*9. Presence of ♫ ♫ , 𝅗𝅥. , |♫. , or an unornamented half note except at the end of a phrase. 100%:2 points

10. Use of nondiatonic note in first part other than 7 of V (or 7 of III in minor movements), third part contains any nondiatonic note, or presence of melodic chromaticism. 50%

11. A simultaneity of more than three notes or less than two sounding voices present for more than three beats. 70%

(For minuets in $\frac{3}{8}$, all rhythmic values halved.)

The minuets of 1, 2, 7, 8, 9, 10, 12, 13, D1, G1, E-flat2, and E-flat3 passed both parts of the profile, while those of 5, 11, and 16 failed both parts (see Chart VI). Thus, Profile I (expositions of fast first or second movements) and Profile II (minuets) agree in every respect with the single exception of Sonata No. 1, which failed the first profile but passed the second.[16] In addition, the minuet of No. 11, which failed, is definitely an authentic movement, being a part of the authentic baryton trio 26, which is entered in the *Entwurf-Katalog*. However, this is not a contradictory result, because the profile was set up for keyboard sonatas, not arrangements from baryton trio movements; authentic movements in one genre may fail the profile of another.

Profile III: Slow Movements

Slow movements were the subject of the third profile. Five exist in the previously-authenticated sonatas (XVI:3, 6, 19, 45, 46), while

---

[16]This is the only contradictory result in the whole study.

seven are present in the doubtful ones.[17] Because of differences in form among the slow movements, the entire movement had to be studied.

For Test I (ranges), the rate of harmonic change per beat was too wide for determining authenticity, but the range of textural change per beat (.183-.235; borderline exceeds by .020 or less) and impacts per beat (greater than 2.50; no borderline) did prove effective. Again, it was possible that a non-Haydn sonata would pass Test I.

Twelve entries made up the slow movement checklist with all traits valid for each of the five authentic works (see Chart VII). All traits were weighted equally because none appeared in either a small number or a large number of the ten non-Haydn pieces (Control Group II). I considered 11 or 12 passing, 8-10 borderline, and below 8 failing, since the lowest consensus sonata score was 11 and the highest a composition in Control Group II scored was 5. All twenty non-Haydn works in Control Group II and Test Group I did not fit the profile, failing at least Test II: checklist (see Chart VIII).

### Chart V. Profile II: Results for the Non-Haydn Works[18]

| Composer | Test I HC/B | Test II Ch | Results R-Ch-Conc. | |
|---|---|---|---|---|
| *Control Group II:* | | | | |
| C.P.E. Bach | .656 | 3.5 | f-f | C |
| Clementi | .513 | 3 | p-f | C |
| Krebs | .676 | 2 | f-f | C |
| Latrobe | .590 | 3 | p-f | C |
| Martini | .460 | 4 | b-f | C |
| Matteson | .433 | 1.5 | f-f | C |
| Paradisi | .530 | 4 | p-f | C |
| Rutini | .666 | 3.5 | f-f | C |
| Schobert | .543 | 3 | p-f | C |
| Wagenseil | .633 | 6 | f-f | C |
| *Test Group I:* | | | | |
| J.C.F. Bach | .686 | 5.5 | f-f | C |
| G. Benda | .436 | 4.5 | f-f | C |

*continued*

---

[17]No. 16/I mixed slow and fast sections and thus could not be fairly evaluated against a profile for slow movements. Also, I did not use XVI:47 bis in Control Group I because its slow movement is in 6/8.

[18]I included a few baroque minuets in these tests for comparison.

*KEYBOARD SONATAS*

## Chart V. Profile II: continued

| Composer | Test I HC/B | Test II Ch | Results R-Ch-Conc. | |
|---|---|---|---|---|
| *Test Group 1:* | | | | |
| Daquin | .366 | 3.5 | f-f | C |
| Lindemann | .292 | 2.5 | f-f | C |
| Mozart | .563 | 2.5 | p-f | C |
| Mozart | .250 | 2.5 | f-f | C |
| Paradisi | .520 | 5 | p-f | C |
| Schwanenberg | .416 | 4 | f-f | C |
| Schwanenberg | .543 | 3.5 | p-f | C |
| Wernicke | .543 | 3 | p-f | C |
| Haydn XVI:5a | .516 | 8.5 | p-p | A |

Scoring. Test I: HC/B .470-.606 (borderline .020); Test II: passing 8.5-12.5, borderline 7.5-8, failing below 7.5.

## Chart VI. Profile II: Results for the Doubtful Works

| Work | Test I HC/B | Test II Ch | Results R-Ch-Conc. | |
|---|---|---|---|---|
| 1 | .583 | 12.5 | p-p | A |
| 2 | .520 | 10 | p-p | A |
| 5 | .443 | 5 | f-f | C |
| 7 | .500 | 8.5 | p-p | A |
| 8 | .560 | 12.5 | p-p | A |
| 9 | .560 | 11.5 | p-p | A |
| 10 | .487 | 12.5 | p-p | A |
| 11 | .333 | 4.5 | f-f | C |
| 12 | .570 | 11.5 | p-p | A |
| 13 | .470 | 10.5 | p-p | A |
| 16 | .443 | 4 | f-f | C |
| D1 | .500 | 9.5 | p-p | A |
| G1 | .470 | 9.5 | p-p | A |
| E-flat2 | .531 | 8.5 | p-p | A |
| E-flat3 | .523 | 8.5 | p-p | A |

Scoring. Test I: HC/B .470-.606 (borderline .020); Test II: passing 8.5-12.5, borderline 7.5-8, failing below 7.5. (For abbreviations, see Chart II.)

KEYBOARD SONATAS

## Chart VII. Profile III: Checklist for Slow Movements
### Positive Traits Appearing in All the Haydn Works

1. Employs triplets and a note value shorter than a sixteenth and eighth notes used frequently. 20% (trait appears in 20% of the Control Group II works)

2. a) Opening harmony lasts at least a half measure but less than two measures, b) closing harmony lasts a measure or less, c) dominant seventh chord appears in the first seven measures, and d) an appoggiatura is not struck simultaneously with the first tonic note in the bass. 30%

3. a) At least two impacts per beat in the opening measure (composite rhythm, b) the melody in the fourth measure does not repeat the rhythm of any preceding measure, c) the rhythms of the fourth and fifth measures are different, and d) all seven diatonic notes appear in the melody by the end of the third measure. 30%

4. At least 33% of the measures have more than two sounding voices and 1/2 texture present for at least four consecutive beats. 50%

5. At least 40% of the measures contain a rest and at least one rest of a quarter note or longer present (not counting rests at the end of the first major part), but no rest of the same value in all parts during the first seven measures. 40%

6. Trills and similar ornaments used frequently but (arpeggiation sign) not used on adjacent chords. 10%

7. Range in left-hand at least G to f¹, right-hand attains at least a c³, and range of a least an octave in the right-hand in the first four measures. 30%

8. a) Texture changes at least three times in the first eight measures, b) first four measures do not contain a simultaneity of more than four notes, and c) the first measure uses two real voices with the highest real voice not doubled. 50%

### Negative Traits Appearing in None of the Haydn Works

9. a) In the melody, ♫. ♫. , ♫. , 𝄻 , |♫♪  or |♪ ♩ ♪ ; or b) in the bass, more than two half notes in a row except for syncopated patterns; or c) Mannheim sigh. 70% (trait appears in 70% of the Control Group II works)

10. Use of Alberti bass, murky bass, or any arpeggiated bass patterns, chords on the downbeat followed by rests in the remainder of the measure, or chords with ♪ ⁊ ♪ ⁊ rhythm as an accompaniment pattern. 70%

11. Use of octave doublings alone in the right-hand or octaves alone in the left-hand for more than three beats, except at the end of a movement. 80%

12. a) In the first eight measures, more than two quarter notes, four eighth notes or eight sixteenth notes in a row, or b) begins with a single sixteenth pickup or a pickup that lasts longer than an eighth note. 70%

**Chart VIII. Profile III: Results for the Non-Haydn Works**

| Composer | Test I-Ranges | | Test II | Results | |
|---|---|---|---|---|---|
| | TC/B | I/B | Ch | R-Ch-Conc. | |
| *Control Group II:* | | | | | |
| Arne | .160 | de | 4 | f-f | C |
| C.P.E. Bach | .126 | de | 2 | f-f | C |
| J.C. Bach | .114 | e | 4 | f-f | C |
| J.C.F. Bach | .255 | e | 4 | b-f | C |
| Cimarosa | .266 | e | 5 | f-f | C |
| Fasch | .260 | e | 3 | f-f | C |
| Paradisi | .091 | e | 5 | f-f | C |
| Sacchini | .224 | e | 4 | p-f | C |
| Scarlatti | .123 | e | 5 | f-f | C |
| Wagenseil | .146 | de | 5 | f-f | C |
| *Test Group I:* | | | | | |
| C.P.E. Bach | .207 | e | 5 | p-f | C |
| G. Benda | .128 | e | 8 | f-b | C |
| Galuppi | .150 | e | 6 | f-f | C |
| Grazioli | .126 | e | 6 | f-f | C |
| Haessler | .277 | e | 3 | f-f | C |
| Martinez | .123 | e | 4 | f-f | C |
| Matielli | .173 | e | 6 | b-f | C |
| Mozart | .139 | e | 8 | p-f | C |
| Rolle | .216 | e | 7 | p-f | C |
| Rutini | .146 | e | 6 | f-f | C |

Scoring. Test I: TC/B .183-.235 (borderline .020), I/B exceeds 2.50; Test II: passing 11-12, borderline 8-10, failing below 8.

The slow movements of 1, 2, 8, 12, and E-flat2 conformed to the profile, while those of 11 and 17 failed both ranges and checklist (see Chart IX). These results agree with those of the two earlier profiles, except, of course, for No. 1, which had previously exhibited conflicting results.

### Chart IX. Profile III: Results for the Doubtful Works

| Work | Test I-Ranges | | Test II | Results |
|---|---|---|---|---|
| | TC/B | I/B | Ch | R-Ch-Conc. |
| 1 | .191 | e | 12 | p-p A |
| 2 | .234 | e | 12 | p-p A |
| 8 | .222 | e | 11 | p-p A |
| 11 | .166 | de | 5 | f-f C |
| 12 | .209 | e | 11 | p-p A |
| 17 | .230 | de | 5 | f-f C |
| E-flat2 | .232 | e | 11 | p-p A |

Scoring. Test I: TC/B .183-.235 (borderline .020), I/B exceeds 2.50; Test II: passing 11-12, borderline 8-10, failing below 8.

Profile IV: Finales

The last profile covered fast nonminuet finales in 2/4 or 3/4, with complete movements studied owing to differences in form. All other types of finales could be excluded from the profile because there were sufficient movements already studied in those sonatas that contained the other types. This allowed a more distinctive profile for the five authentic (XVI:14, 19, 45, 46, 47 bis) and seven doubtful finales in this group; the presence of 3/8 finales might have made drawing up a distinctive profile difficult.

Because of differences in form, no quantitative range worked for finales in 2/4 or 3/4. Nevertheless, a very distinctive profile using just a checklist containing twelve items valid for all five authentic sonatas was possible (see Chart X). I doubly weighted two entries (Nos. 5 and 10) that were valid for none of the ten Control Group II works, yielding a maximum score of 14. The lowest a consensus sonata scored was 11 and the highest a work in Control Group II scored was 5 so I made 11-14 passing; 8-10.5 borderline; and below 8 failing. The twenty non-Haydn finales in Control Group II and Test Group I scored 7 points or less (Chart XI).

## KEYBOARD SONATAS

## Chart X. Profile IV: Checklist for Finales

### Positive Traits Appearing in All the Haydn Works

1. Left-hand attains at least a$^1$, right-hand range includes at least c-sharp$^3$, and treble clef employed in left-hand. 20% (trait appears in 20% of the Control Group II works)

2. Rests of quarter and eighth values used frequently and simultaneous rest in all parts in first twenty-seven measures, but lacks rest in the left-hand that is longer than eight beats. 20%

3. a) 40% of the measures have three or more sounding voices, b) each hand contains two sounding voices at some point, and c) 1/2 texture present for at least two consecutive measures. 30%

4. a) First eight measures in the melody have a range between an octave and two octaves; b) the fifth of the scale appears in the melody before the fifth beat and it or the first degree appears in two different octaves in the first eight measures; and c) disjunct intervals used in the melody by the end of measure three and different note values used by the end of measure four (not counting rests). 50%

*5. Uses a pattern involving a rest on the downbeat in the upper voice such as         or         at least five times.
0%:2points

6. Contains octave doublings in the left-hand lasting at least a measure and a half, but does not use more than two notes at the same time in the right-hand except at the end of movements. 10%

7. At least two impacts per beat in the first measure (composite rhythm), the rhythm of a measure in the melody is repeated in the first five measures, but at least one measure has a different rhythm, and the fifth measure begins with a tonic chord. 30%

8. Upper line includes a melodic seventh, and a pedal of at least four measures is present in any voice (not including one at the end of a movement). 40%

9. Harmony changes at least six times in the first eight measures and texture changes at least three times. 60%

### Negative Traits Appearing in None of the Haydn Works

*10. In the melody, a)         ,         , two sixteenths on the first beat of a measure followed by any value other than another sixteenth, or triplets used for more than a half measure at a time, b) ♫♩ , ♫♩. , ♫♩ except when the last note goes over the barline, or c) more than thirteen unornamented eighth notes in a row. 100%:2 points (trait appears in 100% of the Control Group II works)

11. Opening sonority consists of more than two notes, the second note is longer than the first (not including grace notes), or the first harmonic interval is a bare octave (or equivalent). 60%

12. a) A quarter-note chord on the downbeat followed by rests in the remainder of the measure, chords with the rhythmic pattern ♪ ♪ , or repeated eighth-note chords as an accompaniment pattern; b) ties over the barline in the lowest voice (except those beginning on the first beat of a measure); c) murky bass eighth notes on the same pitch for more than a measure or repeated quarter notes on the same pitch as an accompaniment for more than a measure; or d) doesn't include some kind of patterned accompaniment in the left-hand. 80%

## Chart XI. Profile IV: Results for the Non-Haydn Works

| Control Group II: | Test Group II: |
|---|---|
| C.P.E. Bach-4 (f) | C.P.E. Bach-6 (f) |
| J.C. Bach-1 (f) | Clementi-3 (f) |
| G. Benda-1 (f) | Galuppi-6 (f) |
| Buttstedt-5 (f) | Martinez-2 (f) |
| De Nebra-3 (f) | Martini-3 (f) |
| Mozart-5 (f) | Paradisi-6 (f) |
| Paradisi-1 (f) | Pleyel-4 (f) |
| Platti-3 (f) | Rolle-7 (f) |
| Sacchini-5 (f) | Rutini-5 (f) |
| Wagenseil-4 (f) | Schobert-6 (f) |

Scoring. Checklist: passing 11-14, borderline 8-10.5, failing below 8.

## KEYBOARD SONATAS

Out of the seven doubtful sonatas, four (9, 10, 13, D1) passed and three (16, 17, and E-flat3) failed (see Chart XII).

### Chart XII. Profile IV: Results for the Doubtful Works

| | | |
|---|---|---|
| 9-11 (p) | 13-12 (p) | D1-13 (p) |
| 10-13 (p) | 16-5 (f) | E-flat3-7 (f) |
| | 17-2 (f) | |

Scoring. Checklist: passing 11-14, borderline 8-10.5, failing below 8.

## SUMMARY OF CONCLUSIONS FOR THE SIXTEEN DOUBTFUL SONATAS

The above tests using four profiles for four different types of movements exhibit a great deal of consistency with contradictory results in only one instance (XVI:1). The following discussion relates the outcome of the tests a) to the documentary evidence, b) to opinions of recognized Haydn experts, and c) to other stylistic factors, and presents my conclusions concerning the authenticity of the sixteen doubtful sonatas.

### *XVI:1*

Profiles. I:C, II:A, III:A, contradictory results
Documentary evidence: copy from former Artaria collection
Experts' opinions: general consensus—yes, with reservations from Feder

All six of the Haydn experts mentioned above believe that XVI:1 is authentic, except for Feder who wanted to see more evidence. While the sonata does not appear in the *Breitkopf Catalogue* and while Haydn did not vouch for its authenticity, the presence of a copy from the former Artaria collection presents good, although not conclusive, evidence for its being by Haydn.

XVI:1 is the only sonata that produced conflicting results on the profiles. As stated earlier, since movements II and III passed the tests they may be considered authentic, and there is nothing stylistic in either movement to make one doubt this conclusion. The Andante, in particular, is very typical of Haydn's slow movements, especially with its treatment of triplets (see Ex. 1). On the other hand, the first movement, which failed the profile, does not resemble any of the other opening movements from Haydn's early sonatas. Especially notable is the large extent of Alberti bass patternings and the lack of triplets. A few Haydnesque touches are found in the treatment of ornamentation (especially the typical Haydn ornament ⟨⟩ ) and the figures in m. 15-16 and 46-49 with a quarter-note in the left-hand against  in the right-hand. (This figure appears throughout Haydn's authentic sonatas.) Because there is nothing in the sources to suggest that the first movement is not an original part of the sonata and because the work would be incomplete without it, I must conclude that the movement is authentic and that it failed the profile because it was a compositional experiment. Haydn may have been experimenting with Alberti bass or he may have been writing a piece for his keyboard students to teach them Alberti bass. (XVI:1 is one of the pieces that Feder classifies as a Liebhaber sonata, a small-scale work mainly intended for teaching.)[19]

**Example 1. XVI: 1/II, m. 1-2**

Conclusion (of the present author based on the results of the tests): Authentic.

## XVI:2

Profiles. I:A, II:A, III:A
Documentary evidence: copy from the former Artaria collection
Experts' opinions: general consensus—yes, with reservations from Feder

As was true for XVI:1, only Feder expresses any reservations con-

---

[19]Feder, "Probleme," 100. XVI:3/I seems to be a similar experiment in its use of triplet accompaniment figures.

cerning the authenticity of this sonata, and it survives in a copy from the former Artaria collection. There is nothing atypical of Haydn's style in any of the three movements, and the handling of triplets and skillful treatment of texture in the first movement is especially characteristic. Since all three movements passed the systematic tests and since there is no conflicting documentary evidence, XVI:2 may be regarded as genuine.

Conclusion: Authentic.

## XVI:5

Profiles. I:C, II:C, III:not studied
Documentary evidence: accepted by Haydn in 1803 according to Pohl, in the *Breitkopf Catalogue*, early copy
Experts' opinions: mixed

Despite the evidence supporting the authenticity of this sonata, Feder, Brown, and Landon question its authenticity, although Feder and Landon both think that the minuet might be genuine. From a quick stylistic examination, one might conclude that the sonata is indeed authentic. For example, the first movement contains a number of details that are typical of Haydn, such as the figure ♫♫ to end a phrase, the use of 1/2 texture, and triplets employed as running figures. On the other hand, although the opening theme is very interesting (m. 1-8), the remainder of the first movement consists mainly of filler material. In addition, the composer of the work is obviously writing in large blocks; notice especially m. 16-21, 22-29, and 38-48. The passage from m. 16-21 is merely rhythmically realized harmony (Ex. 2), and most of the first movement lacks melodic or rhythmic distinctiveness. The other two movements also exhibit many traits that are uncharacteristic of Haydn's authentic sonatas. For instance, none of the authentic minuets (including those authenticated in this study) open with 2/1 texture and none of the $\frac{3}{8}$ finales begins with a triplet upbeat or assume such large dimensions.

The profiles reinforce the doubts raised by the general stylistic examination and the previous opinions: both the movements studied did

**Example 2. XVI:5/1, m.16-21**

not fit the profiles (including the minuet that Feder and Landon thought might be genuine), failing both tests.

Conclusion: Spurious.

### XVI:7

Profiles. I:A, II:A, III:not studied
Documentary evidence: accepted by Haydn in 1803 according to Pohl, in the *Breitkopf Catalogue*, early copy
Experts' opinions: probably authentic

The documentary evidence supports the authenticity of this sonata, and none of the six experts disagree. Despite the sonata's brevity, the two movements studied fit the profiles, and since there is nothing atypical stylistically in any of the three movements, it may be considered genuine.

Conclusion: Authentic.

### XVI:8

Profiles. I:A, II:A, III:A, IV:not studied
Documentary evidence: accepted by Haydn in 1803 according to Pohl, in the Breitkopf Catalogue, early copy
Experts' opinions: probably authentic

This sonata, which passed three out of three profiles, is very typical of Haydn's Liebhaber sonata style. There is no reason to seriously doubt its authenticity on documentary or stylistic grounds.

Conclusion: Authentic.

### XVI:9

Profiles. I:A, II:A, III:A
Documentary evidence: accepted by Haydn in 1803 according to Pohl, in the *Breitkopf Catalogue*, early copy
Experts' opinions: probably authentic

Since all movements passed the profiles and there is no conflicting evidence against its authenticity, XVI:9 may be included among the authentic sonatas.

Conclusion: Authentic.

### XVI:10

Profiles. I:A, II:A, III:A
Documentary evidence: accepted by Haydn in 1803 according to Pohl, in the *Breitkopf Catalogue*, early copies
Experts' opinions: probably authentic

Another typical example of the Liebhaber style, all evidence indicates that XVI:10 is by Haydn.

Conclusion: Authentic.

### XVI:11

Profiles. I:not studied, II:C, III:C
Documentary evidence: accepted by Haydn in 1803 according to Pohl, in the *Breitkopf Catalogue*, early copies
Experts' opinions: most regard it as an arrangement

This sonata presents the most complex problem of the sixteen doubtful sonatas. The first movement is undoubtedly by Haydn, also being the finale of the authentic sonata G1 (see below), and the minuet (but not its trio) is shared with baryton trio 26. Feder, Christa Landon, and Brown write that XVI:11 is probably an arrangement, but Landon includes it in his list without comment and Hoboken places 11 rather than G1 among the authentic sonatas.

The first movement appears to be a $\frac{3}{8}$ sonata finale (this type of finale is common in Haydn's keyboard works and none of his authentic sonatas open with a $\frac{3}{8}$ movement) and, therefore, G1 is probably the original version. The second movement, which failed the slow movement profile, is not typical of Haydn's slow movements from the early keyboard sonatas. (See Ex. 3.) Moreover, it does not resemble the style of Haydn's keyboard sonata slow movements from any period. If the movement is authentic Haydn, it is probably an arrangement of a lost work in another genre. The third movement failed the minuet profile, indicating that it was not originally written for solo keyboard. In addition, Feder writes that the trio of the third movement is of questionable authenticity.

**Example 3. XVI:11/2, m. 1-6**

From the above, one may conclude that XVI:11 is an arrangement. If I am right that the second movement is spurious or Feder is correct that the trio is not by Haydn, then the work would have to be considered a factitious arrangement.[20]

---

[20]To avoid confusion, I am using the word factitious rather than spurious to indicate those arrangements not made by Haydn. A factitious arrangement may be formed entirely from authentic movements or may also include spurious movements.

KEYBOARD SONATAS

Conclusion: Arrangement, probably a factitious one that includes material not by Haydn.

## XVI:12

Profiles. I:A, II:A, III:not studied
Documentary evidence: accepted by Haydn in 1803 according to Pohl, in the *Breitkopf Catalogue*, early copy
Experts' opinions: general consensus—yes, although Feder questions the authenticity of the first movement

The only major problem with this sonata is the first movement, which Feder believes may not be by Haydn. However, this movement passed the profile, and I can find nothing in it that makes me doubt its authenticity on stylistic grounds. Moreover, Landon uses this movement as a typical example of Haydn's fondness for series of triplets (see Ex. 4).[21] The second movement also passed its profile, and the sonata may be considered genuine.

**Example 4. XVI: 12/I, m. 1-4**

Conclusion: Authentic.

## XVI:13

Profiles. I:A, II:A, III:A
Documentary evidence: Haydn's statements in 1803 contradictory, in the *Breitkopf Catalogue*, early copy
Experts' opinions: general consensus—yes

The major difficulty with this sonata is that Haydn made contradictory claims concerning its authenticity in 1803.[22] Otherwise, all the documentary evidence and experts' opinions attest to its genuineness. Moreover, none of the movements contain any stylistic details that

[21]Landon, *Haydn: The Early Years*, 225.
[22]Feder, *The New Grove Haydn*, 185-86.

seem uncharacteristic of Haydn. All three movements passed the systematic tests, and the sonata may be included in the authentic category.

Conclusion: Authentic.

## XVI:16

Profiles. I:not studied, II:C, III:C
Documentary evidence: weak, but lacks conflicting attribution
Experts' opinions: general consensus—probably spurious

Weak documentary support and certain stylistic characteristics have caused most modern Haydn scholars to regard this sonata as spurious. The first movement could not be compared against the profiles because it mixes slow and fast sections. This very fact leads one to question the authenticity of this movement, since none of Haydn's early keyboard sonatas are so structured. In addition, the presence of a written-out cadenza is not typical, and the fast sections seem particularly uncharacteristic of Haydn (see Ex. 5). Both the second and third movements failed their profiles, and they contain no details that seem to contradict the conclusion that XVI:16 is not by Haydn.

Conclusion: Spurious.

**Example 5. XVI:16/I, m.18-23**

## KEYBOARD SONATAS

### XVI:17

Profiles. I:C, II:C, III:C
Documentary evidence: accepted by Haydn in 1803 according to Pohl, also attributed to Schwanenberg
Experts' opinions: probably spurious

Although XVI:17 was authenticated by Haydn in 1803 according to Pohl, modern Haydn scholars believe that it was probably written by Johann Gottfried Schwanenberg. Since all three movements failed the profiles, there is no reason to believe that the sonata is by Haydn.

Conclusion: Spurious.

### XVII:D1

Profiles. I:not studied, II:A, III:A
Documentary evidence: weak, but no conflicting attributions
Experts' opinions: mixed

Although Hoboken included this work in his miscellaneous Gruppe XVII:Klavierstücke, most Haydn scholars treat it as a sonata. Hoboken doubts its authenticity and Feder groups it with those sonatas that require more evidence before being considered authentic, but Landon and A. Peter Brown accept it as genuine and Christa Landon includes it in her edition. The lack of other opening variation movements in the early keyboard sonatas makes a stylistic study of the first movement difficult, but it does contain several stylistic features typical of Haydn, including the treatment of texture, the handling of triplets, and the imagination used in deriving variations. Movements II and III both fit the profiles, and movement III, in particular, seems to be characteristic of Haydn. I believe that XVII:D1 is genuine Haydn.

Conclusion: Authentic.

## XVI:G1

Profiles. I:A, II:A, III:not studied
Documentary evidence: weak, but no conflicting attributions
Experts' opinions: mixed

As pointed out earlier, the last movement of G1 and the first movement of 11 are the same. Like D1, the documentary evidence for G1 is weak and previous opinions concerning this sonata are mixed. Movements I and II passed the profiles, and all three movements are typical of Haydn. In addition, the incipits of XVI:G1/I and XIV:7/I are strikingly similar (see Ex. 6). There is little reason to doubt XVI:G1's authenticity.

**Example 6.** XVI: G1/I, m. 1-5

XIV: 7/I, m. 1-3

Conclusion: Authentic.

## KEYBOARD SONATAS

### The Raigern Sonatas
### XVI:E-flat2

Profiles. I:A, II:A, III:A
Documentary evidence: weak
Experts' opinions: probably spurious

### XVI:E-flat3

Profiles. I:A, II:A, ?III:C
Documentary evidence: weak, including a conflicting attribution
Experts' opinions: probably spurious

Of all Haydn's early keyboard sonatas, the Raigern sonatas (XVI:E-flat2 and E-flat3) have generated the most controversy concerning their authenticity. They were discovered in 1961 by Georg Feder, who originally considered them genuine, citing stylistic parallels to authentic works.[23] At that time, Haydn scholars generally accepted their authenticity.[24] However, ten years later, Carsten Hatting uncovered another manuscript for the second sonata that attributed it to a Mariano Romano Kayser, and, since this discovery, the authenticity of both sonatas have been strongly disputed.[25]

Two manuscripts exist for these sonatas: A) the Rutka manuscript that Feder discovered and B) the Roskovszky manuscript found by Hatting. The Rutka manuscript, dating from the mid-1770s, attributes the sonatas to Haydn. This manuscript also contains three other works that are by Haydn (XVI:2, 13, and 14; see above), but, in other cases, Rutka attributed compositions to Haydn that are definitely not by him (three spurious string quartets).

Dating from the mid-1760s, the Roskovszky manuscript contains only E-flat3, with an added finale. On the page preceding this sonata is the comment "Seque Divertimento pour le Clavecin Cembalo Solo. Del Sig.re Mariano Romano Kayser Si Volti." Concerning this attribution, Feder has declared, "The connection of this title with the music following is plausible, if not absolutely certain."[26] The same manu-

---

[23]Feder, "Zwei Haydn zuschriebene Klaviersonaten."
[24]*Haydn Studies*, 107.
[25]Carsten E. Hatting, "Haydn oder Kayser?—Eine Echtheitsfrage," *Die Musikforschung* XXV (1972) 182-87.
[26]Feder, "The Sources of the Raigern Sonatas," 108.

script includes a canzona, an aria, and possibly an allegro that are also attributed to the otherwise unknown Kayser, but contains the minuet from Haydn's keyboard divertimento XIV:4, without an attribution. In addition, the manuscript contains a number of misattributions, as well as misspelled titles ("Suite D. Reces" for "Suite de Pièces") and fanciful tempo indications (like "Lamentevole Amante Pietoso").

Feder presents two hypotheses for the origin of the conflicting attribution: 1) that "Roskovszky copied a sonata by Haydn who was perhaps still unknown to him, and substituted the name of Kayser, known to him from other pieces in the collection" or 2) that "Rutka misread the name of Kayser, and substituted the name of Haydn, whose works were already familiar to him."[27]

Two stylistic studies have been done on the Raigern sonatas. A. Peter Brown was struck by their "impression of redundancy" and "resulting lack of thrust," which differentiated them from the contemporary Haydn keyboard works.[28] Although he did find stylistic details that are characteristic of Haydn (especially the "rather impressive development sections"), he concluded that if they are by Haydn, "they do not convincingly exemplify his keyboard style or his high level of craftmanship."[29] On the other hand, Sonja Gerlach discerned a number of details, especially cadences, that seem typical of Haydn.[30] In addition, she maintained that the Kayser aria also found in the Roskovszky collection differs radically from the sonatas in their harmonic structure and types of cadences.

While Robbins Landon, Feder, Larsen, and Brown consider the Raigern sonatas either questionable or spurious, I believe that a decision, even a tentative one, cannot be made on documentary grounds or general stylistic evidence. The conflicting attribution to Kayser is not definite (see above); neither copyist seems to be particularly reliable; and the general stylistic evidence indicates that the sonatas could be by Haydn, but they could also be by a contemporary who wrote in a similar style.

I believe that Feder's hypotheses explaining the conflicting attribution while possible are highly conjectural, but I would like to suggest

---

[27]Feder, "The Sources of the Raigern Sonatas," 109.
[28]A. Peter Brown, "Haydn's Keyboard Idiom and the Raigern Sonatas," *Haydn Studies*, 111. Brown assumes that they were written in the late 1760s.
[29]*Ibid.*, 115.
[30]Sonja Gerlach, "Remarks on the Structure and Harmony of the Raigern Sonatas," *Haydn Studies*, 115-17.

still another, perhaps equally conjectural, possibility. E-flat3, which contains only two movements, might be incomplete or at least seem incomplete to many observers. Since the Roskovszky manuscript contains a finale not in the other manuscript, Kayser might be the author of this finale, adding it to the otherwise incomplete Haydn sonata.

All five movements contained in the Rutka manuscript passed their respective profiles, and despite the weak documentary evidence and negative opinions, E-flat2 and E-flat3 appear to be authentic Haydn sonatas. However, the movement added in the Roskovszky manuscript did not pass its profile, indicating that it is not by Haydn and thus supporting (but certainly not confirming) my hypothesis concerning its origin.

While the above conclusion disagrees with that of virtually every other Haydn scholar, the possibility that five nonauthentic movements would wrongly pass the profiles is statistically remote; none of over 400 non-Haydn works tested against the various profiles in this study passed or scored uncertain.[31] Concerning the negative documentary evidence, it may be reiterated that both scribes appear to be unreliable and that the presence of a conflicting attribution does not prove that a composition is not by Haydn (see introduction). That the sonatas survive in only one source attributed to Haydn means nothing because several authentic sonatas are lost (XVI:2a-e, g, h). Moreover, it may be repeated that Feder initially accepted these sonatas on stylistic grounds, as did several other Haydn scholars. The treatment of rhythm in E-flat2/I, E-flat2/II, and E-flat3/I is very typical of Haydn's authentic keyboard works, including the frequent use of thirty-second notes, series of sixteenth-note triplets, and the ornament   which Landon believes is a strong indicator of Haydn's authorship (see Ex. 7).[32] Finally, I doubt that a minor composer like Kayser would have been able to produce the extensive and elaborate development sections found in the first movements of both sonatas.

---

[31] I carefully checked and rechecked all aspects of my analyses of E-flat2 and E-flat3 to make absolutely certain that I had made no mistakes. I also searched the sonatas for rhythmic and melodic figures that were not typical of Haydn, without finding a single figure that did not occur in at least one authentic keyboard work.

[32] Landon, "Preface," *Joseph Haydn Klaviertrios: Trio No. 4* (Vienna: Doblinger, 1977). Landon writes, "We believe that in Haydn's use of the ornament   we have perhaps the strongest and most uniquely personal Haydn 'fingerprint' . . . It is, in fact, characteristic that hardly anyone else, except Haydn's pupils . . . uses   in this fashion." Note, however, that XVI:5/I, a sonata that Landon (and I) considers spurious, uses this ornament. (Of course, the sonata may be by a Haydn pupil.)

## KEYBOARD SONATAS

**Example 7. XVI: E flat 2/I, m. 1-4**

Conclusion: Both sonatas authentic, except for E-flat3/III.

## WORKS FOR KEYBOARD FOUR HANDS

Only four works for keyboard four hands have been attributed to Haydn: 1) "Il maestro e lo scolare" (XVIIa:1), an authentic work that is listed in the *Entwurf-Katalog*, 2) a Grand Sonata in C (XVIIa:C1), which is actually by Tommaso Giordani,[33] 3) XVIIa:F1, another spurious work, and 4) the Partita in F (XVIIa:2), a doubtful composition.

XVIIa:2 survives in only one early manuscript. Other than placing it into the doubtful category, no previous opinions have been given about its authenticity.

The existence of only one authentic keyboard duet makes a systematic testing of XVIIa:2 difficult. In addition, XVIIa:1 and XVIIIa:2 are

---

[33]Hoboken, *Haydn Catalogue*, I, 809.

not comparable: XVIIa:1 consists of a set of variations followed by a tempo di minuetto movement while XVIIa:2 comprises a fast binary movement followed by a minuet and trio. XVIIa:2 is a simple work, probably written for teaching. It contains an amount of repetition that is unusual for Haydn, but this may be the result of its didactic function. Otherwise, the work does not contain any trait that would cause one to conclude that it was not by Haydn; I was especially careful in checking for rhythms that are rare in other keyboard genres. Moreover, there are a number of rhythms that are typical of Haydn. In the first movement, one finds the figure ♩ ♪♪♪ several times, while in the minuet, one observes both the figure ♩. ♪♪ and triplets. (Both of these are also present in the tempo di minuetto of XVIIa:1). Still, there is not enough stylistic evidence to decide the authenticity of the piece.

Conclusion: Possibly authentic.

CHAPTER FOUR

# Accompanied Keyboard Divertimentos

INTRODUCTION

Haydn's accompanied keyboard divertimentos for clavier with two violins and cello (or bass) are among his least known works. While this genre must be classified as one of Haydn's "occasional" or "lighter" genres, these divertimentos are delightful and charming works that deserve more attention than they have previously received. Fortunately, all of the accompanied divertimentos that are usually considered authentic are now available in modern edition and several have been recorded[1].

Because these works resemble miniature concertos and can be performed by either solo strings or with a small string orchestra, there has been considerable debate over their classification. Hoboken placed them in *Gruppe XIV: Mehrstimmige Divertimenti mit Klavier*, along with XIV:1, which is scored for keyboard, two horns, violin and bass, and XIV:2, which employs keyboard, two violins, and baryton (extant only in the version for keyboard with violin and cello).[2] Larsen lists XIV:3, 4, 7, 8, 9, 10, and C1-G1 as keyboard ensemble divertimenti, but believes that XIV:11, 12, and 13 should be categorized as concertos.[3] In *Grove*, Feder groups these works and the full-scale concertos

---

[1]There is an excellent recording of XIV:4, 8, 9, 11, 12, and 13 by Jörg Ewald Dähler (pianoforte) with the Ensemble Eduard Melkus on Claves (D 8202). For editions, see Appendix B.
[2]Hoboken, *Haydn Verzeichnis*, 669-80. Hoboken has also wrongly included two compositions (XIV:5 and 6) in this group that are solo keyboard sonatas.
[3]Larsen, *Three Haydn Catalogues*, xviii.

under a single classification "Keyboard Concertos/Concertinos/ Divertimentos."[4] Landon employs both divertimento and concertino to describe these pieces, but seems to prefer concertino because the one extant autograph adopts this title.[5] He also makes a distinction between those compositions that he believes were written for the Morzin family (XIV:11, 12, 13, C2, and XVIII:F2) and those written for the Esterházys (XIV:2, 4, 7, 8, 9, 10). Finally, David Fuller, William S. Newman, Michelle Fillion, and A. Peter Brown prefer similar terms "accompanied keyboard music," "accompanied klavier sonata," "accompanied keyboard divertimenti," and "accompanied divertimenti," respectively.[6] In this study, I shall adopt Fillion's term "accompanied keyboard divertimento." Obviously, this classification also encompasses the keyboard trios, but it is best to treat them separately from the works for keyboard with two violins and cello because of minor differences in style.

Six of the accompanied divertimentos for keyboard with two violins and cello are indisputably by Haydn (out of twelve works studied in this chapter). XIV:3 and 4 appear in the *Entwurf-Katalog*, and 4 also survives in autograph. The principal manuscripts for XIV:7, 8, and 9 were copied by the Esterházy copyist anonymous 23, were in Haydn's library, and were recorded in Haydn's estate catalogue. The missing autograph of XIV:11 was formerly in the Esterházy collection. Although certainly authentic, XIV:10 is not considered here because only the keyboard part is extant.

I shall test the authorship of six other accompanied keyboard divertimentos in this chapter: XIV:12, 13, C1, C2, XVIII:F2, and the Concertino in D, Hob. Deest.[7] The first five of these are plausibly by Haydn, based on documentary and general stylistic evidence. XIV:12 is the best supported of the group from a documentary standpoint. It is preserved in three manuscripts, including one in Kroměříž, and is listed in the *Breitkopf Catalogue* (1772).[8] XIV:13, C2, and XVIII:F2

---

[4]Feder, *The New Grove Haydn*, 178-80.
[5]Landon, *Haydn: The Early Years*, 267-68 and 544-45.
[6]David Fuller, "Accompanied Keyboard Music," *Musical Quarterly* LX (1974) 222-45; William S. Newman, "Concerning the Accompanied Clavier Sonata," *Musical Quarterly* XXXIII (1947) 327-49; Michelle Fillion, *The Accompanied Keyboard Divertimenti of Haydn and His Austrian Contemporaries, c. 1750-1780*, Ph.D. diss., Cornell University, 1982; Brown, *The Keyboard Sonatas of Haydn*, 28.
[7]Deest is the designation given to those works not listed in Hoboken.
[8]*The Breitkopf Catalogue*, 477.

(misclassified by Hoboken as a concerto) survive as unica. The Fürstlich Fürstenbergische Hofbibliotek in Donaueschingen owns the only manuscript for 13, and it is registered in the *Göttweig Catalogue*, along with four probably authentic Haydn compositions XIV:11, XV:36, XVIII:1, and XVIII:2. On the other hand, the source for 13 is apparently corrupt with many wrong notes and other mistakes.[9] The only sources for C2 and F2 are Kroměříž manuscripts. According to Pohl, when evaluating his keyboard works for the Breitkopf & Härtel complete edition in 1803, Haydn initially accepted C1, but he later changed his mind.[10] This work exists in several good manuscripts, but it is not preserved in the scoring for keyboard, two violins, and bass listed in the *Breitkopf Catalogue* of 1772.[11] (I shall test the trio setting in this chapter and try to decide which scoring is the original.)

A. Peter Brown discovered the sole source for the Concertino in D, Hob. Deest, in Kroměříž. It is coupled with a set of variations (XVII:G1) that ends with a minuet and trio, and its three movements are followed by two minuets. From a documentary standpoint, this work is very suspicious.

Although several scholars have given opinions on the authenticity of the works in this genre, the accompanied keyboard divertimentos lack the extensive treatment devoted to the keyboard sonatas, early keyboard trios, and keyboard concertos in several articles by Feder. In *Grove*, Feder marks XIV:12, 13, C2 and XVIII:F2 as "probably authentic," C1 as "? authentic," and Hob. Deest as "probably not authentic."[12] Landon accepts the authenticity of the five most plausible pieces and declares that some of the movements in the Kroměříž manuscript that contains Hob. Deest may actually be by Haydn.[13] Larsen considers 12 and 13 as probably authentic, but regards C1, C2, and, apparently, F2 as spurious.[14] In her discussion of the authenticity of the accompanied keyboard divertimentos, Fillion mainly repeats Feder and Landon and summarizes the major documentary evidence.[15] She is suspicious of the form of C1 (Andante, Presto, Minuet and Trio, Alle-

---

[9]Horst Walter, "Preface," *Joseph Haydn: Concertini* (Munich: Henle, 1968) 5.
[10]Hoboken, *Haydn Verzeichnis*, 678.
[11]*The Breitkopf Catalogue*, 477.
[12]Feder, *The New Grove Haydn*, 179.
[13]Landon, *Haydn: The Early Years*, 225-27, 267-68, and 544-45.
[14]Larsen, *Three Haydn Catalogues*, xviii-xix.
[15]Fillion, *The Accompanied Keyboard Divertimenti*.

gro) and questions the authenticity of Hob. Deest. As one can see, the major disagreement concerns C1, C2, and XVIII:F2.

## THE TESTS

I employed two profiles to test the authenticity of the six doubtful accompanied keyboard divertimentos: one for fast first movements and the other for minuets.

Profile I: Expositions of Fast First Movements

All six of the previously-authenticated accompanied keyboard divertimentos have opening fast movements as do all the doubtful ones, except C1. As is usual with sonata form movements, I only studied expositions for the profile. I found that two ranges were useful for authenticity determination: textural change per beat .197-.263, borderline .020, and harmonic change per beat .565-.670, borderline .040.

I next drew up a checklist with sixteen items for Test II (see Chart I).[16]

### Chart I. Profile I: Checklist for the Expositions of Fast First Movements

#### Positive Traits Appearing in All the Haydn Works

1. In the first measure, a) all parts play in the first half of this measure, b) its texture employs two real voices, c) it has at least two impacts per beat (composite rhythm), and d) it uses a nonornamental note that is shorter than an eighth. 10% (trait appears in 10% of the Control Group II works)

*2. In the first four measures in the melody, a) the rhythm of no more than one measure is repeated, b) the rhythm of the first and fourth measures and second and fourth measures are different, and c) there is no dissonance on the downbeat of a measure (fourths don't count). 0%:2 points

---

[16]The checklist contains more items than usual because it will be employed as the basis for the keyboard trio profile in chapter five.

## ACCOMPANIED KEYBOARD DIVERTIMENTOS

3. a) Uses a nonornamental note value that is shorter than a sixteenth, b) at least four different rhythmic values used in the melody in the first five measures (including ornaments), and c) the first measure (including pickups) employs at least two different rhythmic values (not including rests). 40%

*4. a) Between 40 and 60% of the measures contain exact doubling between the cello and left-hand keyboard (octave placement not considered), b) rhythmic values in the cello equal to or longer than those in the left-hand piano (except at the end of the exposition), and c) cello does not include sixteenth notes (except at the end of the exposition). 0%:2 points

5. a) At least 80% of the measures contain rests and eighth, quarter, and half or whole rests used; b) a rest longer than four beats is present but no rest of six measures or longer in any part; c) keyboard includes at least one quarter rest after the first measure; and d) no simultaneous rest in all voices during the first eight measures. 20%

6. a) Texture changes at least three times in the first eight measures and these measures contain at least one simultaneity containing more notes than parts (one or two violins, bass, keyboard left-hand, keyboard right-hand), and b) the pattern in the left-hand keyboard changes by the beginning of measure seven. 30%

7. Between 40 and 66% of the measures contain textures employing two real voices and at least 66% of the measures include all instruments. 10%

8. a) Keyboard left-hand attains at least $f^1$, first violin goes down to at least $c^1$ or c-sharp$^1$, and cello goes as low as G, and b) in the first eight measures, range of between an octave and a fourth and two octaves in the keyboard right-hand. 10%

9. In the melody, a) all notes of the diatonic scale present in the first four measures, b) dominant pitch found during the first eight beats, c) tonic appears in two different octaves in the first eight measures, and d) the first eight measures include an interval of a tritone or larger. 40%

10. A trill of at least an eighth is used in the first six measures. 40%

11. Opening harmony ends before the middle of the second measure, texture space of exposition's final sonority at least an octave, and exposition's final sonority contains the third or fifth of the chord. 40%

## ACCOMPANIED KEYBOARD DIVERTIMENTOS

### Negative Traits Appearing in None of the Haydn Works

*12. In the right-hand keyboard, a) [♩ ♫] [♩ ♩.♩] , or [♩♪ ♩ ♪] ; b) two sixteenths on the first beat of a measure followed by any value other than another sixteenth; or c) more than two unornamented quarter notes or half notes in a row, except at the end of the exposition, or more than ten unornamented eighth notes in a row. 100%:2 points (trait appears in 100% of the Control Group II works; weighted with two points)

13. In left-hand keyboard, more than sixteen eighth notes, five quarter notes, or forty sixteenth notes in a row. 90%

14. In left-hand keyboard, a) use of Alberti bass in first four measures, 1-3-5-3-1 or 1-3-5-8-5-3-1 accompaniment patterns, murky bass, or bare octaves for more than a beat, or b) chords (three or more notes) used as an accompaniment. 90%

15. a) All voices have the same rhythm for more than two beats (at least three sounding voices), b) exact doubling between the violin and right-hand keyboard for more than fifteen beats (octave placement not considered), or c) only one sounding voice for more than a measure. 80%

16. a) Root position submediant chords in first six measures, b) non-diatonic note in first three measures, c) melodic seventh in left-hand piano, or d) first violin contains chromaticism. 80%

I doubly weighted three entries (nos. 2, 4, and 12) because they were valid for none of the ten works in Control II,[17] producing a maximum score of 19. Because the pieces in this genre have not been extensively studied and because the documentary support for even the most plausible composition (XIV:12) is somewhat weak, it would be dangerous to establish passing on the basis of any of the doubtful divertimentos, as I did with the keyboard sonatas. Instead, I shall employ the second method described in chapter two for determining passing, borderline, and failing: taking the difference between the maximum score (19) and the highest score for a Control Group II work (5) and giving each category (passing, borderline, and failing) one third of the total. 15-19 is passing, 10-14 borderline, and 9 and below failing. All twenty non-Haydn compositions (Control Group II and Test Group I) failed the profile (see Chart II).

[17]Because of the small number of keyboard quartets available, I also used keyboard trios in Control Group II and Test Group I.

## Chart II. Profile I: Results for the Non-Haydn Works

| Composer | Test I-Ranges | | Test II | Results | |
|---|---|---|---|---|---|
| | HC/B | TC/B | Ch | R-Ch-Conc. | |
| *Control Group II:* | | | | | |
| C.P.E. Bach | .445 | .129 | 5 | f-f | C |
| J.C. Bach | .481 | .087 | 5 | f-f | C |
| Eichner | .432 | .079 | 3 | f-f | C |
| Filtz | .560 | .180 | 3 | b-f | C |
| Kozeluch | .435 | .081 | 1 | f-f | C |
| L. Mozart | .300 | .077 | 5 | f-f | C |
| Mozart | .432 | .140 | 4 | f-f | C |
| Pleyel | .565 | .093 | 2 | f-f | C |
| Schobert | .375 | .265 | 3 | f-f | C |
| Toeschi | .560 | .312 | 3 | f-f | C |
| *Test Group I:* | | | | | |
| J.C. Bach | .543 | .113 | 6 | f-f | C |
| Beethoven | .365 | .116 | 5 | f-f | C |
| Gluck | .844 | .086 | 9 | f-f | C |
| Kozeluch | .535 | .077 | 2 | f-f | C |
| Mozart | .635 | .114 | 6 | f-f | C |
| Pleyel | .499 | .098 | 2 | f-f | C |
| Richter | .735 | .115 | 6 | f-f | C |
| Rosetti | .468 | .144 | 6 | f-f | C |
| Schlöger | .570 | .191 | 5 | b-f | C |
| Wagenseil | .723 | .097 | 3 | f-f | C |

Scoring. Test I: HC/B .565-.670 (borderline .040), TC/B .197 -.263 (borderline .020); Test II: passing 15-19, borderline 10-14, failing below 10.
HC/B=harmonic change per beat, TC/B=textural change per beat, Ch-=checklist, R=ranges, Ch=checklist, Conc.=conclusion, A=fits profile, B=results inconclusive, C=failed profile, p=pass, b=borderline, f=fail

Four of the five doubtful movements (XIV:12, 13, C2, and XVIII:F2) passed the profile, while the Concertino in D, Hob. Deest failed (see Chart III).

## Chart III. Profile I: Results for the Doubtful Works

| Work | Test I-Ranges | | Test II | Results | |
|---|---|---|---|---|---|
| | HC/B | TC/B | Ch | R-Ch-Conc. | |
| XIV:12 | .630 | .198 | 17 | p-p | A |
| XIV:13 | .680 | .266 | 18 | b-p | A |
| XIV:C2 | .650 | .210 | 16 | p-p | A |
| XVIII:F2 | .612 | .237 | 16 | p-p | A |
| Hob. Deest | .600 | .450 | 9 | f-f | C |

Scoring. Test I: HC/B .565-.670 (borderline .040), TC/B .197-.263 (borderline .020); Test II: passing 15-19, borderline 10-14, failing below 10.

Profile II: Minuets, not including trios

A second profile was necessary because XIV:C1 had lacked an opening fast movement and to confirm that Haydn did not write the Concertino in D. I created this profile for minuets, not including their trios. XIV:3, 4, 7, 8, and 9 contain minuets, as do XIV:C1, C2, and Hob. Deest.

The ranges of textural change and harmonic change again turned out to be the most effective ranges for Test I (TC/B:.128-.204, borderline .020; HC/B:.333-.386, borderline .020). Fifteen characteristics formed the minuet checklist (see Chart IV).

## Chart IV. Profile II: Checklist for Minuets

### Positive Traits Appearing in All the Haydn Works

#1. Uses a nonornamental note value that is shorter than an eighth and between 66% and 90% of the measures contain a rhythmic value that is shorter than a quarter. 70%:1/2 point (trait appears in 70% of the Control Group II works; weighted with a half point)

2. a) Range of first part in the melody between an octave and an octave and a sixth, b) left-hand keyboard attains at least an $f^1$, c) cello goes down to G, and d) right-hand keyboard attains at least $c^3$. 20%

3. Keyboard left-hand has two sounding voices for at least a measure, but right-hand does not contain more than one note at a time for more than one beat and the keyboard doesn't include simultaneities with more than three notes. 10%

## ACCOMPANIED KEYBOARD DIVERTIMENTOS

4. First measure includes at least two rhythmic values in the melody, has at least four notes in the melody, and has at least 1.66 impacts per beat (composite rhythm). 30%

\*5. a) In first measure all parts play and texture employs at least two real voices; b) two consecutive measures in the melody have the same rhythm and at least two measures (not necessarily consecutive) have only one note value unornamented without rests (not including dotted half notes); and c) two consecutive measures have more than two real voices. 60%:1/2 point

6. First two measures have no more than two harmonies per measure, employ both conjunct and disjunct intervals in the melody, and differ in pitch or rhythm. 40%

7. In first part, a) repeated notes are an important part of the melody, b) the melody uses an interval of a sixth but no interval larger than an octave, c) there is a dissonance at the beginning of a measure during the first five measures, d) a dominant seventh chord is present, and e) the first two measures do not contain trills. 20%

8. Rest of a least a quarter in the first violin and left-hand piano, but no more than one rest in a movement that is shorter than a quarter and no simultaneous rest of the same value in all voices. 10%

9. a) Final harmony is one measure or less, b) it does not include both the third and fifth of the chord, c) it uses bass patterns 8-5-1 or 8-1, d) it is preceded by a I 6-4 - V cadence, e) the last dominant does not include a seventh, and f) the final measure does not use more than two sounding voices in the keyboard. 10%

### Negative Traits Appearing in None of the Haydn Works

10. More than four sixteenths in a row in any voice or uses a nonornamental note value that is shorter than a sixteenth. 50% (trait appears in 50% of the Control Group II works)

11. In right-hand keyboard, use of dotted note, pattern | ♩. | ♫ | ,or more than four repeated notes in a row. 90%

12. a) In cello, dotted half note or more than two eighth notes in a row, or b) in the first violin, more than four repeated notes in a row or triple stops. 90%

13. In left-hand keyboard, a) use of more than two bare octaves in a row, b) a single pitch (not doubled) is repeated without a

break for more than a measure, or c) pattern | ♩ ♩ 𝄾  or | 𝄾 ♩ ♩ for more than a measure at a time. 70%

14. a) Right-hand keyboard rests for more than two beats, left-hand keyboard for more than three beats, or any part for more than four measures, or b) exact rhythmic doubling between the first violin and cello for more than two measures (rests break patterns). 30%

15. Melodic chromaticism in first violin during first part, chromaticism in bass (a quarter rest or longer breaks up a pattern), or 7 of V during first four measures. 90%

(For minuets in 3/8 halve all note values. For instrumentations other than keyboard with two violins and bass, make the highest accompanying instrument equal the first violin and the lowest accompanying instrument equal the bass.)

None of the traits warranted double weighting, but two characteristics (nos. 1 and 5) received only a half point because they appeared in a large percentage of the Control Group II works (60% or more). Since the maximum score was 14 and the highest Control Group II score was 6.5, I made 12-14 passing, 9.5-11.5 borderline, and below 9.5 failing. (Giving each category one third of the difference between 6.5 and 14.) All twenty non-Haydn compositions failed the checklist and scored borderline or failed the ranges (see Chart V).

### Chart V. Profile II: Results for the Non-Haydn Works

| Composer | Test I-Ranges | | Test II | Results | |
|---|---|---|---|---|---|
| | HC/B | TC/B | Ch | R-Ch-Conc. | |
| *Control Group II:* | | | | | |
| J.C. Bach | .550 | .198 | 4.5 | f-f | C |
| J.C. Bach | .497 | .178 | 4 | f-f | C |
| Beethoven | .413 | .156 | 2 | f-f | C |
| Eichner | .466 | .163 | 3.5 | f-f | C |
| Filtz | .416 | .116 | 6.5 | f-f | C |
| Gyrowetz | .433 | .232 | 2 | f-f | C |
| L. Mozart | .356 | .250 | 1.5 | f-f | C |
| Mozart | .513 | .212 | 3.5 | f-f | C |
| Schobert | .566 | .133 | 4 | f-f | C |
| Schobert | .523 | .250 | 3 | f-f | C |

## ACCOMPANIED KEYBOARD DIVERTIMENTOS

### Chart V. Profile II: *continued*

| Composer | Test I-Ranges | | Test II | Results | |
|---|---|---|---|---|---|
| | HC/B | TC/B | Ch | R-Ch-Conc. | |
| *Test Group I:* | | | | | |
| Abel | .469 | .194 | 4 | f-f | C |
| Abel | .506 | .214 | 4.5 | f-f | C |
| Binder | .445 | .085 | 1.5 | f-f | C |
| Evance | .576 | .178 | 2.5 | f-f | C |
| Holzbauer | .533 | .214 | 3.5 | f-f | C |
| Holzbauer | .443 | .222 | 3 | f-f | C |
| Myslivecek | .393 | .131 | 5.5 | b-f | C |
| Pugnani | .430 | .091 | 3.5 | f-f | C |
| Pugnani | .297 | .131 | 4.5 | f-f | C |
| Schobert | .569 | .189 | 0 | f-f | C |

Scoring. Test I: HC/B .333-.386 (borderline .020), TC/B .128-.204 (borderline .020); Test II: passing 12-14, borderline 9.5-11.5, failing below 9.5.

Of the doubtful divertimentos, C1 and C2 passed, while Hob. Deest failed (see Chart VI).

### Chart VI. Profile II: Results for the Doubtful Work

| Work | Test I-Ranges | | Test II | Results | |
|---|---|---|---|---|---|
| | HC/B | TC/B | Ch | R-Ch-Conc. | |
| XIV:C1 | .360 | .143 | 12 | p-p | A |
| XIV:C2 | .333 | .192 | 12 | p-p | A |
| Hob. Deest | .603 | .166 | 6 | f-f | A |

Scoring. Test I: HC/B .333-.386 (borderline .020), TC/B .128-.204 (borderline .020); Test II: passing 12-14, borderline 9.5-11.5, failing below 9.5.

## SUMMARY OF CONCLUSIONS FOR THE SIX DOUBTFUL ACCOMPANIED KEYBOARD DIVERTIMENTOS

### *XIV:12*

Profiles. I:A, only movement tested
Documentary Evidence: survives in three manuscripts and is cited in the *Breitkopf Catalogue*
Experts' opinions: general consensus—probably authentic

The systematic tests support the authenticity of XIV:12. Its first movement passed the profile, and this movement contains several details, such as the figure ♩ ♪♪♪ and the ornament ⟀ , that are very characteristic of Haydn. The other two movements are also typical of Haydn.

Conclusion: Authentic.

### *XIV:13*

Profiles. I:A, only movement tested
Documentary evidence: unicum, listed in the *Göttweig Catalogue*
Experts' opinions: general consensus—yes

Identical in gross form to 11 and 12, XIV:13 seems to be authentic. It passed the profile for fast first movements, and there is nothing in the other two movements to make one seriously doubt the work's authenticity, despite its survival in only one manuscript.

Conclusion: Authentic.

### *XIV:C1*

Profiles. III:A, only movement tested
Documentary evidence: Haydn doubted its authenticity in 1803 according to Pohl, several good manuscripts, in *Breitkopf Catalogue*
Experts' opinions: mixed

---

[18]Landon has published this version as *Diletto Musicale 534* (Vienna: Doblinger, 1976).

## ACCOMPANIED KEYBOARD DIVERTIMENTOS

XIV:C1 is one of the most problematic compositions examined in this study. Despite the negative opinions of Hoboken, Larsen, and Haydn himself, I regard all four movements as authentic, but the original instrumentation is left open to doubt.

The version of XIV:C1 for keyboard, two violins, and bass listed in the *Breitkopf Catalogue* of 1772 has not survived. The work exists in two other version: 1) as a keyboard trio in a manuscript from Kroměříž castle[18] and 2) in two manuscripts in the Austrian National Library as a solo keyboard composition.

Feder prefers the scoring with strings on musical grounds.[19] He puts forth the engaging hypothesis that the version in the Kroměříž manuscript is not a keyboard trio but a keyboard quartet with a missing part because its violin part seems to be a second violin part.

A. Peter Brown seems to favor the keyboard version[20] and Michelle Fillion definitely does.[21] The latter believes that the keyboard trio version is the least credible of the three. Although she declares that deciding between the solo keyboard version and the quartet version is difficult, she concludes that the solo keyboard version is probably the original, mainly based on the lack of variety in texture and the string parts' lack of independence in the quartet scoring.

Reaching a final decision about which version is the original is impossible unless the quartet version turns up, but the existing evidence can be examined and a tentative conclusion made. I concur with Fillion that the trio version is the least plausible of the three. The violin in this version does not imitate the right-hand keyboard at all and never contains the melody. In Haydn's eleven early keyboard trios (for the

---

[19] Feder, "Probleme," 93 and "Haydns Frühe Klaviertrios: Eine Untersuchung zur Echtheit und Chronologie," *Haydn Studien* II (1969-70) 289-316.
[20] A. Peter Brown, "Problems of Authenticity in Two Haydn Keyboard Works (Hoboken XVI:47 and XIV:7)," *Journal of the American Musicological Society* XXVII (1972) 93, 96. In this article, Brown casts doubt on the authenticity of the string parts of XIV:7, because the keyboard is self-sufficient and because there are several awkward details in the string writing. On the other hand, I believe that the treatment of the instruments in this work is comparable to that found in XIV:8 and 9. The keyboard parts of these two compositions are also self-sufficient. In addition, many of the problems that Brown finds in the string parts could be copyist errors. Moreover, I think that the string parts are needed to keep the rhythmic activity moving in m.29-33 in the first movement. Finally, movement I failed the fast first movement keyboard sonata profile from chapter 3 (Ch:7, failing below 8), while movement II failed the minuet profile (Ch:6.5, failing below 7.5).
[21] Fillion, *Accompanied Keyboard Divertimenti*, 103-109.

authenticity of these works see chapter five), the violin imitates the right-hand keyboard at some point, usually extensively, and the violin is important in presenting the melody. Moreover, all eleven trios contain at least one movement that includes some doubling between the violin and right-hand keyboard (both pitch and rhythm the same, minimum two consecutive measures). XIV:C1 has no comparable texture.

I agree with Feder that the violin in the trio scoring often looks like a second violin part. This is especially noticeable at the beginning of the minuet. An alternative hypothesis to Feder's is that the violin in the trio version is a combination of the two violin parts from the quartet version, taking most of its material from the second violin but a few passages from the first.

To determine the appropriateness of the solo keyboard setting, I extracted the keyboard part from C1 and tested it against the profiles for keyboard sonatas in chapter three. Movements I (checklist:6, passing 9-13), III (checklist 5.5, passing 8.5-12.5), and IV (checklist:4, passing 11-14) all failed the profiles, demonstrating that the solo keyboard version is probably not the work's original form.

There is nothing in XIV:C1 to make one think that it could not be a work originally written for keyboard with two violins and bass. The treatment of the instruments seems comparable to that found in XIV:7, 8, and 9. The keyboard part is self-sufficient, but this is also true of XIV:7, 8, 9, and 10. In addition, the string parts, while dispensible, do add to the setting. Finally, there are several places in the trio version that seem to be lacking something. For example, in I, m. 7-9 and 21-22, I believe that there is a need for two violins on the offbeat notes instead of only one.

Primarily by negative evidence, then, I think that the original scoring of XIV:C1 was probably keyboard with two violins and bass.

Fillion has raised another problem concerning this composition: its gross form (I:Adagio, II:$\frac{3}{8}$ Presto, III:Minuet and Trio, IV:$\frac{2}{4}$ Finale); none of Haydn's other keyboard works adopt a four-movement form with a presto second movement in $\frac{3}{8}$. (Symphonies 21 and 22 have similar structures with a duple presto in second place.) From these facts, one might conjecture that XIV:C1 is arranged from two or more authentic pieces. However, no other evidence supports such a conclusion. Each of the work's sources contains all of the movements, and no movement is shared by another extant Haydn composition.

Conclusion: Authentic, the version for keyboard with two violins and bass is probaby the original.

## ACCOMPANIED KEYBOARD DIVERTIMENTOS

### XIV:C2

Profiles. I:A, II:A
Documentary evidence: unicum
Experts' opinions: mixed

Since both movements of XIV:C2 passed the profiles and since neither movement contains any contradictory stylistic evidence, it may be considered authentic, despite the weak documentary support.

Conclusion: Authentic.

### XVIII:F2

Profiles. I:A, only movement tested
Documentary evidence: unicum
Experts' opinions: mixed

Although Hoboken has classified this composition as a concerto, its lack of tuttis and smaller proportions should place it among the accompanied keyboard divertimentos. The lack of solid documentary evidence has caused opposing opinions to arise concerning the work's authorship. Landon and Feder favor its authenticity, while Hoboken includes it among the spurious concertos and Larsen apparently considers it spurious. (He does not list it among the probably authentic works.)

A stylistic examination supports those who favor the work's authenticity. The first movement passes its profile and contains such typically Haydn features as the ornament ⌒ and the presence of triplets. A general stylistic examination of the other two movements reveals nothing that is contradictory; both also evince Haydn's characteristic treatment of triplets, and they employ the typical figure ♪♩♩♩ in the keyboard. F2's gross form, the presence of an adagio rather than a minuet as the middle movement, causes one to group this work with XIV:11, 12, and 13.

Conclusion: Authentic.

# ACCOMPANIED KEYBOARD DIVERTIMENTOS

## Concertino in D, Hoboken Deest

Profiles. I:C, II:C, III:not tested
Documentary evidence: unicum
Experts' opinions: general consensus—no; Landon states that some of the movements in the manuscript may be by Haydn

This concertino seems to be the work of a Haydn imitator. While certain features, such as the treatment of triplets, are characteristic of Haydn, both of the movements tested failed the profiles, and all three movements contain many traits that are not typical of Haydn's keyboard divertimentos. Especially significant is the rapid rate of textural change in the first movement and the quick rate of harmonic change in the minuet. I also tested the keyboard part of the opening movement against the profile for first movements of keyboard sonatas from chapter three, in case the extant instrumentation was not the original. This movement failed both parts of the keyboard sonata profile, scoring 7 points on the checklist (9-13 passing) and markedly higher than normal on the textural change range (.400 vs. the normal range of .119-.180).

As mentioned earlier, Landon thinks that some of the movements found in the Kroměříž manuscript may be authentic. I, however, believe that none of the movements are by Haydn. The set of variations (XVII:G1), also scored for keyboard with two violins and bass, are rather pedestrian and contain no specific traits that are characteristic of Haydn. The minuet that follows fails the keyboard divertimento minuet profile, scoring only two points on the checklist. Finally, the two minuets for keyboard alone failed the checklist for keyboard sonata minuets from chapter three with scores of 5.5 and 3.5 (8.5 to 12.5 passing).

Conclusion: Spurious.

CHAPTER FIVE

# Keyboard Trios

INTRODUCTION

In his important article on the authenticity and chronology of Haydn's early keyboard trios, Georg Feder accepted eleven extant works as genuine, XV:1, 2, 34, 35, 36, 37, 38, 40, 41, C1, and f1, based on both documentary and stylistic evidence.[1] Of these eleven works, though, only one (XV:2, in a manuscript signed by Haydn) is incontestably authentic.[2] While many of the ten remaining works are well-supported by external evidence, they still fall into the doubtful category because they lack entries in the Haydn catalogues and do not exist in autograph or other indisputable sources.

According to Pohl, in 1803, Haydn recognized 1, 34, 35, 36, 37, 38, and 41 as his works and rejected C1.[3] (He was unable to judge 40 and f1 because he could not obtain copies.) However, as was demonstrated in connection with the keyboard sonatas in chapter three, Haydn's memory in his later years was sometimes faulty, so one cannot decide the authenticity of these trios solely on Haydn's statements.

Four of the trios survive in Fürnberg copies: 34 and f1 by Fürnberg-

---

[1]Feder, "Haydns Frühe Klaviertrios," 292-307. See also *The New Grove Haydn*, 180-83. In addition to the eleven extant trios, two possibly authentic works, XV:33 and D1 are lost. Feder regards D1 as questionable.
[2]And this work is probably an arrangement (although an authentic one) from the lost keyboard divertimento XIV:2. Moreover, it is probably the latest of the early keyboard trios (?c1767-71).
[3]*The New Grove Haydn*, 182. For a fuller discussion of Haydn's statements on the authenticity of his keyboard music, see chapter three.

Morzin Copyist No. 1, and 35 and 41 by Fürnberg-Morzin Copyist No. 4. (This copy of 35 may have once been in Haydn's library.) In addition to the Fürnberg copies of f1 and 34, Kroměříž Castle, a major repository of Haydn's early trios, owns manuscripts of 1, C1, and 38. 36 exists in two manuscripts of questionable value and is cited in the *Göttweig Catalogue*. 37 is preserved in ten early copies, as well as several eighteenth-century editions. Seven copies, including several good early manuscripts, survive for 40. Although there is a conflicting attribution to Wagenseil, C1 has several reliable sources attributing it to Haydn. Finally, the *Breitkopf Catalogue* lists eight trios under Haydn's name: 1, 37, C1 (1766); 41 (1767); 38 (1769); 34, 35 (1771); and 36(1774).[4]

Michelle Fillion, in her dissertation on the accompanied keyboard divertimentos of Haydn and his Austrian contemporaries, concludes that from a documentary standpoint the ten trios to be tested in this chapter "are sufficiently well-supported to be considered at least probably by Haydn."[5] Five of these (1, 34, 35, 41, and f1) she regards as almost certainly authentic, based on good copies, their former presence in Haydn's library, or Haydn's authorization for Breitkopf and Härtel's *Oeuvres complettes*. She believes that the five other trios cannot be authenticated, although for the sources of 37, 38, and 40, she is struck by "their number and unanimous attributions to Haydn."[6] On the other hand, she thinks that 36 and C1 have the weakest documentary support of the ten trios. Concerning 36, she declares that "Perhaps XV:36 has been too quickly accepted as a Haydn trio; certainly, it is the most questionable of the eleven printed in *JHW* [the complete works].'"[7] She cites the negative evidence against C1, including the conflicting attribution to Wagenseil. Yet, a stemma she draws up from various manuscripts suggests that the attribution to Wagenseil is a mistake; Haydn's name appears on two separate branches of the stemma. In addition, she states that C1 is much closer in style to Haydn's trios than Wagenseil's.

A. Peter Brown believes that there are no completely spurious works within the ten early trios considered in the present chapter.[8] On

---

[4]*The Breitkopf Catalogues*, 253, 291, 364, 431, 552. As stated in the Introduction, the Breitkopf citations are not completely reliable.
[5]Michelle Fillion, *The Accompanied Keyboard Divertimenti*, 63, 62-75.
[6]Fillion, *op. cit.*, 63.
[7]Fillion, *op. cit.*, 65.
[8]Brown, *The Keyboard Sonatas of Haydn*, 27.

the other hand, he thinks that 1 and C1 can be questioned on the basis of the stylistic inconsistency of the first movements with the two remaining movements.

H. C. Robbins Landon includes fourteen compositions in his edition of the early trios: the ten trios that form the basis of this chapter plus four works that most scholars regard as arrangements (XIV:6=XVI:6, XIV:C1, XV:39, and XV:42 add.)[9] He asserts that all fourteen pieces are genuine, but he is not certain that Haydn originally composed the four added works as trios. (The arrangements in Landon's edition will be treated separately at the conclusion of this chapter.)

Finally, Jens Peter Larsen accepts the authenticity of all ten works, with some slight reservations owing to the lack of documentary evidence.[10] He views it as a mystery that none of these early trios are entered in the *Entwurf-Katalog* or survive in authentic copies.

## THE TESTS

Because only one previously-authenticated trio exists, XV:2 (and at that a relatively late one), a cross-genre study must be employed to test the authenticity of the ten doubtful works. I began with the profiles from the accompanied keyboard divertimentos for keyboard with two violins and bass (see chapter four), a genre that is close in both style and instrumentation to the keyboard trios. I refined the profiles by

1) testing them against XV:2,

2) adjusting them to the requirements of keyboard trio instrumentation,

3) comparing them to the newly-authenticated keyboard divertimentos (XIV:12, 13, C1, C2, and XVIII:F2),[11] and

4) eliminating any part of a trait that I guessed might not be applicable to a different genre.

---

[9]Landon, *Haydn: The Early Years*, 260-62 and "Preface," *Joseph Haydn Klaviertrios: Trio No. 4* (Vienna: Doblinger, 1977). Landon groups XV:2 with later works.
[10]Larsen, *The Three Haydn Catalogues*, xviii-xix.
[11]These works were used only to eliminate characteristics or parts of characteristics. If I was wrong about the authenticity of any of them, it would not effect the keyboard trio results.

The results produced new profiles that should be effective for any of Haydn's early works for keyboard accompanied by a small number of strings. However, because the requirements are now less stringent than they were previously for the accompanied keyboard divertimentos, the profiles must be retested to make certain that no non-Haydn composition will pass.

## Profile I: Expositions of Fast First Movements

The first profile was for the expositions of fast first movements in binary meters. A comparison against XV:2 indicated that the ranges for the comparable accompanied keyboard divertimentos (harmonic change per beat .565-.670, borderline .040; textural change per beat .197-.263, borderline .020) remained valid for the keyboard trios. I retained fifteen of the sixteen characteristics from the accompanied keyboard divertimento profile, although some of the traits were weakened (see Chart I). Consequently, only no. 11 (old no. 12), which had only one small change, was still weighted double. (Traits 2 and 4 had also been weighted double in the accompanied keyboard divertimento profile.) The maximum a work could score on the revised profile was sixteen points.

## Chart I. Profile I: Checklist for the Expositions of Fast First Movements

### Positive Traits Appearing in All the Haydn Works

1. In the first measure, a) the keyboard plays in the first half of this measure, b) its texture employs two real voices, c) it has at least two impacts per beat (composite rhythm), and d) it uses a nonornamental note value that is shorter than an eighth.

2. a) First four measures in the melody contain at least two different rhythmic patterns, b) rhythm of first and fourth measures different, and c) there is no dissonance on the downbeat of a measure (fourths don't count).

3. a) Uses a nonornamental note value that is shorter than a sixteenth, b) at least four different rhythmic values used in the melody during the first five measures (including ornaments but not rests), and c) first measure (including pickups) employs at least two different rhythmic values (not including rests) in the melody.

## KEYBOARD TRIOS

4. a) At least 40% of the measures contain exact doubling between the cello and left-hand piano (octave placement not considered), b) rhythmic values in cello equal to or longer than those in the left-hand piano (except at the end of the exposition or for a beat or less), and c) cello does not include more than four sixteenths in a row.

5. a) At least 70% of the measures contain rests and eighth and quarter rests present, b) keyboard contains at least one quarter rest after the first measure, and c) no simultaneous rest of the same value in all voices during the first seven measures.

6. a) Texture changes at least twice in the first eight measures, b) these measures include a simultaneity in the keyboard with at least three notes, and c) the pattern in the left-hand piano changes by the end of measure three.

7. Between 30% and 66% of the measures contain two real voices and at least 65% of the measures include all instruments.

8. a) Keyboard left-hand attains at least $f^1$ and violin goes down at least as low as G, and b) in the first eight measures in the melody, the range is between an octave and two octaves.

9. In the melody, a) the dominant pitch is present during the first eight beats, b) it or the tonic appears in two different octaves in the first four measures, and c) the first four measures include an interval of a tritone or larger (any rest longer than a sixteenth breaks up a pattern).

10. a) Opening harmony ends before the middle of the second measure, b) texture space of exposition's final chord at least an octave, and c) exposition's final sonority contains the third or the fifth of the chord.

### Negative Traits Appearing in None of the Haydn Works

*11. In the melody, ♩ ♩.♬ , two sixteenths on the first beat of a measure followed by any value other than another sixteenth, or more than two unornamented quarter or half notes in a row (except at the end of the exposition). [2 points]

12. In the keyboard left-hand, a) use of Alberti bass in the first four measures, murky bass in the first half of the exposition, 1-3-5-3-1 or 1-3-5-8-5-3-1 accompaniment patterns, or b) chords (three or more notes) used as an accompaniment.

13. a) All voices have the same rhythm for more than two beats (at least three sounding voices), b) exact doubling between the violin and right-

hand piano for more than fifteen beats, or c) only one sounding voice for more than a measure.

14. In left-hand keyboard (lowest voice), more than thirty-three eighth notes, five quarter notes, or forty sixteenth notes in a row.

15. a) Root position submediant chord in the first six measures (except in minor), b) nondiatonic note in the first three measures or an interval of a seventh in the left-hand keyboard, or c) violin contains melodic chromaticism in the first twenty measures.

I then checked the revised profile against twenty non-Haydn works (Control Group II and Test Group I). Since the quantitative ranges (Test I) remained unchanged, I only tested the checklist (Test II). If none of the twenty non-Haydn pieces pass the checklist, then the new profile may be considered effective. I determined passing, borderline, and failing by examining the ten doubtful works in Control Group I and the four most solidly supported doubtful trios, 34, 35, 41, and f1. (In this case, 35 doesn't have a relevant movement. All the others register at the upper end of the checklist scores.) The highest score for a Control Group II composition was 6 points, while f1 and 41 received 13 points each. Using the first set of scoring criteria described in chapter two, I made 13-16 passing, 9.5-12.5 borderline, and below 9.5 failing. All twenty non-Haydn works failed the profile, scoring eight points or less (see Chart II). The preceding proves that, while the profile was weakened to allow for applicability across genre boundaries, it still distinctly separates authentic Haydn from works by other composers.

### Chart II. Profile I: Results for the Non-Haydn Works

| *Control Group I:* | *Test Group I:* |
|---|---|
| J.C. Bach-6 (f) | C.P.E. Bach-8 (f) |
| Beethoven-3 (f) | J.C. Bach-8 (f) |
| Eichner-6 (f) | J.C. Bach-8 (f) |
| Filtz-5 (f) | Beethoven-5 (f) |
| Kozeluch-4 (f) | Eichner-5 (f) |
| L. Mozart-6 (f) | Mozart-7 (f) |
| Mozart-2 (f) | Mozart-4 (f) |
| Rosetti-5 (f) | Pleyel-4 (f) |
| Schobert-6 (f) | Schobert-7 (f) |

Scoring. Checklist: passing 13-16, borderline 9.5-12.5, failing below 9.5
p=pass, b=borderline, f=fail.

Eight of the ten trios had movements that could be tested by the profile.[12] All movements passed (see Chart III).

### Chart III. Profile I: Results for the Doubtful Works

| Trio | Test I-Ranges | | Test II | Results | |
|---|---|---|---|---|---|
| | HC/B | TC/B | Ch | R-Ch-Conc. | |
| 1 | .607 | .198 | 13 | p-p | A |
| 34 | .590 | .194 | 14 | b-p | A |
| 36 | .625 | .224 | 13 | p-p | A |
| 38 | .598 | .195 | 14 | b-p | A |
| 40 | .615 | .267 | 13 | b-p | A |
| 41 | .660 | .200 | 13 | p-p | A |
| C1 | .662 | .187 | 13 | b-p | A |
| f1 | .620 | .194 | 13 | b-p | A |

Scoring. Test I: HC/B .565-.670 (borderline .040), TC/B .197-.263 (borderline .020); Test II: passing 13-16, borderline 9.5-12.5, failing below 9.5.
HC/B=harmonic change per beat, TC/B=textural change per beat, R=ranges, Ch=checklist, Conc.=conclusion, p=pass, b=borderline, f=fail, A=fits profile, B=results inconclusive, C=failed profile.

Profile II: Minuets, not including trios

The second profile was for minuets not including their trios. I discovered that the textural change per beat range of the accompanied keyboard divertimentos (.128-.204, borderline .020) continued to be valid for the trios, but that the trios exhibited a faster rate of harmonic change (XV:2 scored .423; the accompanied keyboard divertimento HC/B was .333-.386), so I excluded the harmonic change per beat range from the new profile. (However, I shall present the HC/B for the trios at the end of this section in support of the conclusions from the profile.)

[12]No. 35 also has a fast first movement, but its unusual character and 3/4 meter (no 3/4 work was used in drawing up the profile) makes it lie outside of the profile's scope.

I included twelve traits in the revised checklist (see Chart IV). It was based on the accompanied keyboard divertimento checklist for minuets, but certain characteristics were recombined or had portions deleted. Because No. 1 had been weighted with a half point in the keyboard divertimento profile owing to its appearance in a large number of the Control Group II compositions and because the trait remained substantially the same in the new profile, I retained the weighting of this item. I eliminated all other abnormal weightings. The maximum score for the checklist was 11.5.

### Chart IV. Profile II: Checklist for Minuets
### Positive Traits Appearing in All the Haydn Works

#1. Uses a nonornamental note value that is shorter than an eighth and between 55% and 90% of the measures contain a rhythmic value that is shorter than a quarter. [1/2 point]

2. a) Range of first part in the melody at least an octave, b) left-hand attains at least an $f^1$, c) cello goes down to at least G, and d) keyboard right-hand attains at least $c^3$.

3. Keyboard left-hand has two sounding voices for at least two beats and right-hand does not contain more than one note at a time for more than four beats.

4. a) First two measures have at least two different rhythmic values, with at least one impact per beat (composite rhythm), and b) all parts play in the first measure, with at least two real voices.

5. First two measures have no more than two changes of harmony, employ both conjunct and disjunct intervals, and are different in pitch and rhythm.

6. In the first part, a) repeated notes are an important part of the melody, b) at least one interval larger than a fifth is present in the melody, and c) there is a dissonance at the beginning of a measure during the first five measures.

7. Rest of at least a quarter in the violin and left-hand keyboard, but no more than one rest in a movement that is shorter than a quarter.

### Negative Traits Appearing in None of the Haydn Works

8. a) More than eight sixteenths in a row; b) in the cello, three eighth notes in a row (except when all voices have the same rhythm); or, c) in the violin, triple stops or five repeated notes in a row.

9. In the right-hand keyboard, use of a dotted quarter;

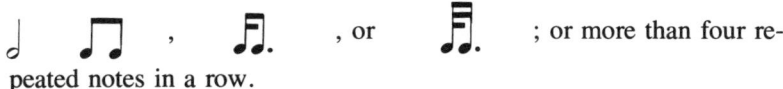
; or more than four repeated notes in a row.

10. In the left-hand, a) more than three bare octaves in a row or bare octaves for more than three beats, b) a single pitch (not doubled) is repeated without break for more than a measure, or c) patterns ♩ ♩ 𝄽 or 𝄽 ♩ ♩ for more than two consecutive measures.

11. a) Right-hand keyboard drops out for more than two beats, left-hand for more than three beats, or any part for more than four measures or b) exact rhythmic doubling between violin and cello for more than two measures (rests break patterns).

12. Melodic chromaticism in first violin during first part, chromaticism in bass during first part (a quarter rest or longer breaks off a pattern), or 7 of V during first four measures.

(For minuets in 3/8 halve all note values. For instrumentations other than keyboard with violin and cello, make the highest accompanying instrument equal the violin and the lowest accompanying instrument equal the bass or cello.)

Passing was 9.5-11.5, borderline 8.5-9 and 8 or below failing, based on the fact that the highest a Control Group II work scored was 7 and that 35 and 41 registered 9.5. All twenty non-Haydn compositions in Control Group II and Test Group I failed the revised checklist (see Chart V).

### Chart V. Profile II: Results for the Non-Haydn Works

*Control Group II:*
Abel-7 (f)
J.C. Bach-3 (f)
Eichner-7 (f)
Filtz-6 (f)
Gyrowetz-2.5 (f)
Holzbauer-5.5 (f)
L. Mozart-2.5 (f)
Mozart-4.5 (f)
Myslivecek-7 (f)
Schobert-6 (f)

*Test Group II:*
Arne-3 (f)
J.C. Bach-7 (f)
Beethoven-5 (f)
Beethoven-5.5 (f)
Eichner-6 (f)
Holzbauer-6 (f)
Pugnani-4 (f)
K. Stamitz-3.5 (f)
Schobert-3.5 (f)
Schobert-5.5 (f)

Scoring. Checklist: passing 9.5-11.5, borderline 8.5-9, failing below 8.5.

Nine of the ten doubtful trios contained minuets, and all nine movements passed both tests (see Chart VI).

### Chart VI. Profile II: Results for the Doubtful Works

| Trio | Test I<br>TC/B | Test II<br>Ch | Results<br>R-Ch-Conc. | |
|------|------|------|------|---|
| 1    | .144 | 10.5 | p-p | A |
| 34   | .138 | 11.5 | p-p | A |
| 35   | .146 | 9.5  | p-p | A |
| 37   | .185 | 9.5  | p-p | A |
| 38   | .138 | 10.5 | p-p | A |
| 40   | .150 | 10.5 | p-p | A |
| 41   | .177 | 9.5  | p-p | A |
| C1   | .166 | 9.5  | p-p | A |
| f1   | .133 | 11.5 | p-p | A |

Scoring. Test I: TC/B .128-.204 (borderline .020); Test II: passing 9.5-11, borderline 8.5-9, failing below 8.5.

A study of the harmonic rhythm of the minuets reinforces these results. All of the nine doubtful movements plus XV:2 fall into a narrow range of harmonic change per beat (.423-.510; see Chart VII).

### Chart VII. Harmonic Change per Beat in the Minuets of the Early Trios

| | | |
|---|---|---|
| 1:.430  | 35:.490 | 41:.466 |
| 2:.423  | 37:.510 | C1:.500 |
| 34:.475 | 38:.453 | f1:.465 |
|         | 40:.510 |         |

## SUMMARY OF CONCLUSIONS FOR THE TEN DOUBTFUL TRIOS

Because all relevant movements fit the profiles and because there is no strong negative documentary evidence for any trio, I believe that all ten early trios are authentic. No. 36, which Michelle Fillion believed was the least supported trio from a documentary standpoint, passed the profile for fast movements in binary meters. In addition, its other two movements contain no stylistic features that are atypical of Haydn. C1, despite its conflicting attribution to Wagenseil, passed both profiles. All of the eight remaining trios fit at least one of the profiles, and their other movements appear to be by Haydn. The only movements that are spurious are two movements that are not included in either of the two complete editions: a spurious minuet and trio from C1 and a spurious adagio that replaces the authentic minuet in 40. Both spurious movements exist in only one source out of several for each trio.[13]

Conclusion: XV: 1, 34, 35, 36, 37, 38, 40, 41, C1, and f1 authentic

## THE ARRANGEMENTS

As mentioned earlier, Landon includes four additional works in his complete edition of Haydn's keyboard trios, but declares that the string parts may not be authentic. My opinion that the original instrumentation of XIV:C1 was probably keyboard, two violins, and cello was given in the previous chapter. My evaluation of the other three trios follows.

### XIV:6

XIV:6 shares three movements with the keyboard sonata XVI:6: they open with the same movement, the order of the minuet and adagio from the keyboard sonata is reversed in the trio version, and the keyboard trio omits XVI:6's finale. The authenticity of the keyboard version is unquestionable, existing in autograph and being entered in the *Entwurf-Katalog*, but the trio instrumentation appears only in the Hummel print of op. 4 and reprints from this edition. The Hummel print also contains three authentic trios, XV:1, 37, and C1; an authentic divertimento for keyboard, two horns, and strings, XIV:1; and XV:39, another questionable keyboard trio (see below). Landon declares that the trio version may be earlier or later than the solo keyboard version.[14]

I applied the profiles for the keyboard trios to XIV:6. Movement I failed its profile (harmonic change per beat .582, textural change per

---

[13] Feder, *The New Grove Haydn*, 182.
[14] Landon, *Haydn: The Early Years*, 261.

beat .180, checklist 12, fail-borderline, conclusion:C), as did the minuet (7.5 on the checklist, fail). These results indicate that the keyboard scoring, not the trio version, is the earliest instrumentation of this work.

On the other hand, the content of the added string parts suggests the participation of a skilled composer, especially in the handling of the short bits of imitation in the violin. While it cannot be definitively proven who wrote the new parts, it is certainly conceivable that Haydn is responsible for the trio arrangement.

Conclusion: Arranged from the original version for solo keyboard, possibly arranged by Haydn.

## XV:39

XV:39 is arranged from several early keyboard sonatas, except for the andante, for which there is no other extant source. Movement I comes from XVI:9/I, III from XVI:8/I (transposed), IV (minuet) from XVI:9/II, IV (trio) from XVI:5/II, and V from XVI:9/III. Landon writes that he is uncertain whether the trio version preceded or is an arrangement of the keyboard movements.[15]

Movements I, III, IV (minuet only), and V passed their profiles in the keyboard sonata chapter (see chapter three). The first movement passed the keyboard trio profile (textural change per beat .200, harmonic change per beat .670, checklist 15, pass-pass, conclusion:A), but the minuet failed its keyboard trio profile (Checklist 7.5, fail). Since all the other movements are derived from keyboard sonatas, one may assume that if movement II, the andante, is authentic, it also comes from a keyboard work. However, a test of this movement (keyboard part only) against the slow movement profile from the keyboard sonatas indicates that it is spurious (it scored only four points on the checklist; 11-12 was passing), an opinion with which Feder concurs.[16] Furthermore, I concluded in Chapter Four that XVI:5 was not authentic Haydn. From the above, one may surmise that XV:39 is a factitious arrangement.

Conclusion: Factitious arrangement made from both authentic and spurious movements, II and IV (trio).

---

[15]Landon, *Haydn: The Early Years*, 261.
[16]Feder, *The New Grove Haydn*, 183.

## KEYBOARD TRIOS

### XV:42

The only source for the two-movement Trio in D, XV:42 in its keyboard trio instrumentation is a Kroměříž manuscript. The second movement is the same as the probably authentic keyboard variations XVII:7, but the first movement does not exist in any other source.

Even a cursory glance at this work suggests that it is a factitious arrangement. The violin doubles the keyboard throughout almost the entire piece, a practice that is atypical of Haydn's authentic trios and that indicates the hand of an unskilled arranger. From examining the string parts and the texture of the keyboard, one must conclude that the original was probably for clavier alone.

The second movement in its solo keyboard form (XVII:7) was recognized by Haydn in 1803 according to Pohl, and it was cited in the *Breitkopf Catalogue* of 1766.[17] Landon believes that it is authentic, while Feder lists it among the "Miscellaneous Keyboard Pieces: Selected Works Attributed to Haydn" without comment.[18] While the small number of authentic keyboard variations from before 1770 precludes an exhaustive stylistic study, a general stylistic examination and a hearing of this movement leads me to conclude that XVII:7 is probably authentic.

The first movement is not a typical Haydn opening movement. It scored only five points on the profile for fast first movements from keyboard sonatas (9-13 passing), and the rhythmic character is completely uncharacteristic of Haydn's authentic keyboard first movements. On the other hand, the movement fits the profile for fast finales in 2/4 or 3/4 from the keyboard sonatas, registering 11 points (11-14 passing). In addition, the rhythmic similarities between this movement and the finale of XVI:13 are striking (see Ex. 1). I believe, therefore,

**Example 1a. XV: 42/I, m. 1-4**

[17]*The Breitkopf Catalogues*, 251.
[18]Landon, *Haydn: The Early Years*, 262 and Feder, *The New Grove Haydn*, 187.

**1b. XVI:13/III, m. 1-6**

that this movement is by Haydn, and it is probably the finale of a lost keyboard sonata.

Conclusion: Factitious arrangement from two authentic keyboard movements. The first movement is extant only in this trio version.

CHAPTER SIX

# String Trios

## CUNY HAYDN STRING TRIO PROJECT

The most comprehensive stylistic authenticity project to date was conducted in several seminars taught by Barry S. Brook at the City University of New York and the Juilliard School of Music, particularly one in the spring of 1981 at CUNY. A Haydn seminar at CUNY in 1975 had undertaken the task of editing the string trio volume for the complete works published by the Haydn Institute.[1] They discovered that outside of the eighteen trios listed in the *Entwurf-Katalog* (twenty-one listed, three of which are lost), it was difficult to decide which of the trios (sixty-three doubtful trios exist) to include in the volume. As a class project, a 1977 seminar applied Paymer's method (see chapter one) to the trios, but a comprehensive authenticity study lay beyond the scope of that seminar.

Brook returned to the authenticity of the string trios in a seminar he taught at CUNY in the spring of 1981.[2] He suggested that each student write a paper on the authenticity of the trios, focusing on a particular element of style or analytical approach. Subjects of the papers in this and other seminars included 1) the Paymer method, 2) general stylistic studies based on the authentic string trios or string quartets, 3) the openings, 4) form, 5) Schenkerian methods, and 6) texture.[3] Although

---

[1] Bruce C. MacIntyre, "The City University of New York: An Unusual Haydn Seminar," *Current Musicology* XX (1975) 42-45.
[2] Participants in that seminar included Chi-Jen Chang, Scott Fruehwald, Andrew Green, Ellen Messina, Bruce MacIntyre, and Albert Wood.
[3] We plan to publish several of these papers, along with a summary of all findings,
*continued*

the students concentrated on their own approach, they were expected to examine each doubtful trio in detail. We brought together the results of the various papers in two weekend meetings at Dr. Brook's home in Hillsdale, N.Y., in the summers of 1981 and 82.

We began our study by eliminating as many of the sixty-three doubtful string trios as we could on documentary grounds. Thirty-two of the sixty-three trios were either lost or convincingly attributed to other composers (V:C9, D2, D5, D6, E-flat1, E-flat6, E-flat7, E-flat8, E-flat9, E-flat10, E-flat12, E-flat13, E1, E3, F2, F3, F4, F5, F6, F8, G2, G6, G7, A1, A4, A5, A6, A7, B2, B3, B5, and B6).[4] That left thirty-one trios, twenty-eight attributed to Haydn alone (C1, C2, C3, C4, C5, C6, C7, C8, D1, D3, D4, d, E-flat2, E-flat3, E-flat4, E-flat5, E-flat11, E2, F1, F7, F9, G3, G5, A3, A8, B1, B4, and B7) and three with questionable conflicting attributions (G1 and A2 to Michael Haydn, and G4 to Ordoñez).[5,6]

## INDIVIDUAL PAPERS

The first stylistic study of the Haydn string trios was done as a group project by the 1977 seminar, using Paymer's method (for a full discussion of Paymer's method, see chapter one). When the 1981 seminar evaluated this study, we found one major problem. Each of us took the

---

when the string trio volume appears. At present, the abstracts of the papers will appear in Barry S. Brook, "Determining Authenticity through Internal Analysis: A Multifaceted Approach," read at the *Internationaler Joseph Haydn Kongress, 1982* in Vienna to be published as a congress report, and they can be consulted at the Music Department at the City University of New York.

[4]C9, D6, E-flat6, E3, F5, F8, G6, G7, A4, and B6 are lost. D2, E-flat1, E1, G2, A1, and B2 are by Michael Haydn; D5, E-flat8, E-flat9, E-flat13, and A7 are probably by Leopold Hofmann; E-flat7 is probably by Gasparini; E-flat10 is probably by Asplmayr; E-flat12, F2, and F6 are probably by Kammel; F4 is probably by J. C. Bach; A5 is probably by Enderle; A6 is probably by Filtz; B3 is probably by Zappa; B5 is probably by Chiesa; and F3 is by Asplmayr or Ivanschiz.

[5]After our study was completed, we discovered that F9 was by Vanhal and B7 by Stamitz. I have included these two trios in my additional tests at the end of this chapter for completeness.

[6]Despite the presence of conflicting attributions for G1, A2, and G4, the documentary evidence suggests that Haydn is the author of all three trios. As mentioned in the introduction, there are a few cases where definitely authentic Haydn works contain conflicting attributions, such as the organ concerto XVIII:2 (in *Entwurf-Katalog*), which is wrongly attributed to Galuppi.

same two doubtful trios and applied the criteria from the 1977 study as we understood them. All five of us came up with different scores. (For example, we each arrived at different percentage of similar activity scores.) These results indicate that, while several scholars can do separate authenticity studies of a group of works and compare their results, each individual investigation must be done by one person to insure consistency in the application of the method. Andrew Green refined the 1977 study as his authenticity project, by eliminating characteristics that appeared to be part of the contemporary vernacular and by developing a system of weighting.

Also in 1981, three of Brook's Juilliard students wrote seminar papers on the authenticity of the string trios. Allen Gimbel and Jeff Langley examined the doubtful trios by comparing them to the string quartets and authentic string trios, respectively, based on isolated aspects of style—chromaticism, formal construction, rhythm, tonal structure, counterpoint, instrumental technique, the element of surprise, and timbral texture. In our Hillsdale meetings, Gimbel stressed that Haydn was a "thinking composer" and that this could be seen in his music. Another Juilliard student, Alan Belkin, studied the themes in Haydn's openings in binary and rounded-binary movements. His criteria included time signatures, use of nonchord tones, length of the first phrase, length of the second phrase, cadence points, material of the first two phrases, relation of peaks, range of first phrase, relation of ranges in first two phrases, combined ranges of first four phrases, unvaried repetition of phrase segments, and diatonic/chromatic melody. Belkin's study was one of the most objective and useful of the papers.

Bruce MacIntyre examined the forms in Haydn's trios, both the cycle and individual movements. MacIntyre found that the eighteen definitely authentic trios employ two or three movements, with a limited number of movement combinations. For individual movements, he isolated four types of binary movements, four types of rounded-binary movements, and seven types of minuets. (Haydn's trios also contain theme and variation movements.) He also studied the ways in which Haydn's trios diverge significantly from "normal patterns" and places in the schemes where Haydn often threw in "elements of surprise."

Two students tried to apply Schenkerian techniques to the trios without initial success in proving authenticity. I believe (in opposition to several people who have worked with the CUNY Haydn String Trio Project) that Schenkerian techniques will probably not work in authenticity studies, because, outside of uncovering the background structure common in most tonal music (such as I-V-I, with 3-2-1 in the upper voice), such techniques tend to concentrate on the uniqueness of a composition rather than traits that are shared among several works. While a graph may indicate that a particular piece treats harmony in a sophisticated manner as one would expect in a work by Haydn, it is still possible that a few other contemporary composers treat harmony in a similarly sophisticated way. If I am wrong about the effectiveness of the Schenkerian approach in testing authenticity, the work in drawing up the large number of graphs required in such a study would probably be prohibitive.

*My Texture Study*

My paper used the same general methods as in this study but covered only one parameter of style—texture—in fast first or second movements in binary or rounded-binary form. Although the method has been refined since this first study, I believe that the results are accurate. I discovered five ranges that were narrow enough for authenticity determination (Chart I) and came up with a checklist that contained twenty items, with each characteristic valid for a least 85% of the trios (see Chart II; the first figure following each item indicates the percentage of Haydn trios a trait appeared in, the second figure the percentage of non-Haydn trios that the trait occurred in).[7]

## Chart I. Ranges in the Authentic Trios

1. % of measures in the exposition and development with 2, 3, or 4 texture (one real voice): 1.4-9%

2. % of measures in the exposition and development with less than three sounding voices: 0-10%

3. Rate of textural change per beat: a) exposition .125-.200
　　　　　　　　　　　　　　　　　　 b) development .075-.165
　　　　　　　　　　　　　　　　　　 c) both .115-.170

Borderline: Ranges 1+2 5%, Ranges 3a-c .020. If a trio has three ranges in the borderline category, it fails Test I.

[7]Some of the traits appeared in a large percentage of the non-Haydn works, but they were retained because they helped distinguish Haydn's treatment of texture from those composers who otherwise treated texture in a similar manner (L. Hofmann, M. Haydn).

*STRING TRIOS*

## Chart II. Checklist for String Trio Fast First or Second Movements in Binary or Rounded-Binary Form

### Positive Traits Appearing in at Least 85% of the Haydn Works

1. First violin dominated texture. A texture is considered to be first violin dominated if it is predominantly homophonic and the first violin presents most of the thematic material. 94%/35.3% (i.e. Haydn/non-Haydn)

2. Two parts against one (2/1 or 1/2) the most frequent texture. 88.2%/82.3%

3. Crossing of the violin parts at least once in a movement. 100%/88.2%

4. Use of more than three sounding voices (double stops) at least once in a movement. 88.2%/76.4%

5. Ending the second part of the movement with the same texture as the first part. 88.2%/58.5%

6. Use of three real voices for at least two consecutive measures. 100%/94%

*7. Use of 1/2 texture for at least two consecutive measures. (-2) 100%/82.3%

8. First and second violins separated by a least an octave and a sixth sometime during the movement. 100%/76.4%

9. Texture space at least three octaves and a third on a single simultaneity at some point in the movement. 100%/76.4%

10. % of measures with more than three sounding voices (exposition and development) 0-17%. 88.2%/76.4%

11. At least three changes of texture in the first eight measures. 100%/58.5%

### Negative Traits Appearing in Less than 6% of the Haydn Works

12. Less than three sounding voices in the first full measure. 0%/17.6%

13. Less than three sounding voices in the first full measure of the dominant section (second theme). 0%/11.8%

14. Less than three sounding voices in the first full measure of the second part of the movement (development). 0%/17.6%

*15. Rate of textural change in the development exceeds that of the exposition by more than .01 points. (Ex., in Hofmann on Chart III, the texture changes at the rate of .165 per beat in the development and .140 per beat in the exposition. The rate of change in the development exceeds that of the exposition by .025.) (-1 to -3) 0%/58.8%

*16. Substantial imitation. (-1 to 3) 0%/11.8% (A small amount of imitation is not atypical in the authentic trios.)

17. Chords to mark the ends of a majority of major sections. (Major sections include the first theme, the transition, the second theme, the closing theme, the development, and the recapitulation.) 0%/23.5%

18. General rhythmic activity in the bass slower than that of the second violin for the majority of the movement. 0%/17.6%

*19. Octaves or unison in all three voices for more than three beats at a time or octaves or unison in the violins with the bass having a separate part or resting for more than two and a half beats at a time. (-1 to -3) 0%/41.2%

20. Parallel thirds or sixths between the violins for more than eight beats at a time. Any different event—a rest of at least a beat or another interval—ends a particular series. 5.9%/23.5%

On the checklist I made 20 points the maximum score. For most items, I subtracted a point when a trait was not valid for a trio, but for No. 7, I subtracted two points because it was especially important in distinguishing Haydn from Michael Haydn, and on Nos. 15, 16, and 19, I subtracted one to three points, depending on the degree of failure. 17-20 was passing, 16 borderline, and 15 or less failing. Thirty-seven non-Haydn trios in Control Group II and Test Group I failed the profile (Charts III and IV).

### Chart III. Results for the Control Group II Works

|  | *Test I-Ranges* | | | | | *Test II* | *Results* |
|---|---|---|---|---|---|---|---|
|  | 1. | 2. | 3a. | 3b. | 3c. | Ch | R-Ch-Conc. |
| Asplmayr | 20.1 | 5.1 | .140 | .163 | .150 | 10 | f-f  C |
| Boccherini | 7.6 | 3.7 | .080 | .118 | .097 | 12 | f-f  C |
| Boccherini | 13 | 6.2 | .148 | .050 | .112 | 13 | f-f  C |
| Gluck | 3.4 | 6.8 | .030 | .063 | .043 | 5 | f-f  C |
| M. Haydn | 2 | 0 | .160 | .049 | .125 | 16 | f-b  C |

## STRING TRIOS

### Chart III. *continued*

| | 1. | 2. | Test I-Ranges 3a. | 3b. | 3c. | Test II Ch | Results R-Ch-Conc. |
|---|---|---|---|---|---|---|---|
| Hofmann | 0 | 0 | .140 | .165 | .150 | 15 | b-f C |
| Holzbauer | 11.1 | 17 | .138 | .158 | .145 | 13 | f-f C |
| L. Mozart | 23 | 0 | .131 | .180 | .143 | 14 | f-f C |
| L. Mozart | 0 | 0 | .045 | .125 | .070 | 16 | f-b C |
| L. Mozart | 8.5 | 0 | .135 | .151 | .141 | 13 | p-f C |
| Ordoñez | 0 | 4.7 | .181 | .222 | .190 | 13 | f-f C |
| Ordoñez | 7.2 | 13.2 | .211 | .219 | .215 | 16 | f-b C |
| Pugnani | 3.1 | 4 | .216 | .179 | .191 | 11 | f-f C |
| Pugnani | 3.1 | 4.2 | .186 | .210 | .195 | 12 | f-f C |
| Sammartini | 14.2 | 0 | .211 | .240 | .222 | 12 | f-f C |
| Schlöger | 1.8 | 5 | .191 | .119 | .146 | 14 | p-f C |
| Tuma | 3.4 | 1.7 | .091 | .195 | .142 | 14 | f-f C |

Scoring. Ranges: see Chart I; Test II: passing 17-20, borderline 16, failing below 16.
Ch=checklist, R=ranges, Conc.=conclusions, p=pass, b=borderline, f=fail, A=fits profile, B=results uncertain, C=failed profile.

### Chart IV. Results for the Test Group I Works

| Work | 1. | 2. | Test I-Ranges 3a. | 3b. | 3c. | Test II Ch | Results R-Ch-Conc. |
|---|---|---|---|---|---|---|---|
| Antes | 10.1 | 3.9 | .135 | .131 | .133 | 14 | b-f C |
| C.P.E. Bach | 0 | 37.2 | .131 | .141 | .135 | 8 | f-f C |
| J. Benda | 0 | 22.2 | .138 | .088 | .112 | 6 | f-f C |
| Boccherini | 2.3 | 0 | .092 | .126 | .108 | 14 | f-f C |
| Filtz | 0 | 1.1 | .075 | .056 | .065 | 17 | f-p C |
| Gassmann | 2.9 | 0 | .196 | .188 | .191 | 16 | f-b C |
| Gluck | 1.2 | 7.4 | .086 | .138 | .104 | 8 | f-f C |
| J.G. Graun | 0.8 | 36.6 | .113 | .171 | .138 | 4 | f-f C |
| M. Haydn | 0 | 0 | .111 | .050 | .084 | 15 | f-f C |
| M. Haydn | 0 | 0 | .156 | .154 | .155 | 15 | b-f C |
| M. Haydn | 6.9 | 18.7 | .043 | .070 | .054 | 7 | f-f C |
| Höckh | 0 | 0 | .084 | .063 | .075 | 16 | f-b C |
| Hofmann | 0 | 0 | .125 | .125 | .125 | 15 | b-f C |
| Mann | 16.9 | 3.4 | .125 | .145 | .133 | 11 | f-f C |
| Monn | 0 | 0 | .067 | .218 | .167 | 11 | f-f C |
| Sacchini | 5 | 7.2 | .125 | .171 | .141 | 13 | b-f C |

## Chart VIII. Profile I: *continued*

*Control Group II:*      *Test Group I:*

| | | | | | | | | |
|---|---|---|---|---|---|---|---|---|
| Schickhard | 15.4 | 7.7 | .078 | .111 | .090 | 11 | f-f | C |
| J. Stamitz | 10.7 | 7.1 | .105 | .084 | .095 | 13 | f-f | C |
| K. Stamitz | 7.5 | 7.2 | .075 | .067 | .072 | 15 | f-f | C |
| Wagenseil | 0 | 0 | .097 | .104 | .103 | 15 | f-f | C |

Scoring. Ranges: see Chart I; Test II: passing 17-20, borderline 16, failing below 16.

Twenty-six doubtful trios (of the 31) contained fast first or second movements in binary or rounded-binary form. Of these seven passed (C1, C4, D1, G3, A2, A3, and B1), while the remainder failed (Chart V).

### Chart V. Results for the Doubtful Works

| Work | Test I-Ranges | | | | | Test II | Results |
|---|---|---|---|---|---|---|---|
| | 1. | 2. | 3a. | 3b. | 3c. | Ch | R-Ch-Conc. |
| C1/I | 4.8 | 4.8 | .195 | .150 | .164 | 17 | p-p C |
| C2/I | 6.2 | 0 | .178 | .275 | .216 | 13 | f-f C |
| C3/I | 4.1 | 6.8 | .192 | .208 | .200 | 15 | f-f C |
| C4/I | 4.5 | 0 | .133 | .152 | .143 | 19 | p-p C |
| C5/I | 2.7 | 5.5 | .110 | .125 | .118 | 8 | f-f C |
| C6/I | 2.3 | 25 | .150 | .131 | .148 | 12 | f-f C |
| C8/I | 10 | 5 | .117 | .176 | .161 | 13 | f-f C |
| D1/I | 3.3 | 0 | .145 | .143 | .144 | 17 | p-p C |
| d/I | 11.2 | 14.2 | .075 | .076 | .075 | 12 | f-f C |
| E-flat3/I | 0 | 0 | .192 | .171 | .180 | 18 | f-p C |
| E-flat4/I | 0 | 6.9 | .111 | .068 | .093 | 15 | f-f C |
| E-flat5/I | 43.6 | 25.8 | .254 | .334 | .274 | 11 | f-f C |
| E-flat11/I | 2.3 | 14.3 | .141 | .154 | .148 | 15 | b-f C |
| E2/II | 4 | 0 | .179 | .111 | .146 | 15 | p-f C |
| F1/I | 4.3 | 17 | .206 | .205 | .206 | 14 | f-f C |
| F9/I | 2.9 | 0 | .101 | .071 | .089 | 19 | f-p C |
| G1/I | 2.9 | 28.3 | .216 | .150 | .167 | 7 | f-f C |
| G3/I | 3 | 6.1 | .131 | .144 | .134 | 17 | p-p C |
| G4/II | 3.7 | 27 | .148 | .150 | .149 | 10 | f-f C |
| G5/I | 10.6 | 0 | .303 | .316 | .309 | 16 | f-b C |
| A2/I | 13.1 | 5.8 | .149 | .172 | .158 | 17 | b-p C |

## STRING TRIOS

### Chart V. *continued*

| Work | | | Test I-Ranges | | | Test II | Results |
|---|---|---|---|---|---|---|---|
| | 1. | 2. | 3a. | 3b. | 3c. | Ch | R-Ch-Conc. |
| A3/I | 1.5 | 0 | .158 | .075 | .121 | 19 | p-p C |
| A8/II | 4.5 | 0 | .140 | .150 | .144 | 14 | p-f C |
| B1/I | 0 | 0 | .144 | .172 | .152 | 18 | b-p C |
| B4/I | 0 | 0 | .094 | .084 | .087 | 16 | f-b C |
| B7/I | 24.6 | 7.3 | .144 | .164 | .151 | 12 | f-f C |

Scoring. Ranges: see Chart I; Test II: passing 17-20, borderline 16, failing below 16.

While re-evaluating the nineteen trios that failed the profile before calling them definitely spurious, I noticed that three of them—F1, G1, and G4—used similar and somewhat unusual contrapuntal techniques. The three movements met the four criteria listed in chapter two on p. 46:

a) they might have failed solely because of the imitation;

b) they might be a member of a previously-unknown subtype;

c) they contained details that seemed typical of Haydn;

d) the other movements could have been written by Haydn.

I discovered three baryton trios (80/I, 82/II, 89/I) that treated texture in a manner similar to the three string trios (see Chart VI) and that none of over 100 non-Haydn string trios movements employed such techniques. The similarities between the six works are so striking that they must all be by the same composer—Haydn.

### Chart VI. Textural Traits Shared by V:F1/I, G1/I, G4/II, XI:80/I, 82/II, 89/I

1. Each trio opens with imitation between the violins at an interval of at least eight beats. The first appearance of the theme is presented by one violin accompanied by the bass and the second appearance begins with only two voices and before it ends either the other violin enters or the imitation is altered.

2. The bass does not participate in the imitation. In non-imitative sections and even sometimes in imitative sections, the bass has the same

general amount of rhythmic activity as the other voices and rhythmic doubling between the second violin and bass occurs.

3. Further imitation involving the main theme occurs at the beginning of the second part and is treated differently than at the beginning of the first part.

4. An imitation at a short time span (two beats or less) occurs in the movement.

5. A texture in which the bass drops out leaving the two violins alone occurs for at least three and a half beats.

6. A texture of 2/1 with the two violins being mostly in sixths or thirds is used extensively in nonimitative sections.

I felt that during the study, I had developed a sense for Haydn's treatment of texture in nonminuet movements. On this basis, I evaluated the five trios that had not contained a fast first or second, binary or rounded-binary movement. I concluded that D3 was probably authentic and that C7, D4, E-flat2, and F7 were probably spurious. Thus, my conclusions from this study were that eleven works—C1, C4, D1, D3, F1, G1, G3, G4, A2, A3, and B1—were by Haydn, while twenty works—C2, C3, C5, C6, C7, C8, D4, d, E-flat2, E-flat3, E-flat4, E-flat5, E-flat11, E2, F7, F9, G5, A8, B4, and B7—were by someone else.

## THE HILLSDALE MEETINGS

We twice met at Dr. Brook's home in Hillsdale, N.Y., to compare the results of the papers and to make final decisions on the authenticity of each work. In addition to our stylistic studies, we examined the documentary evidence and expert opinion on the doubtful trios. As mentioned in the introduction, the documentary evidence was of little help in establishing authenticity, but it was still useful to know that C6, C7, C8, D4, d, E-flat3, E-flat4, E-flat5, E-flat11, E2, F7, F9, G5, A8, B4, and B7 were unica. In *Grove*, Feder marked D3, F1, G1, and A2 as "probably authentic," A3, D1, B1, G3, and G4 as "?authentic," C3, C2, C1, C4, C5, and E-flat4 as "doubtful," and C6, C7, C8, d, E-flat2, E-flat3, E-flat5, E-flat11, E2, F7, F9, G5, A8, D4,

## STRING TRIOS

and B4 as probably not authentic.[8] Landon rated only those works he considered "indubitably genuine": C1, C2, C3, C4, C5, D1, D3, F1, G1, G3, G4, A2, and B1.[9] Finally, Larsen regarded C1, C3, C4, C5, D1, D3, F1, G1, G3, A2, A3, and B1 as possibly authentic.[10] As one can see from the above, the major disagreement concerns C1, C2, C3, C4, C5, G4, and A3.[10]

When we compared the results of our seminar papers, we found that they sometimes differed,[11] but that after discussing each trio in detail we generally agreed whether the work was authentic or not. (Our discussion also covered stylistic features not examined in the papers.) We concluded that ten works, C1, C4, D1, D3, F1, G1, G3 (first two movements), G4, A2, and B1 were authentic and that seventeen works, C2, C5, C6, C7, D4, d, E-flat2, E-flat3, E-flat4, E-flat5, E-flat11, E2, F7, G5, A8, B4, and B7 were spurious. We disagreed about the authenticity of four works—C3, C8, F9, A3, the majority of the group leaning toward calling these trios probably authentic. We decided to include the four works in the volume with a note stating that there were some stylistic questions about their authenticity, if no new evidence was found before our volume went to press.

### V:F9

The most interesting work of the disputed group was F9. On hearing a tape of this composition, we thought that the finale sounded remarkably like a Haydn finale. I maintained, though, that the first and second movements could not possibly be by Haydn: the first movement had failed my tests (see above) and the melodic style of both movements seemed foreign to Haydn. (More like Mozart's style. It includes Mannheim sighs, figures like ♪♪♪♪♩ , and the phrasing is too symmetrical.) Two others thought that if the work was by Haydn, it must be from the late 1770s or early 1780s, which is much later than the other string trios. However, the rest of the group believed that the trio was probably authentic, based on hearing the work, especially the skillful handling of the element of surprise.

---

[8]Feder, *The New Grove Haydn*, 166-67. Feder does not mention B7.
[9]Landon, *Haydn: The Early Years*, 220-21.
[10]Larsen, *Three Haydn Catalogues*, xvi.
[11]This is because some of the approaches were more effective than others.

A few weeks after our last meeting while searching through the *Breitkopf Catalogue* for the themes of the doubtful trios, I noticed the incipit of F9 listed under Vanhal's name.[12] In addition, this trio had been published with five other Vanhal trios in Paris as op. 22 by Heina (c. 1777). The melodic style of the first movement is especially close to that found in several authentic Vanhal first movements. Moreover, Vanhal often imitated Haydn's style, and the element of surprise is often as skillfully used in his works as it is in Haydn's. We now accept the trio as being by Vanhal.

We decided that the reason that the majority of the group erred was that they relied too heavily on intuition (in this isolated instance) rather than the objective tests that strongly suggested that the composition was spurious. Obviously, Vanhal was imitating Haydn's style in the finale, but Vanhal could not imitate Haydn's hidden communicators.

Vienna Haydn Conference

At the Vienna Haydn Conference in 1982, Dr. Brook reported on the results of his authenticity seminar and other authenticity research done under his guidance.[13] His conclusions were favorably received, and the participants accepted that stylistic methods could be used for authenticity determination. Especially notable was that on hearing C2 the large majority agreed with our conclusion that Haydn could not have written the trio, despite Landon's strong opinion that it was authentic and its existence in three early manuscripts.

## FURTHER TESTS

The studies done for Dr. Brook's seminars were, in many ways, experimental. While I firmly believe that the conclusions of our Hillsdale meetings are reliable, I thought that I should do one more set of tests, before making final decisions about the authenticity of the doubtful string trios. I chose minuet or tempo di menuetto movements since most of the trios contained such a movement and since these types of movements had not been studied in as much detail as other types of movements in our previous studies. I discovered that minuet and

---

[12]*Breitkopf Catalogue*, 636.
[13]Brook, "Determining Authenticity Through Internal Analysis."

## STRING TRIOS

tempo di menuetto movements, while similar in many ways, differed to the extent that two profiles had to be employed.

Profile I: Minuets

Nine previously-authenticated trios (V:6, 7, 8, 15, 16, 17, 18, 20, 21) and nineteen doubtful ones contain minuets. To evaluate the authenticity of the nineteen doubtful works, I set up a profile based on the nine authentic works, consisting of a checklist with twelve characteristics (see Chart VII).

### Chart VII. Profile I: Checklist for String Trio Minuets
#### Positive Traits Appearing in All the Haydn Works

1. a) First measure has at least one impact per beat but less than two (composite rhythm), b) at least two different rhythmic patterns in first four measures, and c) opening harmony ends before the downbeat of measure two. 30% (trait appears in 30% of the non-Haydn works)

2. Final harmony a) lasts three beats or less, b) uses three sounding voices and two real voices, c) doesn't include the third of the triad, d) employs bass patterns 8-5-1, 1-8, 1-8-1 or 1, and e) has no more than three notes in the bass or two in the violin. 20%

#### Negative Traits Appearing in None of the Haydn Works

3. In first violin during first part, a) more than one half note, nine quarter notes, six triplets, or twelve sixteenths in a row, b) ties over the barline except those beginning on the downbeat of a measure, or c) thirty-seconds except for [rhythmic figures shown], followed by any value other than another sixteenth. 70%

4. In bass during first part, a) ties over the barline other than those beginning on the downbeat of a measure, b) two measures in a row with different repeated pitches, or c) triplets or sixteenths other than [rhythmic figure shown], more than five eighth notes in a

## STRING TRIOS

row, | 𝅗𝅥. | , | ♫ , 𝅗𝅥. , | 𝅗𝅥 𝅗𝅥 | , | 𝄽 ♩ 𝄽 | , | 𝅗𝅥 𝄽 | 𝅗𝅥 𝄽 | , or | 𝄽 ♫ ♩ | .

5. In first violin, a) during first measure more than four eighths or sixteenths in a row, 𝅗𝅥. , | 𝅗𝅥 ♫ ♩ | , or first note shorter than a quarter, b) during second measure | 𝅗𝅥 ♩ | or more than two eighths or sixteenths in a row, or c) pickups other than a single quarter. 50%

6. In first violin, a) the first note not the first or fifth of the scale, b) more than two unornamented repeated notes in a row except at the end, or c) the following rhythms repeated in consecutive measures in the first part: | ♫ ♩ ♩ | | 𝅗𝅥 ♩ ♫ | , | 𝅗𝅥. ♪ ♩ | , | ♬ ♩ | , | 𝅗𝅥 ♬ | 𝅗𝅥 ♩ ♫ | , | 𝅗𝅥 ♬♬ | , | 𝅗𝅥. ♫♫ | , | 𝅗𝅥 ♫ ♫ | , | ♫ ♩ | or d) chromaticism in any part in the first four measures. 50%

7. a) In first part, first violin rests longer than a dotted quarter or second violin or cello rests longer than three beats, except at end; no rest of a quarter or longer before the end of the first part; or rest shorter than an eighth in the first part, or b) rest longer than four beats in the first or second violin in the second part. 60%

8. In first measure of second part, a) first violin employs more than four eighths, four sixteenths, or three triplets in a row, b) second violin has dotted quarter or two eighth notes on the first beat, or c) bass not present. 60%

9. a) Only one sounding voice for more than two measures, unison or octave passages in all three voices for more than a measure or in first measure, or first and second violins doubled exactly for more than four measures from the beginning or b) double stops used in second part or in first two measures or triple stops used anywhere, or c) first violin opens with an ascending triad beginning on 1 or first six notes all in the tonic triad. 70%

10. a) Bass not present by second beat, eighths or sixteenths in first three measures other than ♩. ♪ , or only one rhythmic value in bass (including rests) during first part, b) in first measure bass, | 𝅗𝅥 𝄽 | , two intervals that are larger than a

third, or the second degree of the scale, or c) | 𝅗𝅥 𝅗𝅥 | more than once during first three measures or same pitch repeated more than ten times in bass. 60%

11. Note sustained longer than seven beats in any voice; in first part in any voice syncopation; or more than two eighth notes in a row at beginning. 50%

12. a) On beats two or three of penultimate measure, more than one sixteenth or eighth in a row in first or second violin, half note in violins, or any value other than a quarter or rest in the bass, b) descending interval larger than a fifth in first violin during this measure, c) on first beat half note in first violin or rest in bass, or d) triplets vs. sixteenths in the two violins. 50%

Each item appeared in all previously-authenticated works, but 50% or less of the ten non-Haydn works in Control Group II.[14] No trait warranted abnormal weighting. I determined passing by taking the lowest score of those trios that were considered authentic by everyone—Larsen, Feder, Landon, and the seminar (D3, F1, G1, A1), which was 10. The highest Control Group II score was 6, so I made 10-12 passing, 9 borderline, and below 9 failing. All twenty non-Haydn works in Control Group II and Test Group I failed, scoring 7 points or less (See Chart VIII).

### Chart VIII. Profile I: Results for the Non-Haydn Works

*Control Group II:*
J.C. Bach-3 (f)
M. Haydn-4 (f)
L. Hofmann-6 (f)
Kammel-3 (f)
Le Duc-6 (f)

*Test Group I:*
Camerloher-6 (f)
Dittersdorf-7 (f)
Filtz-6 (f)
Gassmann-6 (f)
Kirmayr-6 (f)

[14]Control Group II and Test Group I for both the minuet and tempo di menuetto profile contained works of both types, since they resemble each other closely. Whether the trios contain or do not contain a basso continuo or are for solo or orchestral performance was not considered because one cannot be sure about these features in the doubtful trios; only the three main voices were studied. Also, for scorings of violin, viola (rather than second violin), bass, read viola instead of second violin on the checklist.

L. Mozart-6 (f)        Mann-7 (f)
Ordoñez-2 (f)          Porsile-3 (f)
Schlöger-6 (f)         Sammartini-7 (f)
Tuma-6 (f)             K. Stamitz-5 (f)
Wagenseil-6 (f)        Vanhal-7 (f)

Scoring. Passing (p):10-12, borderline (b):9, failing (f), 8 and below.

Of the nineteen works tested against the profile, C1, C4, D3, F1, G1, and A2 passed, while C3, C5, C7, C8, d, E-flat2, E-flat3, E-flat4, E-flat5, E-flat11, A8, B4 and B7 failed (see Chart IX).

### Chart IX. Profile I: Results for the Doubtful String Trios

C1-10 (p)       D3-10(p)         F1-10 (p)
C3-6 (f)        d-7 (f)          G1-12 (p)
C4-11 (p)      E-flat2-7 (f)     A2-12 (p)
C5-7 (f)       E-flat3-7 (f)     A8-5 (f)
C7-7 (f)       E-flat4-7 (f)     B4-7 (f)
C8-7 (f)       E-flat5-7 (f)     B7-7 (f)
               E-flat11-6 (f)

Scoring. Passing:10-12, borderline:9, failing:8 and below.

Profile Ia: Tempo di Menuetto Movements

With modifications based on the six authentic trios containing tempo di menuetto movements (V:1, 2, 3, 11, 12, 19), the minuet profile could be applied to the eight doubtful trios with tempo di menuetto movements (C2, D1, D4, F7, G3, G4, B1, and A3). Twelve traits were still present (see Chart X), and I retained the previous scoring of 10-12 passing, 9 borderline, and below 9 failing. The six authentic tempo di menuetto movements scored 10 to 12 points on the revised profile (1-10, 2-10, 3-10, 11-12, 19-10), while ten non-Haydn movements in Test Group I scored 7 points or less (Chart XI).

*STRING TRIOS*

## Chart X. Profile Ia: Checklist for String Trio Tempo di Minuet Movements

### Positive Traits Appearing in All the Haydn Works

1. a) One to three impacts per beat in opening measure (composite rhythm), b) opening harmony lasts from two beats to eight beats, c) at least two different rhythmic patterns in first three measures, and d) all instruments play in the first measure with three notes or less in the bass.

2. Final harmony a) lasts three beats or less, b) does not use dotted quarter in any voice, c) employs three sounding voices and two real voices, d) adopts bass patterns 8-5-1, 1-8, 1-8-1, or 1, and e) has no more than three notes in the bass or two in the violin.

### Traits Appearing in None of the Haydn Works

3. In first violin during first part, a) more than one half or nine unornamented quarters in a row, b) ties over the barline except those beginning on the downbeat of a measure, or c) [rhythmic figures], followed by any value other than another sixteenth, thirty-seconds at the beginning of a beat, [rhythmic figure], or triplets and sixteenths in the same measure.

4. In bass during first part, a) two measures in a row with different repeated pitches, b) triplets, more than six eighths or eight sixteenths in a row (except at end of section, or c) [rhythmic figures], other than [rhythmic figure]

5. In first violin, a) during first measure, more than four eighths or six sixteenths in a row, [rhythmic figures], on first beat eighths, sixteenths, or thirty-seconds, or on second beat four sixteenths or b) pickups of any kind.

6. In first violin, a) first note not the first or fifth of the scale, b) more than three repeated notes in the first part, or c) the following rhythms repeated in consecutive measures in the first part: |♪♪♩ ♩|, |♩ ♩ ♪♪|, |♩. ♪♩|, |♪♪♪♪ ♩|, |♩ ♪♪♪♪|, or |♩ ♪♪♪|.

7. a) in first part, first violin rests longer than a dotted quarter, second violin longer than four beats, or cello longer than three beats, except at end; no rest of a quarter or longer before the end of the first part; rest not present in final measure of first part; or b) rests longer than four beats in violins during second part.

8. In first measure of second part, a) first violin employs more than eight eighths or six sixteenths, b) second violin or bass more than three notes, or c) a part not present.

9 a) Only one sounding voice for more than a measure, except at end; unisons or octaves in all sounding voices for more than a measure, or violins doubled exactly in first measure or b) double stops in first two measures.

10. a) Bass not present by second beat, eighths or sixteenths in first three measures of bass, or only one rhythmic value in bass (including rests) during first part, b) in first measure bass, disjunct intervals, except as a part of the tonic triad in order, or c) in bass, sixteenths in consecutive measures, in first four measures a rest longer than a quarter, or more than seven quarter notes in a row at the beginning.

11. Note sustained longer than seven beats in any voice, in first part in any voice syncopation, or more than two notes in any voice at the beginning.

12 a) On beats two or three of penultimate measure, more than one sixteenth or eighth in a row in first or second violin or in bass value other than a quarter or a rest, b) in this measure, rest on downbeat in bass, or c) descending interval larger than a fifth in this measure.

### Chart XI. Profile Ia: Results for the Non-Haydn Works

*Asplmayr*-5 (f)        *Le Duc*-5 (f)
J.C. Bach-7 (f)         Monn-4 (f)
M. Haydn-6 (f)          Ordoñez-2 (f)
Hofmann-6 (f)           J. Stamitz-7 (f)
Kammel-7 (f)            Wagenseil-4 (f)

Scoring. Passing:10-12, borderline:9, failing:8 and below.

*STRING TRIOS*

Four of the doubtful movements (D1, G4, A3, and B1) passed the profile, while four did not (C2, D4, F7, G3) (see Chart XII).

### Chart XII. Profile Ia: Results for the Doubtful String Trios

| C2-6 (f) | F7-6 (f) | G4-10 (p) |
| D1-10 (p) | G3-5 (f) | A3-10 (p) |
| D4-7 (f) | | B1-10 (p) |

Scoring. Passing:10-12, borderline:9, failing:8 and below.

## CONCLUSIONS

The results of the new tests agree with those of my original paper, and basically, with the CUNY Haydn String Trio Project. (G3 showed conflicting results on the tests, but I believe that this is because the first two movements are authentic while the last two are not. These two spurious movements appear in only one of G3's sources. Also, a middle movement that appears in two related sources for D1 is probably spurious.) The three times I disagree with the majority opinion of the CUNY Haydn String Trio Project concern those trios that we were still uncertain about after our last Hillsdale meeting. The authenticity of A3, which we had leaned toward supporting, has been corroborated. C3, and C8, which the majority of the group had also thought probably authentic but which I believed were spurious, failed the new tests. (In chapter two, I demonstrated that it was very unlikely that the first movement of C3 was by Haydn.)[15] Four trios (C6, E2, F9, G5) could not be retested because they lacked a relevant movement. However, F9 has been proven to be by Vanhal (see above), while C6, E2, and G5 were trios that the group was absolutely certain were not by Haydn based on all stylistic tests.

Conclusion: 11 authentic trios—C1, C4, D1 (two movements only), D3, F1, G1, G3 (first two movements only), G4, A2, A3, B1; 20 spurious trios—C2, C3, C5, C6, C7, C8, D4, d, E-flat2, E-flat3, E-flat4, E-flat5, E-flat11, E2, F7, F9 (Vanhal), G5, A8, B4, B7 (J. Stamitz).

---

[15]In addition, C3's gross form is a factor against its authenticity. None of Haydn's authentic string trios adopt a four movement form or a $\frac{3}{8}$ opening movement.

CHAPTER SEVEN

# Opus 3 String Quartets

## INTRODUCTION

Until the 1960s, the op. 3 string quartets had generally been accepted as authentic Haydn, dating from when Pleyel had included them in his collection of Haydn's complete string quartets (1801-02). Although Larsen, in 1939,[1] had expressed reservations because of the total absence of early sources, other Haydn scholars, including Marion Scott, Donald Tovey, and Adolf Sandberger, did not doubt their authenticity. In 1960, László Somfai wrote the first article that seriously questioned Haydn's authorship of op. 3, mainly based on stylistic factors.[2] Four years later, Alan Tyson demonstrated that the name Hoffstetter had been erased from the engraving plates of the first edition of the first two quartets.[3] This discovery caused most Haydn scholars to place op. 3 in the spurious category and to ascribe them tentatively to Romanus Hoffstetter (1742-1815), the only person of this surname who could have been the composer. Nevertheless, a few important questions remain, including

1) was the erasure of Hoffstetter's name a fraudulent act or the correction of a mistake?

---

[1]Larsen, *Die Haydn Überlieferung*, 150.
[2]László Somfai, "A klasszikus kvartetthangzás megszületése Haydn vonósnégyeseiben," *Zenetudományi tanulmányok* VIII (1960) 295-420 and "Zur Echtheitsfrage des Haydn'schen 'Opus 3'," *The Haydn Yearbook* III (1965) 153-65.
[3]Alan Tyson and H. C. Robbins Landon, "Who Composed Haydn's Op. 3?" *The Musical Times* CIII (1964) 506-07.

2) if Hoffstetter was the composer of the first two quartets, did he write the entire set? and

3) could Haydn have written any of the remaining quartets?

All extant sources for op. 3 derive from a Bailleux print of 1777. The print was engraved by two different persons: nos. 3-6 by a Madame Annereau and nos. 1-2 by a yet unidentified engraver. In addition, Madame Annereau altered a few details of the plates for nos. 1 and 2, including the deletion of Hoffstetter's name.[4] His name had originally appeared at the beginning of all four parts of quartets 1 and 2, and it can be faintly seen in some of the extant copies of the print that were made after the plates had become worn.

Pleyel used the Bailleux print as the basis for the edition of op. 3 in his collection of Haydn's complete quartets. A thematic index of Haydn's quartets prefaced Pleyel's edition, and two letters indicate that Haydn approved this inventory.[5] Johann Elssler based his list of Haydn's quartets in the *Haydn Verzeichnis* on Pleyel's catalogue.

A large amount of negative evidence contradicts Haydn's authorship of op. 3. First, of course, there is the conflicting attribution to Hoffstetter. As mentioned in the introduction, most Haydn scholars regard a conflicting attribution as strong evidence against a work's authenticity. Second, the complete lack of early sources casts considerable suspicion on op. 3. Haydn's other early quartets exist in a large number of good early manuscripts, averaging forty extant copies.[6] For stylistic reasons, op. 3, if by Haydn, must have been written well before op. 9 (1769/70). Yet, the earliest extant source is the Bailleux print of 1777. In any case, this print must be considered a peripheral source and, hence, a poor witness for authenticity, because it was produced in Paris, far from Haydn's control. Finally, op. 3 does not appear in the *Entwurf-Katalog*, which, according to Tyson, seems "especially comprehensive for the years 1765-77 and which contains all the Op 9, Op 17 and Op 20 quartets."[7]

---

[4]Alan Tyson, "Bibliographic Observations on Bailleux's Edition," *Haydn Studies*, 95-98. Tyson says that Madame Annereau's engraving style is readily identifiable in her freelance lettering and her engraving punches.
[5]Reginald Barret-Ayres, "Not Proven," *Haydn Studies*, 104.
[6]James Webster, "Relations between the Documentary and Stylistic Evidence," *Haydn Studies*, 100.
[7]Tyson and Landon, "Who Composed Op. 3?" 506.

## OPUS 3 STRING QUARTET

While most scholars now agree that op. 3 is not by Haydn, Reginald Barret-Ayres holds a more conservative view.[8] Although the evidence raises strong suspicions against Haydn as the author of op. 3, he believes that the case against Haydn (or for Hoffstetter) is "not proven." He raises several points that support Haydn's case, including

1) Haydn's approval of the Pleyel edition,

2) the presence of op. 3 in the *Haydn Verzeichnis* of 1805,

3) Marion Scott's explanation of how Bailleux had obtained the quartets, and

4) the appearance of many of Haydn's "thumbprints" in these quartets.

Based solely on the documentary evidence, one might share Barret-Ayres's view that while the external evidence against the authenticity of op. 3 is very strong, the non-authenticity of the six quartets has not been definitively demonstrated. I would like to test the hypothesis that Haydn might have written some of the quartets. Remember that Hoffstetter's name appears only on the first two quartets and that two separate engravers produced the Bailleux print; it is very possible that more than one composer might be responsible for op. 3. Printers in the eighteenth century sometimes filled out an incomplete set of works by one composer (quartets were generally published in groups of six) with one or more pieces by another. This explanation still leaves several unanswered questions, especially the lack of good early sources for those quartets that Haydn might have written. Yet, one cannot rule out the possibility that the dissemination of these quartets was an exception to the norm. In any case, a thorough stylistic study of op. 3 should demonstrate whether or not Haydn was the author of any of the six quartets.

## THE TESTS FOR HAYDN'S AUTHORSHIP OF OP. 3

The case against Haydn's authorship of any of the op. 3 quartets can be corroborated by comparing them against two profiles from the early

---

[8]Barret-Ayres, "Not Proven," 103-105 and *Joseph Haydn and the String Quartet* (London: Barrie & Jenkins, 1974).

authentic quartets (one for fast first movements and another for 2/4 finales), using quantitative ranges.[9]

Profile I: Expositions of Fast First Movements

An examination of the expositions of opening fast movements of Haydn's op. 1, op. 2, and op. 9 quartets[10] produced a range of harmonic change per beat (HC/B) of .610 to .690 (borderline .020) and a range of textural change per beat of .207 to .312 (borderline .020). As one can see in Chart I, none of the five op. 3 quartets with fast first movements fit the profile. In op. 3, no. 1, op. 3, no. 4, and op. 3, no. 6, the rate of harmonic change per beat is much slower than is normal for early Haydn quartets, while, in op. 3, no. 3 and op. 3, no. 5, it is too fast. Furthermore, the rate of textural change is too slow in all the quartets, except no. 5.

### Chart I. Profile I: Quantitative Ranges in Op. 3, First Movements

| Work | HC/B | TC/B | Results |
|---|---|---|---|
| op. 3, no. 1 | .445 (f) | .100 (f) | C |
| op. 3, no. 3 | .716 (f) | .166 (f) | C |
| op. 3, no. 4 | .420 (f) | .059 (f) | C |
| op. 3, no. 5 | .812 (f) | .258 (p) | C |
| op. 3, no. 6 | .490 (f) | .107 (f) | C |

Scoring. Ranges: HC/B .610-.690 (borderline .020), TC/B .207-.312 (borderline .020).
p=pass, b=borderline, f=fail, A=fits profile, C=fails profile

Profile II: $\frac{2}{4}$ Finales

A study of the first part of $\frac{2}{4}$ finales from the op. 3 quartets provides similar results. In Haydn's op. 1, op. 2, and op. 9, the harmonic change per beat for such movements is .555- .680 (borderline .040),

---

[9]To prove nonauthenticity, it is not necessary to employ two separate tests (both quantitative ranges and checklist). As stated in chapter two, a work is regarded as not fitting the profile if it fails either test.
[10]These quartets encompass all the years in which Haydn could have written op. 3.

while the textural change per beat is .187-.264 (borderline .020). Although three of the five quartets containing $\frac{2}{4}$ finales score borderline on the textural change range, all five have rates of harmonic change per beat that are much slower than is normal for Haydn (see Chart II).

### Chart II. Profile II: Quantitative Ranges in Op. 3, 2/4 Finales

| Work | HC/B | TC/B | Results |
|---|---|---|---|
| op. 3, no. 1 | .250 (f) | .147 (f) | C |
| op. 3, no. 2 | .304 (f) | .155 (f) | C |
| op. 3, no. 3 | .438 (f) | .177 (b) | C |
| op. 3, no. 5 | .375 (f) | .278 (b) | C |
| op. 3, no. 6 | .490 (f) | .270 (b) | C |

Scoring. Ranges: HC/B .555-.680 (borderline .040), TC/B .187-.264 (borderline .020).

Therefore, when compared to the authentic quartets, each of the ten op. 3 movements tested, including at least one from each quartet, failed their profiles; in my opinion, Haydn had nothing to do with op. 3.

## DID HOFFSTETTER WRITE OP. 3?

With the case against Haydn confirmed, the question remains, who wrote op. 3? Several writers have accepted Hoffstetter as the composer of all six quartets.[11] For example, Hubert Unverricht writes that "Further researches by Finscher and Unverricht have established his [Hoffstetter's] authorship with a fair degree of certainty."[12] Others are not so sure. James Webster believes that the attribution to Hoffstetter is not completely convincing, declaring that Bailleux in Paris is just as poor a witness for a south German monk as he is for the Esterházy kapellmeister.[13] Ludwig Finscher asserts that "the possibility, suggested by the bibliographical evidence in Bailleux's edition, that 'Op. 3' was not by one composer but by two or even several should be taken very

---

[11]For instance, Tyson and Landon, "Who Composed Op. 3?" 507 and Hubert Unverricht, "Roman Hoffstetter," *The New Grove*, VII, 631.
[12]Unverricht, *op. cit.*
[13]Webster, "Relations Between the Documentary and Stylistic Evidence," 100.

seriously."[14] Finally, in the most recent article on op. 3, Øivind Eckhoff proposes that op. 3, nos. 1-4 and 6 were written by one composer, while op. 3, no. 5 was written by someone else.[15]

To compare op. 3 with authentic Hoffstetter, I set up two profiles (Profile III: fast first movements; Profile IV: minuets), based on seven Hoffstetter quartets, most of which were scored from early editions.[16]

Profile III: Expositions of Fast First Movements
from Hoffstetter's String Quartets

The third profile was for the expositions of fast opening movements from Hoffstetter's string quartets. Two ranges, textural change per beat .097-.187 (borderline .020) and harmonic change per beat .350-.555 (borderline .040), were used in Test I. I discovered that an abnormally large number of the ten non-Hoffstetter quartets in Control Group II met the criteria of Test I (see Chart IV), but I retained Test I because all of the relevant movements in Haydn's op. 1, op. 2, and op. 9 had failed.

On the other hand, Test II (checklist) produced a clear distinction between Hoffstetter and non-Hoffstetter quartets. Twelve items made up the checklist with nos. 1, 4, 11, and 12 weighted double because they were valid for none of the ten non-Hoffstetter works in Control Group II (see Chart III). Because the maximum score was 16 and the highest Control Group II score was 4, I made 13-16 passing, 9-12 borderline, and below 9 failing (giving each category ⅓ of the difference between 16 and 4). As one can see in Chart IV, twenty non-Hoffstetter compositions (Control Group II and Test Group I) failed the checklist, indicating its effectiveness.

---

[14]Ludwig Finscher, "Comments on Style," *Haydn Studies*, 103.
[15]Øivind Eckhoff, "The Enigma of Haydn's Opus 3," *Studia musicologica norvegica* IV (1978) 9-43.
[16]This group consists of six op. 1 quartets (Amsterdam c. 1770) plus a quartet from c. 1765. I did not use op. 2 (Mannheim 1780) because these quartets are probably too late for comparison with op. 3.

*OPUS 3 STRING QUARTET*

## Chart III. Profile III: Checklist for the Expositions of Fast First Movements

### Positive Traits Appearing in All Seven Hoffstetter Works

*1. Uses 1/2/1 texture (second violin and viola share one real voice) with the middle voices having the melody and at least two consecutive measures have texture 4 (one real voice). 0%: 2 points (traits appear in none of the non-Hoffstetter works in Control Group II; weighted with two points)

2. a) Uses dotted eighth notes several times, b) in ?/8 meter uses ties over the barline or in ?/2 or in ?/4 meter two sixteenths at the beginning of a measure followed only by another sixteenth and ♩♫ ♩. not used. 30%

3. Rest of two beats or longer present, but no rest shorter than an eighth and no simultaneous rest of the same value in the first nine measures. 30%

*4. Exposition ends with only one real voice, final harmony includes both the third and the fifth of the chord, and final cadence V-I. 0%:2 points

5. First and second violins separated by a least an octave at some point and viola and cello doubled exactly for more than one and a half measures (octave placement not considered), not including those passages where one of the violins also doubles these parts. 30%

6. Texture space of at least three octaves on a single simultaneity and first violin does not go below bb. 10%

7. In the first violin, same pitch sustained or reiterated for at least two measures, and, in first three measures, an interval of a fourth or fifth but no interval larger than a fifth. 10%

8. In the first measure, a) at least 1.75 impacts per beat in ?/2 or ?/4 or three impacts per beat in ?/8 meter (composite rhythm); b) melody uses at least two different note values including an eighth (ornaments not counted); c) melody does not include a note value longer than a dotted quarter in ?/2 or ?/4 meter or longer than a dotted eighth in ?/8 meter; and d) in the melody, relationship between the longest and shortest note no more than 3 to 1. 30%

## OPUS 3 STRING QUARTET

### Negative Traits Appearing in None of the Seven Hoffstetter Works

9. a) 1/1/1/1 texture present for more than a measure, or b) either violin drops out for more than two measures, cello drops out for more than three and a half measures, or one part alone for more than four beats. 60% (trait appears in 60% of the Control Group II works)

10. a) In first four measures, a nondiatonic note, or a dissonance on the downbeat of a measure (fourths don't count), or, b) in the first violin in the first two measures, the tonic is not present in two different octaves. 90%

*11. In the first violin, a) in ?/2 or ?/4 meter, more than six triplets, six unsyncopated quarters, or two unsyncopated half notes in a row, or a whole note that is not tied over the barline; b) in ?/8 meter, more than one unornamented dotted quarter or more than ten eighth notes in a row or any triplets; or c) in any meter, triplets other than eighth note triplets, thirty-second notes except with the figure ♩.♫ , or a dotted half that doesn't go over the barline. 100%:2 points

*12. In the bass, a) in ?/2 or ?/4 meter, more than one sixteenth at a time, except when doubling another voice, or more than one half note or whole note at a time; b) in ?/8 meter, more than four sixteenth notes at a time except when doubling another voice, more than six dotted quarters in a row, or ♩ ♪ more than three times in a row; or c) in any meter, murky bass for more than one and a half beats, a note tied over the barline, or a dotted half. 100%:2 points

### Chart IV. Profile III: Results for Non-Hoffstetter Works

| Composer | Test I-Ranges | | Test II | Results |
|---|---|---|---|---|
| | HC/B | TC/B | Ch | R-Ch-Conc. |
| *Control Group II:* | | | | |
| Boccherini | .365 | .166 | 0 | p-f  C |
| Cambini | .426 | .173 | 1 | p-f  C |
| Cannabich | .241 | .176 | 2 | f-f  C |
| Dittersdorf | .365 | .144 | 2 | p-f  C |
| Haydn | .610 | .270 | 2 | f-f  C |
| M. Haydn | .369 | .142 | 3 | p-f  C |
| Mozart | .512 | .158 | 1 | p-f  C |

## OPUS 3 STRING QUARTET

**Chart IV. Profile III: Results for Non-Hoffstetter Works**

| Composer | Test I-Ranges | | Test II | Results | |
|---|---|---|---|---|---|
| | HC/B | TC/B | Ch | R-Ch-Conc. | |
| Richter | .473 | .178 | 2 | p-f | C |
| Rosetti | .402 | .144 | 2 | p-f | C |
| A. Stamitz | .285 | .107 | 4 | f-f | C |
| *Test Group I:* | | | | | |
| Haydn | .640 | .256 | 7 | f-f | C |
| Haydn | .672 | .242 | 8 | f-f | C |
| M. Haydn | .382 | .156 | 8 | p-f | C |
| Mozart | .433 | .219 | 5 | f-f | C |
| Richter | .495 | .236 | 2 | f-f | C |
| Starzer | .947 | .169 | 3 | f-f | C |
| Toeschi | .295 | .209 | 4 | f-f | C |
| Tomasini | .258 | .166 | 4 | f-f | C |
| Vogler | .436 | .128 | 6 | p-f | C |
| Wendling | .422 | .125 | 3 | p-f | C |

Scoring. Test I: HC/B .350-.555 (borderline .040), TC/B .097-.187 (borderline .020); Test II: passing 13-16, borderline 9-12, failing below 9.

I then tested the five op. 3 quartets that began with fast movements. Op. 3, no. 1 turned out to be authentic, while op. 3, nos. 3, 4, 5, and 6 failed the profile (see Chart V). (Op. 3, no. 2 begins with a set of slow variations.)

**Chart V. Profile III: Results for Op. 3 String Quartets**

| Work | Test I-Ranges | | Test II | Results | |
|---|---|---|---|---|---|
| | HC/B | TC/B | Ch | R-Ch-Conc. | |
| op. 3, no. 1 | .445 | .100 | 15 | p-p | A |
| op. 3, no. 3 | .716 | .166 | 5 | f-f | C |
| op. 3, no. 4 | .420 | .059 | 8 | f-f | C |
| op. 3, no. 5 | .812 | .258 | 8 | f-f | C |
| op. 3, no. 6 | .490 | .107 | 7 | p-f | C |

Scoring. Test I: HC/B .350-.555 (borderline .040), TC/B .097-.187 (borderline .020); Test II: passing 13-16, borderline 9-12, failing below 9.

## OPUS 3 STRING QUARTET

Profile IV: Minuets from Hoffstetter's String Quartets

The fourth profile, for minuets without trios, helped confirm the above results and tested the one quartet, op. 3, no. 2, that lacked an opening fast movement.[17] Test I, quantitative ranges, again proved to be somewhat inconclusive, with only one range (textural change per beat .106-.151, borderline .020) being narrow enough for authenticity determination.

The checklist in Test II comprised twelve entries, with the first item, which did not appear in any of the ten non-Hoffstetter quartets in Control Group II, being given two points instead of one (see Chart VI). Passing was 11-13, borderline 9-10, and failing 8 and below, using the same criteria that were employed in the previous profile. Again, all twenty non-Hoffstetter quartets failed the checklist (see Chart VII).

### Chart VI. Profile IV: Checklist for Minuets
#### Positive Traits Appearing in All Eight Hoffstetter Minuets

*1. At least two changes of texture in the first part but does not use four real voices or one real voice for more than a measure at a time. 0%:2 points (trait appears in 0% of the non-Hoffstetter works; weighted with two points)

2. Final harmony a) includes the third or the fifth of the chord, b) lasts no longer than a measure, c) uses the bass patterns 1, 8-1, or 8-5-1, and d) employs no more than two real voices or five sounding voices. 40%

3. a) Uses a note value of a sixteenth or shorter, with a value shorter than an eighth present in the first violin before the third beat of the third measure, and b) in the first violin, no ties over the barline and no thirty-seconds except for ♩. ♪♪ . 10%

4. First violin does not go below b, and, in the first part, its range is between an octave and an octave and a fifth. 50%

5. In first violin, a) there is no interval larger than a seventh in the first part, b) a restruck suspension is employed, and c) no pedal of two measures or longer is present. 30%

---

[17] I employed eight Hoffstetter minuets in setting up the profile because one quartet contained two minuets.

*OPUS 3 STRING QUARTET*

6. In the first measure, a) the first violin contains between three and five notes including a quarter or a half, b) cello has no more than three notes, and c) all parts play by the fifth beat. 30%

### Negative Traits Appearing in None of the Eight Hoffstetter Minuets

7. Contains a rest that lasts more than eight beats or a rest that is shorter than a quarter. 90% (trait appears in 90% of the non-Hoffstetter works)

8. In the first violin, a) ♪♩. or four sixteenths on the second beat of a measure; b) more than two dotted halves in a row, half notes in consecutive measures, or more than eight unornamented eighth notes in a row; or c) in first part, a dotted quarter. 80%

9. a) Octave or unison passages in all voices or exact doubling between the violins for more than two beats at a time (octave placement considered), or b) does not contain exact rhythmic doubling between the first violin and the second violin or viola for at least six consecutive measures and first and second violins do not have exact rhythmic doubling for at least four beats at a time four times in a movement. 50%

10. a) A pickup other than ♩ , ♩.♪ , ♪♪♪ (3), b) a half note beginning on a second beat, or c) in the penultimate measure of the first or second part, ♪♪♪♩ (3) ♩. 50%

11. a) Melodic chromaticism in the first violin or cello in the first part (rests break up patterns) or consecutive half steps anywhere in the first violin; b) nondiatonic note in the violins or viola in the first four measures; c) triple stops; or d) does not include a dominant seventh chord in the first part. 70%

12. a) In the bass, ties over the barline, murky bass for two or more beats, more than four sixteenths in a row, dotted quarter, double stops, thirty-second notes, a dotted half that doesn't double another part, or b) bass uses only one note value. 70%

### Chart VII. Profile IV: Results for Non-Hoffstetter Works

| Composer | Test I<br>TC/B | Test II<br>Ch | Results<br>R-Ch-Conc. | |
|---|---|---|---|---|
| *Control Group II:* | | | | |
| Albrechtsberger | .138 | 5 | p-f | C |
| Boccherini | .196 | 2 | f-f | C |
| Dittersdorf | .235 | 2 | f-f | C |
| Haydn | .141 | 6 | p-f | C |
| Haydn | .158 | 4 | b-f | C |
| M. Haydn | .236 | 4 | f-f | C |
| Mozart | .250 | 2 | f-f | C |
| Richter | .083 | 6 | f-f | C |
| Rosetti | .143 | 2 | p-f | C |
| Starzer | .713 | 2 | f-f | C |
| *Test Group I:* | | | | |
| Abel | .166 | 4 | b-f | C |
| Boccherini | .200 | 4 | f-f | C |
| Haydn | .135 | 7 | p-f | C |
| Holzbauer | .159 | 4 | b-f | C |
| Holzbauer | .141 | 6 | p-f | C |
| Richter | .000 | 6 | f-f | C |
| Rosetti | .181 | 5 | f-f | C |
| Starzer | .153 | 6 | b-f | C |
| Tomasini | .116 | 5 | p-f | C |
| Tomasini | .111 | 6 | p-f | C |

Scoring. Test I: TC/B .106-.151 (borderline .020), Test II: passing 11-13, borderline 9-10, failing below 9.

Op. 3, no. 1 and no. 2 fit the profile, while nos. 3, 5, and 6 failed (see Chart VIII). (Op. 3, no. 4 does not contain a minuet.) The results for op. 3, no. 1 on Profile IV seem somewhat problematic, since it scored borderline (10 points) on the checklist. Normally, a composition is put into Category A (fits profile), if it passes one test and scores borderline on the other, as op. 3, no. 1 does. However, the presence of only one range in Test I does create some question. On the other hand, because this minuet scored only one point below passing, because the highest a non-Hoffstetter quartet scored was 8, and because the first movement passed its profile, I believe that I can safely include the op. 3, no. 1 minuet in Category A.

## Chart VIII. Profile IV: Results for Op. 3 String Quartets

| Work | Test I TC/B | Test II Ch | Results R-Ch. Conc. | |
|---|---|---|---|---|
| op. 3, no. 1 | .143 | 10 | p-b | A |
| op. 3, no. 2 | .141 | 11 | p-p | A |
| op. 3, no. 3 | .138 | 5 | p-f | C |
| op. 3, no. 5 | .194 | 6 | f-f | C |
| op. 3, no. 6 | .100 | 8 | b-f | C |

Scoring. Test I: TC/B .106-.151 (borderline .020), Test II: passing 11-13, borderline 9-10, failing below 9.

## CONCLUSION

As one can see from the above, the tests indicate that op. 3, nos. 1 and 2 are by Hoffstetter, while op. 3, nos. 3-6 are not. I suspect that nos. 3-6 were written by at least two different composers and that it is possible that four composers were involved. Most significantly, the rates of harmonic change per beat in the expositions of the first movements of Nos. 3 and 5 (.716 and .812) are much faster than those for nos. 4 and 6 (.420 and .490). I tried to identify the authors of nos. 3-6 by comparing them to authenticated works by other composers without success.[18] Unless new sources are found, the authors of these quartets will probably never be discovered.

---

[18]To do this properly, it would have been necessary to set up profiles for all composers who wrote string quartets in the 1750s, 60s, and 70s, an undertaking which is obviously beyond the scope of this study. Still, if the real composer or composers of op. 3 wrote a sufficient number of previously-authenticated quartets, I believe that they could be identified using the methods of this investigation.

CHAPTER EIGHT

# Divertimentos

## INTRODUCTION

In Haydn's day, the term divertimento might have been attached to most of the works examined in this study. The term did not designate a genre; rather, it represented the new wave of classical instrumental music sometimes including the symphony, although in Austria it was generally applied to works for one on a part. Moreover, unlike our modern conception "divertimento," the term did not necessarily signify light music. Finally, in the eighteenth century, the term was interchangeable with cassation, notturno, serenade, and, sometimes, partita.

In this chapter, however, I shall study the authenticity of those works listed in Group N "Divertimentos Etc. for 4+ String and/or Wind Instruments (str. qts, works with baryton, lira organizzata excepted)" in Feder's *Grove* worklist (generally, the same as Hoboken Gruppe II).[1] Definitely authentic extant compositions contained in this list are Hob II: 1, 2, 3, 7, 8, 9, 11, 14, 15, 16, 17, 20, 21, 22, 23, 24, 33, 34, 35, 36, 37, and 38.[2] Doubtful works that will be tested in this chapter include II:18, 19, 39, D6, D8, D9, D10, D11, D18, D22 add., D23 add., F2, F12, G1, G4, G9/C12, A1, B4, and a flute quartet in C

---

[1] Feder, *The New Grove Haydn*, 158-61.
[2] 1, 2, 3, 7, 8, 9, 11, 17, 20, 21, 22, and 38 are in the *Entwurf-Katalog*, while 14, 15, 16, 23, and 24 exist in autograph. Only one of the six Scherzandos (33-38), 38, is in the *Entwurf-Katalog*, but it is likely that the remainder were recorded on missing pages (see Landon, *Haydn: The Early Years*, 282). All six exist in many good, early sources. II:4, 5, 10, 12, 13 and 20bis are lost.

that is not in Hoboken (Hob. Deest).[3] A chart showing the instrumentation of the divertimentos appears below.

## Chart I. Instrumentation of the Divertimentos

### A. Authentic Works

II:1—flute, oboe, two violins, cello, bass.

II:2—two violins, two violas, bass.

II:3—two oboes, two horns, two bassoons.

II:7—two oboes, two horns, two bassoons.

II:8—two flutes, two horns, two violins, bass.

II:9—two oboes, two horns, two violins, two violas, bass.

II:11—flute, oboe, two violins, cello, bass.

II:14—two clarinets, two horns.

II:15—two oboes, two horns, two bassoons.

II:16—two english horns, two horns, two violins, two bassoons.

II:17—two clarinets, two horns, two violins, two violas, bass.

II:20—two oboes, two horns, two violins, two violas, bass.

II:21,22—two horns, two violins, viola, bass.

II:23—two oboes, two horns, two bassoons.

II:24—flute, two english horns, bassoon, two horns, solo violin, two violins, cello, violone.

II:33-38—flute/two oboes, two horns, two violins, bass.

### B. Doubtful Works

II:18—flute, two horns, violin, viola, bass.

II:19—flute, (two horns), violin, viola, bass.

II:39—four violins, two basses.

II:D6—flute, violin, viola, bass.

II:D8—flute, two violins, viola, bass.

---

[3] I have added D10 and D11 to Feder's list.

## DIVERTIMENTOS

II:D9, D10, D11-G4—flute, violin, viola, bass.

II:D18—two oboes, two horns, two bassoons.

II:D22—four horns, violin, viola, bass.

II:D23—two oboes, two horns, two bassoons.

II:F2—oboe, bassoon, two horns, violin, viola, bass.

II:F12—two oboes, two horns, two bassoons.

II:G1—two oboes, two horns, two violins, two violas, bass.

II:G9/C12—two oboes, two horns, two bassoons.

II:A1—two violins, two violas, bass.

II:B4—oboe, violin, viola da gamba, bass.

Quartet in C, Hob. Deest—flute, violin, viola, cello.

The authenticity of the doubtful divertimentos has not been examined as extensively as that of other genres, but Feder, Larsen, and Landon give opinions on most of them. Feder includes G1, D22, D18, and G9/C12 among Haydn's authentic divertimentos.[4] He groups the rest of the doubtful pieces cited above (except D10 and D11, which he does not mention and obviously considers spurious) with the selected doubtful and spurious works, marking D23 as "?authentic," 18 and 19 as "probably by Vanhal" and D6 as "probably by L. Hofmann." Larsen believes that 18, 19, and 39 are dubious, while all those divertimentos entered under letter designations in Hob. Gruppe II are spurious except D18 and G1, which are probably authentic.[5] Of those works not listed in Volume I of Hoboken, he thinks that G9/C12 and D23 may be authentic. Landon regards D18, D22, G1, A1, and G9/C12, and D23 as authentic and D8, D9, D10, D11, and G4 as spurious.[6] In addition, he marks II:39 as "genuine ?" in the index.[7] In summary, the scholars who have previously examined these compositions generally agree that D18, D22, D23, G1, and G9/C12 are probably authentic and that most or all of the remainder are probably spurious. The major disagreement concerns 39 and A1.[8]

[4]Feder, *The New Grove Haydn*, 159-61.
[5]Larsen, *Three Haydn Catalogues*, xv-xvi, xxiv.
[6]Landon, *Haydn: The Early Years*, 180-83, 188, 270-73, 523, 622.
[7]Landon, *Haydn: The Early Years*, 618.
[8]Because of the diversity within this genre, I shall give the documentary evidence with the discussion of the individual works at the end of the chapter rather than in the introduction.

*DIVERTIMENTOS*

## THE TESTS

As one can see in Chart I, the divertimentos fall into three groups by instrumentation: those for strings alone, those for mixed strings and winds, and those for winds alone. (In addition, I included the op. 1 and 2 string quartets in Control Group I to provide a large enough sample of works for strings alone.) I discovered that a single "cross-genre" profile could be formulated for the string and mixed string and wind works, and that this profile could be modified for the wind divertimentos.[9] I created profiles for two separate types of movements: Ia and Ib for fast first or second movements in some type of sonata form and IIa and IIb for minuets.

Profiles Ia and Ib: Fast First or Second Movements in Sonata Form

The first profile (Ia) was for fast first or second movements in sonata form, based on seventeen authentic movements for either strings or strings and winds from Hob. II and III.[10] (I withheld five other authentic movements so that the completed profile could be tested to make certain that it passed authentic works.)[11] Because the profile had to be applicable across genre boundaries, quantitative ranges were not used.[12] The great diversity within the seventeen authentic movements made drawing up the checklist particularly difficult. Consequently, I employed twenty non-Haydn works in Control Group II and concentrated on negative characteristics. I created a checklist with twenty-one items that were valid for at least 85% of the seventeen Haydn movements (at least 15 of 17), but 60% or less of the twenty non-Haydn pieces in Control Group II (see Chart II).

### Chart II. Profile Ia: Checklist for Fast First Movements

#### Positive Traits Appearing in at Least 85% of the Haydn Works

*1. In first measure, bass includes four notes or less and seventh of scale not present in the melody. 45%/one point (trait appears in 45% of the

---

[9]II:9 and 16 were not available for this study.
[10]II:1, 2, 11, 17, 21, 33, 34, 35, 36, 37, and III:1, 2, 4, 6, 7, 8, 10.
[11]II:6, 8, 20, 22, 38.
[12]As stated in chapter two, quantitative ranges are generally too wide for authenticity determination in cross-genre studies.

non-Haydn works in Control Group II/given one point because it appears in less than 100% of the Haydn works in Control Group I)

2. a) Texture changes at least three times in the first ten measures, b) bass pattern changes by measure six, and c) first four measures include a dominant seventh chord or leading tone chord. 40%/two points

*3. a) In exposition, rest of over one and a half measures in some voice, b) rest of an eighth present but no sixteenth rest, c) lacks rest longer than a beat in first two measures' melody, and d) bass enters by measure six. 55%/one point

4. a) Movement's final sonority lasts no more than four beats, uses two real voices or less, does not have the following rhythmic patterns in bass: 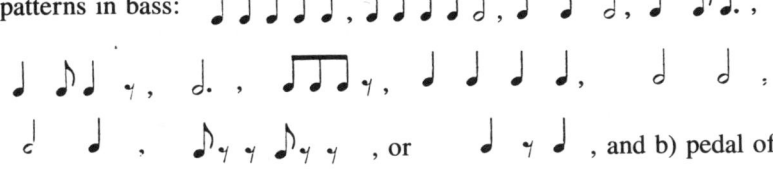, and b) pedal of three measures or longer not present at end. 40%/two points

*5. a) In first five measures' melody, a measure's rhythmic pattern is repeated, but at least one measure's pattern is different, b) melody uses a value of an eighth or shorter in the first measure, and c) melodic seventh present in top voice during movement. 50%/one point

## Negative Traits Appearing in 15% or Less of the Haydn Works

6. In the exposition, ties over the barline in the bass, triplets in the bass, or bass range less than an octave in the first eight measures. 35%/two points

*7. In bass during exposition, a) no more than two half notes, one dotted half note, three quarter notes (except at the end of the exposition), or four dotted quarter notes in a row (all of the above except when all voices have the same rhythm); b) more than four sixteenths in a row except when doubling another voice; c) a trill in the cello or bass; or d) in $\frac{3}{8}$ or $\frac{6}{8}$, ♩♫ or more than three ♩ ♪ . 20%/one point

*8. In main voice, a) more than two unornamented, unsyncopated quarter notes, two unornamented dotted quarter notes, or two unornamented half notes in a row (all of the above except when

all voices have the same rhythm); b) ♫. or ♫ ;
c) in $\frac{?}{2}$ or $\frac{?}{4}$ meter, |♪♩♪ or |♫♩ ; d) in $\frac{?}{8}$,
♫♪⁊ , or , ♫♫ , ♫ rest . 30%/one point.

9. a) Nondiatonic note in first two measures, b) chromaticism in main voice or bass during first twelve measures, or c) figure like ♫♫ or ♫♫ in the main voice during the expo-
f e e d     g f f e
sition.
55%/two points

10. a) Mannheim sigh during first ten measures; b) in $\frac{3}{8}$, first strong beat in main voice dotted quarter or second interval an octave leap; or c) in $\frac{6}{8}$, sixteenth not employed during exposition. 50%/two points

11. a) Pickup other than a single eighth; b) in $\frac{6}{8}$, any pickup, c) first note longer than a dotted half; or d) in $\frac{6}{8}$, a note of a dotted quarter or longer on the first beat in any voice. 55%/two points

*12. In exposition, a) regular suspension, b) eighths or sixteenths repeated on the same note for more than three measures in the main voice, or c) note tied over the barline during the first four measures. 55%/one point

*13. a) In $\frac{?}{2}$ or $\frac{?}{4}$ meter, presence of ♫♫ in bass more than once during the exposition or first forty measures (whichever comes first); or b) in any voice in exposition, more than six triplets in a row or ♩ ♪.♪ (except at the end of the exposition). 40%/one point

14. a) At the beginning all voices have the same rhythm but not the same pitches for more than two measures, b) unison-octave passages in all sounding voices (at least three voices, texture remains the same throughout) for more than three measures; or c) exposition ends with less than four sounding voices, bass not in exposition's final sonority, or violins have double stops in last measure of the exposition. 55%/two points

15. a) In exposition, more than fifty-eight consecutive eighth notes in a row in any voice; b) in $\frac{3}{4}$, two dotted half notes in a row in strings; or c) in $\frac{3}{4}$ or $\frac{4}{4}$ ♩ ♪ . 55%/two points

## DIVERTIMENTOS

16. In exposition, whole notes in the strings. 50%/two points

17. a) In the main voice during the exposition [♩♫♫♩] , b) more than fourteen eighth notes in a row at the beginning of the piece, and c) use of murky bass for more than two beats on the same pitch. 60%/two points

18. a) In main voice, half notes in adjacent measures ($\frac{4}{4}$ and $\frac{3}{4}$ only); or b) more than two thirty-second notes in a row or thirty-seconds that don't sound at the end of a beat (such as [♩.♬] ). 45%/two points

19. a) Note in viola lasting two measures or longer; b) viola and bass doubled exactly for more than ten measures (octave placement not considered); or c) double stops in second viola, cello, or bass. 50%/two points

20. a) More than fifteen consecutive sixteenths, sixteenth triplets, or thirty-seconds in a row during the first eight measures in the melody; b) in $\frac{3}{8}$, ties over the barline in the exposition (except those beginning on a downbeat); or c) in $\frac{4}{4}$, [♩. ♫] in exposition. 60%/two points

21. In exposition in any voice, a) in $\frac{4}{4}$, half note beginning on the second beat of a measure, b) [♫♩̌] in main voice, or, c) in 6/8, note sustained longer than three and a half measures in any voice. 60%/two points

I weighted those traits that were valid for all the Haydn movements with two points, while those characteristics that were valid for less than 100% of the Haydn works received one point (marked * on Chart Two), producing a maximum score of 34. The lowest that one of the five compositions that were withheld from Control Group I scored was 30, so I made 30-34 passing. The highest Control Group II score was 21, so I made 26-29 borderline and below 26 failing. (The midpoint between 21 and 30 is 26; everything above 26 was given to the borderline category and everything below to the failing category.) All twenty-three Haydn pieces passed the profile, while all thirty non-Haydn works (Control Group II and ten compositions in Test Group I) failed (see Chart III).

*DIVERTIMENTOS*

## Chart III. Profile Ia: Results for the Non-Haydn Works

*Control Group II:*

J.C. Bach-13 (f)
J.C.F. Bach-15 (f)
W.F.E. Bach-10 (f)
Boccherini-20 (f)
Boccherini-21 (f)
Cambini-12 (f)
Dittersdorf-13 (f)
Dittersdorf-17 (f)
Förester-15 (f)
M. Haydn-20 (f)

Hofmann-21 (f)
Krommer-20 (f)
L. Mozart-20 (f)
Mozart-21 (f)
Mozart-11 (f)
Peter-15 (f)
Starzer-18 (f)
Toeschi-14 (f)
Tomasini-19 (f)
Vanhal-21 (f)

*Test Group II:*

Asplmayr-21 (f)
Cannabich-22 (f)
Cannabich-22 (f)
Hoffmeister-25 (f)
Holzbauer-19 (f)

Mica-16 (f)
Mozart-9 (f)
Richter-22 (f)
Rosetti-12 (f)
Wendling-18 (f)

Scoring. Checklist: passing 30-34, borderline 26-29, failing below 26. p=pass, b=borderline, f=fail.

I then tested the doubtful works for strings alone or mixed strings and winds against the profile. D22 and G1 passed, while 18, 19, 39, D6, D8, D9, D10, D11, F2, G4, A1, and the flute quartet in C (Hob. Deest.) failed (see Chart IV).

## Chart IV. Profile Ia: Results for the Doubtful Haydn Works

18-25 (f)
19-14 (f)
39-25 (f)
D6-22 (f)
D8-23 (f)

D9-22 (f)
D10-24 (f)
D11-23 (f)
D22-30 (p)
F2-16 (f)

G1-31 (p)
G4-25 (f)
A1-20 (f)
B4-12 (f)
*C-25 (f)

Scoring. Checklist: passing 30-34, borderline 26-29, failing below 26.
*Hob. Deest.

I discovered that Profile Ia could be adapted for wind divertimentos with some deletions and some additions to compensate for the deletions (see Chart V).

*DIVERTIMENTOS*

## Chart V. Profile Ib: Checklist for Fast First Movements

### Positive Traits Appearing in at Least 85% of the Haydn Works

*1. In first measure, melody includes four notes or less and seventh of the scale is not present in the melody during the first two measures. [one point] (Trait given one point because it appears in less than 100% of the Haydn works in Control Group I)

2. a) Texture changes at least three times during the first ten measures, b) a dominant seventh or leading tone chord is present in the first eleven measures, and c) the opening harmony lasts at least a measure. [two points]

*3. a) In the exposition, rest of an eighth but no sixteenth rest, b) bass enters by measure eight, and c) ties over the barline beginning on a downbeat used in some voice. [one point]

4. Movement's final sonority a) lasts no more than two beats, b) uses no more than two real voices, c) has all parts except the bass with the same rhythm, and d) uses bass patterns ♩ , ♪ , ♫♩ , or ♫ . [two points]

5. a) In first five measures, a measure's rhythmic pattern is repeated but at least one measure's pattern is different; b) dotted quarter used in some voice, and c) bass employs at least three different rhythmic values. [two points]

### Negative Traits Appearing in 15% or Less of the Haydn Works

*6. Ties over the barline in the bass, triplets in the bass, or bass range less than an octave in the first eight measures. [one point]

*7. In bass during the exposition, a) no more than two half notes, one dotted half note, three quarter notes (except at the end of the exposition), two unornamented dotted quarters, or two unornamented half notes in a row (all of the above except when all voices have the same rhythm), b) more than four sixteenths in a row except when doubling another voice, or c) in $\frac{3}{8}$ or $\frac{6}{8}$, or more than three ♩♫♩ . [one point]

*8. In main voice, a) more than three unornamented, unsyncopated quar-

## DIVERTIMENTOS

ter notes, two unornamented dotted quarter notes, or two unornamented half notes in a row (all of the above except when all voices have the same rhythm); b) pattern ♫. or ♪. ; c) in $\frac{?}{2}$ or $\frac{?}{4}$, ♫ ♩ ; d) in $\frac{?}{8}$, ♫♪., ♫♫ , or ♫ rest , or e) two sixteenths on the first beat of a measure followed by any value other than another sixteenth. [one point]

9. a) Nondiatonic notes in first two measures; b) chromaticism in main voice or bass during first ten measures; c) first two measures do not contain a disjunct interval; d) first eight measures do not employ repeated notes in the melody; or e) pattern like

♫♫♫ or ♫♫♫ in main voice. [two points]
f e e d      e d d c

10. a) Mannheim sigh during first eight measures; b) in $\frac{6}{8}$ sixteenth value not employed during the exposition; c) in $\frac{3}{8}$, ♫♫♫♫ not used; or d) dissonance on downbeat in first five measures except for pedal in bass. [two points]

11. a) Presence of a pickup; b) first note shorter than an eighth or c) opening bass note ♩., ♩, ♪, ♩., or ♪. in duple meter or longer than a quarter in $\frac{?}{8}$. [two points]

*12. In the main voice during the exposition, a) regular suspension; b) eighths or sixteenths repeated on same note for more than three measures; or c) note tied over the barline in first four measures. [one point]

13. In the exposition, a) in any voice more than six triplets in a row; b) in $\frac{?}{2}$ or $\frac{?}{4}$ does not use a half note in main voice; or, in $\frac{3}{8}$, employs a dotted half in main voice. [two points]

*14. a) At beginning, the same rhythm in all voices but not the same pitches for more than two measures; b) unison-octave passages in all sounding voices for more than three and a half measures or twelve beats (at least three voices, texture remains the same throughout); c) exposition ends with less than four sounding voices; or d) bass does not sound on exposition's final sonority. [one point]

15. a) Range of an octave or less in main voice during first eight measures or b) second part begins with old material in full texture. [two points]

16. In exposition, a) more than fifty-eight consecutive eighths in any voice; b) in $\frac{3}{4}$, more than two consecutive dotted halves in any voice; or c) in $\frac{3}{4}$ or $\frac{4}{4}$, 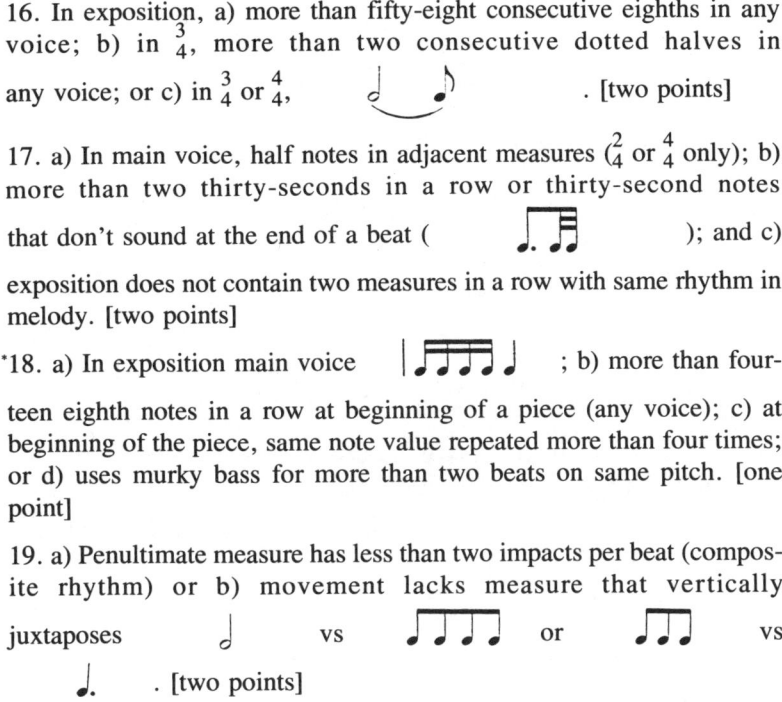 . [two points]

17. a) In main voice, half notes in adjacent measures ($\frac{2}{4}$ or $\frac{4}{4}$ only); b) more than two thirty-seconds in a row or thirty-second notes that don't sound at the end of a beat ( ); and c) exposition does not contain two measures in a row with same rhythm in melody. [two points]

*18. a) In exposition main voice  ; b) more than fourteen eighth notes in a row at beginning of a piece (any voice); c) at beginning of the piece, same note value repeated more than four times; or d) uses murky bass for more than two beats on same pitch. [one point]

19. a) Penultimate measure has less than two impacts per beat (composite rhythm) or b) movement lacks measure that vertically juxtaposes    vs    or    vs   . [two points]

Because the number of items remained the same and because the lowest an authentic wind divertimento scored was 30, I retained the scoring criteria from Profile Ia: passing 30-34, borderline 26-29, and failing below 26. I believe that the new profile is stronger than the old one because of the additions, but the revised profile must still be tested to make certain of this. Ten non-Haydn works in Test Group I failed the profile, with a maximum score of 20( see Chart VI). (The maximum score of a non-Haydn divertimento in Profile Ia was 25.)

### Chart VI. Profile Ib: Results for the Non-Haydn Works

*Test Group I:*
J.C. Bach-20 (f)            Mozart-13 (f)
Beethoven-18 (f)            Mysliveček-15 (f)
Druschetzky-18 (f)          Rosetti-18 (f)
M. Haydn-18 (f)             Sacher-19 (f)
Krommer-20 (f)              Stranensky-19 (f)

Scoring. Checklist: passing 30-34, borderline 26-29, failing below 26.

*DIVERTIMENTOS*

Of the doubtful compositions, D18, D23, and G9/C12 passed, while F12 failed (see Chart VII).

### Chart VII. Profile Ib: Results for the Doubtful Works

D18-30          G9/C12-30 (p)          F12-20 (f)
                D23-31 (p)

Scoring. Checklist: passing 30-34, borderline 26-29, failing below 26.

Profiles IIa and IIb: Minuets

Profile IIa was for minuets without their trios, based on thirty authentic minuets.[13] (Ten movements were withheld to test the profile.)[14] I drew up a checklist with fourteen characteristics, again concentrating on negative traits (Chart VIII).

### Chart VIII. Profile IIa: Checklist for Minuets

#### Positive Traits Appearing in All the Haydn Works

1. a) First full measure has between one and two impacts per beat (composite rhythm) and at least two parts play in this measure, b) at least two different rhythmic patterns in the melody of the first three measures, and c) the third and fourth measures have different rhythmic patterns. 40%

2. a) Final harmony lasts one to four beats, b) last measure has no more than two real voices and employs bass patterns 8-5-3-1, 8-5-1, 1-8-1, 8-1, or 1, c) no pedal involved in final measures, d) a dotted half not employed in the last measure, and e) tritone not present in the melody of the penultimate measure. 50%

3. Opening harmony no more than a measure (four beats if includes pickup) and dominant pedal not present in the first four measures. 50%

---

[13]II:2, 8 (first minuet), 17 (first minuet), 21, 22, 33, 34, 35, 36, 37, 38, and III:1, 2, 3, 4, 6, 7, 8, 10 (second minuet), 12 (second minuet).
[14]II:1, 6, 8 (second minuet), 11, 17 (second minuet), 20, III:10 (first minuet), 12 (first minuet).

## DIVERTIMENTOS

### Negative Traits Appearing in None of the Haydn Works

4. In bass during first part, a) 𝅗𝅥., |𝄽 𝅘𝅥 𝄽 |, ties over the barline, more than one sixteenth at a time, or more than four eighth notes in a row; b) |𝅘𝅥 𝅘𝅥 𝄽 | in consecutive measures or |𝅘𝅥 𝄽 𝄽 in consecutive measures or every other measure; or c) double stops in the bass. 50%

5. In main voice in first part, a) more than two consecutive measures with half notes or dotted half notes, more than eight sixteenths or nine triplets in a row, or thirty-seconds on the second beat of a measure; b) |♪𝄾 ♪𝄾 ♪𝄾 , |♫♫ followed by any value other than a triplet, 𝄽 ♫|♫♫♫, |♫ 𝄽 𝄽 , |♫ 𝅘𝅥 , |𝅘𝅥.♪ , |♫ 𝅘𝅥 ♫ , or |♫ 𝅘𝅥 𝄽 ; or c) less than four different rhythmic values used. 30%

6. a) In first measure melody, more than four sixteenths, four eighths, or three triplets in a row, ♪ on first two beats, |𝅘𝅥 ♫ 𝅘𝅥 , ♫. , ♫ , |𝅘𝅥 ♫♫ , |𝅘𝅥 𝅘𝅥 ♫ , |𝅘𝅥 𝅘𝅥 , pickup other than 𝅘𝅥 , ♫ , or 𝅘𝅥.♪ or value following pickup other than 𝅘𝅥 or ; b) first two measures have patterns |𝅗𝅥 𝅘𝅥 |𝅗𝅥 𝅘𝅥 𝅘𝅥 , |𝅗𝅥 𝅘𝅥 |𝅗𝅥 ♫ , or dotted half followed by triplets; c) first full measure melody begins with third of the scale, 1 followed by tonic triad, 5-1-5, 1-5-1, or two quarter notes that are separated by a second. 50%

7. a) More than four eighth notes in a row in an accompanying voice during the first part, b) triple stops, c) syncopated accompaniment in first part, or d) accompaniment pattern involving eighths or sixteenths repeated more than once. 50%

8. a) In first three measures in bass, an eighth or two consecutive sixteenths (except when doubling all sounding voices); b) in first measure bass, two intervals that are larger than a third, melodic pattern involving 7 other than 1-7-1, involving 6 other than 1-3-6, involving 4 other than 1-4, or patterns 5-1-5, 8-1, or 1-8 without other pitches; c) eighth notes

## DIVERTIMENTOS

in consecutive measures in bass during first part; or d) in accompanying voice in first part, more than four sixteenths in a row or in first four measures in bass [♩ ♩] three times. 50%

9. First three notes in the melody the same or, in main voice during first part, rest on first beat or eighth rest on second beat. 50%

10. a) In main voice during first measure of second part, more than two eighths or sixteenths; b) in first eight measures of second part, more than eleven consecutive eighth notes in an accompanying part; or c) syncopated accompaniment in this part. 50%

11. a) Repeated notes in the melody in each of the first three measures, more than five repeated notes in a row in main voice, or three measures in a row in main voice just repeated notes (a-a-a, b-b-b, c-c-c) or b) note sustained longer than twelve beats in first part. 50%

12. a) In last measure of first part, any voice has more than three notes, melody has more than two or penultimate measure of this part has an accompanying voice containing six eighth notes, tritone present in melody here but not penultimate measure of piece, or b) last five notes of melody quarter notes. 50%

13. a) In melody in first part, [♩. ♫] on the same pitch (except in the first two measures), four sixteenths and an eighth or two eighths and triplets in the same measure, rest [♫♫] or rest [♩. ♪] or b) in first three measures [♩ ♩] [♫♩] , [♫♫♩ ♫♫] , [♩. ♫♫] , or [♩. ♫♫♫] . 50%

14. a) In first ten measures in any voice, [♩. ♫] , [♫♫♫] , [♩♩] , [♩ ♩] or b) in first measures, Mannheim sigh or [♫♩] . 50%

Each trait was valid for all thirty minuets, but 10% or less of the ten Control Group II works. No characteristic warranted weighting. The minimum score of the ten Haydn divertimentos withheld from Control Group I was 12 and the maximum score of the Control Group II compositions was 8, so I designated 12-14 as passing, 11 borderline, and below 11 failing. All thirty-six Haydn works passed the profile; all twenty non-Haydn pieces (Control Group II and Test Group I) failed (see Chart IX).

*DIVERTIMENTOS*

### Chart IX. Profile IIa: Results for the Non-Haydn Works

*Control Group II:*
Boccherini-4 (f)
Dittersdorf-8 (f)
M. Haydn-5 (f)
Hoffstetter-7 (f)
Holzbauer-6 (f)
Krommer-6 (f)
Mozart-8 (f)
Peter-6 (f)
Richter-8 (f)
Vanhal-8 (f)

*Test Group I:*
Albrechtsberger-7 (f)
Asplmayr-10 (f)
J.C. Bach-7 (f)
Boccherini-10 (f)
Förester-9 (f)
M. Haydn-8 (f)
Hoffmeister-10 (f)
Mozart-8 (f)
Pichl-9 (f)
Starzer-10 (f)

Scoring. Checklist: passing 12-14, borderline 11, failing below 11.

Both minuets of G1 and the second minuet of D22 passed, the second minuet of D22 scored borderline, and those of 18, 19, 39, D6, D8, D9, D10, D11, F2, G4, A1, and the flute quartet in C (Hob. Deest.) failed (see Chart X).

### Chart X. Profile IIa: Results for the Doubtful Haydn Works

| | | |
|---|---|---|
| 18-10 (f) | D8-10 (f) | F2-10 (f) |
| 18-9 (f) | D9-10 (f) | G1-12 (p) |
| 19-7 (f) | D10-10 (f) | G1-13 (p) |
| 19-10 (f) | D11-9 (f) | G4-4 (f) |
| 39-9 (f) | D22-12 (p) | A1-9 (f) |
| D6-10 (f) | D22-11 (b) | C-9 (f) |
| | F2-10 (f) | |

Scoring. Checklist: passing 12-14, borderline 11, failing below 11.

Again, the profile for strings or mixed strings and winds could be altered to evaluate the wind divertimentos (see Chart XI).

### Chart XI. Profile IIb: Checklist for Minuets

**Positive Traits Appearing in All the Haydn Works**

1. a) First full measure has at least one but less than two impacts per beat (composite rhythm) and at least two parts play in this measure, b)

## DIVERTIMENTOS

at least two different rhythmic patterns in the melody of the first three measures and the third and fourth measures have different rhythmic patterns, and c) all voices do not have the same rhythm in the first three measures with at least three sounding voices, except for a dotted quarter.

2. a) Final harmony lasts one to four beats, b) last measure has no more than two real voices and employs bass patterns 8-5-3-1, 8-5-1, 1-5-1, 1-8-1, 8-1, or 1, c) a dotted half note not employed in the last measure, and d) tritone not present in the melody of the penultimate measure.

3. Opening harmony no more than a measure (four beats if includes pickup) and dominant pedal not present in the first four measures.

### Negative Traits Appearing in None of the Haydn Works

4. In bass during first part, a) | 𝄽 ♩ 𝄽 |, more than one sixteenth at a time, or more than four eighth notes in a row; b) | ♩ ♩ 𝄽 |, | ♩. 𝄽 ♩ |, or | ♩ 𝄽 ♩ | n consecutive measures or | ♩ 𝄽 𝄽 | in consecutive measures or every other measure; c) double stops; or d) bass has only one rhythmic value and no rests or a measure's rhythmic pattern is repeated more than twice except for just quarters.

5. In main voice during first part, a) more than two consecutive measures with half notes or dotted half notes or more than eight triplets in a row; b) | ♪ 𝄽 ♪ 𝄽 ♪ 𝄽 |, | ♫♫ ♫♫ | followed by any value other than a triplet, 𝄽 ♫ | ♫♫♫♫ |, | ♫ 𝄽 𝄽 |, | ♫♫ ♩ |, | ♩. ♪ ♩ |, | ♫♫ ♩ ♫♫ |, or | ♫♫ ♩ 𝄽 |; or c) less than four different rhythmic values used.

6. a) In first measure melody, more than four sixteenths, four eighths, or three triplets in a row, ♩.♪ on first two beats, | ♩ ♫♫ ♩ |, ♫., ♫♫, | ♩ ♫♫♫ |, | ♩ ♩ ♫ |, | ♩ ♩ |, pickup other than ♩, ♫, or ♫., or value following pickup other than ♩ or ♩.; b) first two measures have patterns | ♩ ♩ | ♩ ♩ |, | ♩ ♩ | ♩ ♫ |, or dotted half fol-

## DIVERTIMENTOS

lowed by triplets; or c) first full measure melody begins with the third of the scale, 1 followed by tonic triad, 5-1-5, 1-5-1, or two quarter notes that are separated by a second.

7. a) More than four eighth notes in a row in an accompanying voice during the first part, b) triple stops, c) syncopated accompaniment in first part, d) accompaniment pattern involving eighths or sixteenths more than once, e) note value sustained longer than seven beats in first part, or f) nondiatonic note in first part other than 7 of V.

8. a) In first three measures in bass, an eighth or two consecutive sixteenths (except when doubling all sounding voices); b) in first measure bass, two intervals that are larger than a third, melodic pattern involving 7 other than 1-7-1, involving 6 other than 1-3-6, involving 4 other than 1-4, or patterns 5-1-5, 8-1, or 1-8 without other pitches; c) eighth notes in consecutive measures in bass during first part; d) in accompanying voice in first part, more than four sixteenths in a row or in first measure bass | ♩ ♩ | three times; or e) in bass during penultimate measure, 6 or 7 or 2 other than followed by 5 or more than three notes.

9. a) First three notes in melody the same; b) in main voice during the first part, rest on first beat or eighth rest on second beat, or c) rest in first part that is shorter than an eighth.

10. a) In main voice during first measure of the second part, more than two eighths or sixteenths; b) in first eight measures of second part, more than eleven consecutive eighth notes in an accompanying part; or c) syncopated accompaniment in this part.

11. Repeated notes in the melody in each of the first three measures, more than five repeated notes in a row in main voice, or three measures in a row in main voice just repeated notes (a-a-a, d-d-d, e-e-e).

12. a) In last measure of first part, any voice has more than three notes, melody has more than two, or bass rests on first beat, b) penultimate measure of the first part has an accompanying voice containing six eighth notes, tritone present in melody here but not in penultimate measure of the piece, or last five notes of melody quarter notes.

13. a) In melody in first part, ♩.♪ on the same pitch (except in the first two measures), four sixteenths and an eighth or two eighths and triplets in the same measure, rest ♪♪♪| or rest ♩. ♪| ; b) in first three measures, |♪♪ ♩ ♪♪ ,

## DIVERTIMENTOS

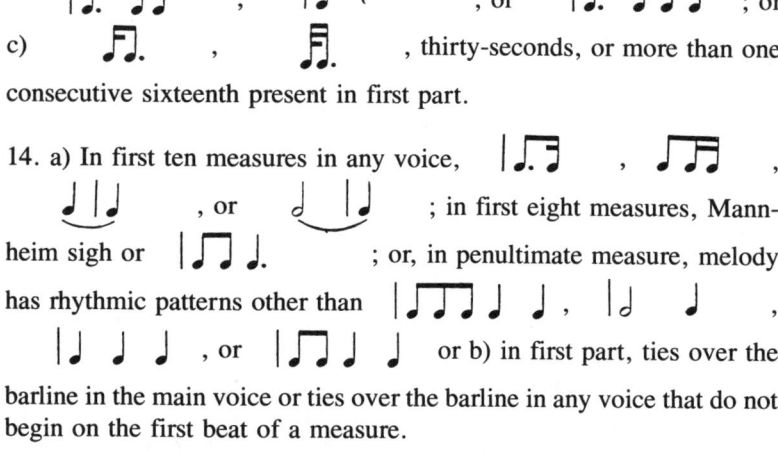

c) ♫. , ♫. , thirty-seconds, or more than one consecutive sixteenth present in first part.

14. a) In first ten measures in any voice, |♩.♫ , ♫♫ , ♩|♩ , or ♩|♩ ; in first eight measures, Mannheim sigh or |♫♩. ; or, in penultimate measure, melody has rhythmic patterns other than |♫♫♩ ♩ , |♩ ♩ , |♩ ♩ ♩ , or |♫♩ ♩ or b) in first part, ties over the barline in the main voice or ties over the barline in any voice that do not begin on the first beat of a measure.

I tested the revised profile (IIb) with ten non-Haydn works (Test Group I), with a maximum score of 9 (see Chart XII). (The maximum non-Haydn score of Profile IIa was 10.) Because the minimum score of the authentic wind divertimentos was again 12, I retained the scoring of Profile IIa (12-14 passing, 11 borderline, 10 and below failing.)

### Chart XII. Profile IIb: Results for the Non-Haydn Works

*Test Group I:*
J.C. Bach-7 (f)          Kammel-6 (f)
Dittersdorf-9 (f)        Krommer-9 (f)
Druschetzky-7 (f)        Masek-7 (f)
F.X. Dusek-7 (f)         Mozart-7 (f)
Hoffmeister-8 (f)        Schenk-9 (f)

Scoring. Checklist: passing 12-14, borderline 11, failing below 11.

Both minuets of D18 and G9/C12 and the single minuet of D23 passed, while both minuets of F12 failed (see Chart XIII). The results of Profiles IIa and IIb correspond to those of Profiles Ia and Ib.

### Chart XIII. Profile IIb: Results for the Doubtful Works

D18-13 (p)        D23-13 (p)          F12-8 (f)
D18-14 (p)        G9/C12-12 (p)       F12-7 (f)
                  G9/C12-13 (p)

*DIVERTIMENTOS*

Scoring. Checklist: passing 12-14, borderline 11, failing below 11. Note: when the same work is listed twice, the first indicates the work's first minuet; the second, the work's second minuet.

## SUMMARY OF CONCLUSIONS FOR THE DOUBTFUL DIVERTIMENTOS

### *II:G1*

Profiles. I:A, First Minuet:A, Second Minuet:A
Documentary evidence: several good, early manuscripts; in *Breitkopf Catalogue*
Experts' opinions: very probably authentic

Although G1 does not appear in the *Entwurf-Katalog* or *Haydn Verzeichnis* and does not survive in autograph, the existence of several good, early sources, including ones in Lambach Abbey, the Pachta Archives (now in the National Museum Prague), and the archives of the Counts von Clam Gallas, has led most Haydn scholars to accept the work as authentic. The systematic tests support the work's genuineness; the three movements tested passed the profiles. In addition, the other movements are typical of Haydn. Because of instrumentation and general stylistic factors, this divertimento should be grouped with II:9 and 20.

Conclusion: Authentic.

### *II:D22*

Profiles. I:A, First Minuet:A, Second Minuet:B
Documentary evidence: unicum
Experts' opinions: general consensus—probably authentic

Robbins Landon discovered the sole source for this work in Prague in 1959. The manuscript had been copied for Count Christian Clam Gallas and was formerly in Friedland Castle. Despite the lack of solid documentary evidence, the Haydn scholars who have commented on this divertimento consider it probably genuine. The opening movement and first minuet passed the profiles, while the second minuet scored borderline. (The second minuet still scored higher than any non-Haydn piece.) In addition, the fourth movement (second minuet) contains the post horn call also found in Haydn's Symphony No. 31 (see Example 1).

**Example 1a. Posthorn Call from II: D22/IV**

**1b. I: 31/I**

Conclusion: Authentic.

The Authentic Wind Divertimentos

### II:D18

Profiles. I:A, First Minuet:A, Second Minuet:A
Documentary evidence: a few early sources and the *Göttweig Catalogue*
Experts' opinions: general consensus—probably authentic

### II:G9/C12

Profile. I:A, First Minuet:A, Second Minuet:A
Documentary evidence: two early sources
Experts' opinions: general consensus—probably authentic

### II:D23

Profiles. I:A, Minuet:A
Documentary evidence: one early manuscript
Experts' opinions: general consensus—probably authentic, but not as strong as for the other two works

Haydn was exposed to Bohemian wind band music when he worked for Count Morzin in Lukavec. Five definitely authentic wind divertimentos are extant (II:3, 7, 14, 15, and 23), while at least four other authentic works are lost (II:4, 5, 12, 20bis). Of the large number of other wind divertimentos that are attributed to Haydn, three are usually considered probably authentic: D18, D23, and G9/C12.

D18 exists in three sources: 1) in Kroměříž, 2) in Melk, and 3) formerly in Göttweig, and it is entered in the *Göttweig Catalogue*. The three movements tested passed the profiles, and the composition may be considered authentic.

G9/C12 survives in two versions: one in the Clam Gallas Archives in Prague in G and one in Kroměříž in C. Landon believes that the piece was originally in G.[15] He conjectures that someone transposed the G version to C because of the "fearfully high horns." He adds that such parts are not unusual for Haydn, citing II:3, which is also in G. The three movements of G9/C12 that were tested against the profiles passed, and the composition is genuine.

D23 survives in only one source, a manuscript in the Clam Gallas Archives in Prague. Landon accepts it as authentic, while Feder marks it as "?authentic." Both the first movement and minuet fit the profiles, and, like D18 and G9/C12, D23 may be included among Haydn's genuine wind band works.

Conclusion: D18, D23, and G9/C12 authentic.

Other Wind Divertimentos Attributed to Haydn

## II:F12

Profile. I:C, First Minuet:C, Second Minuet:C
Documentary evidence: unicum
Experts' opinions: probably not authentic

Most of the other wind band divertimentos ascribed to Haydn (including several that are recorded) have been attributed to other composers or are so weakly supported from a documentary viewpoint and are so stylistically inconsistent that there is little possibility that any are authentic.[16] Only F12, existing as a unicum in Kroměříž, is listed among the selected doubtful and spurious compositions in Feder's worklist. All three of the movements from F12 that were evaluated

---

[15]Landon, *Haydn: The Early Years*, 270.
[16]The six Feldparthien (II:41-46) lie outside of the time period of this study. Most Haydn scholars regard them as spurious. A systematic stylistic study of these Feldparthien is virtually impossible because there are no comparable contemporary works.

## DIVERTIMENTOS

against the profiles failed, and this work too may be labeled as spurious.

Conclusion: Not authentic.

The Flute Quartets in Hummel's Op. 5

### II:D9

Profiles. I:C, Minuet:C
Documentary evidence: weak
Experts' opinions: general consensus—probably not authentic

### II:D10

Profiles. I:C, Minuet:C
Documentary evidence and experts' opinions: same as D9

### II:D11

Profiles. I:C, Minuet:C
Documentary evidence and experts' opinions: same as D9

### II:G4

Profiles. I:C, Minuet:C
Documentary evidence and experts' opinions: same as D9

Around 1767, the publisher Hummel of Amsterdam issued a set of six flute quartets under Haydn's name. Two of the compositions are factitious arrangements of authentic Haydn works (II:1 and 11), while the four other pieces—D8, D9, D10, D11, and G4—exist only in this instrumentation. Like the op. 3 string quartets, these flute quartets do not survive in any contemporary manuscript sources; all extant sources derive from the Hummel print. Because of the source situation, modern Haydn scholars have labeled these flute quartets as probably spurious.[17]

Listening to recordings of these quartets leads me to conclude that they are very attractive works, but not by Haydn. This was confirmed

---

[17]In 1933, C. S. Smith wrote an article on Haydn's flute music in which he considered the flute quartets authentic on stylistic grounds. Smith, "Haydn's Chamber Music and the Flute," 435-40. In the 1930s before Larsen's study, many works that contained false attributions to Haydn were regarded as genuine.

by the systematic tests: all the movements from D9, D10, D11, and G4 that were tested failed the profiles.

Conclusion: D9, D10, D11, and G4 spurious.

Other Works for Flute and Strings Attributed to Haydn

### II:D6

Profiles. I:C, Minuet:C
Documentary evidence: also attributed to L. Hofmann
Experts' opinions: probably by Hofmann

### II:D8

Profiles. I:C, Minuet:C
Documentary evidence: weak
Experts' opinions: probably not authentic

The Flute Quartet in C (Hob. Deest.)

Profiles. I:C, Minuet:C
Documentary evidence: weak
Experts' opinions: probably not authentic

I examined three more works for flute and strings in this study: D6, D8, and the flute quartet in C (Hob. Deest.). Landon and Feder include D8 in their lists of doubtful and spurious compositions without comment; Feder marks D6 as "probably by L. Hofmann," and the only mention of the flute quartet in C is in Feder's worklist. All three works are spurious; the first movement and the minuet of each divertimento failed the profiles.

Conclusion: D6, D8, and the flute quartet in C—spurious.

### II:18 and 19

### II:18

Profiles. I:C, First Minuet:C, Second Minuet:C
Documentary evidence: in *Haydn Verzeichnis*; attributed to Vanhal in only source
Experts' opinions: probably by Vanhal

## DIVERTIMENTOS

### II:19

Profiles. I:C, First Minuet:C, Second Minuet:C
Documentary evidence: in *Haydn Verzeichnis*; attributed to Vanhal in three manuscripts
Experts' opinions: probably by Vanhal

II:18 and 19 are among the spurious works that are entered in the *Haydn Verzeichnis*. The manuscript sources for these divertimentos (one for 18 and three for 19) attribute the two compositions to Vanhal, and modern Haydn scholars generally accept these attributions. My systematic examination of both pieces supports the conclusion that they were not written by Haydn.

Conclusion: 18 and 19—spurious, probably by Vanhal.

### II:39

Profiles. I:C, Minuet:C
Documentary evidence: numerous prints and several catalogue entries
Experts' opinions: general consensus—no; Landon—"genuine?"

The well known "Echo Divertimento" II:39 is usually included among Haydn's dubious compositions. It is presented under Haydn's name in several catalogues, including the *Breitkopf Catalogue* (1767), the *Sarasin Catalogue*, and the *Sigmaringen Catalogue*, and it exists in several eighteenth century prints. However, there are no extant contemporary manuscripts and the earliest known print is from the 1790s.

Both of the movements studied failed the profiles. One could argue that the special character of the work (the use of echo effects) might have made these movements fail the tests, but after a careful examination of the entire divertimento, I believe that there is little possibility that it is by Haydn.

Conclusion: Spurious.

### II:F2

Profiles. I:C, First Minuet:C, Second Minuet:C
Documentary evidence: weak
Experts' opinions: probably spurious

## DIVERTIMENTOS

A very weakly supported divertimento from a documentary viewpoint, F2 is generally thought to be spurious. Three movements failed the profiles, and the work is not authentic.

Conclusion: Spurious.

### II:A1

Profiles. I:C, Minuet:C
Documentary evidence: unicum, listed in the *Göttweig Catalogue*
Experts' opinions: Landon considers it authentic

Robbins Landon discovered the sole source of A1, manuscript parts from Raigern Abbey, in Bruno.[18] He writes that he realized at once that the work was by Haydn; he had known the incipit from the *Göttweig Catalogue*. He concluded that the piece was an early composition, possibly "the earliest surviving piece of chamber music by Haydn, 'warts and all.' "

Despite Landon's opinion, the documentary evidence supporting A1's authenticity is weak. As Landon relates, its only source is full of copying errors and also contains schoolboy mistakes in the partwriting. Furthermore, the *Göttweig Catalogue* is not a reliable witness for Haydn authenticity; it contains many misattributions to Haydn, including among the divertimentos II:G7, III:D3, D4, E-flat7, and E2. Moreover, no other Haydn expert mentions this work as being even possibly authentic.

My stylistic tests indicate that A1 is spurious; the two movements tested did not fit the profiles. While the slight possibility exists that A1 might have failed because it was an early work, other early compositions have passed the profiles in other genres. For example, I believe that the string trio V:C4 is one of the earliest if not the earliest of Haydn's string trios and that it is much earlier than any of the eighteen authentic trios that were used in drawing up the profiles. Yet, it scored higher on the checklist for fast first movements than any other doubtful and several previously-authenticated trios. A1 is probably by a contemporary of Haydn working in Austria or Bohemia who wrote in a similar style.

Conclusion: Spurious.

---

[18]Landon, *Haydn: The Early Years*, 180.

# DIVERTIMENTOS

## II:B4

Profiles. I:C

Documentary evidence: weak, including conflicting attributions to C. F. Abel and J. C. Bach

Experts' opinions: probably spurious

According to Arnold Dolmetsch, Auguste Tolbecque had made a copy of this divertimento from Haydn's autograph.[19] Nevertheless, neither of the work's two movements could be seriously confused for a composition by Haydn. It has also been attributed to C. F. Abel and J. C. Bach, both of whom wrote gamba music.

Conclusion: Spurious

---

[19]Arnold Dolmetsch, "Preface," *Divertissement pour Hautbois, Violin, Viola da Gamba et Basse par Joseph Haydn* (London: Oxford University Press, 1929). Dolmetsch gives no source for Tolbecque's "autograph." Apparently, Tolbecque mistook a copyist's manuscript for a Haydn autograph.

CHAPTER NINE

# Concertos

INTRODUCTION

Most of Haydn's extant, previous-authenticated concertos date from before 1770. These include two violin concertos (VIIa:1 and 3), a cello concerto (VIIb:1), a horn concerto (VIId:3), a concerto for violin and keyboard (XVIII:6), and four keyboard concertos (XVIII:1, 2, 3, and 4). All of these concertos, except the horn concerto, are authenticated by the *Entwurf-Katalog*; the horn concerto survives in autograph. Among Haydn's later authentic concertos are the second cello concerto (VIIb:2), the trumpet concerto (VIIe:1), the D major keyboard concerto (XVIII:11), and five concertos for two lire organizzata (VIIh:1-5), which seem more like divertimentos than concertos. Finally, several authentic works that are listed in the *Entwurf-Katalog*, the *Haydn Verzeichnis*, or other primary sources are lost, including a violin concerto (VIIa:2), a cello concerto (VIIb:3),[1], a violine concerto (VIIc:1), two baryton concertos (XIII:1 and 2), a flute concerto (VIIf:1), a bassoon concerto, a horn concerto (VIId:1), and a concerto for two horns (VIId:2).[2]

[1]This concerto might be the same as VIIb:1; the incipits are similar (almost a variation of one upon the other), and the *Entwurf-Katalog* does occasionally list the same work twice.
[2]Two spurious concertos should be mentioned because they are still performed and recorded under Haydn's name. Although Haydn did write a flute concerto in D (lost), it is not the same as the extant flute concerto listed in the *Breitkopf Catalogue* of 1771. This concerto is by Leopold Hofmann. The very fine oboe concerto (VIIg:C1), although lacking a conflicting attribution, is definitely not by Haydn, a conclusion that is easily reached on a single hearing. Haydn's name was added to the sole surviving manuscript in Zittau. Landon believes that it is in the style of the Bohemians. Landon, *Haydn: The Early Years*, 519.

## CONCERTOS

Most of the authenticity problems in Haydn's concertos concern the keyboard works. In addition to the four definitely authentic keyboard concertos listed above, eight doubtful keyboard concertos are extant (XVIII:5, 7, 8, 9, 10, E-flat1, F3, and G1). Four of these pieces have conflicting attributions: 5 and 7 to Wagenseil, 8 to Leopold Hofmann, and F3 to Johann Georg Lang and Johann Stamitz. 5 and 8 are probably listed in the *Entwurf-Katalog*; two keyboard concertos are recorded there without incipits. Both concertos survive in three manuscripts. The first and third movements of 7 are later versions of the keyboard trio XV:40. 9, 10, E-flat1, and G1 survive as unicum, while F3 exists in three sources with three different attributions. Finally, 5, 7, 8, 9, and 10 are entered in the *Breitkopf Catalogue* under Haydn's name, while 9 is also in the catalogue of the Schloss Zeil with a Haydn attribution.[3]

Feder believes that concertos 3, 4, and 11 are for harpsichord, while the remainder of those concertos he considers authentic (1, 2, 5, 8, and 10) are for organ based on the range of their solo parts.[4] Larsen prefers to say that "3, 4, and 11 are definitely not organ concertos, whereas the other concertos were composed to fit both instruments."[5]

In *Grove*, Feder marks 5, 8, and 10 as "probably authentic," 7 and 9 as "doubtful," E-flat1 and G1 as "probably not authentic," and F3 as "probably by Lang."[6] Larsen lists 5, 7, 8, 9, and 10 as probably authentic and considers the remainder spurious.[7] Landon regards 5, 10, and, apparently, 8 as authentic, but he is uncertain about 9 and says that 7 is probably an arrangement of XV:40.[8] For 8, he declares that the attribution to Hofmann is not far-fetched since Hofmann wrote a number of keyboard concertos and his style was similar to Haydn's. Concerning 9, he believes that 1767 is early for a falsification of a Haydn concerto, but with the lack of documentary evidence he does not wish to assert the work's authenticity on style alone. He seems to regard the remainder of the concertos attributed to Haydn (including

---

[3]*Breitkopf Catalogue*, 134, 254, 193, 431 and Landon, *Haydn: The Early Years*, 521.
[4]Georg Feder, "Wieviel Orgelkonzerte hat Haydn geschrieben?" *Die Musik Forschung* XXIII/4 (1970) 440-444. If 7 and 9 were authentic Haydn concertos, they would be organ concertos, based on Feder's criteria.
[5]Larsen, *Three Haydn Catalogues*, xix.
[6]Feder, *The New Grove Haydn*, 178-80.
[7]Larsen, *Three Haydn Catalogues*, xix. As mentioned in chapter four, Larsen includes XIV:11, 12, and 13 among the organ concertos rather than the keyboard ensemble divertimentos.
[8]Landon, *Haydn: The Early Years*, 196-218, 261, 521.

E-flat1, F3, and G1) as spurious.⁹ In sum, the three scholars agree that 5, 8, and 10 are probably authentic and that E-flat1, F3, and G1 are probably spurious, but they disagree about the authenticity of 7 and 9.

Only two nonkeyboard concertos are considered in this chapter: the Violin Concerto in D (VIId:4) and the Horn Concerto in D (VIId:4). Although it lacks good documentary evidence supporting its authenticity, VIIa:4 is usually considered genuine by Haydn scholars. Feder accepts it as authentic in *Grove*, Landon states that "there are just enough elements of Haydn's early style in all three movements to allow it to remain in the list of genuine early works," and Larsen labels it probably authentic.[10] Other than a manuscript in the Gesellschaft der Musikfreunde in Vienna and a set of parts formerly in the Breitkopf and Härtel archives, its major documentary claim to genuineness is an entry in the *Breitkopf Catalogue* of 1769, where it is entered beside VIIa:1.[11] Obviously, those who have accepted the work's authenticity do so primarily on stylistic grounds.

In contrast to VIIa:4, the horn concerto VIId:4 is generally regarded as spurious by most Haydn scholars. Paul R. Bryan, in an article on the treatment of the horn in the works of Mozart and Haydn, declares that the range and technical demands of the solo part are different from that of authentic compositions.[12] On the other hand, Landon does not rule out the slight possibility that the concerto is genuine, although he views Michael Haydn as a more likely candidate.[13] The only eighteenth century copy of this concerto is from Zittau, and the work appears in the *Breitkopf Catalogue* of 1781.[14] From a stylistic standpoint, this citation in the *Breitkopf Catalogue* is well after the time that Haydn could have written the concerto.

## THE TESTS

To insure a large group of previously-authenticated works for the profile, I used all the early authentic concertos regardless of solo in-

---

[9]Landon, *op. cit.*, 521-22.
[10]Feder, *The New Grove Haydn*, 156; Landon, *Haydn: The Early Years*, 518; and Larsen, *Three Haydn Catalogues*, xxiv.
[11]*Breitkopf Catalogue*, 354.
[12]Paul R. Bryan, "The Horn in the Works of Mozart and Haydn: Some Observations and Comparisons," *Haydn Yearbook* IX (1975) 202-03.
[13]Landon, *Haydn: The Early Years*, 519.
[14]*Breitkopf Catalogue*, 132.

strumentation. I examined tutti sections to avoid differences among solo instruments.

Profile I: First Movements Opening Tuttis

In the first profile, I employed the opening tuttis of first movements from nine authentic concertos (VIIa:1 and 3, VIIb:1, VIId:3, and XVIII:1, 2, 3, 4, 6). In Test I, the ranges were harmonic change per beat .400-.680 (borderline .040) and textural change per beat .166-.256 (borderline .020). Twelve traits formed the checklist in Test II (see Chart I). Only trait 6, which appeared in 70% of the ten non-Haydn works in Control Group II, was weighted abnormally with a half point. 9.5-11.5 was passing, 8.5-9 borderline, and below 8.5 failing, based on the second set of scoring criteria in chapter two. Twenty non-Haydn works in Control Group II and Test Group I failed the profile (Chart II).

## Chart I. Profile I: Checklist for First Movement Opening Tuttis
### Positive Traits Appearing in All the Haydn Works

1. a) All parts play in the first full measure, b) opening harmony lasts no longer than two measures, and c) at least three different rhythmic patterns in the first four measures, with the second and third and second and fourth measures having different patterns. 30% (trait appears in 30% of the non-Haydn works)

2. Texture at the end of the first tutti one real voice and final harmony two or three beats. 20%

3. a) Texture changes at least three times in the first ten measures, b) pattern in the bass changes by the fifth measure, and c) dominant seventh appears in the first seven measures. 50%

4. a) Range in first violin during the first eight measures at least an octave and a sixth, b) bass attains a middle c, c) bass range of at least an octave in the first five measures, and d) the violins separated by at least an octave and a fifth at some point. 20%

5. a) At least four different rhythmic values used in the melody during the first five measures (including ornaments), b) dominant appears in two different octaves in first violin during first four measures, c) a sixteenth note appears in the first violin during the first seven measures,

## CONCERTOS

and d) both conjunct and disjunct intervals in the melody by the end of measure three. 30%

*6. At least 85% of the measures contain a value of an eighth or shorter and at least 12% of the measures have three real voices. 70%: one half point

### Negative Traits Appearing in None of the Haydn Works

7. In first violin, a) more than four quarters or one unornamented half note in a row or b) 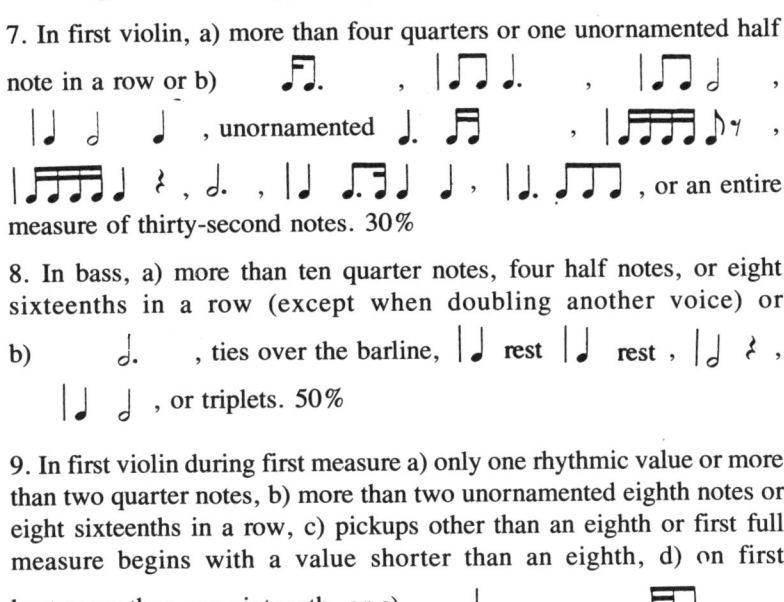, or an entire measure of thirty-second notes. 30%

8. In bass, a) more than ten quarter notes, four half notes, or eight sixteenths in a row (except when doubling another voice) or b) 𝅗𝅥., ties over the barline, |𝅗𝅥 rest |𝅗𝅥 rest , |𝅗𝅥 𝄾 , |𝅗𝅥 𝅗𝅥 , or triplets. 50%

9. In first violin during first measure a) only one rhythmic value or more than two quarter notes, b) more than two unornamented eighth notes or eight sixteenths in a row, c) pickups other than an eighth or first full measure begins with a value shorter than an eighth, d) on first beat more than one sixteenth, or e) 𝅗𝅥. , ♫♩ , ♩.♪ , ♫♫ , or |♩.♫ . 20%

10. a) Uses a nondiatonic note in the first four measures, b) first three pitches in the first violin the same, c) first interval (other than after a pickup) a perfect fourth, or d) employs exact rhythmic doubling between the two violins for the first eight measures. 50%

11. a) Rest of two measures or longer in any string part, b) simultaneous rest of the same value in all parts during the first fourteen measures, c) a whole note in the strings, or d) last two notes in the melody during the first measure the same. 40%

12. a) Note sustained longer than eight beats in any voice, b) more than six consecutive notes on the same pitch in the first violin, c) figure like ♬♬ or ♬♬ in the first violin, or d) more
   f e e d        g f f e
than twelve eighth notes in a row in any voice at the beginning. 40%

## Chart II. Profile I: Results for the Non-Haydn Works

| Composer | Test I-Ranges | | Test II | Results | |
|---|---|---|---|---|---|
| | HC/B | TC/B | Ch | R-Ch-Conc. | |
| *Control Group II:* | | | | | |
| Albrechtsberger | .645 | .191 | 6.5 | p-f | C |
| C.P.E. Bach | .356 | .082 | 4.5 | f-f | C |
| J.C. Bach | .405 | .109 | 5.5 | f-f | C |
| Boccherini | .432 | .125 | 4 | f-f | C |
| Cimarosa | .555 | .108 | 5.5 | f-f | C |
| Devienne | .315 | .136 | 2 | f-f | C |
| Dittersdorf | .425 | .086 | 1.5 | f-f | C |
| J.G. Graun | .650 | .125 | 6 | f-f | C |
| Krommer | .357 | .108 | 1.5 | f-f | C |
| Wagenseil | .334 | .168 | 3.5 | f-f | C |
| *Test Group II:* | | | | | |
| J. Benda | .513 | .076 | 3 | f-f | C |
| Brixi | .446 | .138 | 2 | f-f | C |
| M. Haydn | .456 | .123 | 3 | f-f | C |
| Kraus | .392 | .096 | 3.5 | f-f | C |
| Mestrino | .438 | .215 | 3.5 | p-f | C |
| Mozart | .435 | .126 | 2.5 | f-f | C |
| J.F. Reichardt | .657 | .088 | 5.5 | f-f | C |
| Schobert | .416 | .156 | 3.5 | b-f | C |
| K. Stamitz | .348 | .106 | 2.5 | f-f | C |
| Viotti | .334 | .186 | 5.5 | f-f | C |

Scoring. Test I: HC/B .400-.680 (borderline .040), TC/B .166-.256 (borderline .020); Test II: passing 9.5-11.5, borderline 8.5-9, failing below 8.5.

HC/B=harmonic change per beat, TC/B=textural change per beat, Ch=checklist, R=ranges, Conc.=conclusion, A=passes profile, B=results inconclusive, C=failed profile, p=pass, f=fail.

Of the ten doubtful works tested, VIIa:4 and XVIII:5, 8, and 10 fit the profile, and VIId:4 and XVIII:7, 9, E-flat1, F3 and G1 did not (see Chart III).

## Chart III. Profile I: Results for the Doubtful Works

| Work | Test I-Ranges | | Test II | Results | |
|---|---|---|---|---|---|
| | HC/B | TC/B | Ch | R-Ch-Conc. | |
| VIIa:4 | .665 | .175 | 10.5 | p-p | A |
| VIId:4 | .517 | .147 | 8 | b-f | C |
| XVIII:5 | .557 | .176 | 10.5 | p-p | A |
| XVIII:7 | .710 | .344 | 7.5 | f-f | C |
| XVIII:8 | .400 | .187 | 9.5 | p-p | A |
| XVIII:9 | .560 | .213 | 4.5 | p-f | C |
| XVIII:10 | .675 | .175 | 10.5 | p-p | A |
| XVIII:E-flat1 | .243 | .095 | 6.5 | f-f | C |
| XVIII:F3 | .366 | .116 | 6.5 | f-f | C |
| XVIII:G1 | .401 | .111 | 6 | f-f | C |

Scoring. Test I: HC/B .400-.680 (borderline .040), TC/B .166-.256 (borderline .020); Test II: passing 9.5-11.5, borderline 8.5-9, failing below 8.5.

Profile II: Slow Movements Opening Tuttis

The only other portion of a movement that seemed comparable among a large number of concertos was the opening tutti of slow movements. I required that the minimum length of such a section be seventeen beats. Because of the differing lengths of these opening tuttis, only the checklist could be used. I drew up a checklist with twelve items based on eight authentic concertos (the slow movement of VIIa:1 lacks an opening tutti) (see Chart IV). 10-12 was passing, 9 borderline, and below 9 failing, again, employing the second set of scoring criteria in Chapter Three. Twenty non-Haydn concertos (Control Group II and Test Group I) failed the checklist (see Chart V).

## Chart IV. Profile II: Checklist for Second Movement Opening Tuttis

### Positive Traits Appearing in All the Haydn Works

1. a) In first violin during first four measures, at least three different rhythmic patterns, with first and third measures and third and fourth measures having different rhythms, b) first measure employs at least two real voices, and c) first note in the melody the first or fifth of the scale. 60%

2. a) Texture changes during first six measures, b) three real voices used at some point in first tutti, and c) dominant seventh or seventh resolving to tonic present in first three measures. 30%

3. a) In first violin during first four measures, range of at least an octave and a third, b) both conjunct and disjunct intervals used in first three measures melody, and c) there is a dissonance present on the downbeat of a measure during the first six measures (including perfect fourths with the bass). 30%

4. a) In first twelve measures, there is at least one measure where the viola and bass are not rhythmically doubled and b) value of a sixteenth or shorter used in the melody of the first five measures. 40%

### Negative Traits Appearing in None of the Haydn Works

5. In first violin, a) more than one half, two unsyncopated, unornamented quarters, or eight eighth notes in a row or b)

, eighth-note triplets,

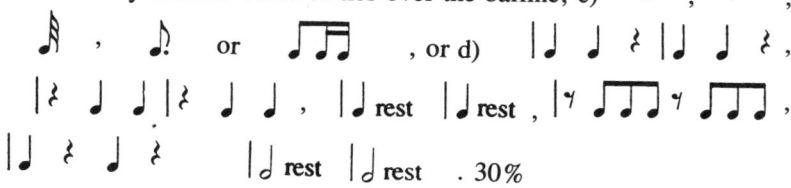, or a Mannheim sigh. 30%

6. In bass, a) two or more half notes in a row, b) sixteenths that are not doubled by another voice or ties over the barline, c) 𝅗𝅥 , 𝅗𝅥. , 𝅘𝅥𝅮 , 𝅘𝅥𝅮. or 𝅘𝅥𝅯𝅘𝅥𝅯 , or d) | 𝅘𝅥 𝅘𝅥 𝄽 | 𝅘𝅥 𝅘𝅥 𝄽 , | 𝄽 𝅘𝅥 𝅘𝅥 | 𝄽 𝅘𝅥 𝅘𝅥 , | 𝅗𝅥 rest | 𝅗𝅥 rest , |𝄼 𝅘𝅥𝅯𝅘𝅥𝅯𝅘𝅥𝅯 𝄼 𝅘𝅥𝅯𝅘𝅥𝅯𝅘𝅥𝅯 , | 𝅘𝅥 𝄽 𝅘𝅥 𝄽 | 𝅗𝅥 rest | 𝅗𝅥 rest . 30%

7. a) Nondiatonic notes in first two measures or melodic chromaticism in first four or b) more than four eighth notes in a row in an inner voice at the beginning. 40%

8. Rest of a measure or longer in any part after the beginning or simultaneous rest of the same value in all voices during the first eleven measures. 20%

9. a) Bass in first measure includes only one pitch without rests (except constant eighths), b) first two notes in the melody the same pitch, c) three repeated notes in a row in first measure melody, or d) triple stops used. 40%

# CONCERTOS

10. Opening harmony lasts longer than a measure or only one real voice for more than three beats. 30%

11. In first measure melody, a) presence of half note, syncopated quarter note, 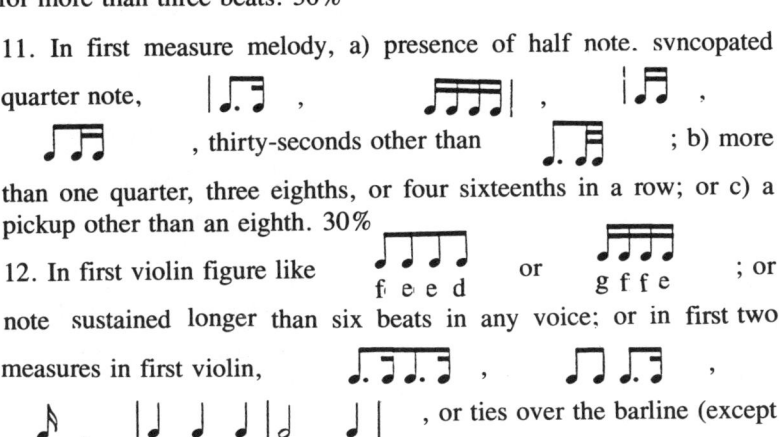, thirty-seconds other than ; b) more than one quarter, three eighths, or four sixteenths in a row; or c) a pickup other than an eighth. 30%

12. In first violin figure like f e e d or g f f e ; or note sustained longer than six beats in any voice; or in first two measures in first violin, , or ties over the barline (except those beginning on a downbeat). 30%

### Chart V. Profile II: Results for the Non-Haydn Works

*Control Group II:*
Albrechtsberger-3 (f)
C.P.E. Bach-5 (f)
J.C. Bach-1 (f)
Boccherini-5 (f)
Cimarosa-3 (f)
Devienne-5 (f)
Dittersdorf-5 (f)
J.G. Graun-4 (f)
Krommer-5 (f)
Wagenseil-7 (f)

*Test Group I:*
J. Benda-7 (f)
Brixi-8 (f)
Dittersdorf-4 (f)
M. Haydn-8 (f)
Kraus-6 (f)
Mozart-5 (f)
Reichardt-4 (f)
Schobert-5 (f)
K. Stamitz-5 (f)
Viotti-6 (f)

Scoring. Checklist: passing 10-12, borderline 9, failing below 9.

VIIa:4 passed the checklist, while VIId:4, XVIII:9, and XVIII:E-flat1 failed (see Chart VI). (The remainder of the concertos did not contain a slow movement, opening tutti.) These results agree with those of Profile I.

### Chart VI. Profile II: Results for the Doubtful Concertos

VIIa:4-10 (p)         XVIII:9-6 (f)
VIId:4-5 (f)          XVIII:E-flat1-7 (f)

Scoring. Checklist: passing 10-12, borderline 9, failing below 9.

## CONCERTOS

## SUMMARY OF CONCLUSIONS
## FOR THE DOUBTFUL CONCERTOS

### *VIIa:4*

Profiles. I:A, II:A
Documentary evidence: two manuscripts, listed in *Breitkopf*
Experts' opinions: authentic

Despite weak documentary support, modern Haydn experts consider the Violin Concerto in G (VIIa:4) as very probably authentic. My stylistic tests support the work's authenticity; it passed both profiles, and none of the three movements contain any stylistic traits that are not typical of Haydn.

Conclusion: Authentic.

### *VIId:4*

Profiles. I:C, II:C
Documentary evidence: unicum, listed in *Breitkopf*
Experts' opinions: General consensus—not authentic

Most Haydn experts regard this horn concerto as spurious, although Landon does not want to rule out the slight possibility that it might be by Haydn. Paul R. Bryan believes that the treatment of the solo horn in VIId:4 differs from that of authentic works. Both of the movements tested failed the profiles.

Conclusion: Spurious.

### *XVIII:5*

Profiles. I:A
Documentary evidence: possibly listed in the *Entwurf-Katalog* without incipit
Experts' opinions: probably authentic

XVIII:5 is probably one of the two keyboard concertos referred to in the *Entwurf-Katalog* without incipits. A set of parts in the Burgerländisches Landsmuseum in Eisenstadt originally had Haydn's name, but Wagenseil's name was later substituted. Two other manuscripts, however, contain Haydn attributions. Based on a systematic examination of the first movement and general stylistic examination of the other two movements, I consider XVIII:5 genuine.

Conclusion: Authentic.

## XVIII:7

Profiles. I:C
Documentary evidence: listed in *Breitkopf*, partially based on XV:40, conflicting attribution to Wagenseil
Experts' opinions: mixed

XVIII:7 is an extremely problematic work as regards its authenticity. Its first and third movements are obviously later versions of the comparable movements of XV:40, an authentic keyboard trio (see chapter five), but a conflicting attribution to Wagenseil exists in a Kroměříž manuscript. Larsen considers the concerto genuine Haydn, while Feder labels it doubtful (probably spurious).

The first and last movements are close to their XV:40 counterparts, with the exception of the opening and closing tuttis in each movement. These tuttis are based on XV:40 but also contain new material. To me this new material does not seem to be by Haydn.

I could not test the second movement against the slow movement profile because it begins with a keyboard solo. It does not seem particularly like Haydn, but it contains nothing that seems unlike Haydn either.

The main criterion on which I have made a judgment concerning this concerto is the systematic test of the first movement. It failed the profile, but previous tests have demonstrated that arrangements of a work, even those made by the original composer, may fail the profile of another genre. Nevertheless, the way the concerto failed leads me to believe that it is probably not by Haydn. Both the textural change range and harmonic change range are faster than any pre-1770 work by Haydn that I have examined.

Based on the profile and the treatment of the material in the opening and closing tuttis of the outer movements, I believe that XVIII:7 is probably not by Haydn. Could Wagenseil have adapted a Haydn trio for use as a concerto?

## CONCERTOS

Conclusion: Later arrangement of XV:40, probably not by Haydn.

### XVIII:8

Profiles. I:A
Documentary evidence: possibly listed in the *Entwurf-Katalog* without incipits, also attributed to Leopold Hofmann
Experts' opinions: most authentic, slight reservations from Landon

XVIII:8 is probably the other keyboard concerto listed in the *Entwurf-Katalog* without an incipit. One of the three principal manuscripts (from the Berlin Staatsbibliotek) originally contained the name Hofmann but this was later replaced by Haiden. Landon believes that the attribution to Hofmann is not far-fetched, but most Haydn scholars consider the work probably authentic. XVIII:8 passed the first movement profile, and there is nothing unlike Haydn in the other movements.

Conclusion: Authentic.

### XVIII:9

Profiles. I:C, II:C
Documentary evidence: listed in the *Breitkopf Catalogue* and the catalogue of the Schloss Zeil
Experts' opinions: mixed

Of the doubtful keyboard concertos, XVIII:9 is the most disputed: Larsen regards it as probably authentic, Feder considers it doubtful, and Landon is uncertain. A general stylistic examination causes one to question the work's authenticity. Especially suspicious is the passage from m. 15-20 in the first movement, which consists merely of rhythmically realized harmony with half notes in the first violin and ♩ ♪♪♪ in the other two voices (see example 1). In general, the concerto seems unimaginative. Both of the movements tested failed the profiles, and the concerto does not appear to be by Haydn.

**Example 1. XVIII: 9, m. 15-20**

Conclusion: Spurious.

## XVIII:10

Profiles. I:A
Documentary evidence: unicum, cited in *Breitkopf*
Experts' opinions: probably authentic

XVI:10 exists as a unicum in the collection of the Gesellschaft der Musikfreunde, Vienna, and it is entered in the *Breitkopf Catalogue*. A general stylistic examination turned up nothing that seems atypical of Haydn, and the first movement passed its profile.

Conclusion: Authentic.

## XVIII:E-flat1

Profiles. I:C, II:C
Documentary evidence: unicum
Experts' opinions: probably spurious

Surviving as a unicum, XVIII:E-flat1 is one of the least supported of the doubtful keyboard concertos from a documentary standpoint. A general stylistic examination also casts suspicion on this work's authenticity, the pedestrian accompaniments being especially uncharacteristic. Both of the movements examined did not fit the profiles, and E-flat1 seems to be spurious.

Conclusion: Spurious.

CONCERTOS

## XVIII:F3

Profiles. I:C
Documentary evidence: weak, conflicting attributions to Lang and J. Stamitz
Experts' opinions: probably by Lang

F3 survives in three sources:

1) a manuscript from the Kloster Einsiedeln, Switzerland, attributed to Haydn,

2) a print by Longman, Lukey, and Company attributed to Johann Stamitz, and

3) a manuscript in the Staatsbibliotek Preussicher Kulturbesitz in West Berlin ascribed to Johann Georg Lang.

In addition, the *Breitkopf Catalogue* of 1766 lists the concerto under Lang's name.[15]

Shelley Davis has argued convincingly that XVIII:F3 is probably by Lang based on documentary and general stylistic evidence.[16] It is especially significant that the Berlin manuscript seems to be the most credible source because it is copied in a professional hand and it is the most complete of the three sources. Based on my systematic examination of the first movement and general stylistic examination of the other two movements, I believe that F3 is not by Haydn. Based on the documentary evidence, I agree with Davis that Lang rather than Stamitz is probably the composer.

Conclusion: Spurious, probably by Lang.

## XVIII:G1

Profiles. I:C
Documentary evidence: unicum
Experts' opinions: probably spurious

---

[15]*Breitkopf Catalogue*, 254.
[16]Shelley Davis, "Regarding the Authenticity of the 'Haydn' Keyboard Concerto Hoboken XVIII:F3," *Haydn Studies*, 121-26.

## CONCERTOS

The incipit of this concerto resembles that of the authentic concerto VIIa:4 (see example 2) and employs the characteristic Haydn ornament ⌒. Despite this, the concerto is not by Haydn. Modern Haydn scholars regard the work as probably spurious, and the first movement failed the profile. The other two movements do not show any signs of being by Haydn.

**Example 2. XVIII: G1 and VIIa: 4**

Conclusion: Spurious.

CHAPTER TEN

# Conclusion

## THE AUTHENTICITY OF HAYDN'S EARLY MULTIMOVEMENT INSTRUMENTAL WORKS

The preceding investigation has tested the authenticity of all of the doubtful multimovement pre-ca. 1770 instrumental compositions (not including groups of dances or marches) that according to Haydn scholars might be by Haydn. A number of very doubtful compositions were not examined stylistically because their attributions to Haydn are completely far-fetched. For example, Feder includes thirty-six works in the category "Appendix S: Miscellaneous Chamber Music for 2-3 Strings and/or Wind Instruments: Works Attributed to Haydn," which I did not study.[1] Of these thirty-six compositions, only one single-movement piece (IV:G2) might be the work of Haydn. In the instrumental genres not examined in this study, including the symphonies and string quartets other than op. 3, there are no questions concerning authenticity, except for an occasional individual movement.[2]

On the basis of this study and *the assumption that the method and the application of the method are valid*, the following conclusions may be drawn:

Keyboard Sonatas (Hob. XVI)

Concerning the keyboard sonatas, the most startling conclusion is

---

[1] Feder, *The New Grove Haydn*, 175-76.
[2] Feder, *The New Grove Haydn*, 146-91, and "Apokryphe 'Haydn'—Streichquartette" *Haydn Studien* III (1973-74) 125-50.

that the two Raigern Sonatas (XVI:E-flat2 and E-flat3) are authentic. In addition, I expunged XVI:5 and 16 from the standard list of authentic sonatas, showed that XVI:11 was a factitious arrangement, and corroborated the authenticity of 1, 2, 7, 8, 9, 10, 12, 13, G1, and XVII:D1. I also confirmed that XVI:17, which is also attributed to Schwanenberg, is not by Haydn.

Works for Keyboard Accompanied by Strings (Hob. XIV and XV)

For the accompanied keyboard divertimentos for keyboard with two violins and bass, I discovered that most of the doubtful ones attributed to Haydn—XIV:12, 13, C1, C2, and XVIII:F2—were authentic but that the highly suspect Concertino in D, Hob. Deest., was spurious. The ten early keyboard trios (XV:1, 34, 35, 36, 37, 38, 40, 41, C1, and f1) that most Haydn scholars regard as probably authentic passed the stylistic tests. However, the four arrangements that Robbins Landon included in his edition of the keyboard trios—XIV:6, XIV:C1, XV:39, and XV:42—were not originally intended for this scoring; and XV:39 contains a spurious movement.

String Trios and Quartets (Hob. V and III)

Concerning the works for strings alone, the string trios had the most authenticity problems. Of the thirty-one trios that could not be judged on documentary grounds (at the start of the study), eleven (V:C1, C4, D1, D3, F1, G1, G3, G4, A2, A3, and B1) appear to be authentic, while the rest are spurious. These conclusions differ significantly from Landon's;[3] three works he considers "indubitably genuine"—C2, C3, and C5, I regard as spurious, and I included one trio—A3—among the authentic compositions that he didn't mention. In my op. 3 chapter, I concluded that Haydn did not write the op. 3 string quartets, and that Hoffstetter composed only the first two.

Divertimentos (Hob. II)

The results of my divertimento study (for four or more strings and/ or winds not including string quartets or works with baryton) agree with those of most standard lists. Five works (II:D18, D22, D23, G1,

[3]Landon, *Haydn: The Early Years*, 220-22.

CONCLUSION

and G9/C12) that are generally considered probably authentic but that lack solid documentation passed the stylistic tests. All the other doubtful compositions falling into this category, including II:A1, which Landon calls authentic; II:18 and 19, which are listed in the *Haydn Verzeichnis*; and the well-known *Echo Divertimento* (II:39), seem to be spurious.

Concertos (Hob. VII and XVIII)

Concerning the keyboard concertos, I showed that XVIII:5, 8, and 10 are authentic, that XVIII:7 is probably a factitious arrangement, and that XVIII:9, E-flat1, F3, and G1 are spurious. I also decided that the violin concerto VIIa:4 is by Haydn, while the horn concerto VIId:4 is not.

## FINAL COMMENTS ON THE METHOD

It is my belief that this study has proven the effectiveness of stylistic methods in establishing authenticity. Only one doubtful work (out of ninety-eight) showed conflicting results on the profiles.[4] In addition, none of over 400 non-Haydn pieces that were tested against the profiles passed or scored borderline. In only two related cases—the Raigern Sonatas, XVI:E-flat2 and E-flat3— did I disagree with *all* the major experts who had previously given opinions on the authenticity of the doubtful works.[5] Concerning the major Haydn scholars, I differed with Larsen ten times, Feder five times, and Landon ten times.[6,7]

Based on the results of this study, I strongly believe that a stylistic approach can be just as reliable as one based on documents in deter-

---

[4] This does not include authentic works that contain a spurious movement.
[5] The stylistic evidence from my systematic examination very strongly supports the authenticity of these two sonatas, with all five movements tested passing the profiles (see chapter three).
[6] When they give definite opinions. I regard ?authentic or ?doubtful as a definite opinion. Also, when a list of possibly authentic works excludes a composition that I have called authentic, I consider that to be a disagreement.
[7] In addition, I believe that Hoboken has misclassified forty-six early instrumental works (he gave spurious works or arrangements authentic numbers, such as XVI:15 or XVI:17, and he gave authentic pieces letter designations, such as II:G1), including nine keyboard sonatas, three accompanied keyboard divertimentos, four keyboard trios, eleven string trios, six string quartets, eight divertimentos, and five concertos.

## CONCLUSION

mining authorship.[8] In all authenticity studies, one should examine both the stylistic and documentary evidence. In those cases where the documentary evidence is conclusive, one need not undertake a systematic stylistic examination,[9] but when the external evidence is ambiguous, style should be the main factor in deciding authorship.

While I maintained the same general method throughout this study, my ideas about certain aspects of the method have changed as I worked on the analyses. Initially, I believed that quantitative figures, such as the rate of textural change or harmonic change, were the most important factors in authenticity determination. However, the checklists turned out to be the most reliable indicators of authorship. None of over 400 non-Haydn movements examined in this study passed the checklist (Test II), but several did pass the quantitative ranges (Test I). In addition, the quantitative ranges are useless in most cross-genre studies. While I believe that it is best to employ both quantitative ranges and checklists in an authenticity study, I do admit that establishing the quantitative ranges involves a considerable amount of work; it is certainly possible to do a reliable authenticity study based on checklists.

In doing this study, I discovered what types of criteria do or do not work best on the ranges and in the checklists. For the ranges, the rates of textural change and harmonic change are usually narrow enough to use. In previous investigations, I had also employed the percentage of measures with particular types of texture (such as the percentage of measures with full texture), but these types of ranges were usable in only isolated instances in this study.

Negative traits turned out to be most effective for the checklists. Especially useful were those items that involved rhythms that Haydn never or rarely employed. I discovered that the easiest way to obtain checklist characteristics was to isolate certain parts of movements (the opening measure, the first four measures, the last measure), particular voices (the main voice, the bass), one element of style (harmony, rhythm, range, texture), or a combination of these.[10] I tried to avoid those traits that I assumed were a part of the contemporary vernacular. Other traits that were generally ineffectual for a variety of reasons (at

---

[8]At least with multimovement works when more than one movement is tested.
[9]Because there is usually less work involved in a documentary study than in a stylistic one.
[10]For more information on how to draw up the checklist, see Appendix D.

## CONCLUSION

least from my analytical approach) included aspects of gross form, kinds of keys, proportions of sections (such as the dominant area occupies 10-45% of the movement), cadences, lengths of movements, phrasing, time signatures, relations between themes, the use of minor mode, the large-scale harmonic structure, and orchestration. For example, Haydn's works are often cited for their so-called "monothematicism" (their first and second themes are related). While Haydn does often relate first and second themes by reusing motives, he does not do this all the time, and this practice is also frequently used by other composers. Similarly, phrasing is difficult to employ because Haydn's compositions have such a wide variety of phrase structures. Although Haydn's phrases and combination of phrases in his early works are often asymmetrical, he also sometimes adopts regular phrasing.

The main advantage of my method is that it allows for considerable variation within a composer's style and a wide margin of error on the part of the analyst, through the use of borderline categories, two separate tests for most profiles, and the study of more than one movement from most compositions. While this study was done with considerable care and all aspects checked and rechecked, mistakes are undoubtedly present. However, the margin of error built into this method compensates for the small number of inevitable mistakes. That only one composition (XVI:1) showed conflicting results confirms this.[11]

---

The preceding study has demonstrated one effective method for determining authenticity by style. It is hoped that musicologists working in other periods will use these or other techniques to solve the many authenticity problems that are still with us.

*Fine Laus Deo*

---

[11]Of course, XVI:1 was extensively re-examined to make certain that I had made no errors during the testing.

APPENDIX A

# Lists of Haydn's Early Works in Selected Instrumental Genres

The following charts give my conclusions on the authenticity of Haydn's early multimovement instrumental compositions in those genres that were examined in this study. I have placed the works for each genre in up to five categories: 1a. Previously-Authenticated Works, 1b. Works Authenticated in this Study, 2a. Works Proven Spurious in this Study, 2b. Other Selected Spurious Works Listed in Hoboken or Feder, plus Selected Lost Works, and 3. Selected Arrangements (mainly ones discussed in the text). Dates are mostly from Feder in *The New Grove Haydn*. (-=before, ( )=not documented, -?=possibly composed by.) No entry has been given for the string quartets because my conclusions do not alter the standard list. Compositions are listed in Hoboken number order, except for the divertimentos where works are grouped together by type in a manner similar to that of Feder.

## A. EARLY KEYBOARD SONATAS

1a. Previously-Authenticated Works

| Work | Date | *Authentication* |
|---|---|---|
| 1. XVI:3 in C | (?c1765) | Entwurf-Katalog |
| 2. XVI:4 in D | (?c1765) | Entwurf-Katalog |
| 3. XVI:5a in D[1] | (c1767-70) | Entwurf-Katalog |

[1]=XIV:5, survives incomplete.

## APPENDIX A

| Work | Date | Authentication |
|---|---|---|
| 4. XVI:6 in G | -1766 (-?1760) | Autograph |
| 5. XVI:14 in D | -1767 (-?1760) | Entwurf-Katalog |
| 6. XVI:19 in D | 1767 | Autograph |
| 7. XVI:45 in E-flat | 1766 | Autograph |
| 8. XVI:46 in A-flat | -1788 (c1767-70) | Entwurf-Katalog |
| 9. XVI:47 bis in e | (?1765) | Haydn Verzeichnis[2] |

1b. Works Authenticated in this Study

| Work | Date | Previous Opinions |
|---|---|---|
| 10. XVI:1 in C | (?c1750-55) | probably authentic |
| 11. XVI:2 in B-flat | (-?1760) | probably authentic |
| 12. XVI:7 in C | -1766 (-?1760) | probably authentic |
| 13. XVI:8 in G | -1766 (-?1760) | probably authentic |
| 14. XVI:9 in F | -1766 (-?1760) | probably authentic |
| 15. XVI:10 in C | -1767 (-?1760) | probably authentic |
| 16. XVI:12 in A | -1767 (?c1750-55) | probably authentic; Feder: ? I doubtful |
| 17. XVI:13 in E | -1767 (-?1760) | probably authentic |
| 18. XVI:E-flat2 | (?c1755) | probably spurious |
| 19. XVI:E-flat3[3] | (?c1764) | probably spurious |
| 20. XVI:G1 | (-?1760) | mixed |
| 21. XVII:D1 | ? | mixed |

21 authentic early keyboard sonatas extant[4]

2a. Works Proven Spurious in this Study

| Work | Date | Previous Opinions |
|---|---|---|
| 1. XVI:5 in A | -1763 (?c1750-55) | mixed |
| 2. XVI:16 in E-flat | (?c1750-55) | majority: spurious |
| 3. XVI:17 in B-flat | -1768 | probably by Schwanenberg, though in HV. |

3. Selected Arrangements

| Work | Date | Comments |
|---|---|---|
| 1. XVI:11 in G | -1767 | factitious arrangement: I=XVI:G1/III, II=probably spurious andante, III=minuet |

[2]later F major version.
[3]Added finale in Roskovszky manuscript spurious.
[4]Seven lost sonatas (XVI:2a-e, g, h) are listed in the *Entwurf-Katalog*.

## APPENDIX A

| Work | Date | Comments |
|---|---|---|
| 2. XVI:15 | -1785 | from XI:26 with probably spurious trio. factitious arrangement from II:11. |

### B. ACCOMPANIED KEYBOARD DIVERTIMENTOS (EXCLUDING TRIOS)

1. Previously-Authenticated Works

| Work | Date | Authentication |
|---|---|---|
| 1. XIV:1 in E-flat[1] | -1766 | Entwurf-Katalog |
| 2. XIV:2 in F[2] | ?c1767-71 | Entwurf-Katalog |
| 3. XIV:3 in C | -1771 (-c1767) | Entwurf-Katalog |
| 4. XIV:4 in C | 1764 | Autograph |
| 5. XIV:7 in C | -c1767 | Copy from Haydn's estate. |
| 6. XIV:8 in C | c1768-72 | Same XIV:7 |
| 7. XIV:9 in F | -c1767 | Same as XIV:7 |
| 8. XIV:10 in C[3] | ?c1764-7 | Elssler copy |
| 9. XIV:11 in C | 1760 | lost autograph |

1b. Works Authenticated in this Study

| Work | Date | Previous Opinions |
|---|---|---|
| 10. XIV:12 in C | -1772 (-c1767) | probably authentic |
| 11. XIV:13 in G | -c1767 | probably authentic |
| 12. XIV:C1[4] | -1772 (-c1767) | mixed |
| 13. XIV:C2 | -c1767 | mixed |
| 14. XVIII:F2 | -c1767 | mixed |

14 authentic works extant, 12 of which are for keyboard with two violins and bass

2a. Works Proven Spurious in this Study

| Work | Date | Previous Opinions |
|---|---|---|
| 1. Concertino in D | ? | probably not authentic |

[1]Scored for harpsichord with two horns, violin, bass.
[2]Scored for harpsichord with two violins and baryton. Extant only in keyboard trio version.
[3]String parts not extant.
[4]Scoring disputed. I believe that the version for keyboard with two violins and bass is the original. Extant only in keyboard trio and solo keyboard scorings.

## APPENDIX A

### 2b. Selected Lost and Spurious Works

| Work | Date | Comments |
|---|---|---|
| 1. XIV:C3 | -1766 | by Wagenseil |
| 2. XIV:E-flat1 | ? | by Steffan |
| 3. XIV:F1 | -1774 | by Schmittbauer |
| 4. XIV:F2 | ? | by J.C. Bach, op. 22, no. 2 |
| 5. XIV:G1 | -1774 | lost, probably spurious. |

## C. EARLY KEYBOARD TRIOS

### 1a. Previously-Authenticated Works

| Work | Date | Authentication |
|---|---|---|
| 1. XV:2 in F[1] | ?c1767-71 | Manuscript signed by Haydn |

### 1b. Works Authenticated in this Study

| Work | Date | Previous Opinions |
|---|---|---|
| 2. XV:1 in g | -1766 (?1760-62) | probably authentic |
| 3. XV:34 in E | -1771 (-?1760) | probably authentic |
| 4. XV:35 in A | -1771 (?c1764/5) | probably authentic |
| 5. XV:36 in E-flat | -1774 (-?1760) | probably authentic |
| 6. XV:37 in F | -1766 (-?1760) | probably authentic |
| 7. XV:38 in B-flat | -1769 (-?1760) | probably authentic |
| 8. XV:40 in F | (?c1760) | probably authentic |
| 9. XV:41 in G | -1767 (-?1760) | probably authentic |
| 10. XV:C1 | -1766 (-?1760) | probably authentic |
| 11. XV:f1 | -?1760 | probably authentic |

11 early keyboard trios extant

### 2b. Selected Lost and Spurious Works

| Work | Date | Comments |
|---|---|---|
| 1. XV:33 in D | -1771 (?1760) | lost, probably authentic |
| 2. XV:D1 | -1771 | lost, probably spurious |

[1]Same as XIV:2.

## APPENDIX A

### 3. Selected Arrangements

| Work | Date | Comments |
|---|---|---|
| 1. XIV:6 | -1767 | arranged from XVI:6. |
| 2. XIV:C1 | -1772 (-c1767) | version for keyboard, two violins, bass probably the original. |
| 3. XV:39 | -1767 | factitious arrangement; I=XVI:9/I, II:spurious, III=XVI:8/I, IV=XVI:9/II and XVI:5/II (spurious), V=XVI:9/III. |
| 4. XV:42 | ? | factitious arrangement from two authentic keyboard works; I:extant only in this version, II=XVII:7. |

## D. STRING TRIOS

### 1. Previously-Authentic Works

| Work | Date | Authentication |
|---|---|---|
| 1. V:1 in E | -1767 | Entwurf-Katalog |
| 2. V:2 in F | -1767 | Entwurf-Katalog |
| 3. V:3 in b | -1767 | Entwurf-Katalog |
| 4. V:4 in E-flat | -1767 | Entwurf-Katalog |
| 5. V:5 in B (lost) | -?1765 | Entwurf-Katalog |
| 6. V:6 in E-flat | -?1765 | Entwurf-Katalog |
| 7. V:7 in A | -?1765 | Entwurf-Katalog |
| 8. V:8 in B-flat[1] | -?1765 | Entwurf-Katalog |
| 9. V:9 in E-flat (lost) | -?1765 | Entwurf-Katalog |
| 10. V:10 in F | -1767 | Entwurf-Katalog |
| 11. V:11 in E-flat | -1765 | Entwurf-Katalog |
| 12. V:12 in E | -1767 | Entwurf-Katalog |
| 13. V:13 in B-flat | -?1765 | Entwurf-Katalog |
| 14. V:14 in b (lost) | -?1765 | Entwurf-Katalog |
| 15. V:15 in D | -1762 | Entwurf-Katalog |

[1]Uses viola instead of second violin.

# APPENDIX A

| Work | Date | Authentication |
|---|---|---|
| 16. V:16 in C | -1766 | Entwurf-Katalog |
| 17. V:17 in E-flat | -1766 | Entwurf-Katalog |
| 18. V:18 in B-flat | -1765 | Entwurf-Katalog |
| 19. V:19 in E | -1765 | Entwurf-Katalog |
| 20. V:20 in G | -1766 | Entwurf-Katalog |
| 21. V:21 in D | ?c1765 | Entwurf-Katalog |

Ib. Works Authenticated in this Study[2]

| Work | Previous Opinions |
|---|---|
| 22. V:C1 | mixed |
| 23. V:C4 | mixed |
| 24. V:D1[3] | probably authentic |
| 25. V:D3 | probably authentic |
| 26. V:F1 | probably authentic |
| 27. V:G1 | probably authentic |
| 28. V:G3[4] | probably authentic |
| 29. V:G4 | mixed |
| 30. V:A2 | probably authentic |
| 31. V:A3 | mixed |
| 32. V:B1 | probably authentic |

32 authentic trios, 3 of which are lost

2a. Works Proven Spurious in this Study

| Work | Previous Opinions |
|---|---|
| 1. V:C2 | mixed |
| 2. V:C3 | mixed* |
| 3. V:C5 | mixed |
| 4. V:C6 | probably spurious |
| 5. V:C7 | probably spurious |
| 6. V:C8 | mixed* |
| 7. V:D4 | probably spurious |
| 8. V:d | probably spurious |
| 9. V:E-flat2 | probably spurious |
| 10. V:E-flat3 | probably spurious |
| 11. V:E-flat4 | probably spurious |

[2]and in the CUNY String Trio Project. Those works that I believe are spurious but that the group (as of Aug. 1982) thought were authentic, I have marked * under previous opinions.
[3]Two movements only.
[4]Only first two movements authentic. III and IV in a single copy spurious.

## APPENDIX A

| Work | Previous Opinions |
|---|---|
| 12. V:E-flat5 | probably spurious |
| 13. V:E-flat11 | probably spurious |
| 14. V:E2 | probably spurious |
| 15. V:F7 | probably spurious |
| 16. V:F9[5] | mixed* |
| 17. V:G5 | probably spurious |
| 18. V:A8 | probably spurious |
| 19. V:B4 | probably spurious |
| 20. V:B7[6] | probably spurious |

2b. Selected Lost and Spurious Works

| Work | Comments |
|---|---|
| 1-6. V:D2, E-flat1, E1, G2, A1, B2 | by M. Haydn |
| 7-17. V:C9, D6, E-flat6, E3, F5, F8, G6, G7, A4, B6 | lost, probably spurious |

For other attributions see chapter six (footnote 4).

[5]By Vanhal.
[6]By J. Stamitz

## E. DIVERTIMENTOS FOR FOUR OR MORE STRINGS OR WINDS
(excluding string quartets and works with baryton)

1a. Previously-Authenticated Works

| Work | Instrumentation | Date | Authentication |
|---|---|---|---|
| 1. II:9 | 2ob, 2hn, 2vn, 2va, b | -1764 | Entwurf-Katalog |
| 2. II:17 | " (2cl for 2ob?) | -c1765 | Entwurf-Katalog |
| 3. II:20 | " +(bn) | -1763 (-?1757) | Entwurf-Katalog |
| 4. II:24 | fl, 2eng hn, bn, 2hn, solo vn, 2vn, vc, vle | ?1761-62 | Autograph |
| 5. II:2 | 2vn, 2va, b | -1763 (?1753/4) | Entwurf-Katalog |
| 6. II:10[1] | ? | -1765 | Entwurf-Katalog |

## APPENDIX A

| Work | Instrumentation | Date | Authentication |
|---|---|---|---|
| 7. II:13[1] | ? | -c1765 | Entwurf-Katalog |
| 8. II:8 | 2fl, 2hn, 2vn, b | -1767 | Entwurf-Katalog |
| 9. II:21 | 2hn, 2vn, va, b | -1763 (-?1761) | Entwurf-Katalog |
| 10. II:22 | " | -1764 (-?1760) | Entwurf-Katalog |
| 11. II:1 | fl, ob, 2vn, vc, db | -1768 | Entwurf-Katalog |
| 12. II:11 | " | -1765 | Entwurf-Katalog |
| 13. II:33 | fl/2ob, 2hn, 2vn,b | -1765 | Many good sources |
| 14. II:34 | " | " | Many good sources |
| 15. II:35 | " | " | Many good sources |
| 16. II:36 | " | " | Many good sources |
| 17. II:37 | " | " | Many good sources |
| 18. II:38 | " | " | Entwurf-Katalog |
| 19. II:3 | 2ob, 2hn, 2bn | -1766 | Entwurf-Katalog |
| 20. II:7 | " | -1765 | Entwurf-Katalog |
| 21. II:15 | " | 1760 | Autograph |
| 22. II:23 | " | -1765 (?1760) | Autograph |
| 23. II:14 | 2cl, 2hn | 1761 | Autograph |
| 24. II:16 | 2 eng hn, 2hn, 2vn, 2bn | 1760 | Autograph |
| 25. II:20bis[1] | ? | -c1765 | Entwurf-Katalog |
| 26. II:4[1] | 2cl, 2hn, 2bn | -?c1765 | Entwurf-Katalog |
| 27. II:5[1] | 2cl, 2hn, ?bn | -?c1765 | Entwurf-Katalog |
| 28. II:12[1] | ? | -c1765 | Entwurf-Katalog |

1b. Works Authenticated in this Study

| Work | Instrumentation | Date | Previous Opinions |
|---|---|---|---|
| 29. II:D22 | 4hn, vn, va, b | ?c1763 | probably authentic |
| 30. II:G1 | 2ob, 2hn, 2vn, 2va, b | -1768 (?1760) | probably authentic |
| 31. II:D18 | 2ob, 2hn, 2bn | -1765 (?c1760) | probably authentic |
| 32. II:G9/C12 | " | -1766 (?c1760) | probably authentic |
| 33. II:D23 | " | ? | probably authentic |

# APPENDIX A

| Work | Instrumentation | Date | Previous Opinions |
|---|---|---|---|

33 authentic works, 6 of which are lost

## 2a. Works Proven Spurious in this Study

| Work | Instrumentation | Date | Previous Opinions |
|---|---|---|---|
| 1. II:18 | fl, 2hn, vn va, b | ? | probably by Vanhal |
| 2. II:19 | fl, (2hn), vn, va, b | ? | probably by Vanhal |
| 3. II:39 | 4vn, 2b | -1767 | mixed |
| 4. II:D6 | fl, vn, va, b | -1767 | probably by Hofmann |
| 5. II:D9 | " | -1768 | probably spurious |
| 6. II:D10 | " | " | probably spurious |
| 7. II:D11 | " | " | probably spurious |
| 8. II:G4 | " | " | probably spurious |
| 9. Deest in C | " | ? | probably spurious |
| 10. II:D8 | fl, 2vn, va, b | ? | probably spurious |
| 11. II:A1 | 2vn, 2va, b | -1762 | Landon: authentic |
| 12. II:B4 | ob, vn, va da gamba, b | ? | probably spurious |
| 13. II:F2 | 2ob, 2hn, vn va, b | ? | probably spurious |
| 14. II:F12 | 2ob, 2hn, 2bn | ? | probably spurious |

1. lost.

fl=flute, ob=oboe, cl=clarinet, eng hn=english horn, bn=bassoon, hn=horn, vn=violin, va=viola, vc=cello, b=bass, db=double bass, vle-=violone.

## F. EARLY CONCERTOS

### 1. Previously-Authenticated Works

| Work | Date | Authentication |
|---|---|---|
| 1. VIIa:1 (vn) | -1769 (?c1761-5) | Entwurf-Katalog |
| 2. VIIa:3 (vn) | -1771 (?1765-70) | Entwurf-Katalog |
| 3. VIIb:1 (vc) | -?c1761-5 | Entwurf-Katalog |
| 4. VIId:3 (hn) | 1762 | Autograph |
| 5. XVIII:1 (kb) | ?1756 | Entwurf-Katalog |
| 6. XVIII:2 (kb) | -1767 | Entwurf-Katalog |

## APPENDIX A

| Work | Date | Authentication |
|---|---|---|
| 7. XVIII:3 (kb) | -1771 | Entwurf-Katalog |
| 8. XVIII:4 (kb) | -1781 (?c1770) | Entwurf-Katalog |
| 9. XVIII:6 (vn+kb) | -1766 | Entwurf-Katalog |

1b. Works Authenticated in This Study

| Work | Date | Previous Opinions |
|---|---|---|
| 10. VIIa:4 (vn) | -1769 | probably authentic |
| 11. XVIII:5 (kb) | -1763 | probably authentic |
| 12. XVIII:8 (kb) | -1766 | probably authentic |
| 13. XVIII:10 (kb) | -1771 | probably authentic |

3 extant violin concertos, 1 early cello concerto, 1 horn concerto, 7 early keyboard concertos, and 1 double concerto for violin and keyboard.

2a. Works Proven Spurious in This Study

| Work | Date | Previous Opinions |
|---|---|---|
| 1. VIId:4 (hn) | -1781 | probably spurious |
| 2. XVIII:9 (kb) | -1767 | mixed |
| 3. XVIII:E-flat1 (kb) | ? | probably spurious |
| 4. XVIII:F3 (kb) | -1766 | probably by Lang |
| 5. XVIII:G1 (kb) | ? | probably spurious |

2b. Selected Lost and Spurious Works[1]

| Work | Date | Previous Opinions |
|---|---|---|
| 1. VIIa:2 (vn) | ?c1761-5 | lost, authentic (EK) |
| 2. VIIf:D1 (fl) | -1771 | by L. Hofmann |
| 3. VIIg:C1 (ob) | ?c1800 | spurious |

3. Selected Arrangements

| Work | Date | Comments |
|---|---|---|
| 1. XVIII:7 | -1766 | probably a factitious arrangement; labeled authentic by Larsen. |

vn=violin, vc=cello, hn=horn, kb=keyboard, fl=flute, ob=oboe.

[1]For other lost concertos, see chapter nine.

APPENDIX B

# Editions of Authentic and Doubtful Works Attributed to Haydn and Hoffstetter

Whenever possible, I have used editions from the complete works produced by the Haydn Institute in Köln (*Joseph Haydn: Werke*. Munich: Henle, 1958- ). Other editions employed are as follows (information from the editions supplemented by library catalogue cards):

Chapter Three (Keyboard Sonatas):

1. XVI:17—*J. Haydn Werke, XIV/1*. (Leipzig: Breitkopf & Härtel, 1907-33.)

2. XVIIa:1—Paris; Carli, c1820.

3. XVIIa:2—ed. Douglas Townsend. (London: Ditson, 1956)


Chapter Four (Accompanied Keyboard Divertimentos):

1. XIV:3—ed. Wilhelm Weisman. (Leipzig: C. F. Peters, c1952)

2. XIV:4—ed. Gertrud Wertheim. (London: Boosey & Hawkes, c1955)

3. XIV:7—ed. László Kalmár. (Budapest: Edition Musica, c1972)

4. XIV:8—ed. György Balla. (Budapest: Editio Musica, c1973)

## APPENDIX B

5. XIV:9—ed. László Kalmár. (Budapest: Editio Musica, c1972)

6-10. XIV:11-13; XVIII:F2—ed. Horst Walter. (Munich: Henle, 1969)

11. XIV:C1—ed. H. C. Robbins Landon. (Vienna: Doblinger, 1975)

12. XIV:C2—ed. H. C. Robbins Landon. (Vienna: Doblinger, 1969)

13. Concertino in D, Hob. Deest—rough score provided by A. Peter Brown. Also parts from Kroměříž.


Chapter Five (Keyboard Trios):

1-4. XIV:6, XIV:C1, XV:39, XV:42—ed. H. C. Robbins Landon. (Vienna: Doblinger, 1974-75)


Chapter Six (String Trios):

String trios—work copies provided by the Haydn Institute and scores produced by students at the City University of New York.


Chapter Seven (Op. 3):

1. Op. 3—ed. Wilhelm Altman. (London: Eulenberg, 1957?)

2. Hoffstetter op. 1—scored by the author from parts in the Library of Congress, listed as Joseph Haydn, *Op. 21* published by Bérault, 1774.

3. Hoffstetter, Quartet (c1765) in *Chamber Music*, ed. Hubert Unverricht. (Cologne: Arno Volk Verlag, 1975)


Chapter Eight (Divertimentos):

1. II:1—ed. Walter Upmeyer. (Kassel: Nagels Verlag, c1937)
(flute quartet version)

2. II:2—(Wolfenbüttel: Möseler Verlag, c1958)

3. II:3—ed. H. C. Robbins Landon. (Vienna: Doblinger, c1959)

4. II:7—ed. H. C. Robbins Landon. (Vienna: Doblinger, c1959)

5. II:8—ed. Kurt Janetzky. (Leipzig: Pro Musica Verlag, c1953)

## APPENDIX B

6. II:11—ed. H. C. Robbins Landon. (Vienna: Doblinger, c1961)

7. II:14—ed. H. C. Robbins Landon. (Vienna: Doblinger, c1959)

8. II:15—ed. H. C. Robbins Landon. (Vienna: Doblinger, c1959)

9. II:17—ed. Hubert Steppan. (Vienna: Doblinger, c1960)

10. II:18—scored by the author from parts in the Muzeum České Hudby, Prague.

11. II:19—scored by the author from parts in the Kungl. Musikaliska Akademiens Bibliotek, Stockholm.

12. II:20—ed. H. C. Robbins Landon. (Vienna: Doblinger, c1962)

13. II:21—ed. Arthur Egidi. (Berlin: C. F. Vieweg, c1936)

14. II:22—ed. Ewald Lassen. (Frankfurt: C. F. Peters, 1962)

15. II:23—ed. H. C. Robbins Landon. (Vienna: Doblinger, c1959)

16-21. II:33-38—ed. H. C. Robbins Landon. (Vienna: Doblinger, c1961)

22. II:39 (Berlin: T. Trautwein, c1840)

23. II:D6—ed. Frank Nagel. (Frankfurt: Henry Litolff's Verlag, 1971)

24. II:D8—ed Hermann Scherchen. (Leipzig: Gebrüde Hug, 1940?)

25. II:D9 (New York: Schirmer, 1963?)

26-27. II:D10-11—scored by the author from the London: R. Bremner print in the Princeton University Library.

28. II:D18—ed. H. C. Robbins Landon. (Vienna: Doblinger, c1959)

29. II:D22—ed. H. C. Robbins Landon. (Vienna: Doblinger, c1960)

30. II:D23—ed. H. C. Robbins Landon. (Vienna: Doblinger, c1959)

31. II:F2—ed. Kurt Janetzky. (Leipzig: Peters, 1970)

32. II:F12—ed. Kurt Janetzky. (London: Musica Rara, c1969)

33. II:G1—ed. H. C. Robbins Landon. (Vienna: Doblinger, 1959)

34. II:G4 (New York: Schirmer, 1963?)

35. II:G9/C12—ed. H. C. Robbins Landon. (Vienna: Doblinger, c1959

36. II:A1—Haydn Institute work copy.

37. II:B4—ed. Arnold Dolmetsch. (London: H. Milford, 1929)

38. Flute Quartet in C, Hob. Deest—ed. Herbert Köbel. (Zurich: Hug, c1969)

# APPENDIX B

Chapter Nine (Concertos):

1. VIId:3 (London: Boosey & Hawkes, c1954)

2. VIId:4—ed. H. H. Steves. (London: Boosey & Hawkes, c1954)

3. XVIII:1—ed. M. Schneider. (Wiesbaden: Breitkopf & Härtel, c1953)

4. XVIII:2—rough draft provided by Horst Walter of the Haydn Institute.

5. XVIII:3—ed. Ewald Lassen. (Mainz: B. Schott's Söhne, 1958)

6. XVIII:4—ed. K. Schubert. *Nagels Musik-Archiv, Nr. 86.* (Hanover: A. Nagel, 1932)

7. XVIII:5—ed. H. Schultz. (Leipzig: Musikwissenschaftlichen Verlag, 1937)

9. XVIII:7—ed. K. Weelink. (Amsterdam: A Cuypstr, 1962) (contains added viola part!).

10. XVIII:8—ed. H. C. Robbins Landon. (Vienna: Doblinger, c1962)

11. XVIII:9—advance copy of complete works edition provided by Horst Walter of the Haydn Institute.

12. XVIII:10—ed. Horst Walter. (Munich: Henle, 1969)

13. XVIII:E-flat1—scored by the author from manuscript parts in the Staatsbibliotek Preussicher Kulturbesitz, Berlin.

14. XVIII:F3—same as XVIII:E-flat1.

15. XVIII:G1—rough score from manuscript in Kroměříž provided by A. Peter Brown.

APPENDIX C

# Comments on the Non-Haydn Works and a Sample of Non-Haydn Works Used

The non-Haydn works employed in chapters three to nine were drawn from the collections of the New York Public Library, Library of Congress, Library of the Graduate Center of the City University of New York, and the Ph.D. Program in Music at the Graduate Center of the City University of New York, including unpublished compositions scored by students in Professor Brook's seminars at the City University of New York, Juilliard School of Music, and Brigham Young University. It is possible that a few of the works are not by the authors stated on their title pages, but this is not important as long as they have no possibility of being by Haydn.

Selection of the works was not made by random sampling. A random sample would have been possible only if all eighteenth-century compositions in a particular genre were easily available, which, of course, is not the case. In selecting the pieces, I was very careful to include several compositions by Haydn's Austrian contemporaries in each profile, especially his brother Michael, Leopold Hofmann, Wagenseil, Monn, Vanhal, Gassmann, Dittersdorf, and Mozart. In addition, I carefully chose a balanced group of compositions by both major and minor composers.

Because of space limitations, it was possible to include only the last name of a composer (or the last name of a composer and initials) on the charts in chapters three to nine. When initials are not given, one may assume that the composer is the most famous possessor of a particular name. Thus, only Mozart is given for Wolfgang Amadeus Mozart, but L. Mozart is given for his father. When the same composer appears more than once in a particular chart or in both Control Group II and Test Group I, they are obviously different works. The non-Haydn pieces are in the same genres as the authentic and doubtful Haydn works, with any qualifications in a particular chapter given in the footnotes.

Frequently, the non-Haydn compositions used for one profile in a chapter

## APPENDIX C

are different from those of another profile in the same chapter (first movement group different from minuet group). This is because pieces do not always contain all relevant movements and because the work on the dissertation had to be done in several libraries. I also decided that it might be best to choose movements from different works, such as an opening movement from one Mozart sonata and the minuet from another Mozart sonata, to provide a larger sample.

The chronological limits of the non-Haydn works exceed those of the Haydn compositions in each profile. This is necessary because while an authentic composition cannot be expected to pass a profile from a different time period, it must be demonstrated that non-Haydn works from an earlier or later time will not fit the profile. Of course, there are limits beyond which one need check; obviously, a Schumann sonata will not fit a distinctive profile set up for eighteenth-century compositions.

Limitations of space make a complete listing of the over four hundred non-Haydn movements studied impractical.[1] I thought it appropriate, however, to give all of the non-Haydn works employed in a particular chapter as an example. I have chosen the concerto chapter listing because it is the shortest. The information has been taken from the title pages supplemented by library catalogue cards.

[1]A complete listing of the non-Haydn works would require *over fifty pages* (dissertation version).


A. Concertos. Control Group II: First Movements

1. Albrechtsberger, Johann Georg. *Harp Concerto*, ed. Olivér Nagy. (Budapest: Zeneműkiadó Vállat, 1964)

2. Bach, Carl Philipp Emanuel. *Harpsichord Concerto in C Minor, wq. 31.* (Kassel: Nagels Verlag, 1976)

3. Bach, Johann Christian. *Harpsichord Concerto in D, op. 13, no. 2*, ed. Ludwig Landshoff. (Frankfurt: Peters, 1933)

4. Boccherini, Luigi. *Flute Concerto in D, op. 27*, ed. Sydney Beck. (New York: New York University/New York Public Library, 1934)

5. Cimarosa, Domenico. *Concerto for Two Flutes in G*, ed. Fernard Oubradous. (Paris: Editions Musicales Transatlantiques, 1963)

6. Devienne, Francois. *Flute Concerto in D*, ed. Sherwood Dudley. (Paris: Heugel, 1971)

## APPENDIX C

7. Dittersdorf, Karl Ditters van. *Harp Concerto*, ed. Karl Hermann Pilney. (New York: Peters, 1958)

8. Graun, Johann Gottlieb. *Oboe Concerto in C Minor*, ed. Hermann Tottcher. (Hamburg: Musikverlag Hans Sikorski, 1953)

9. Krommer, Franz. *Clarinet Concerto in E-flat, op. 36*, ed. Melinda Berlász. (Budapest: Editio Musica, 1975)

10. Wagenseil, Georg Christoph. *Harpsichord Concerto in C*, ed. Walter Upmeyer. (Berlin: Dieweg, 1936)


B. Concertos. Control Group II: Slow Movements

All of the works are the same as those used for the first movement profile with the following exception (the Johann Christian Bach op. 13, no. 2 did not have a relevant slow movement):

1. Bach, Johann Christian. *Bassoon Concerto in E-flat*, ed. J. Wojciechowski. (Hamburg: Musikverlag Hans Sikorski, 1953)


Concertos. Test Group I: First Movements

1. Benda, Jiří. *Keyboard Concerto in F Minor*, in *Musica Antiqua Bohemica*. (Prague: Editio Artia, 1960)

2. Brixi, František Xaver. *Organ Concerto in F*, in *Musica Antiqua Bohemica*. (Prague: Editio Artia, 1956)

3. Haydn, Michael. *Violin Concerto in A*, ed. Charles Sherman. (Vienna: Doblinger, 1968 (Diletto Musicale Nr. 194))

4. Kraus, Joseph Martin. *Violin Concerto in C*, ed. W. Lebermann. (Wiesbaden: Breitkopf & Härtel, c1957)

5. Mestrino, Niccolò. *Fourth Violin Concerto*. (New York: The New York Public Library, 1934)

6. Mozart, Wolfgang Amadeus. *Violin Concerto in D, K. 218*. (Leipzig: Breitkopf & Härtel, 1878)

7. Reichardt, J. F. *Violin Concert in E-flat*, ed. H. Lugershausen. (Kassel: Nagel, 1955)

*APPENDIX C*

8. Schobert, Johann. *Keyboard Concerto in E-flat, op. 12*, ed. Hugo Riemann in *Denkmäler Deutscher Tonkunst, 1. Folge, vol. 39*. (Leipzig: Breitkopf & Härtel, 1909)

9. Stamitz, Karl. *Concerto for Clarinet and Bassoon in B-flat*, ed. Johannes Wojciechowski. (Hamburg: Musikverlag Hans Sikorski, 1954)

10. Viotti, Giovanni Battista. *Piano Concerto in G Minor*, ed. Reno Giazotto. (Milan: Ricordi, 1960)


D. Concertos. Test Group I: Slow Movements

All of the works are the same as those used for the first movement profiles with the following exception (the Mestrino lacked a slow movement):

1. Dittersdorf, Karl Ditters van. *Violin Concerto in D, K. 167*. Budapest: (Zeneṁukiadó Vállat, 1967)

APPENDIX D

# A Method for Drawing Up the Checklists

Several methods of drawing up the checklists of positive and negative traits are possible. It seems useful to give the reader my method for doing so.

I start with all relevant works (Control Group I) in front of me, as well as a sample of non-Haydn pieces.[1] After acquainting myself with all the authentic compositions, I concentrate on one work at a time. For example, I might look at the opening measure of the first composition, trying to determine which positive characteristics might be consistent throughout the group. I then search through all the authentic pieces to retain, modify, or reject the particular trait. If the final trait is present in all authentic compositions (or 85% or more of the authentic works with a large group of authentic pieces), I put it in a list of potential characteristics. When I have discovered all the traits that are evident for a particular authentic piece, I move on to the next authentic work; certain traits seem more obvious in certain compositions. Next, I examine a group of non-Haydn works to determine negative characteristics (traits that appear in a majority of the non-Haydn pieces, but are present rarely in the Haydn works). For each negative characteristic, I search through the authentic compositions to make certain that it is absent from all authentic works (or 85% or more of the authentic compositions with a large group of authentic pieces.)

After I have completed the list of potential characteristics, I draw up a grid like the one in Example I (see Example I at the end of this appendix). At the top, I place the composer of the Control Group II works (ten to twenty non-Haydn works) and on the left-hand side the number of each trait. A "+" means that a characteristic is valid for a piece (is present for a positive trait, absent for a negative one), while a "-" means that it isn't. When I have examined all the Control Group II pieces, I can determine the percentage of

---

[1] It is often best to begin by determining the quantitative ranges for Test I, because checklist characteristics can frequently be discerned from the quantitative charts (like Chart I in chapter two.)

231

## APPENDIX D

works each trait appeared in, and, on this basis, decide whether an item should be retained and what its weighting should be. I make signs for each trait for visibility indicating the outcome, crossing off characteristics that are rejected and putting 2 for double weighting, 1 for normal weighting, and 1/2 for half weighting. Finally, I determine the score for each Control Group II work.

If the score of a particular Control Group II work is too high, I compare that composition against the authentic Haydn pieces to see how it differs and then I modify the checklist. (Therefore, the grid will not end up as neat as it is in Example I.) When the checklist contains enough traits and when each Control Group II work scores well below the maximum score, the checklist is complete, and it can be tested further against Test Group I (another group of ten to twenty non-Haydn works.)

As one can see from the above, the checklists may undergo considerable change when tested against Control Group II. However, no changes should be made in the checklist during the comparison against Test Group I. If Test Group I proves that the profile is not effective, a new Test Group I must be used to test the profile after it has been revised.

To give a concrete example of how the checklists work, I have chosen Profile IV from chapter three (Charts X-XII). Chart X presents a checklist of

### Example I. Sample Grid for Checklists

*COMPOSER*

|     | Trait | I | II | III | IV | V | VI | VII | VIII | IX | X | Total | Weight |
|-----|-------|---|----|-----|----|----|----|----|------|----|----|-------|--------|
| 2   | 2 | - | - | - | - | - | - | - | - | - | - | 0% | 2 |
| 1   | 4 | - | + | - | + | - | + | - | + | - | + | 50% | 1 |
| 1/2 | 5 | + | + | + | + | + | + | + | - | - | - | 70% | 1/2 |
| 1   | 6 | + | - | + | - | + | - | + | - | + | - | 50% | 1 |
| 1   | 7 | - | - | - | - | - | - | - | - | + | + | 20% | 1 |
| 2   | 8 | - | - | - | - | - | - | - | - | - | - | 0% | 2 |
| 1   | 10 | + | + | - | - | - | - | + | - | - | - | 30% | 1 |
| Total |  | 2.5 | 2.5 | 1.5 | 1.5 | 1.5 | 1.5 | 2.5 | 1 | 2 | 2 |  | 8.5 |

Sample explanation: Each of the ten non-Haydn works in Control Group II contained Trait 1, so this trait was rejected. None of the Control Group II works included Trait 2, so this trait was retained in the profile and weighted double. To obtain the score of Composer I's work, one adds the weightings of the three traits it passed ($1+1+0.5=2.5$; rejected traits — Nos. 1, 3, 9 — were disregarded).

## APPENDIX D

twelve items, nine positive ones and three negative ones. Most traits received one point; I gave nos. 5 and 10 two points each because they were valid for none of the Control Group II works. A composition fails a particular characteristic if it lacks any part of a positive trait or contains any part of a negative trait. Thus, if in the tested work, the left-hand does not attain at least an $a^1$, it fails trait 1, and if the same piece includes a ♫. it fails trait 10.

On Chart XII, XVI:9 scores 11 points because it passed ten of the twelve traits, including no. 10, which was weighted double. It failed no. 5 (two points) because it lacked the required accompaniment pattern, and it failed no. 6 because it lacked octave doublings in the left-hand. XVI:10 scored 13 points, failing trait 9, because it had only one change of texture in the first eight measures. Both XVI:9 and 10 passed Profile IV (passing 11-14). XVI:16 failed the profile because it passed only five traits (nos. 1, 2, 3, 6, 8).

APPENDIX E

# Two Examples of the Analysis of Quantitative Ranges

This appendix presents two extended examples of the analysis of quantitative ranges. Two types of ranges are illustrated: 1) textural ranges and 2) the rate of harmonic change. For the textural ranges, I draw up a chart that contains measure numbers and the type of texture for each measure. To determine the rate of textural change, I count the number of changes of texture and divide by the number of beats. One establishes the percentage of measures with a particular type of texture (such as "the percentage of measures with three real voices") by calculating the number of measures with that texture and dividing by the total measures. For harmonic rhythm, I count the number of changes of harmony and divide by the number of beats.[1]

Obviously, some scholars will disagree with aspects of my analyses. This is why a single scholar must do an entire authenticity study to insure consistency.

[1] Further information on drawing up the quantitative ranges appears in chapter two.

**Chart I. Texture in the Exposition of the Haydn Keyboard Sonata XVI:33/I**

| 1 | 2 | 3 | 4 | 5 | 6 | 7 | 8 | 9 | 10 | 11 | 12 | 13 | 14 | 15 |
|---|---|---|---|---|---|---|---|---|---|---|---|---|---|---|
| $\frac{1}{2}$ | 3 | $\frac{1}{2}$ | $\frac{2}{1}$ | $\frac{1}{2}$ | | $\frac{2}{1}$ | 3 | $\frac{1}{2}$ | | $\frac{1}{1}$ | 2 | 1 | $\frac{2}{1}$ | 1 |

## APPENDIX E

| 16 | 17 | 18 | 19 | 20 | 21 | 22 | 23 | 24 | 25 | 26 | 27 | 28 | 29 | 30 |
|---|---|---|---|---|---|---|---|---|---|---|---|---|---|---|
| $\frac{2}{1}$ | 1 | $\frac{1}{1}$ | | | | $\frac{1}{2}$ | 3 | | $\frac{1}{4}$ | | $\frac{1}{1}$ | | | |

| 31 | 32 | 33 | 34 | 35 | 36 | 37 | 38 | 39 | 40 | 41 | 42 | 43 | 44 | 45 |
|---|---|---|---|---|---|---|---|---|---|---|---|---|---|---|
| | | | | | | | | | $\frac{1}{2}$ | | 1 | $\frac{1}{1}$ | | |

| 46 | 47 | 48 | 49 | 50 | 51 | 52 | 53 | 54 | 55 | 56 | 57 | 58 | 59 | 60 |
|---|---|---|---|---|---|---|---|---|---|---|---|---|---|---|
| 1 | $\frac{1}{\frac{1}{1}}$ | $\frac{1}{2}$ | $\frac{1}{1}$ | 1 | | | | | $\frac{1}{3}$ | | $\frac{1}{2}$ | $\frac{1}{1}$ | | 6 |

| 61 | 62 | 63 | 64 | 65 | 66 | 67 | 68 |
|---|---|---|---|---|---|---|---|
| $\frac{1}{2}$ | $\frac{2}{2}$ | $\frac{1}{1}$ | 6 | $\frac{1}{2}$ | $\frac{2}{2}$ | 4 $\frac{1}{2}$ | 4 |

### Chart II. Changes of Harmony in the Exposition of XVI:33/I

Changes of Harmony=71

### Chart III. Quantitative Ranges in the Exposition of XVI:33/I

1. Textural Change per Beat=40 changes of texture ÷ 136 beats=.294

2. % of measures with 1/1 texture=29 measures ÷ 68 measures=42.6%

3. % of measures with more than three sounding voices=10 measures ÷ 68 measures=14.7%

4. Harmonic Change per Beat=71 changes of harmony ÷ 136 beats=.522

Note: For Ranges 2 and 3, I count any measure that partially contains the relevant texture.

*APPENDIX E*

## Chart IV. Texture in the Exposition of the Haydn String Quartet Op. 33, No. 4/I

| 1 | 2 | 3 | 4 | 5 | 6 | 7 | 8 | 9 | 10 | 11 | 12 | 13 | 14 | 15 |
|---|---|---|---|---|---|---|---|---|----|----|----|----|----|----|
| $\frac{1}{3}$ | 4 | $\frac{1}{3}$ | 4 | $\frac{2}{2}$ | 4 | $\frac{2}{2}$ | 4 | $\frac{1}{3}$ | 4 | 1 | $\frac{1}{3}$ | $\frac{4}{2}$ | 54 | 61 | $\frac{1}{3}$ |

(m. 9 column shows $\frac{1}{3}\frac{2}{1}$ under measure 10–11)

| 16 | 17 | 18 | 19 | 20 | 21 | 22 | 23 | 24 | 25 | 26 | 27 | 28 | 29 | 30 | 31 |
|----|----|----|----|----|----|----|----|----|----|----|----|----|----|----|----|
| 4 | $\frac{1}{\frac{1}{1}}$ | $\frac{1}{\frac{1}{1}}$ | $\frac{1}{\frac{1}{1}}$ | $\frac{1}{\frac{1}{1}}$ | $\frac{2}{\frac{2}{1}}$ | $\frac{2}{2}$ | $\frac{1}{\frac{1}{1}}$ |  | $\frac{1}{3}$ |  | $\frac{1}{1}$ | $\frac{1}{1}$ | $\frac{2}{\frac{1}{1}}$ | $\frac{1}{\frac{2}{1}}$ | $\frac{1}{\frac{3}{1}}$ | $\frac{1}{4}$ | 1 |

## Chart V. Changes of Harmony in the Exposition of Op. 33, No. 4/I

Changes of Harmony = 70

## Chart VI. Quantitative Ranges in the Exposition of Op. 33, No. 4/I

1. Textural Change per Beat = 33 changes of Texture ÷ 124 beats = .266

2. % of measures with double-stops = 4 measures ÷ 31 measures = 12.9%

3. % of measures with less than four instruments playing = 2 measures ÷ 31 measures = 6.5%

4. Harmonic Changes per Beat = 70 changes of harmony ÷ 124 beats = .565

Note: In m. 17-19, there are three different 1/1/1 textures. These count as three changes of texture.

Note: For Range 2, it is easier to look at the music than at the chart.

# APPENDIX E

**Example 1**
**XVI:33/I**

## APPENDIX E

**Example 1**—*Continued*

## APPENDIX E

Example 1—*Continued*

240

# APPENDIX E

Example 1—*Continued*

## *APPENDIX E*

### **Example 2**

# APPENDIX E

Example 2—*Continued*

## APPENDIX E

Example 2—*Continued*

244

## APPENDIX E

Example 2—*Continued*

## APPENDIX E

Example 2—*Continued*

# APPENDIX E

Example 2—*Continued*

APPENDIX F

# Selected Checklist Terms

The following pages give my definitions of unusual or often ambiguously-defined terms that I have employed in the checklists or quantitative range charts. The figures in parentheses following most terms indicates its first appearance on a chart. The first figure is the chapter, the second is the chart, and the third is the trait. (ex. 3-III-5=chapter three, Chart III, Trait Five.) I have also included entries on pitch symbols and texture symbols.

**Alberti Bass**—accompaniment pattern often found in classical keyboard sonatas, which is named after the composer Domenico Alberti. It consists of broken triads in this sequence—lowest, highest, middle, highest (ex. I). (2-VIII-9)

**Example 1.**

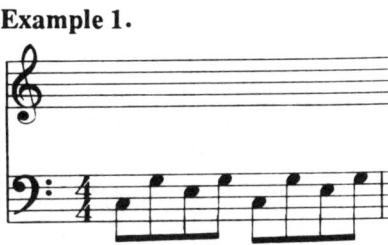

**Appoggiatura**—an unprepared dissonance that occurs on a strong beat and resolves by step (ex. 2). (3-VII-2)

**Example 2.**

APPENDIX F

**Composite rhythm**—the rhythm created by the combination of all voices in a texture. For example, if in a measure from a four-part work, the voices have the rhythms ♩ ♫♩ , ♫ ♩ , ♩ ♩ , and ♩. , the composite rhythm is ♫ ♫ ♩ . (2-X-5)

**Conjunct intervals**—melodic intervals that are a major second or smaller (major seconds, minor seconds, unison). (4-IV-6)

**Disjunct intervals**—melodic intervals that are larger than a major second. (3-X-4)

**Hammerstroke opening**—a cliche opening usually associated with the Northern Italian concerto and later used in eighteenth-century symphonies. It employs a rhythm like ♩ 𝄾 ♩ 𝄾 with forte chords as an attention getting device (ex. 3). (2-VIII-7)

**Example 3.**

**Mannheim sigh**—a type of dissonance usually associated with the eighteenth-century Mannheim school. The dissonance occurs on the first half of a strong beat and resolves to the harmonic note on the second half of that beat with the harmonic note repeated on the next weak beat (ex. 4). (2-VIII-7)

**Example 4.**

**Melodic chromaticism**—at least two consecutive minor seconds in the same voice. ex. C-C-sharp-D. (2-X-9) (Same as chromaticism)

*APPENDIX F*

**Murky bass**—accompaniment pattern that employs broken octaves (ex. 5). (3-VII-10)

**Example 5.**

**Octave doublings** or **bare octaves**—a part is doubled exactly at the octave above or below. In this study, the term is used only when the octave doublings are the only thing happening in a part. Most frequently found in the left-hand keyboard (ex. 6). (2-III-17)

**Example 6.**

**Patterned accompaniments**—an accompaniment pattern that is repeated several times, such as  , etc. Not limited to standard accompaniment patterns, such as Alberti bass or murky bass. (2-III-16)

**Pitch class**—notes of the same letter name in any octave. Thus, C, $c^1$, and $c^2$ are different pitches but of the same pitch class. (2-X-4)

**Pitch symbols**—In any key or any octave, 1=tonic pitch, 2=supertonic pitch, 3=mediant pitch, 4=subdominant pitch, 5=dominant pitch, 6=submediant pitch, 7=leading tone or subtonic pitch. In C major, 1-3-5=C-E-G; in D major 1-3-5=D-F-sharp-A. (ex. 7).

## Example 7.

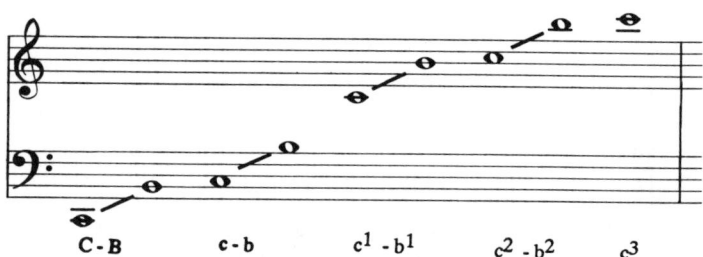

C - B    c - b    $c^1 - b^1$    $c^2 - b^2$    $c^3$

**Real voice**—a melodically-rhythmically independent part. Two lines that employ different rhythms and melodic contours are independent, while two lines that employ parallel thirds or sixths are dependent. Many textures are not as clear-cut as in the preceding examples, and the analyst must decide whether a line is independent or dependent, based on directional, intervallic, and, especially, rhythmic factors. (2-II-12)

**Regular suspension**—a dissonance on a strong beat that is preceded by the same note in a consonant context to which it is tied and that resolves downward by a step (ex. 8). (8-II-12)

### Example 8

**Restruck suspension**—a dissonance on a strong beat that is preceded by the same note in a consonant context, reattacked, and resolved downward by step (ex. 9). (9-VI-5)

### Example 9.

# APPENDIX F

**Simultaneity**—all the pitches that sound together vertically at a particular point in time. If in a 4/4 measure the highest voice has ♩. ♪ ♩ with the pitches $c^2$-$d^2$-$e^2$, the middle voice has 𝅗𝅥 𝅗𝅥 with the pitches $g^1$-$c^2$, and the lowest voice has 𝅝 with the pitch $c^1$, the three simultaneities in that measure would be $c^1$- $g^1$-$c^2$, lasting for a dotted quarter; $c^1$-$g^1$-$d^2$, lasting for an eighth; and $c^1$-$c^2$-$e^2$, lasting for a half. (2-II-3)

**Sounding voice**—the number of parts playing at a particular time, regardless of the number of real voices. Thus, if an oboe, two violins, and a cello are playing, there are four sounding voices. (3-IV-5)

**Texture space**—the distance between the lowest and highest notes in a texture. It can be calculated for a simultaneity, a section of a composition, or an entire work. If the highest note in a simultaneity is $c^2$ and the lowest note is c, the texture space is two octaves.

**Texture symbols**—such as 2, 3/1, 2/1/2/1. The number of numerals represents the number of real voices, the numbers added together the number of sounding voices, and an individual numeral the number of sounding voices that present a single real voice. Ex. 2=two sounding voices, one real voice; 3/1=four sounding voices (3+1), two real voices; 2/1/2/1=six sounding voices, four real voices; 3/1/1=five sounding voices, three real voices; 3/1/2/1/1=eight sounding voices, five real voices.

# Bibliography

Atlas, Allan. "Conflicting Attributions in Italian Sources of the Franco-Netherlandish Chanson, c. 1465-c. 1505: A Progress Report on a New Hypothesis," *Music in Medieval and Modern Europe: Patronage, Sources, and Texts*, ed. Iain Fenlon. (Cambridge, England: Cambridge University Press, 1981) 249-93.

Barrett-Ayres, Reginald. *Joseph Haydn and the String Quartet*. (London: Barrie and Jenkins, 1974)

──────────. "Not proven," *Haydn Studies: Proceedings of the International Haydn Conference, Washington, D. C., 1975*, ed. Jens Peter Larsen, Howard Serwer, and James Webster. (New York: Norton, 1981) 103-05.

Benton, Rita. "A Resumé of the Haydn-Pleyel Trio Controversy with Some Added Contributions," *Haydn-Studien* IV (1978) 114-17.

Berenson, Bernard. *The Study and Criticism of Italian Art, Second Series*. (London: G. Bell, 1902)

Berry, Wallace. *Structural Functions in Music*. (Englewood Cliffs, N. J.: Prentice Hall, 1976)

Brantley, Daniel Lawrence. *Disputed Authorship of Musical Works: A Quantitative Approach to the Attribution of the Quartets Published as Haydn's Opus 3*. Ph.D. diss., University of Iowa, 1977.

Brinegan, Claude. "Mark Twain and the Quintus Curtius Snodgrass Letters: A Statistical Test of Authorship," *Journal of the American Statistical Association* LVIII (1963) 85-96.

Brook, Barry S., ed. *The Breitkopf Thematic Catalogue, 1762-1787*. (New York: Dover, 1966)

# BIBLIOGRAPHY

————————. "Determining Authenticity Through Internal Analysis: A Multifaceted Approach," read at the *Internationaler Joseph Haydn Kongress, 1982*, to be published as a congress report.

————————. "Piracy and Panacea: On the Dissemination of Music in the Eighteenth-Century," *Proceedings of the Royal Musical Association* CII (1975-76) 13-36.

Brown, A. Peter. "The Chamber Music of Carlos d'Ordoñez: A Bibliographic and Stylistic Study," *Acta Musicologica* XLVI (1974) 222-72.

————————. "Haydn's Keyboard Idiom and the Raigern Sonatas," *Haydn Studies: Proceedings of the International Haydn Conference, Washington, D. C., 1975*, ed. Jens Peter Larsen, Howard Serwer, and James Webster. (New York: Norton, 1981) 111-15.

————————. "Notes on Some Eighteenth-Century Viennese Copyists," *Journal of the American Musicological Society* XXXIV (1981) 325-38.

————————. "Problems of Authenticity in Two Haydn Keyboard Works (Hoboken XVI:47 and XIV:7)," *Journal of the American Musicological Society* XXV (1972) 85-97.

————————. *The Solo and Ensemble Keyboard Sonatas of Joseph Haydn: A Study of Structure and Style.* Ph.D. diss., Northwestern University, 1970.

————————. "The Structure of the Exposition in Haydn's Keyboard Sonatas," *Music Review* XXXVI (1975) 102-29.

Brown, A. Peter and James T. Berkenstock with Carol Vanderbilt Brown. "Joseph Haydn in Literature: A Bibliography," *Haydn Studien* III (1973-74) 173-352.

Bryan, Paul R. "The Horn in the Works of Mozart and Haydn: Some Observations and Comparisons," *Haydn Yearbook* IX (1975) 198-225.

Crane, Fredrick and Judith Fiehler. "Numerical Methods of Comparing Musical Styles," *The Computer and Music*. (Ithaca, N.Y.: Cornell University Press, 1970) 209-22.

Cudworth, Charles L. "Notes on the Instrumental Works Attributed to Pergolesi," *Music and Letters* XXX (1949) 321-28.

————————. "Ye Olde Spuriosity Shoppe, or Put it in the Anhang," *Music Librarian Association Notes* XII (1954) 25-40; XII (1955) 540-41.

Davis, Shelley. "Regarding the Authenticity of the 'Haydn' Keyboard Concerto Hob. XVIII:F3," *Haydn Studies: Proceedings of the International*

# BIBLIOGRAPHY

*Haydn Conference, Washington, D. C., 1975*, ed. Jens Peter Larsen, Howard Serwer, and James Webster. (New York: Norton, 1981) 121-26.

Dolmetsch, Arnold. "Preface," *Divertissement pour Hautbois, Violin, Viola da Gamba et Basse par Joseph Haydn*. (London: Oxford University Press, 1929)

Eckhoff, Øivind. "The Enigma of Haydn's Opus 3," *Studia musicologica norvegica* IV (1978) 9-43.

Ellegard, Alvan. *A Statistical Method for Determining Authorship*. (Gothenberg, Sweden: Elanders Boktryckeri Aktiebolag, 1962)

Feder, Georg. "Apokryphe 'Haydn'—Streichquartette," *Haydn-Studien* III (1973-74) 125-50.

_____. "Die Bedeutung der Assoziation und des Wertvergleichs für das Urteil in Echtheitsfragen," *International Musicological Society: Report of the Eleventh Congress Copenhagen 1972*, ed. Henrik Glahn et al. (Copenhagen: Wilhelm Hansen, 1974) 365-77.

_____. "Die beiden Pole im Instrumentalschaffen des jungen Haydn," *Der junge Haydn*, ed. Vera Schwarz. (Graz: Akademische Druck- und Verlagsanstalt, 1972) 192-201.

_____. "Haydns frühe Klaviertrios: Eine Untersuchung zur Echtheit und Chronologie." *Haydn-Studien* II (1969-70) 289-316.

_____. "Introductory Statement," to "Roundtable: Source Problems, Authenticity and Chronology, List of Works," *Haydn Studies: Proceedings of the International Haydn Conference, Washington, D. C., 1975*, ed. Jens Peter Larsen, Howard Serwer, and James Webster. (New York: Norton, 1981) 74-75.

_____. "Manuscript Sources of Haydn's Works and Their Distribution," trans. Eugene Hartzell, *The Haydn Yearbook* IV (1968) 102-39.

_____. "Probleme einer Neuordnung der Klaviersonaten Haydns," *Festschrift Friedrich Blume*, ed. Anna Abert and Wilhelm Pfannkuch. (Kassel: Bärenreiter, 1963) 92-103.

_____. "The Sources of the Two Disputed Raigern Sonatas," *Haydn Studies: Proceedings of the International Haydn Conference, Washington, D. C., 1975*, ed. Jens Peter Larsen, Howard Serwer, and James Webster. (New York: Norton, 1981) 107-111.

_____. "Vorwort," *Klaviersonaten, 1. Folge-JHW*. (Munich: Henle, 1970)

## BIBLIOGRAPHY

⸺⸺⸺⸺. "Wieviel Orgelkonzerte hat Haydn geschrieben?" *Die Musikforschung* XXIII (1970) 440-44.

⸺⸺⸺⸺. "Zwei Haydn zugeschriebene Klaviersonaten," *Bericht über den Internationalen musikwissenschaftlichen Kongress Kassel, 1962*, ed. Georg Reichert and Martin Jus. (Kassel: Bärenreiter, 1963)

⸺⸺⸺⸺. Fillion, Michelle. *The Accompanied Keyboard Divertimenti of Haydn and his Austrian Contemporaries, c 1750-1780*. Ph.D. diss., Cornell University, 1982.

Fruehwald, Scott. "A Method for Determining Authenticity by Style," *Journal of Musicological Research* V (1985).

⸺⸺⸺⸺. "The Chronology of Haydn's Early Keyboard Trios: A Method for Determining Chronology by Style," *Journal of Musicological Research*, in press.

Fuller, David. "Accompanied Keyboard Music," *The Musical Quarterly* LX (1974) 222-45.

Geiringer, Karl. *Haydn: A Creative Life in Music*, 3rd edition with Irene Geiringer. (Berkeley, Ca.: University of California Press, 1982)

Gerlach, Sonja. "On the Chronological Correlation of Haydn's Scoring and the Esterházy Musicians," *Haydn Studies: Proceedings of the International Haydn Conference, Washington, D. C., 1975*, ed. Jens Peter Larsen, Howard Serwer, and James Webster. (New York: Norton, 1981) 93-94.

⸺⸺⸺⸺. "Remarks on the Structure and Harmony of the Raigern Sonatas," *Haydn Studies: Proceedings of the International Haydn Conference, Washington, D. C., 1975*, ed. Jens Peter Larsen, Howard Serwer, and James Webster. (New York: Norton, 1981) 115-117.

Gotwals, V., ed. *Joseph Haydn: Eighteenth-Century Gentleman and Genius*. (Madison, Wisconsin: University of Wisconsin Press, 1963)

Hatting, Carsten E. "Aspects of Texture in the Two Raigern Sonatas," *Haydn Studies: Proceedings of the International Haydn Conference, Washington, D. C., 1975*, ed. Jens Peter Larsen, Howard Serwer, and James Webster. (New York: Norton, 1981) 118.

⸺⸺⸺⸺. "Haydn oder Kayser?—Eine Echtheitsfrage," *Die Musikforschung* XXV (1972) 182-187.

Hoboken, Anthony van. *Joseph Haydn: Thematisch-bibliographisches Werkverzeichnis, Vol. I: Instrumentalwerke, Vol. II: Vokalwerke, Vol. III: Register, Addenda, und Corrigenda*. (Mainz: B. Schotts Söhne, 1957, 1971, 1978)

# BIBLIOGRAPHY

Hoel, Paul G. *Elementary Statistics.* (New York: John Wiley, 1960)

Hucke, Helmut. "Pergolesi," *Die Musik in Geschichte und Gegenwart*, ed. Friedrich Blume. (Kassel/Basel: Bärenreiter, 1962) X, 1058.

Jenkins, Newell and Bathia Churgin. *Thematic Catalogue of the Works of Giovanni Battista Sammartini.* (Cambridge, Mass.: Harvard University Press, 1967)

Kleinbauer, W. Eugene. *Modern Perspectives in Western Art History.* (New York: Holt, Rinehart, and Winston, 1971)

Landon, Christa. "Vorwort," *Sämtliche Klaviersonaten.* Vols. I-III. (Vienna: Universal Edition, 1963) Vol. I, iv-xxv; Vol. II, iii-xvi; Vol. III, iv-xviii.

Landon, H. C. Robbins. "Doubtful and Spurious Quartets and Quintets Attributed to Haydn," *Music Review* XVIII (1957) 213-21.

_____. "Haydn and Authenticity: Some New Facts." *Music Review* XVI (1955) 138-40.

_____. *Haydn: Chronicle and Works*, 5 vols. (Bloomington: Indiana University Press, 1976-80)

_____. "Haydniana (I)," *The Haydn Yearbook* IV (1968) 199-206.

_____. "Preface," *Joseph Haydn Klaviertrios. Trio No. 4* (Vienna: Doblinger, 1977)

_____. "Problems of Authenticity in Eighteenth-Century Music," *Instrumental Music: A Conference at the Isham Memorial Library, May 4, 1957*, ed. David G. Hughes. (Cambridge, Mass.: Harvard University Press, 1959) 31-56.

_____. *The Symphonies of Joseph Haydn.* (London: Universal Edition, 1955)

Larsen, Jens Peter. "Haydn und das 'kleine Quartbuch,' " *Acta Musicologica* VII (1935) 111-23.

_____. *Die Haydn Überlieferung.* (Copenhagen: Einar Munksgaard, 1939)

_____. *The New Grove Haydn*, with worklist by Georg Feder. (New York: Norton, 1983)

_____. "A Survey of the Development of Haydn Research: Solved and Unsolved Problems," *Haydn Studies: Proceedings of the International Haydn Conference, Washington, D. C., 1975*, ed. Jens Peter Larsen, Howard Serwer, and James Webster. (New York: Norton, 1981) 14-25.

———. *Three Haydn Catalogues*. (New York: Pendragon Press, 1979)

———. "Über Echtheitsprobleme in der Musik der Klassik." *Die Musikforschung* XXV (1972) 4-16.

LaRue, Jan. *Guidelines for Style Analysis*. (New York: Norton, 1970)

———. "Major and Minor Mysteries of Identification in the 18th-Century Symphony," *Journal of the American Musicological Society* XIII (1960) 181-96.

———. "Mozart Authentication by Activity Analysis: A Progress Report," *Mozart-Jahrbuch* (1978-79) 209-214.

———. "Mozart or Dittersdorf." *Mozart-Jahrbuch* (1971-72) 40-49.

———. "A New Figure in the Haydn Masquerade," *Music and Letters* XL (1959) 132-39.

———. "Remarks on Activity Analysis," *Haydn Studies: Proceedings of the International Haydn Conference, Washington, D. C., 1975*, ed. Jens Peter Larsen, Howard Serwer, and James Webster. (New York: Norton, 1981) 102-03.

———. "Three Notes of Non-Authenticity," *Haydn-Studien* II (1969) 69-70.

Lowens, Irving. "Haydn in America," *Haydn Studies: Proceedings of the International Haydn Conference, Washington, D. C., 1975*, ed. Jens Peter Larsen, Howard Serwer, and James Webster. (New York: Norton, 1981) 35-48.

Mendel, Arthur. "Some Preliminary Attempts at Computer-Assisted Style-Analysis in Music," *Computers and the Humanities* IV (1969) 41-52.

———. "Toward Objective Criteria for Establishing Chronology and Authenticity: What Help Can the Computer Give?" *Josquin des Pres: Proceedings of the International Josquin Festival Conference*, ed. Edward E. Lowinsky with Bonnie J. Blackburn. (London: Oxford University Press, 1976) 297-308.

Mendenhall, T. C. "The Characteristic Curve of Composition," *Science* IX (1887) 237-49.

# BIBLIOGRAPHY

Mosteller, Frederich and David L. Wallace. *Inference and Disputed Authorship: The Federalist*. (Reading, Mass.: Addison-Wesley, 1964)

Nakano, Hiroshi. "Über das Echtheitsprobleme des 'Streichtrios C Dur (Hob. V:C4)' von Joseph Haydn," *Quarterly of the Japanese Aesthetics Society* XVII (1966) 35-38.

Newman, William S. "Concerning the Accompanied Clavier Sonata," *The Musical Quarterly* XXXIII (1947) 327-49.

_____, chairman. "Problems of Authenticity—The Raigern Sonatas," *Haydn Studies: Proceedings of the International Haydn Conference, Washington, D. C., 1975*, ed. Jens Peter Larsen, Howard Serwer, and James Webster. (New York: Norton, 1981) 107-20. Roundtable with contributions by Georg Feder, A. Peter Brown, Sonja Gerlach, and Carsten Hatting. See individual entries.

Nowak, Leopold. *Joseph Haydn: Leben, Bedeutung, und Werke*, 3rd edition. (Zurich: Amalthea, 1966)

O'Donnel, Bernard. "Stephan Crane's *The O'Ruddy*: A Problem in Authorship Determination," *The Computer and Literary Style*, ed. Jacob Leed. (Kent, Ohio: Kent State University Press, 1966) 107-115.

Paisley, William J. "Identifying the Unknown Communicator in Painting, Literature, and Music: The Significance of Minor Encoding Habits," *Journal of Communication* XIV (1964) 219-237.

Paymer, Marvin E. *The Instrumental Music Attributed to Giovanni Battista Pergolesi: A Study in Authenticity*. Ph.D. diss., City University of New York, 1977.

Plath, Wolfgang. "Vorwort," in *Wolfgang Amadeus Mozart. Neue Ausgabe Sämtlichen Werke. Serie X: Supplement*. (Kassel: Bärenreiter, 1980)

Rosen, Charles. *The Classical Style: Haydn, Mozart, and Beethoven*. (New York: Norton, 1972)

Schwarting, H. "Über die Echtheit dreier Haydn-Trios," *Archiv für Musikwissenschaft* XXII (1965) 169-82.

Sherman, Lucius A. "Some Observations upon the Sentence-Length in English Prose," *University of Nebraska Studies* I (1888) 119-30.

Sisman, Elaine. *Haydn's Variations*. Ph.D. diss., Princeton University, 1978.

Smith, C. S. "Haydn's Chamber Music and the Flute," *The Musical Quarterly* XIX (1933) 435-40.

# BIBLIOGRAPHY

Somfai, László "A klasszikus kvartetthangzás megszületése Haydn vonósnégyeseiben," *Zenetudományi tanulmányok* VIII (1960) 153-65.

──────────────, chairman. "Problems of Authenticity—'Opus 3,' " *Haydn Studies: Proceedings of the International Haydn Conference, Washington, D. C., 1975*, ed. Jens Peter Larsen, Howard Serwer, and James Webster. (New York: Norton, 1981) 95-106. Roundtable with contributions by Alan Tyson, Hubert Unverricht, James Webster, Jan LaRue, Ludwig Finscher, Reginald Barret-Ayres. See individual entries.

──────────────. "Zur Echtheitsfrage des Haydn'schen 'Opus 3,' " *The Haydn Yearbook* III (1965) 153-65.

Spitzer, John. *Authorship and Attribution in Western Art Music*. Ph.D. diss., Cornell University, 1983.

Steglich, R. "Eine Klaviersonate Johann Gottfried Schwanenbergs in der Joseph Haydn Gesamtausgabe," *Zeitschrift für Musikwissenschaft* XV (1932-33) 77-79.

Steinberg, Lester S. "A Numerical Approach to Activity and Movement in the Sonata-Form Movements of Haydn's Piano Trios," *Haydn Studies: Proceedings of the International Haydn Conference, Washington, D. C., 1975*, ed. Jens Peter Larsen, Howard Serwer, and James Webster. (New York: Norton, 1981) 515-22.

Tyson, Alan. "Bibliographical Observations on Bailleux's Edition," *Haydn Studies: Proceedings of the International Haydn Conference, Washington, D. C., 1975*, ed. Jens Peter Larsen, Howard Serwer, and James Webster. (New York: Norton, 1981) 95-98.

──────────────. "Haydn and Two Stolen Trios," *Music Review* XXII (1961) 21-27.

Tyson, Alan and H. C. Robbins Landon. "Who Composed Haydn's Op. 3?" *Musical Times* CV (1964) 506-07.

Unverricht, Hubert. "Roman Hoffstetter," *The New Grove Dictionary of Music and Musicians*, ed. Stanley Sadie. (London: MacMillan, 1980) VII, 631.

──────────────. "Summary of the Documentary Facts Relevant to the Question of Haydn's Authorship," *Haydn Studies: Proceedings of the International Haydn Conference, Washington, D. C., 1975*, ed. Jens Peter Larsen, Howard Serwer, and James Webster. (New York: Norton, 1981) 98-99.

Walter, Horst, "Preface," *Joseph Haydn: Concertini*. (Munich: Henle, 1968)

## BIBLIOGRAPHY

Webster, James. "External Criteria for Determining the Authenticity of Haydn's Music," *Haydn Studies: Proceedings of the International Haydn Conference, Washington, D. C., 1975*, ed. Jens Peter Larsen, Howard Serwer, and James Webster. (New York: Norton, 1981) 75-81.

_____. "Prospects for Haydn Biography after Landon," *The Musical Quarterly* LXVIII (1982) 476-95.

_____. "Relations between the Documentary and Stylistic Evidence," *Haydn Studies: Proceedings of the International Haydn Conference, Washington, D. C., 1975*, ed. Jens Peter Larsen, Howard Serwer, and James Webster. (New York: Norton, 1981) 99-102.

_____. "Toward a History of Viennese Chamber Music in the Early Classical Period," *Journal of the American Musicological Society* XXVII (1974) 212-47.

Wolf, Eugene. "Authenticity and Stylistic Evidence in the Early Symphony: A Conflicting Attribution between Richter and Stamitz," *A Musical Offering*, ed. Edward H. Clinkscale and Claire Brook. (New York: Pendragon Press, 1977) 273-94.

Yule, George. *The Statistical Study of Literary Vocabulary*. (Cambridge, England: Cambridge University Press, 1944)

Wackernagel, Bettina. *Joseph Haydns frühe Klaviersonaten: ihre Beziehungen zur Klaviermusik um die Mitte des 18. Jahrhunderts*. (Tutzing: Schneider, 1975)

# Index

Abel, C. F., 190
Accompanied keyboard divertimentos, 101
Activity Analysis, 26
Annereau, 152
Atlas, Allan, 4

Bach, J. C., 190
Barret-Ayres, Reginald, 153
Beethoven, Ludwig van, 15
Belkin, Alan, 133
Benton, Rita, 51
Berenson, Bernard, 18
Berry, Wallace, 46, 47
Brantley, Daniel Lawrence, 24, 25, 26, 37
Breitkopf and Härtel, *Oeuvres Complèttes,* 8, 68, 85, 87, 88, 89, 91, 102, 112, 113, 118, 129, 142, 188, 192, 193, 200, 201, 202, 203, 204
Brook, Barry S., 12, 131, 132, 142
Brown, A. Peter, 10, 68, 69, 87, 90, 93, 96, 102, 103, 118
Bryan, Paul R., 193, 200

CUNY Haydn String Quartet Project, 13
    String Trio Project, 17, 61, 149
Chugin, Bathia, 3, 12
Concertino in D, 103, 108
Crane, Frederick, 24
Crane-Fiehler, 37
Cudworth, Charles, 36

*Index*

Dähler, Jörg Ewald, 101
Davis, Shelley, 204
Dittersdorf, Karl Ditters von, 28, 29
Dolmetch, Arnold, 190

*Echo Divertimento*, 209
Eckhoff, Oivind, 156
Elssler, Johann, 152
*Entwurf-Katalog*, 1, 8, 51, 67, 77, 98, 102, 127, 151, 183, 191, 192, 200, 202
Esterházys, Symphonies 6 - 8, 15
Esterházys, (XIV:2, 4, 7, 8, ,9, 10), 102

Feder, Georg, 1, 10, 51, 68, 85, 86, 87, 88, 89, 90. 91, 95, 96, 97, 101, 103, 113, 114, 115, 117, 129, 140, 145, 167, 185, 187, 192, 202, 207, 209
*Federalist Papers*, the, 20
Fiehler, Judith, 24
Fillion, Michelle, 102, 103, 113, 118, 126
Finscher, Ludwig, 155
Fontaine, Pierre, 24
Forster, William, 50, 51
Fuller, David, 102

Galuppi, Baldassare, 8
Geiringer, Karl, 14
Gerlach, Sonja, 96
Gimbel, Allen, 133
Giordani, Tommaso, 98
*Göttweig Catalogue*, 103, 112, 118, 189
Green, Andrew, 133
Grenon, Nicolas, 24

Harold (or Haroldt), Joseph George, 10
Hatting, Carsten, 95
Haydn, Joseph, 6, 50
   Flute Concerto in D, 191
   Opus 1, string quartets, 15, 25, 154
   Opus 2, string quartets, 15, 25, 154
   Opus 3, string quartets, 24, 25, 151, 153, 155, 159, 160, 162, 163, 187, 207, 208

Opus 9, 25
Opus 13, piano sonatas, 50
    conclusion, 163
String Trios, C3, 15, 40, 46, 63
Symphony No. 31, 184
*Verzeichnis*, 1, 8, 9, 10, 51, 151, 153, 183, 187, 191
Haydn, Michael, 6, 132
Hucke, Helmut, 36
Hoboken, Antony, 68, 70, 101, 113, 115
    catalogue, 209
    II:1, 165, 166
    II:2, 15, 165, 166
        conclusion, 188
    II:3, 165, 166, 184
    II:4, 184
    II:5, 184
    II:7, 165, 166, 184
    II:8, 165, 166
    II:9, 165, 166
    II:11, 165, 166
    II:12, 184
    II:14, 165, 166, 184
    II:15, 165, 166, 184
    II:16, 165, 166
    II:17, 165, 166
    II:18, 165, 166, 172, 179, 182, 187, 188, 209
    II:19, 165, 166, 167, 172, 179, 188, 209
        conclusion, 188
    II:20, 165, 166
    II:20bis, 184
    II:21, 165, 166
    II:22, 165, 166
    II:23, 165, 166, 184
    II:24, 165, 166
    II:33, 165, 166
    II:34, 165
    II:35, 165
    II:36, 165
    II:37, 165
    II:38, 165, 166
    II:39, 165, 166, 167, 172, 179, 188, 209
        conclusion, 188

*Index*

II:A1, 165, 167, 172, 179, 189, 209
   conclusion, 189
II:B4, 165, 167, 190
   conclusion, 190
II:D6, 165, 166, 167, 172, 179, 187
   conclusion, 187
II:D8, 165, 166, 167, 172, 179
   conclusion, 187
II:D9, 165, 167, 179, 186, 187
   conclusion, 186
II:D10, 165, 167, 172, 179, 186, 187
II:D11, 165, 172, 179, 186, 187
   conclusion, 186
II:D11-G4, 167
II:D18, 165, 167, 176, 184, 185, 208
   conclusion, 184
II:D22 add, 165, 167, 172, 179, 183, 208
   conclusion, 184
II:D23 add., 165, 167, 176, 182, 184, 185, 208
   conculsion, 185
II:F2, 165, 167, 172, 179, 188, 189
II:F12, 165, 167, 176, 182, 185
   conclusion, 186
II:G1, 165, 167, 172, 179, 183, 208
   conclusion, 183
II:G4, 165, 172, 179, 186
   conclusion, 187
II:G9/C12, 165, 167, 176, 182, 184, 185, 209
   conclusion, 184
IV:G2, 207
V:1, 146
V:2, 146
V:3, 146
V:6, 143
V:7, 143
V:8, 143
V:11, 146
V:12, 146
V:15, 143
V:16, 143
V:18, 143
V:19, 146
V:20, 143, 149

*Index*

V:21, 143
V:A1, 132, 145
V:A2, 138, 140, 141, 146, 208
V:A3, 132, 138, 140, 141, 146, 149, 208
V:A4, 132
V:A5, 132
V:A7, 132
V:A8, 132
V:B1, 132, 138, 140, 141, 146, 149, 208
V:B2, 132
V:B3, 132
V:B4, 140, 141, 146, 149
V:B5, 132
V:B6, 132
V:B7 G. Stamitz, 140
V:C1, 132, 138, 140, 141, 146, 149, 208
V:C2, 132, 138, 140, 141, 146, 149
V:C3, 61, 132, 140, 141, 146, 149
V:C4, 132, 138, 140, 141, 146, 149, 189, 208
V:C5, 132, 140, 141, 146, 149
V:C6, 132, 140, 141
V:C7, 132, 140, 141, 146, 149
V:C8, 132, 140, 141, 146, 149
V:C9, 132, 149
V:D1, 132, 138, 140, 141, 146, 208
V:D2, 132
V:D3, 132, 140, 141, 145, 146, 149, 208
V:D4, 132, 140, 141, 146, 149
V:D5, 132
V:D6, 132
V:d, 138, 149
V:E1, 132
V:E2, 132, 140, 149
V:E3, 132
V:E-Flat1, 132, 142
V:E-Flat2, 132, 141, 142, 146, 149
V:E-Flat3, 132, 141, 142, 146, 149
V:E-Flat4, 132, 141, 142, 146, 149
V:E-Flat5, 132, 142 142, 149
V:E-Flat7, 132
V:E-Flat8, 132
V:E-Flat10, 132
V:E-Flat11, 132, 140, 146, 149

*Index*

V:E-Flat13, 132
V:F1, 132, 139, 140, 145, 146, 149, 208
V:F2, 132
V:F3, 132
V:F4, 132
V:F5, 132
V:F6, 132
V:F7, 132, 140, 141, 146, 149
V:F8, 132
V:F9, 132, 140, 141, Vanhal
V:G1, 139, 140, 141, 145, 146, 149, 208
V:G2, 132
V:G3, 132, 1138, 140, 141, 146, 149, 208
V:G4, 110, 139, 140, 141, 149, 208
V:G5, 132, 140, 141, 149
V:G6, 132
V:G7, 132
VIIa:1, 191, 194
VIIa:2, 191
VIIa:3, 191, 194
VIIa:4, 191, 193, 194, 196, 199, 200, 205, 209
conclusion, 200
VIIB:1, 194
VIIb:1, 191
VIIb:2, 191
VIIb:3, 191
VIIc:1, 191
VIID:3, 194
VIId:1, 191
VIId:2, 191
VIId:3, 191
VIId:4, 193, 196, 199, 200, 209
   conclusion, 200
VIIe:1, 191
VIIf:1, 191
VIIg:C1, 191
VIIh:1, 191
VIIh:2, 191
VIIh:3, 191
VIIh:4, 191
VIIh:5, 191
XIV:3, 8, 108
XIV:4, 108

## Index

XIV:6, 127, 208
XIV:7, 108, 113, 114
XIV:7/I, 94
XIV:8, 114
XIV:9, 108
XIV:10, 114
XIV:11, 112, 208
XIV:12, 106, 107, 112, 115, 119, 208
   conclusion, 112
XIV:13, 107, 112, 115, 119, 208
   conclusion, 112
XIV:C1, 102, 104, 108, 111, 112, 113, 114, 119, 127, 208
   conclusion, 114
XIV:C2, 103, 107, 108, 111, 115, 119, 208
   conclusion, 115
XV:1, 117, 118, 119, 126, 127, 208
XV:2, 117, 119, 120, 123, 126
XV:3, 9, 50, 55
XV:4, 9, 50, 55
XV:34, 117, 118, 122, 126, 127, 208
XV:35, 117, 118, 126, 127, 208
XV:36, 118, 126, 127, 208
XV:37, 117, 118, 126, 127
XV:38, 117, 126, 127,208
XV:39, 119, 126, 128, 208
XV:40, 117, 118, 126, 127, 208
XV:41, 118, 122, 126, 127, 192, 201, 202, 208
XV:42, 119, 129, 192, 208
XV:C1, 117, 118, 119, 127, 208
XV:F1, 117, 118, 122, 126, 127, 208
XVI:1, 67, 69, 70, 75, 77, 82, 85, 86, 101, 208, 211
   conclusion, 86
XVI:2, 67, 69, 70, 75, 77, 82, 86, 87, 95, 101, 208
   conclusion, 88
XVI:2a, 67
XVI:2b, 67
XVI:2c, 67
XVI:2d, 67
XVI:2e, 67
XVI:2g, 67
XVI:2h, 67
XVI:3, 67, 71, 75, 77, 101
XVI:4, 67, 71, 75, 96, 101

*Index*

XVI:5, 68, 69, 70, 75, 77, 101, 114, 208
   conclusion, 88
XVI:5a, 67
XVI:6, 67, 71, 75, 77, 127
XVI:7, 67, 68, 69, 70, 74, 75, 77, 101, 114, 208
   conclusion, 88
XVI:7/I, 94
XVI:8, 67, 68, 69, 70, 74, 75, 77, 82, 89, 101, 114, 208
   conclusion, 88
XVI:8/I, 128
XVI:9, 67, 68, 69, 70, 74, 75, 77, 89, 101
   conclusion, 89
XVI:9/I, 128
XVI:10, 67, 68, 69, 70, 74, 75, 77, 89, 101, 114, 208
XVI:11, 67, 69, 82, 89, 91, 101, 102, 208
   conclusion, 91
XVI:12, 67, 68, 69, 70, 77, 82, 91, 101, 102, 208
   conclusion, 91
XVI:13, 67, 68, 69, 75, 7795, 101, 102, 103, 129
   conclusion, 92
XVI:14, 67, 71, 75, 82, 95
XVI:16, 67, 68, 69, 70, 92, 208
   conclusion, 92
XVI:15, 67
XVI:16/I, 78
XVI:17, 67, 68, 69, 70, 75, 82, 93, 208
   conclusion, 93
XVI:19, 67, 71, 77, 82
XVI:19, 67, 71, 77, 82
XVI:24, 50
XVI:25, 50
XVI:26, 50
XVI:45, 67, 71, 77, 82
XVI:46, 67, 71, 77, 82
XVI:47, 67, 71, 78, 82, 113
XVI:C1, 101, 104
XVI:C1-G1, 101
XVI:C2, 102, 103
XVI:D1, 93, 94, 208
   conclusion, 94
XVI:D-flat2, 95
XVI:D-flat3, 95

*Index*

XVI:E-flat2, 6, 68, 69, 75, 77, 82, 98, 208
    conclusion, 97
XVI:E-flat3, 6, 68, 69, 75, 77, 208
    conclusion, 98
XVI:E-flat3add, 67, 70
XVI:G1, 67, 68, 69, 70, 75, 77, 90, 94, 208
XVI:G1/I, 94
XVII:7, 129
XVIIa:F1, 98
XVIIa:1, 99
XVIIa:2, 99
XVII:D1, 67, 68, 69, 70, 77, 93, 94
    conclusion, 94
XVII:G1, 116
XVIII:1, 191, 194
XVIII:2, 8, 191, 194
XVIII:3, 191, 194
XVIII:4, 191
XVIII:5, 192, 193, 196, 200, 209
    conclusion, 201
XVIII:6, 191, 194
XVIII:7, 192, 196, 201, 209
    conclusion, 202
XVIII:8, 192, 193, 196, 202, 209
XVIII:9, 192, 196, 199, 202, 209
    conclusion, 203
XVIII:10, 192, 193, 194, 203, 209
    conclusion, 203
XVIII:11, 191
XVIII:E-flat1, 192, 193, 196, 199, 203, 209
    conclusion, 203
XVIII:F2, 102, 103, 104, 107, 115, 119, 208
    conclusion, 115
XVIII:F3, 192, 193, 196, 204, 209
    conclusion, 204
XVIII:G1, 10, 192, 193, 196, 204, 209
    conclusion, 205
Deest, 103, 108
Deest Concertino in D, 103, 107, 116, 208
    conclusion, 116
Deest, Quartet in C, 165, 167, 172, 179, 187
Hoffstetter, Romanus, 25, 26, 151, 153, 155, 156, 160, 163, 208

*Index*

Hofmann, Leopold, 8, 167, 187, 191, 192, 202

Jenkins, Newell, 2, 12
Josquin des Pres, 23

*Katalog Kees*, 1
Kayser, Mariano Romano, 6, 95, 96
Kleinbauer, W. Eugene, 18

LaRue, Jan, 5, 8, 12, 26, 27, 28, 29, 30, 31, 32, 3, 37
Landon, Christa, 68, 69, 89, 93
Landon, H. C. Robbins, 10, 11, 14, 61, 68, 69, 87, 88, 90, 91, 93, 96, 101, 103, 115, 119, 127, 129, 142, 145, 167, 183, 187, 188, 189, 191, 192, 202, 208, 209
Lang, Johann Georg, 192, 204
Langley, Jeff, 133
Larsen, Jens Peter, 1, 8, 10, 17, 68, 69, 70, 96, 101, 103, 113, 145, 151, 167, 192, 201, 202, 209
Le Duc, 51
Lockwood, Lewis, 23
Longhi, Roberto, 18
Longman and Broderip, 51

MacIntyre, Bruce, 133
Mendel, Arthur, 23
Mendenhall, T.C., 20
Moran, August de, 19
Morelli, Giovanni, 13, 18
Mosteller, Frederich, 20
Mozart, Wolfgang Amadeus, 28, 29

Newman, William S., 102

Offner, Richard, 18
Ordoñez, 10, 11, 14, 132

Paisley, William, 14, 18, 20, 21, 37
Paymer, Marvin E., 1, 4, 12, 17, 33, 34, 35, 36, 37, 132
Pergolesi, Giovanni Battista, 4, 12, 33, 34, 35, 36
Pleyel, Ignaz (Ignace) Joseph, 9, 50, 51, 52, 54, 55
Pohl, C.F., 68, 87
Pohl, Carl Ferdinand, 68, 87, 88, 91, 93, 112, 117, 129
Pope-Hennessy, John, 19

## Index

*Raigern Sonatas*, 67, 70, 96. *See also* Hoboken XVI, 6
Renaissance chanson, 4
Richardson the Elder, Johnathan, 18
Richter, 31, 32

Sammartini, Giovanni Battista, 3, 12
Sandberger, Adolf, 151
*Sarasin Catalogue*, 188
Schwanenberg, 68, 69, 70, 93, 208
Scott, Marion, 151, 153
Sherman, Lucius A., 20
*Sigmaringen Catalogue*, 188
Somfai, László, 151
Spitzer, John, 4
Stamitz, Johann, 31, 32, 192, 204
Steglich, Rudolf, 70
Steinberg, Lester S., 29, 30

Tolbecque, Auguste, 190
Tovey, David, 151
Tovey, Donald, 151
Tyson, Alan, 51, 151, 152

Unverricht, Hubert, 155

Vanhal, Georg Christoph, 187, 188
Vanhal, Johann Baptist, 142, 167
Vide, Jacques, 24
Vienna Haydn Conference, 142

Wagenseil, Georg Christoph, 118, 192, 201
Wallace, David, 20
Webster, James, 2, 7, 11, 155
Wolf, Eugene, 12, 31, 32, 37
Works for Keyboard Four Hands, (conclusion), 99

**LIBRARY OF DAVIDSON COLLEGE**